RED MOUNTAIN BURNING

A NOVEL

BOO WALKER

ALSO BY BOO WALKER

A Marriage Well Done

Red Mountain

Red Mountain Rising

An Unfinished Story

Writing as Benjamin Blackmore:

Lowcountry Punch

Once a Soldier

Off You Go: A Mystery Novella

Cover design by JD Smith

For my beta readers

SONG DOGS DON'T DIE

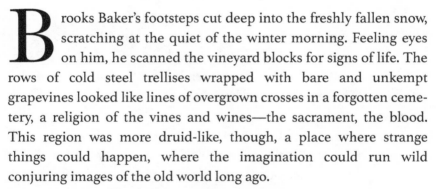

Brooks Baker's footsteps cut deep into the freshly fallen snow, scratching at the quiet of the winter morning. Feeling eyes on him, he scanned the vineyard blocks for signs of life. The rows of cold steel trellises wrapped with bare and unkempt grapevines looked like lines of overgrown crosses in a forgotten cemetery, a religion of the vines and wines—the sacrament, the blood. This region was more druid-like, though, a place where strange things could happen, where the imagination could run wild conjuring images of the old world long ago.

A ghostly and thrilling chill crept up his spine as if he were traversing a burial ground, walking over graves. It wasn't danger that he felt, more the raw energy of Red Mountain, the mystical place in the desert of eastern Washington State that had found him when he'd desperately needed finding.

Once Brooks reached a plateau, he twisted and gazed west through the last of the falling snowflakes drifting from pink clouds over apple and cherry orchards. Ice sheets floated down the frigid Yakima River. Somewhere out there, past the farms and the rolling hills, stood the sharp peaks and evergreen forests of the Cascades.

Brooks looked down at his house on the shore of the river, where a plume of smoke rose from the chimney. His home was full of life— at least, for now. His girlfriend, Adriana, and her son, Zack, were inside stoking a fire and cooking breakfast. Their current living arrangement was the closest Brooks had ever come to having a family of his own, but he had an agonizing suspicion it wouldn't last for much longer.

Turning back, he worked his way southeast through the maze of roads threading through the vines. He found a snow-covered Red Mountain mesmerizing and inspiring, like gazing at the stars while at sea, and the edginess he'd felt waned. A hawk soared by, and he wondered if those were the eyes he'd sensed watching him.

"It's quiet here," a voice said, gruff and English, sneaking by like a phantom whisper.

Brooks spun around to find Otis Till standing a few feet into a row with his arms crossed. A smirk rose on the man's face.

"Well played," Brooks said, watching his breath turn to fog in the cold. "You're starting to melt into the land."

Otis had left England as a teenager, but his English accent hadn't left him. "The only way to know these vines is to match their stillness."

Brooks had noticed Otis speaking in other dimensions lately, as if the wise man now crossing into his late sixties had seen things Brooks had yet to see. Otis wore a weathered red wool sweater and brown corduroy pants. A tweed cap covered his head.

"Aren't you cold?" Brooks asked.

Otis stepped toward him, coming out from the row. The older man shook his head. "Nah, it's refreshing."

The two men shook hands, and Brooks felt the excitement and anticipation of the man known as the grapefather, a warrior-farmer preparing for the next vintage. Never had Brooks met such an artist. Never had he encountered a man more dedicated to his craft.

"As cold as it is," Brooks said, "I'm hearing it'll be another hot year."

"I've heard the same," Otis admitted with the same disappointment he might have if his party had lost an election. "Too many more of these scorchers and we might have to replace our vines with agave plants and start producing tequila."

"Let's not go there. How's Joan?"

"Still hiding my pork rinds and trying to make me do the twist on a yoga mat."

Brooks could never get enough of Otis's grumpy humor. "Someone has to keep you in line."

"And Adriana and Zack?" Otis asked.

"They're cold." An image of Florida—palm trees and turquoise water—passed Brooks's inner vision. "She's not used to this kind of winter. I think she's feeling a little trapped."

What Brooks didn't say was that Adriana had been having awful nightmares involving her ex-husband, Michael, who Adriana, her mother, and her son had fled from two years earlier. With her lawyer's help, Adriana had organized the perfect escape. By the time she was driving over the California state line, Michael had been put in handcuffs. He'd been sent to California State Prison to serve three-to-five for felony domestic battery.

It was this past August when Michael had gotten out early and tracked his family down, surprising them one night at Margot Pierce's house. Brooks had tried to protect Adriana and Zack, but Michael had hit him with a baseball bat and knocked him unconscious. If it hadn't been for Margot, who'd stopped the attack with a butcher knife, Michael would very possibly have gotten away with taking Adriana and Zack. The only good that had come from the incident was that Michael had been sent back to prison for another five years.

Adriana had mentioned the appeal of moving to Florida more than once and had asked Brooks if he had any interest. The question plagued his mind like Chinese water torture. Could he ever leave *la Montaña Roja*, as Adriana called it?

As if climbing into his thoughts, Otis said, "You can't go anywhere." His eyes searched west over Benton City. "It may come as a surprise, but no matter how much I listen to Joan, I won't be around forever. Someone will need to carry on here, to lead this bunch of vagabonds."

Brooks stomped on the snow, widening the flattened area around his feet. "Jake will always be here."

Otis shook his head. "No, it's you. Jake understands wine, that's for sure. But not like you. You're the one making his wines. You're the one who makes them sing. Without you, his vines would lose their..." Otis's voice trailed off into the cold wind. "They'd lose their power. It's you who's out there talking to them. His vines are part of your destiny."

A bird—maybe a magpie—squawked from down a distant row.

"That's a big responsibility to put on me," Brooks said. "I'm just trying to survive the days. I don't have the ability to look off into the future." He stared at the snow while he contemplated his mentor's remarks.

Like a teacher reprimanding his favorite student, Otis shook his finger at Brooks. "You do, Brooks. You must. The burden is on you whether you like it or not. They may call me the grapefather, and perhaps I can carry that name. But they'll bury me with it soon, and we'll need someone who understands where this mountain is going. Think back to Burgundy. Think of the men and women who put their land before themselves, even during the great wars. You, Brooks, must preserve the resilience of our *terroir*."

Brooks watched a truck move slowly along Demoss Road. "I think we've found this mountain can take care of herself."

"As much as I'd like to believe that," Otis said, "every good piece of land needs a steward, like a good flock needs a shepherd." Otis waved a hand in the air. "All this is yours. I need you to be here after I'm gone."

It was impossible to imagine letting Otis down after all the man had done for him.

Brooks turned and looked to the top of the mountain. "Oh, c'mon. Don't go saying your goodbyes yet. You're not even seventy. Let's have this talk in another decade or two."

"I'm tired, Brooks." Otis dusted the snow off his tweed cap. "Who knows? Maybe I'll come back as a coyote to keep an eye on you."

"I don't doubt it, but that's a long way off." Brooks felt the weight of his mentor's charge settle onto his shoulders.

2

SPRING BERRIES

Otis's words lingered through January and February in Brooks's mind like a haunting melody. Was there any doubt that this mountain was his calling?

As the winds of March started to blow, the new vintage officially began. The hardworking men and women of the mountain had pruned all the vines, and the clippings lay dying around the trunks. Soon, there would be buds, and then flowers, and then baby grape clusters.

Brooks had been head winemaker at Lacoda since the musician Jake Forester had plucked him from Otis Till's employment four years earlier. Brooks had assisted Jake in designing a gravity-flow winery that was cut three stories down into the earth, allowing them to use gravity as opposed to pumps to move the wine from one vessel to the next.

Brooks was currently in the cellar, thirty feet high at the top of a stack of barrels, having monkeyed up there as usual. He pulled out the bung and stuck his wine thief deep into the barrel of Minnesota wood. Drawing the thief out, he filled the crystal glass in his free hand.

Situating himself to a more comfortable lean, he looked down at the clean concrete floors and at the rows of barrels stacked high in the air, thinking back on the past vintage, the one that had brought him Adriana. For an orphan who had never had a girlfriend growing up, it was funny to think that two consecutive vintages had brought him the two loves of his life.

Abby and Adriana.

Abby had been his first love, and he'd asked for her hand in marriage. During their engagement, however, she'd admitted to cheating on him with Jake's wife, Carmen Forester, on a drunken night earlier in their relationship. Having trust issues, Brooks wasn't able to get past her infidelity and had ended their relationship. When he'd thought he'd never love again, Adriana had walked into his life.

He spun the stem in his hand, freeing the aromas, and stuck his nose into the glass. Oh God, how savory it was. A twinge of pencil lead overtaken with gamey notes, those savory qualities that might scare off someone with a less adventurous palate. Smoked meats and Gouda, mushrooms, earth—a wine that instantly transported you to a long wooden table with iron straps and an antique, wax-caked candelabra. A wine so dinner-worthy that it almost put a cut of lamb in front of you, begging a slow meal with the ones you love.

"Don't get too lost in it," someone said down below.

Jake Forester wore black jeans and a denim button-down. The sleeves were rolled up, revealing his ink. Though he was fifteen years older than Brooks, people had often asked if the two of them were brothers. They both had dark hair and tattoos and dressed like bikers. But Brooks could list their differences for days. Having led a famous band for most of his life, Jake had a confidence that only a rock star could possess. He could walk onto a stage with 70,000 people and have them eating out of his hands after one note. His entrance into any room carried the same weight.

Brooks had flashes of that confidence, the kind that comes from being a well-known—dare he think *famous*?—winemaker, but his past never stopped nipping at his heels. It hadn't been easy to come back from growing up a runaway. Jake trusted everyone until that person did him wrong. Brooks trusted no one, even the ones he loved most. He couldn't afford the scarring that came from being let down.

Brooks looked up to the man he was looking down on at the moment. His proximity to Jake Forester had saved him in many ways. Otis had taught Brooks the art of the vine. Jake had taught Brooks the art of life.

His boss put his hands on his waist and peered up at Brooks. "How are they tasting?"

"Like Red Mountain." Brooks eased down one barrel at a time. He didn't spill a drop from the glass as he plopped down onto the concrete next to Jake. "See for yourself."

Jake spun the glass in circles and sniffed. The two men thought about wine differently too. Jake had found his love of wine by tasting all the greatest vintages. The great collectors of the world loved to open up their cellars to rock stars. Before he'd ever picked a grape, Jake had drunk the finest vintages of all the great houses in Europe. He'd drunk grand crus for breakfast. He'd flown into Barolo on a helicopter. He'd broken bread with Daganeau, Mondavi, and Gravner, to name only a few.

Brooks had cut his teeth on wine with a pair of shears and a shovel—by blade and dust. Though Otis had shared many wonderful bottles from his cellar in the eight years they'd worked together, Brooks's education was rooted in the soil.

Tapping into his deep database of tasted wines, Jake thought for a moment and returned his eyes to Brooks. "Reminds me of '04 Côte-Rôtie. Younger and fresher, of course."

Brooks shook his head, not sure if he'd ever enjoyed an '04.

Jake handed the glass back to Brooks. "I need to run something by you," he said in a sobering, deeper tone.

It was fair warning that bad news was coming. Brooks found himself more like Otis these days, expecting the worst. "What is it?"

Jake looked both ways, making sure they were alone. "Carmen wants to come work for the winery."

A bitter taste hit Brooks's tongue, and it wasn't the finish of the Red Mountain syrah. It took thirty seconds before he could even begin to process the news. Was Jake asking for Brooks's approval or issuing a warning? What was Brooks supposed to say? Should he protest? Jake was his boss but also a friend. Brooks had never seen someone stand by his wife like Jake had for Carmen—even through the addiction, the rehab, the relapses. Speaking against the idea might get Brooks in trouble. Recognizing Jake's devotion to his marriage, Brooks had to assume he'd already made up his mind.

"You're not saying anything," Jake said.

Brooks drew in a breath, still debating a reply. The fact was that it was a terrible idea. She would quite possibly ruin everything. "What's she planning on doing?" he finally asked.

It wasn't that Brooks hated Carmen. Even after the former super-model had slept with Brooks's fiancée and destroyed their engagement, he'd moved past it and forgiven her. He loved the rest of Carmen's family too much to hold a grudge the rest of his life. But she was a storm chaser who loved and attracted toxic drama. She *also* happened to be newly sober, which was nothing short of a recipe for disaster.

"I want her to run the front of the house. She won't get in the way of what you do in the cellar. In fact, she'll take some of the things you don't want to manage off your plate. You'll still be head winemaker and general manager, but she'll run events, the tasting room, and the wine club. You don't enjoy those parts anyway. Now you can focus even more on the vines and wines."

Brooks's head swam as the last bastion of his secure world crumbled. Amid all the shit that had fallen down around him, he'd found peace at Lacoda. If there was one thing Carmen was good at, it was yanking the rug out from under anything secure.

What do you say to a man who's committed to his wife? A man who's forgiven her a thousand more times than she deserved? A man who's chosen his wife above all else?

There's only one way to respond, Brooks thought. *I must respect the line of command.*

"You're the boss, Jake." Brooks turned and poured the leftover wine from his glass into a barrel.

Jake ran a hand through his hair. "I know you're not happy."

Even if he wasn't going to say as much, Brooks wasn't going to deny it. "You don't think it's a bad idea to invite someone struggling with addiction into the belly of the beast?" He heard a forklift run its forks under a pallet around the corner.

Jake shrugged. "If Carmen can't handle it, we'll pull her out. She wants to spend more time with me and needs something to do out here. She sure as hell isn't going to take up knitting. She wants to be a part of this thing we're building, especially now that Emilia's going to work for us through the summer. On top of that, you and I both know Carmen needs to stop traveling. These photo shoots, the endorsement trips, that's what's getting her in trouble. The people in the fashion industry run hard and fast, and that's not what she needs. She needs the safety and quiet of Red Mountain. And she needs a job out here," he added, "something to get her mind off herself."

"Understood." There wasn't much more to say. Brooks wouldn't dare admit that, for the first time in months, he could seriously see himself following Adriana and Zack to Florida.

This was the beginning of the end. Somehow, someway, Brooks knew for certain that their brotherhood would suffer because of this news. Most likely, by the end of it all, only one of them would remain standing on the mountain. Carmen was that powerful, that much of a toxic web weaver, and she would always be first in Jake's world. Above his children. Above the *terroir*. Hell, even above himself. No man in Washington valued the union of a marriage more, even if he went to his grave protecting it.

3

SIZE EIGHT

"I know as well as anyone that a second wedding isn't supposed to be as big," Margot Pierce told her sweet terrier mutt, Philippe. "But you know what? I don't care. My first wedding was a billion years ago, and I can barely remember it. Remi Valentine is the love of my life, and I intend to have a befitting ceremony."

The winds of March had finally slowed, and April had brought the warm and teasing days of spring, reminding Margot of why she'd left everything behind in Vermont to open a bed and breakfast—or inn, as she most often called it—on the other side of the country.

Philippe was in the center of her plush, white comforter, watching her put away clothes, his head moving back and forth as though he were sitting center court at a tennis match. Margot was taking her midmorning break to get caught up before returning to her inn for the rest of the day. Now that the season had started again, she was booked almost every night—which was great for the business plan and not so great for her personal life.

As she held and folded a pair of her fiancé's boxers, she found herself giddy at the idea of second chances and doing this wedding the right way. Remi had proposed in such grand fashion on the stage behind Lacoda, and she wanted their small wedding to be equally magical.

Margot already had her list of bridesmaids. They weren't inviting many out-of-town guests, but Margot's best friend, Erica, who lived in Vermont, was definitely first on the list and would serve as maid of honor. Joan, Emilia, and Adriana would also be included, as well as Remi's estranged daughter, if she resurfaced.

As Margot hung a pair of wool pants, she glanced at the neighboring closet, which was full of Remi's things. "Philippe, I'm still getting used to this whole one-closet thing. I'm happy to share most everything with him, but let's be honest. I may need more space."

When she reached the bottom of the basket, Margot set it near the door, approached Philippe on the bed, and leaned over for a kiss. "Come down when you're ready, *mon chou*."

She pulled on a pair of jeans, a flannel shirt, and a sweater. As she was closing her closet door, she couldn't help but take a look at the stunning antique white wedding dress she and Joan had found on a recent trip to Seattle. It was a form-fitting, size-eight stunner that she somehow needed to fit into by September. A size eight was the pot of gold at the end of the rainbow, but Margot was determined to lose the necessary weight. Knowing she would have ripped it at the seams, she hadn't even attempted to try it on before she'd bought it.

A size eight.

Ha!

She'd worn a size eight in college and also toward the end of her marriage, the year she'd committed to winning back her husband by dropping almost every ounce of fat on her body. It was nice to take a sabbatical from eating from time to time, and this was the perfect excuse. A size twelve would have been much more doable. In fact, that's what Joan had suggested. But when Margot balked, Joan had said, "I'm certainly not going to stand in the way of what will make you happy."

Margot had thought about Joan's words a lot lately, but she wasn't ready to address her body image problems quite yet. Maybe *after* the wedding and honeymoon.

Though she'd done it a million times, Margot counted the months out loud. "May, June, July, August, September. Less than six months." She'd been exercising (walking with a smattering of jogging) and eating much healthier (no more second helpings), but she needed to do more. She was already dreading the difficulties of her old diet again, the one that had worked back in Vermont, where she ate mostly air and ran far, far away from any refined carbohydrates. *Oh, the things we women put ourselves through,* she thought.

Margot looked at the lace dress one last time. A bride dreams her whole life of wearing such a work of art. She stuck out a finger. "You're slipping easily onto my body in September. Believe me. You just wait."

Saying goodbye to her adorable little doggie, Margot left the bedroom and descended the stairs. It was odd not finding Adriana and Zack at the dining room table, eating their cereal as usual. Margot's former roommates had moved down to Brooks's house, where he and Adriana had formed their own family of sorts. Considering that Margot's fiancé had been living in an Airstream on his gentleman's farm along the Yakima River, it was *he* who would have to move to her.

She was delighted to hear Remi burst through the door and announce his presence with his latest silly entrance.

"Honey, I'm a gnome!" He smiled with his bushy black eyebrows. He was tall and burly and spoke with a low, husky voice, but his jokes reminded her how playful he could be.

She rolled her eyes. "You're such a ding-dong."

"Oh, I should have rung the bell then." He pressed an imaginary button in the air. "Ding-dong, the gnome's home."

Margot stood on her tiptoes to kiss him. "I forgot to ask you to pick up radishes."

He was chewing gum, and his breath smelled like cinnamon. "Uh-oh."

She followed him to the kitchen. He set the cloth bags on the kitchen counter and reached inside. Drawing out a bunch of radishes, he said, "It's a good thing I'm a mind-reading gnome."

"Oh, you *did* get them," she said, thinking, *That's the way it should be between lovers.* She held up a nearly empty carafe of coffee. "Did you want any more before I pour this out?"

"No, thanks." Remi produced a box about two feet long and skinny. "I bought you a gift."

"A bug zapper?" she asked, squishing her face together in insult. "You know I don't kill bugs." As a matter of fact, even if Margot found a black widow in her bathtub, she'd go out of her way to capture the pest and escort it back outside.

"That's just it," he said, opening the box. "It doesn't zap them." Wielding the new toy like a light saber, he said, "It sucks them up gently so you can return them to the wild unharmed."

Margot curiously took her new toy. "How have I not owned this all along? Sure beats my cup-and-piece-of-paper technique." Margot kissed him again. "Are you buttering me up for something?"

Remi's head kicked back. "Now *you're* the one reading minds." His face straightened, growing serious. "I'm not exactly slathering you with butter—though that would be fun—but something has come up. Amber called while I was in the store."

Margot was taken aback. She knew Remi and his ex-wife texted about Carly sometimes, but Margot had no idea they were speaking on the phone. "When's the last time you spoke with her?"

"By phone? It's been a long time."

Margot wanted to believe him.

He leaned against the counter. "Carly is not doing well at all. I knew she was unhappy, but this is bad. Amber doesn't think she's doing drugs, but she's really down and out. She's sworn off college, and Amber's threatening to kick her out of the house."

Margot sighed and put a hand on his arm. "I'm so sorry. Have you tried calling her?" Remi had kept Margot apprised of his estranged seventeen-year-old daughter's difficulties during her senior year, but Margot hadn't known it was this serious.

Remi shook his head, and Margot was reminded of his pain. She couldn't imagine going years without talking to Jasper. Carly hadn't even reached out to congratulate Remi on their engagement.

Margot lost herself in Remi's dark, sad eyes as she waited for more.

"I need to do something about it," Remi said. "Enough is enough. I thought I might go down there and talk to Carly. Not that I can do any good, but I have to try." Carly and Amber had been living in San Francisco since the divorce.

Margot's bleeding heart sank. "Of course, honey. Please do whatever you need to do. Do you want..." She paused, wondering if she should keep her big mouth shut. "Do you want to ask her if she wants to come stay with us for a little while? The mountain seems to cater well to the lost."

Remi smiled. "I'd love for her to come up and visit, but..."

Though the thought terrified Margot, she wanted to put Remi and Carly first. "Before you fly down there, why don't you offer her a trip up?"

"I don't know why she'd talk to me now," he said defeatedly.

"Well, it sounds like she's no longer mommy's girl. Maybe she's ready, Remi. Call her. Fly down there. Whatever it takes."

"I just don't want all this to get in the way of us. Not that it *would*. That's not what I mean. But more...get in the way of this year and our wedding."

He'd said exactly what Margot was thinking, and she felt the burn of worry in her chest. She tried desperately not to dwell on it. "I'd do anything in my power to help you get your daughter back. Good God, let's get some perspective here. Our wedding and my size-eight dress, or a young woman—your daughter—finding her way in the world?"

She half-believed what she was saying. Yes, putting the other first in a relationship was supposedly the secret to a love that lasts forever, and it was so important to Remi to reunite with his daughter. But would it be at the cost of his marriage to Margot? Though raising Jasper had been a piece of cake, Margot was well aware of how easily a troubled teenager could rip families apart.

4

EX-LOVERS

Margot spent the next few days trying not to drown in the busyness of her inn and the community she'd built around it. Though she now had the help of Adriana and two part-timers as well, the work never seemed to end. Not only was the inn full most of the time, but Margot was also expanding her operation. She offered daily picnic lunches to wine enthusiasts touring the mountain and even the occasional dinner for those who didn't want to drive into Richland. She'd also jumped into the lucrative wedding business, which she was starting to regret. Being engaged herself, she could empathize with the high-maintenance brides, parents, and planners, but that didn't make working with them any easier.

On Wednesday, after serving their guests a beautiful breakfast including homemade blueberry scones and the choice of an egg or tofu scramble, Margot helped Adriana with the dishes and then slipped out for her midmorning break. Remi was spending his days working on his farm, so her house was quiet. She waltzed up the stairs and into the bathroom, where she ran hot water for a bath.

Margot unzipped her dress and let it fall to the floor. Hesitantly turning to the mirror, she gave a quick look up and down. "Margot

Pierce, shame on you. A few more pounds, and you'll be able to sell tickets for whale watching. The first whale ever spotted in the desert!"

She pinched the fat around her stomach. "Captain Ahab," she called out. "We've spotted her fifty feet off the starboard bow. Prepare the harpoon."

In a slightly different sailor voice, she said, "We'll need more than a harpoon, matey. Send for the Royal Navy!"

Swallowing a smile at her own absurdity, she let her hands fall to her sides and took a step closer to the mirror. This was Margot Pierce in all her glory. Maybe Remi was losing his eyesight, which might explain his hunger for her, a craving that could often be quite ravenous in the best of ways.

Margot lifted up her breasts. "Captain Ahab, we'll need a pulley system if we're to get the beasts on board."

"Stop it," Margot finally said, squelching this absurd self-bashing. Though she could turn almost anything into a joke, this loathing had to stop. Her friend Joan would pinch her and tell her not to give any light to this dark voice. Margot closed her eyes, breathed in love, and let all the self-hate and fear go.

Now collected, she lifted her eyelids and dropped her shoulders. With her arms at her side, she looked at the mirror as affectionately as she could. "I love you, stomach. You're not quite where I want you, but I still love you. And you, breasts. You're more than a few handfuls, and you droop like you're both geriatric, but I still love you." She directed her eyes down. "Thighs, I love you most of all."

She addressed her entire body. "But we need to clean ourselves up for this wedding. I am not walking down the aisle like a bulldozer in antique white."

She stopped, becoming aware of how absurd she sounded, speaking to her body as if each part had a brain. "Okay, I'm losing my mind. But still. Do you all get my point? Things are about to change around here. No more pastries. No more *pommes frites*. No more rosé at lunch. Well, okay, that might be pushing it. A glass of rosé at lunch as long as I don't pair it with anything more than a leaf of lettuce—or a *tear* off a leaf. Trust me, the effort will be worth it in the end. Just imagine us strutting down the aisle, each person staring in disbelief. And then Remi casting his eyes at his new bride, his jaw dropping to the floor."

After a long soak in the tub, she dressed in something flowy and comfortable and went downstairs. Bursting out the front door of her home, she stepped into a stunning spring day on Red Mountain. After a brutal, snowy winter, the vines were coming alive all around her. The birds were singing major-keyed songs. Her chickens were happily pecking in the dirt. Her old-world inn further down the drive —her dream come true—looked outrageously beautiful with its weathered cream stucco and pastel yellow shutters. The landscaping had filled out since opening just over a year ago. Though the roses weren't blooming yet, the tulips and daffodils burst with vibrant color. The black locusts lining the gravel drive had grown several feet. The honeysuckle vines had crept up the walls. And the orderly patches of grass were bright and green. No longer was she the new kid on the block. No longer was she a woman chasing a dream.

Margot was now *living* her dream and was an entrepreneur, an innkeeper, and a chef. Though she could easily fall into the trap of disliking her body, she still basked in the pride of knowing she'd broken free of her philandering husband and jumped, blindfolded, into the unknown, trusting that the world would somehow catch her and put her back on her feet. It surely had, so far. Remi was at the forefront of that happy thought, captaining their life into the exciting unknown.

With Philippe at her heels, she did her daily stroll through the garden between the house and inn. She checked the water and food in the chicken coop, noticing Enrique had polished the crystal chandelier that hung almost absurdly in the center above the thick bed of fresh hay. Nothing but the finest for her ladies, the closest they'd ever get to a Ritz-Carlton. After delivering a basket of blue, hazelnut brown, and green eggs to the inn, she returned to her house.

She and Philippe climbed into her Volvo for the short drive down to Remi's place by the river. She saw his white T-shirt first, in the center of his four acres. He was lost in a long line of old Concord grapes that had come with the house. Beyond him, the Yakima River ran strong and high, full with the cold water running east from the spring ice melts. She parked in the gravel drive near the garage where he kept a few vessels of fermenting wine and mead *and* a growing collection of old motorcycles.

Philippe shot out of the car and ran down to find Henri, Remi's Boston terrier, who Margot was sure had the largest eyeballs of any canine on earth. The two dogs met by the garden, which was twice the size of Margot's at the inn, and chased each other into the forest of English walnut trees.

Margot weaved through the small orchard of apple, peach, pear, and plum trees and down the hill to the block of Concord vines. "You've got your work cut out for you," she said.

Remi pulled off his gloves and kissed her. He smelled like an honest morning's efforts. "It's funny. For some reason, I thought farming would be so much easier than my old life. It's quite the opposite."

Margot had come to the same conclusions with her entire dream. "It's a rude awakening, isn't it? I guess there's no running from what has to be done."

"As long as it's the right endeavor, then I don't mind."

It had taken losing his family for Remi to realize the severity of his workaholic ways. Two years ago, he'd walked away from his business as a developer in Seattle to chase the simpler life on Red Mountain. Though he was extremely wealthy, he'd chosen to live in this Airstream in order to unplug and simplify. His eagerness to rediscover himself and reconnect with nature was one of the many reasons Margot had fallen in love with him.

"What's on the agenda today?" she asked.

He looked at the vine cutting he was training upward with green tape. "I'm trying to fill some of these gaps with new plantings." He looked up guiltily. "In my rookie days of learning to drive a tractor, I may have knocked a few vines out of the ground."

"How dare you!"

"Believe me, I've beat myself up about it."

Margot crossed her arms and changed the subject. "So, did you try Carly?"

"Yeah, I tried. She didn't answer."

"Give her a little while. When's the last time you actually called her?"

"Last year." He wiped the sweat from his forehead. "If I don't hear back soon, I'll fly down."

Margot felt a sudden fear rise at the idea of Remi going down to San Francisco to do more reconnecting—this time, with his old life, his daughter and ex-wife.

"This whole thing is really messing me up," he admitted. "It's funny what a seventeen-year-old can do to your psyche."

"Don't I know," Margot agreed, trying not to think of Remi falling back in love with his ex. Margot would readily admit he'd given no reason for her to be suspicious or worried, but she couldn't help having the feelings.

Speaking of seventeen-year-olds, though, her son, Jasper, had been nothing if not perfect all his life. She couldn't wait for him to come home for the summer, but the glass-half-empty in her was terrified he'd call soon to say he was staying in Boston. Though she'd support his decision, Margot wasn't sure she could handle the news.

Moving on, Margot said, "So, as you know, I'm jumping into a major diet soon. Like the craziest ever. Probably in the next couple of days."

Remi inclined his head and studied her. "I think you're perfect just the way you are."

"Thank you. And I almost believe you. But you've seen my dress. It's expecting big things from me—or, I mean, little things. And I plan on delivering."

Remi held an open hand toward her. "I support you either way."

"That's why I love you," Margot admitted. "But this means something to me, to give us the skinny Margot."

"Now, hold on. I like your curves. Stop saying you're overweight, or you'll make me start worrying about myself." He patted his adorable belly. "I could stand to lose a few."

Margot rolled her eyes. "Give me a break."

He smiled, flashing his gorgeous white teeth. "If you don't stop talking about your body, I'll be forced to undress and examine you myself."

Margot's legs quivered. She put her hand on his waist and pulled him close. "I welcome that, Mr. Valentine, though I'm also open to taking this to the Airstream."

Remi glanced up the hill and then back at her. He made a long effort, looking her up and down. Then he reached for the buttons of her shirt, undoing the first one. In a low whisper that sent shivers up her spine, he asked, "How about a peek at those curves?"

Margot undid the next two buttons for him and pulled her shirt open. He sure knew how to make her feel comfortable.

He ran a finger from her left clavicle down. In an even deeper voice, imitating a man of great authority, a police officer, he said, "I'd like to investigate further, ma'am. Will you please step inside my vehicle while I run your tags?"

"Is that what you call these?" she asked.

Continuing his game, he spoke into the fake microphone pinned to his sleeve. "Whiskey, Tango, we have a beautiful blonde who appears to be armed and dangerous and carrying weapons of mass distraction. Permission to investigate further. I'm recommending a strip search." Ignoring her laughter, he paused with a serious face to listen to an imaginary operator. "Roger. I'll be very thorough. Over and out."

Putting his eyes back on her, he grinned, and Margot beamed with the thought of marrying this man. She undid the last of her buttons and let her shirt fall to the sides. For a woman often uncomfortable with her body, Remi could extinguish even the most powerful insecurity.

He swallowed and touched her breasts, those big hands, fingers light as feathers.

Margot loved how playful he could be. Tapping into her theater roots, she put on her best dazed-blonde persona. "My boots don't come off very easily, officer."

Remi wrapped his hand around her lower back and forcefully pulled her to him. "You can leave them on. But the rest has to go." He kissed her neck. "Now let's get moving before I have to take you downtown."

"Yes, sir!"

Remi escorted her toward his RV. As he pulled open the door and she climbed the steps, Margot's heart skipped a beat, and she felt a wave of reservations, that familiar fear of things too good to be true. There was a time when she'd felt this same exact thirst for her ex, Rory, the man who'd ultimately decided his career and secretary's open mouth were more important than Margot. She wanted to believe in love that lasted a lifetime, love that was meant to be, and so much of her knew that she'd found the perfect man. But something was telling her Remi was still hiding skeletons in his closet that would need outing before she officially said, "I do."

5

THE GRUMPY WISE MAN

Otis Till pulled back the curtains and peeked out the window of the house he and his deceased wife had built twenty-three years ago after uprooting their family from Sonoma to pursue a new grape-growing frontier in Washington State. As a way to hold onto his youth and to pay homage to the old world, they'd built their home and the winery in the style of an English countryside cottage. He looked up past his vineyard and winery, farther up the drive, to what had become the future flagship site of Drink Flamingo.

Everyone had thought they'd chased the box-wine empire off the mountain, but their Chief Visionary Officer, Harry Bellflour, had slipped in and bought the old Davidson property next to Till Vineyards. Before Bellflour, it had been Henry Davidson who had tormented Otis, but in a much more serious and violent way. Otis and Henry had been in a feud of sorts that had ended when Henry had shot Joan Tobey two years ago and nearly killed her. Henry had gone to prison, and Joan had recovered, but the guilt of that day still attempted to strangle Otis on quiet nights.

Squinting, Otis could make out Bellflour leading a group of men in business-casual attire across the property. April was nearly over, as were the spring rains, and dust rose with the men's steps. Bellflour was flapping his fat hands around like a slimy salesman, and Otis could only imagine what kind of bullshit web the man was spinning.

When Otis had first learned late last year that Drink Flamingo had bought this cursed ten acres that abutted his own ten acres on the southeastern side, he'd nearly fallen to the ground. He remembered clutching his chest and feeling the pain of an entire life wasted as he imagined the worst.

This same man had nearly gotten away with building a trashy theme park at the gates of Red Mountain, right on the highway near the exit to the appellation. If he had, anyone who'd come to taste the wines of Red Mountain would have first seen this eyesore with gaudy and noisy carnival rides, a lazy river, an RV park, giant pink flamingos, and God knew what else.

Thankfully, Bellflour had been forced to bail on the plans. He'd discovered in the final hour that the property didn't have enough water to support his shoddy vision, so he'd sold the nearly worthless land to a newcomer, Remi Valentine, who would be marrying Margot in the fall. Otis often thought of the day Joan had popped a cork at Margot's house to celebrate the collapse of Drink Flamingo's takeover of the mountain. The news had spread throughout the wine world, and Otis had proudly read in the trade journals—even a well-placed mention in *Decanter*—that Red Mountain had protected herself.

But had she? Otis wondered.

He wasn't as bullheaded as he used to be about boxed wine. In fact, after being swayed by Brooks, who was more up to speed with the trends, Otis had taken a full turn in his opinion. Alternative packaging had become the rage among the new guard of winemakers, and many interesting wines had popped up in cans and boxes from all over the world.

Still, nothing—*nothing*—Drink Flamingo did was interesting. If some fifth-generation farmer in Beaujolais was putting his unfiltered organic gamay into a box, that was okay with Otis. But Harry Bellflour might as well be pissing in those dreaded black boxes featuring pink flamingos and terrible slogans like *Drink inside the box* or *Quit your day job, but never quit drinking Flamingo.*

In the continued fashion of Otis's ominous bad luck—that damn black cat constantly clawing at him—his nemesis would now be his neighbor. The irony was not lost on anyone, especially Otis. He put his heart and soul into his wines and into Red Mountain the same way Yo-Yo Ma danced his bow across the strings of his Montagnana cello. Otis had created a piece of property so special that visitors often came to pay homage to his piece of land like they might walk the rows of Romanée-Conti in Burgundy, kissing the ground and tasting the soil. Many had referred to their visits to Red Mountain as pilgrimages.

How in God's name could Otis continue to shepherd this land with a corporate beast like Drink Flamingo staking its claim?

Having riled himself up to a boiling pot of fury, Otis let go of the curtains and turned with a tense jaw to the woman eating a poké bowl at the kitchen table. With all due respect to the woman he loved, how could she go on smiling euphorically with a terror like Bellflour only a few hundred yards away?

Otis already knew what she'd say if he expressed how he felt. Not that he hadn't done so a nearly infinite number of times since he'd first heard the news of Drink Flamingo's next chess play.

She'd say, "Don't let anyone else drive your emotions. Just let go." Or, "Attachment is suffering. Why tie your own happiness to your neighbor's actions?"

Damn it. If she weren't right all the time, he'd happily jump into an argument with her. With all this anger, he'd jump into an argument with a damn brick right now.

Catching himself from senselessly putting her in the crosshairs, he still couldn't avoid dumping his emotions on her. He said through gritted teeth, "If he puts up a giant flamingo in the yard, I will burn the whole thing to the ground." So much for keeping his thoughts to himself.

Joan Tobey finished chewing. "Darling, you must stop worrying."

He paced the kitchen floors. "Stop worrying? I'm not sure you've grasped the severity of the situation. This guy is not going to put up something classy. We've already gotten a taste of his style. Expect the worst and double it. This is a winery where decisions are made by men in ties who live and die by Excel sheets and PowerPoint presentations. They couldn't change an implement on a tractor if their lives depended on it."

"It's their property," she said, clearly tired of this discussion. "You know as well as anyone that the idea of Red Mountain is to be open to all."

"There must be exceptions," Otis insisted, looking at the bowl of rabbit food she'd prepared for him. Oh, he'd kill for a hamburger right now. Even after two years of adjusting to her diet, he'd eat a hamburger the size of Texas if she'd let him. His only hope for cheating now was cramming a bag of chips down his gullet at Home Depot.

He shook his head at his own grumpiness. How could anyone, especially him, think a bad thought of her at all? He loved her more and more every day and was forever grateful that she'd recovered from the gunshot that had nearly killed her. Though he didn't always show it, he would choose her over his vines if it came down to it.

He kissed the top of her head, her short gray hair. "I know I sound like a broken record, but there must be rules. If Bellflour turns this place into some kind of Disneyland, I'll stick my pocket knife right in his side and let him bleed out on my vines."

Joan sighed. "I'm afraid the challenges never stop coming."

"Oh, that is perhaps the one thing I know more than any other. Especially in my case."

Joan's phone rang on the counter, and she answered.

Otis sat down at the table and stared at his breakfast, remembering Joan's go-to quote whenever he scoffed at a giant bowl of vegetables. *Remember, Otis, food is medicine.*

Picking up a pair of chopsticks, he fumbled around, attempting to grab a cube of sweet potato. After a weak effort, he cast them to the side of the plate and retrieved a fork. Once he was finally eating —or *grazing*, which is what it really felt like—he couldn't help but listen to her conversation. Evidently, she was talking to a complete stranger.

"What are you selling?" she asked.

Ah, a spam caller. Otis braced himself. They'd been here before. Joan couldn't stand it when Otis all but barked at spam callers. She was always quick to explain how difficult their job was and that he should go out of his way to be courteous. Leading by example, Joan was no stranger to carrying on ten-minute conversations with these privacy invaders. Otis was starting to believe she carried on with these intruders just to grate at his nerves.

In the same grateful tone she might use to decline a second pour of coffee from a server, she said, "No, thank you, I'm not looking for life insurance. Where are you located? Oh, I love Utah. It's been a few years, but when I was much younger, I used to ski there all the time. How's the weather this time of year?" Joan smiled as she listened, her patience a wire brush on Otis's tense spine.

"Kids? No, I don't have any children. But I have the most wonderful partner."

She glanced at Otis, and he now knew she was indeed making a point.

Otis spun his hands in the air. "Okay, Mother Teresa, can we wrap this up? I get it."

Joan ignored him and sprang from her seat. "No, I'm on Red Mountain in Washington State." She smiled and listened.

How could she possibly care so much about this idiot on the other end? Otis wondered.

"No, it's not wet at all," Joan continued, apparently finding a thrill in her little chat. "We're a long way from Seattle. In wine country. Yes, everyone thinks that it rains all the time. The Cascades actually get most of the precipitation. Enough about me. Your job must be terribly challenging at times..."

Joan walked into the living room to continue her conversation as Otis muttered mockingly, "Your job must be terribly challenging...bollocks!"

Otis needed out of there. He donned his tweed cap and stormed out the front door with a last shake of his head. The noon sun had warmed the cool morning, but summer was still a good ways out. Jonathan, his Great Pyrenees guard dog, came running up to the fence. "If I let you out, will you go take a chunk out of the fat one's leg?"

Jonathan put his giant paws on the fence.

"Suit yourself. I'll be back down in a minute." Otis worked his way up the hill, past the vineyard he'd been farming for more than two decades. Glancing along the cordons of the vines, he saw that the buds were swelling, reminding him that harvest would be there before he knew it.

Passing his winery, he looked through the giant open doors in the back and exchanged a wave with Elijah, who was hosing down a tank. As his assistant winemaker turned back to his work, Otis returned his attention to the new site of Drink Flamingo's flagship. He'd heard they were running some sort of social media campaign to come up with a name, and Otis was quite sure whatever they came up with would rival *Drink Flamingo* for the worst name in wine since *bunghole*, which referred to the hole bored into a barrel.

In place of Davidson's doublewide and junkyard, the framing had gone up for Drink Flamingo's tasting room and winery. To Otis, the cookie-cutter design looked like the beginnings of a McMansion that belonged in a gated community with some absurd suburban name like Swallowtail at Hampton Downs. Otis had no problems with such a community, but he did take issue with the knuckleheads at Drink Flamingo thinking this concept would work among the other wineries that had a more European mien. This wasn't the suburbs, by God!

A giant hole had been dug behind the McMansion, and Otis feared it might be evidence of an upcoming swimming pool. What was Bellflour up to? The rest of the land had been cleared for planting vines. Next to a John Deere tractor were piles of vineyard poles and huge spools of wire. Otis wondered what varieties they might be planting. Most likely cabernet sauvignon. It was the obvious choice, the easiest variety to sell, and the surefire suggestion his Excel-loving, suit-and-tie board members would offer.

Cresting the hill, Otis stopped at his property line. Only a gravel road fit for tractors separated his favorite syrah block from this travesty. If he could, he would cover his vines' eyes, just as he might shield a child from witnessing a bloody murder.

Bellflour stood in the middle of the future vineyard with the four men circling him. Otis felt sick as his enemy reached down and gathered a handful of Red Mountain soil, then tossed it in front of him. The act was no different than the devil bathing in holy water. The dusty soil caught in the air and hung like ashes and smoke.

When Bellflour finished his demonstration and the air cleared around them, he caught sight of Otis and led the men in Otis's direction.

Otis held his ground, ready for whatever might come. He reminded himself of his new motto. "W.W.J.D? What would Joan do?"

And then, to himself, he said grumpily, "Do the opposite."

6

WHAT LONELY LOOKS LIKE

When the five men drew near, Bellflour said with a shit-eating grin, "Howdy, neighbor."

Otis felt a quick urge to bulldoze the man into the dirt. If the nitwit wasn't careful, Otis would drop to all fours, run over, and take a bite out of his leg. Being a good boy, though, Otis stuffed his hands in his pocket and nodded. Had this been 100 years earlier, he would have put his hand on his six-shooter.

Judging by his attire, Bellflour was growing accustomed to living in the country. He wore heavy leather boots and blue jeans. He was a big man with a swollen belly that pushed at his short-sleeve button-down. A large gold watch adorned his hairy arms. Small red veins covered his nose like fine cracks in glass.

Keeping his hands in his pockets, Otis asked, "How you gentlemen doing today?"

"Haven't seen you in a while," Bellflour said, stopping a few feet away—too far to shake hands.

Otis assumed Bellflour didn't want to embarrass himself by sticking out a hand and having Otis ignore it. Which is exactly what Otis would have done. And, as the notion crossed his mind, he couldn't resist. He took a couple of steps closer, crossing into Drink Flamingo territory.

He offered his hand to Bellflour. "I do my best to avoid you."

Bellflour reached for Otis's hand skeptically.

That was just too easy, Otis thought. With his own smug grin, he pulled his hand back. It was the game of a child, but it gave Otis a modicum of satisfaction.

A guy in a Patagonia vest snickered, followed by the others.

Looking past Bellflour as if he weren't worthy of eye contact, Otis said, "I was hoping you'd change your mind about this place."

Bellflour chuckled. "Here I was just telling these men how much I admired you. After all, I might have been chewed up by those coyotes last year had you not jumped into the fray. I owe you for that, Otis."

"I'll consider us even if you'll sell me your property and go shit on another mountain."

"I'm not sure I ever want to leave this place," Bellflour confessed. "We're excited to get our vines into the ground and see what all the fuss is about."

"You and I both know you couldn't grow a weed out here."

Bellflour turned back to his unfinished property. "That might be true. But I partner with the best." He gestured toward the other men and introduced them. Two were Drink Flamingo associates. The other two were contractors who'd flown up from Napa. A winemaker and vineyard manager. Nice enough men with names Otis knew well. Drink Flamingo was no doubt paying a pretty penny for their involvement.

Otis addressed the others. "So you're all as intent as Bellflour on ruining this land?"

Bellflour extracted a cigar from his shirt pocket and rolled it back and forth with his fat fingers. "Oh, lighten up, Otis. As much credit as you're due for your contributions, you're getting old and grumpy."

"You don't need to tell me that," Otis hissed.

"You ask what we're planning," Bellflour said. "We're going to make one of the best cabernets Washington State has ever tasted."

Otis *tsk-tsked* and held up a finger. "You don't make wine on Red

Mountain, Bellflour. We're not making soft drinks here. Haven't you learned yet? You don't make wine. You *grow* it."

Bellflour shook his head, but he knew better than to argue wine philosophy. If he had taken the bait, Otis would easily have wiped the floor with him.

Saving Bellflour, one of the other men chimed in. For some reason, maybe the fine cut of his shirt or the clean haircut, Otis felt as though he was the one with the money. "These will be high-scoring wines, Mr. Till. People will pay big money to have us in their cellars."

Otis shook his head and wondered where to start. People so quickly turned to scores when they didn't know what they were talking about. Should he try to teach them a lesson today—or bite his tongue? What would Joan do? She was probably still on the phone with the Utah spammer.

Oh, fuck it.

"You know," Otis started, "the problem with you guys is you're putting money first. I get it. We all have to feed our families, and some of us have to make our board members smile. But you're going about it ass backward. Gentleman, breathe this air for a moment. You're in a holy place. Put your knees in the Red Mountain dust and pay tribute. *Try* to understand her. If you do that, she'll give you all the treasures of the earth." Otis locked eyes with one of the Drink Flamingo henchmen. "I didn't start out by opening a business checking account and filing for papers. The first thing I did was put my ear to the ground."

He glanced at Bellflour, just *waiting* for him to throw up a challenge, to dare and try to dance with the grapefather.

The vineyard manager up from Napa nodded eagerly. "I respect you tremendously, Otis. Your name far precedes you down in California, and I know exactly what you mean. I hope to make you proud with what we're doing."

Otis pinched his chin and scrutinized the man, judging his intentions. "You're surrounding yourself with questionable company, my friend."

The man pressed his lips together, and Otis could almost read what he wanted to say—that Drink Flamingo money was just too good to turn down.

Otis raised a hand, shook his head, and bounced his eyes from one man to the next. "If you don't put the mountain first in your decisions, you'll suffer the consequences."

"Sounds like a threat to me," Bellflour said, lighting his cigar with a silver Zippo.

Otis stared at the orange flame. "I don't need to threaten anyone here. This mountain takes care of herself." As he said the words, Otis hoped she would continue to do so.

Bellflour puffed hard, the orange going red, and a cloud of smoke swarmed around him.

"And Bellflour," Otis continued, "if she doesn't protect herself, there are a few good men and women here who damn sure will. Don't forget that."

Bellflour pulled the stubby cigar away with his fat fingers. "Ah, Otis. I was hoping we were done with all the bickering and threats."

The grapefather tilted his cap to the man and turned away. "I was too."

Otis caught himself angrily stomping back down the gravel drive and slowed to a more calculated meandering. The grapefather had to be wiser about the situation, not a hothead running around chomping at people like Pac-Man.

How could he deal with a neighbor whose agenda was the exact opposite of his own? Part of him wished he were back in the Middle Ages, where he could settle the war the old-fashioned way. With stricter laws and lawyers, his hands were tied.

⟿

OTIS FOUND Joan sitting in the living room under the painting Otis's Aunt Morgan had done of him, an arresting picture of Otis on all fours, howling at the moon. He couldn't look at the painting without remembering that night that Morgan had shined a light on him well past midnight and scolded him for howling in his birthday suit.

"It's lovely to have gotten to know you," Joan said into the phone.

Otis clapped his hand to his forehead. "Oh, don't tell me you're still on the phone with this buffoon."

Joan gave him the evil eye and returned to her conversation.

Otis looked back at Morgan's painting. It had been a long time since he'd howled with the coyotes. Knowing he couldn't listen to another word of this agonizingly long phone call, he pivoted back toward the kitchen, raising both hands in the air in frustration.

After wearing out the floors in the kitchen with his feet, he finally heard her end the call. Returning to the living room, he said, "The whole world's crashing on top of us, and here you are, delighting in a phone call with a stranger who wants to sell something that you don't need."

She clasped her hands together. "If you don't lighten up, I'm going to send you to your room, Otis. You sound like a five-year-old. The poor guy gets yelled at and hung up on all day long. The least I could do is treat him like he's human."

"You're treating him like he's your best—" Otis stopped himself and sighed. "I don't mean to take it out on you."

"Well, you are."

"I'm truly sorry." Otis did feel like a five-year-old as he traipsed toward her and collapsed onto the couch. "I can't share this mountain with that man, let alone be his neighbor. It looks like they're putting in a pool, Joan."

"What's wrong with a pool? We do live in the desert."

He crossed his arms. "It's the principle of the thing. No farmer has time to sit by the pool."

"Your farmer's tan is testament to that," she said, apparently trying to lighten his mood.

Her humor was lost on him. He shook his head in defeat and breathed through a notion that he'd not yet said out loud. "Something tells me this is my last vintage here. I can feel it in my bones. It terrifies me to think what this mountain might become."

"Oh, quit talking like you're dying. You're in your late sixties. You've got a long way to go."

He drew in a lengthy breath. "Yeah, but I'm running low on fight, my love."

"Then don't fight. Go be you. Focus on your wines. Not his."

Otis removed his cap and folded it in half. "I think this could be it. Seriously." A heaviness settled into his chest.

Joan took his cap and placed it back on his head. "And what would you do with all your time if you weren't out there working your land?"

Otis turned to her and met her diamond eyes. He could see freedom for a moment, but then it dashed away like a disappearing light. "As long as I'm with you, I'm not sure I care."

"That's very sweet of you. But we both know you'd go crazy without your vines. I'm not sure I could stand being with a 'retired' Otis. Talk about a handful."

He had to admit, a retired Otis did sound like a disaster. "That's why this whole mess is so confusing. What would you do if a man had invaded your land? A thousand years ago, I would have run him through with a sword. What now? Run? Fold the hand I was dealt? What would I do with the land? For a long time, I thought I'd leave it to Brooks, but I wouldn't wish this tainted *terroir* on anyone now."

"I've already told you what I'd do, Otis. I'd forget about him and focus on your own vines." She nestled into him. "Let everything outside of this property drift away."

~

"WE'LL SEE YOU GENTLEMEN SOON," Harry Bellflour said, offering a final wave to the two consultants from Napa who were climbing into their rental car. Once they'd pulled away, he turned to his colleagues, the Drink Flamingo controller and the new CEO, Wendall. "I think they'll do," he said with confidence.

Wendall was still trying to establish his dominance in the company and frequently spoke with his arms crossed. "Yeah, they'll be fine. I wonder about Otis Till, though. Will he be a problem?"

Bellflour often wanted to punch Wendall right in his giant nose, but he needed the man on his side. After the fiasco last year with the project near the highway, Bellflour was skating on thin ice with the members of the board.

He pulled on his Padrón cigar, enjoying the gentle burn of the Nicaraguan leaves. "Nah, he's just an old man holding onto the past. He's harmless."

Wendall kicked the dirt. "We need to get to the airport. You sure we'll have the winery up by the end of September?"

Bellflour turned and looked at the frame of the building. He'd had a few hiccups, but things were going as planned now.

"Yes," he said. "I'm confident. In fact, I've already committed to buying several tons of cabernet. We don't have a choice." They would have to wait at least two years to get any fruit off the vines they'd planted on the estate, so, in the meantime, they would purchase fruit from other Red Mountain wineries.

Not only was Bellflour intent on meeting the deadline in order to save face, but he also felt a burning need to fire back at Otis and the rest of his clueless neighbors. They'd tried to laugh him off the mountain, crucifying him in the media. No one waged war with Bellflour, and he'd prove it soon enough. It didn't matter that Otis had saved his life—maybe he'd have a statue done of the grapefather and put it poolside as a way of saying thanks. The old man was still a bastard and needed to be knocked off the playing board.

Wendall straightened his collar. "No more mistakes, Harry."

Bellflour felt the tendons in his own neck tighten. He'd had nothing to do with the screwup with the water rights on last year's property, but here he was, still taking the blame.

"The facility will be operational, and the tasting room will be open," Bellflour said. "I give you my word."

Until their own vines bore fruit, they would mostly serve offerings from their boxed-wine collection. Bellflour was also working on a frozen-sangria project and had filed paperwork for the trademark to the name *Fro-gria*. If he could get that project up and running in time, he could also serve Red Mountain Fro-grias.

Wendall smoothed his hands together. "I don't need to tell you what another PR disaster would do to us. I'm *still* cleaning up this whole Red Mountain mess."

Bellflour could hear the threats of last chances in his new boss's tone. His fingers tightened around the cigar. "We learned a lot about this mountain last year...and about the people. Nothing can stop us now."

"I do love the idea of using a social media campaign to name the winery," Wendall admitted.

Bellflour smiled proudly. "Why not let the millennials do all the marketing for us?"

Showing the board he was as plugged in to modern times as ever, Bellflour had suggested they have one of their fans name the winery, and their PR team had put together a brilliant social media contest that was underway. The person who named their flagship winery would get an all-expenses-paid trip to the grand opening at the end of September and a lifetime membership to the wine club.

"I look forward to hearing what they come up with," Wendall said.

"There are already some great ideas on the table. I'll send you some favorites soon."

The three men shook hands, and Bellflour offered a last wave as they rounded the yet-to-be paved driveway.

"Good riddance," he whispered, watching their rental car disappear down Sunset Road. He was always the guy on the ground, the man getting things done, and it was so easy for those chumps from corporate to fly up here and point fingers and bark orders. It was he —Bellflour—who uprooted and moved every time they started a new project and needed someone to manage the thick lists of to-dos.

7

NORMALCY

On the third of May, Brooks woke with the dread of Carmen's first day bearing down on him. He spent an hour with his hands behind his head, staring at the ceiling fan, wondering how Carmen would ruin what he and Jake had built at Lacoda. Because it wasn't a question that began with *if.* Not at all. Carmen was a ticking time bomb. No, the question was *when* would Lacoda come crashing down? Could Brooks pull off another vintage? Two? Or would Carmen come in fast and furious, destroying all that was good about the winery in a matter of days?

As the morning sun poked through the blinds, Brooks let it all go, hoping his worry was unwarranted. If they were lucky, Carmen would try out the gig for a week or two and then choose something else to do with her time. With her newfound sobriety, she was surely going to be all over the place until something stuck.

Brooks rolled toward Adriana and kissed one of the scars on her cheek. "Good morning, sunshine."

The lines marking her face had come from a day toward the end of her marriage when her husband, now her ex-husband, had flung her into a china cabinet. They weren't the only scars left from that day. When she opened her eyes, he saw a very strong woman who was fighting to get back to the person she had been before her abusive marriage. That's why Brooks kept feeding her slack when she sometimes turned a cold shoulder to him.

"*Buenos días,*" she said. She often slipped into her native tongue.

Never knowing whether she'd wake up hot or cold, he edged closer and pushed a hair away from her forehead. "How'd you sleep?"

Adriana covered a yawn. "Okay. It took me forever to fall asleep."

"I wasn't snoring, was I?" She'd never mentioned it, but Abby had said something a couple of times.

Adriana glanced at him and then to the ceiling. A subtle shake of her head. "No, I was just thinking too much. My mother used to call it *mente desbocada.* The runaway mind."

Unable to resist his Mexican temptress lying naked in the sheets next to him, Brooks slid his hand down her side. "I call this the runaway finger."

She caught his hand and pushed him away. "Oh no, you don't. Zack will be up any moment."

Brooks conceded and turned away before she could see his disappointment. Every time he thought he was getting somewhere, she would pull back, and not only sexually. Her affection toward him was a roller coaster of screaming downhills followed by slow upward ascents. He couldn't help but wonder if she was questioning her love for him.

~

THE COFFEE WAS JUST KICKING in when seven-year-old Zack came barreling into the kitchen, bright-eyed and beaming, as if he'd been up for hours. "Did you know there's a giant island of plastic in the Pacific Ocean? And only a small part of the items we put in the big blue bins actually get recycled?"

Brooks looked up from his iPad, where he was catching up on the latest wine news while his first cup of coffee worked its way through his veins. "Slow down, my man. Once you get to be my age, it takes a minute to wind up the engine. How do you know all this, anyway?"

Zack wore green pajamas, and his hair stuck out in every direction. He'd just lost an upper front tooth and spoke with a slight lisp. "Lots of animals, like turtles, get trapped in all the plastic. Sometimes they die."

"Is this what you're learning about in camp?" Adriana asked, turning from the stove.

Zack nodded while sticking a finger up his nose.

Brooks pointed at him and asked, "You mining for gold up there?"

Having already heard this comment from Brooks a hundred times, Zack pulled his finger from his nose and dropped a few more facts about plastic.

Adriana eventually interrupted him. "I'd better get a kiss in the next five seconds or else."

Zack ran to her and wrapped himself around her leg. "I'm hungry."

"That makes two of us," Brooks chimed in, standing up from the table, breathing in the simmering concoction of cilantro, jalapeños, and eggs. He couldn't get enough of Adriana's cooking; the savory smells constantly filled the kitchen. She'd learned from her mother first, and had mastered the flavors of the Yucatan, and now, under Margot's tutelage, she'd taken her skills to the next level.

"Just a few more minutes, *mis amores*."

Even just this term of endearment was enough to make Brooks want to keep trying. He knew deep down how much she cared. It was just a matter of supporting her while she fought her demons.

Zack ran up to Brooks and smacked his shoulder. "Tag, you're it." With that, he raced out of the room.

Brooks set down his coffee and bulleted after him. He made monster sounds as he stomped up the stairs and into Zack's room, which no longer resembled the guest room it used to be. Brooks and Adriana had worked hard to make him feel at home here. Now it was full of toys and art projects—the boy's room Brooks had never had growing up.

In his best attempt at scary-yet-silly, Brooks whispered, "You can't run forever, little boy."

Zack shrieked, and Brooks jerked his head toward the closet and growled.

The boy he was coming to love yelled louder this time, and the feeling of fatherhood rose up through Brooks and bloomed into a smile. He was so happy to be there for Zack and to give him the life Brooks had never known as a child. What was even more beautiful about their relationship was that it wasn't one-sided. It wasn't about Brooks helping a young boy who needed a father figure. This relationship was good for Brooks too. And whether they were playing games or fishing or chatting about life, Brooks enjoyed their time together as much or more than Zack did.

With his smile still stretched wide, Brooks crept toward the closet and whipped open the door. "You're mine!"

Zack sprang out with a shout.

Brooks snatched up Zack and squeezed him tight, feeling the boy's heart pounding with excitement. Dropping him on the bed, Brooks commenced to tickle Zack until he screamed "Uncle!" at the top of his lungs.

As they descended the stairs in exhaustion, both red-faced and breathing heavily, Brooks rubbed Zack's head. "Let's sneak up on your mom," he whispered. "I think she needs a good scare."

They both snuck down the stairs, careful not to let them creak. With Brooks at the lead, they slipped through the hall toward the kitchen. Brooks saw the hot plates of enchiladas Adriana had prepared for them steaming next to the stove, and the kitchen was thick with the aromas of Mexican cuisine.

Adriana had taken her seat at the table to drink coffee and was looking at her phone.

Brooks and Zack crept toward her, one quiet foot at a time, both barely able to suppress their laughter. Just before revealing themselves, Brooks caught a glimpse of the image on Adriana's screen.

Palm trees, white sand, and turquoise water.

Florida.

He stopped and let Zack go ahead of him. A frown rushed over Brooks as he now knew for sure that he was losing her, little by little, day by day. It had been a while since he'd seen her looking at tropical pictures. He'd hoped she'd changed her mind.

Apparently not.

Sometimes, she made it so damn hard to love her. He was all in, but he needed her to be committed too. As he'd told her before, there were no winemaking gigs in Florida to be had—at least, none that he'd be interested in.

Zack put a hand on his mom's shoulder. "Mommy!"

Adriana let out a yell and nearly jumped out of her chair. Before acknowledging her son, she quickly put her phone face down on the table mat.

When she turned, she grabbed her son's shirt. "Not nice, young man." Then she looked at Brooks.

He had to dig deep to force his lips to curl up and pretend he hadn't seen the truth of what was on her mind.

8

MARGOT'S LAST STAND

O ne thing about Margot and diets: she liked to go out in style. Her diets were always a cold-turkey kind of thing, wake up one morning and go. But first, she had to enjoy one last day of pure hedonism, a way to shake all her urges out of the tree. Today was Margot's last stand before 166 days of unsatisfied temptation.

Remi was down at his place but had promised he'd be back by noon to join her in this day of debauchery. It was eleven now. Already full of food ideas, Margot walked into her kitchen, tied on an apron, and got started. Her world could be divided up into two camps: sweet and savory. She couldn't have one without the other—at least, not on this most special day. And how could she possibly kick off a diet without her deep fryer? The savory portion of today's gluttony would begin with Champagne and *pommes frites*, which already set her up for the "sweet" decision. Since the fryer was out, why not do mini doughnuts? Oh God, how gluttonous could one girl be?

Well, potatoes and doughnuts were just the beginning. As with all her last stands (and there had been more than a few), she'd make sure they had enough food to munch on all day long, whenever the mood struck. Why not cheese and chocolate too? How about deviled eggs? Oh, was that gelato in the freezer?

Margot had made mini doughnuts so many times in her life that she'd memorized the recipe. Once the dough was ready, she covered it in cellophane to let it rise. Sadly, she hadn't soaked potatoes for the *frites* overnight, but that was okay. She could at least soak them for a little while to extract some of the starch. She ran the russet potatoes through her french fry attachment on the food processor, marveling as it easily cut out the perfect shape for bistro *frites*. Then she dropped them in a saltwater bath so they'd at least have a chance of crisping to perfection.

Taking her favorite vintage breadboard off the pot rack, she went to work on a cheese plate. Having stocked the kitchen in the inn the day before, she had an abundance of cheeses from cow and sheep milk. She cut off chunks of a Cotswold from the UK, a surprisingly delicious vegan smoked cashew cheese from Oregon, and a *Challerhocker* from Switzerland, which all of her guests at the inn had loved.

To accompany the cheese, Margot searched the fridge shelves for ideas. Finding the bunch of radishes Remi had bought, she washed and dried them, then dipped their tips in tempered butter, finishing them with a pinch of black Cyprus salt flakes. Once they were on the board with the butter hardening, she added a few dried Red Mountain apricots from Remi's harvest last year, some homemade pickles, and a handful of pecans and walnuts. She found some chickpeas in a Ziploc bag that hadn't been blended into hummus yet, so she took a couple of handfuls, mixed them with olive oil and herbs, and tossed them in the oven on 400 degrees. The ideas kept coming until the board started to look embarrassing.

Just as she was setting a pink Champagne from Duval-Leroy into a bucket of ice, Remi came walking in, right on time. Entering the kitchen area, he looked at their feast. "Oh, I didn't realize we were hosting the entire mountain today. Are they all climbing in bed with us?"

He reached for a radish, but Margot slapped his hand. "No, sir. I want you showered before you touch me or any of my food." She turned on the fryer to the left of the stove, then said, "Meet me in bed in fifteen?"

~

BY THE TIME Remi walked out of the bathroom in his robe, Margot had gotten the dogs comfortable on their beds with homemade treats, and she'd set two trays of food in the middle of the four-poster, king-sized bed.

Remi's wet hair was combed back, and he'd shaved again, his face shining. He looked at the cheese plate and then the tray holding the *frites* and doughnuts. "I think you should go on diets more often."

"Ha, ha," she said slowly.

Once they'd climbed into bed and shared a toast, Remi asked about their honeymoon. "Are you still thinking Europe?"

As she sipped her pink bubbles, Margot saw a vision of the two of them strolling hand in hand along the Seine at sunset, the Eiffel Tower lit up above them. Then again, a gondola in Venice sounded just as nice. Not that she'd be against a resort in the Caribbean—with their own infinity pool up on a cliff looking out over the crystal-clear water.

"I can't decide," she admitted. "How much can we get done in two weeks?"

"Is that all? I was thinking we'd go for months."

"Two weeks during harvest is already going to be a lot on Adriana." She popped an apricot into her mouth, thinking how lucky she was to have Adriana at all. A year ago, she couldn't have left the mountain for longer than an hour without things falling apart.

Remi dipped a *frite* into a Dijon mustard that Margot ordered from France by the bucket. "I think she'll be just fine. You know, Amber and I didn't even go on a honeymoon. I had to be in Portland the day after our wedding for a meeting, and then we just never got around to it. I will not let the same thing happen to us."

Margot broke a *frite* in half and tossed it down to the dogs.

"There's something so romantic about France. You and I could get in a lot of good trouble in Paris."

"I like good trouble."

Fifteen minutes and one glass of Champagne later, Margot took the remote control off the bedside table. "We'd better get started. I have the perfect movie."

"*Hallmark*, I hope," Remi said. "I'm *sooooo, sooooo* tired of CIA operatives hunting down terrorists. Who wants to sit on the edge of their seat? Give me a drama-free happily ever after that will keep me guessing all the way through the opening—and I do mean *opening* —credits."

"Are you done?" she asked, unable to suppress her smile. What could be better than a lazy day with Remi Valentine?

"I don't know why Hallmark movies don't win more Oscars," he said, apparently still full of sarcasm. "That last one we watched... what was it?"

"*A Kiss Forever*?"

"That's the one. How did that not win best film of the year? I'm talking about riveting, tour-de-force performances that really affected me. Deep down. I'm still shook up."

Margot rolled her eyes. "You're so mean. I do think you'll like this one, though."

Navigating the screen, she found the one she wanted. "Here it is. *A Romance in the Vines*."

"Get out of here," he said. "I'm so in, you don't even know."

It didn't take long for Remi to start poking fun. After the first scene with the lead lady's winemaker love interest, he said, "This guy is the next Cary Grant. I mean, wow. Do you think they'll end up together at the end? Gosh, I hope so."

Margot slapped his thigh. "Will you hush?"

A few scenes later, the two lovebirds in the movie were having their first date at a restaurant near the man's winery. Margot was thinking how cute they were together when Remi said, "Look, he's holding the wine glass by its bowl. Someone may want to tell this head winemaker of this very fancy, if not slightly fake-looking, winery to hold the glass by the stem." Remi chuckled as he pointed to the screen. "Look at him twirling the glass. Oh God, I can't watch. If he calls the wine *smooth*, I will fall over."

Margot and everyone else on the mountain knew *smooth* was the most overused descriptor in the wine world.

The winemaker on the television looked up from his glass and said, "It's very smooth."

Remi's mouth fell open, and he raised his hands high. "Smooth! He said it. You realize you're marrying a man who not only reads minds but can also see the future."

Once Remi finished gloating, Margot asked, "Are we doing this the whole movie? Is that what's happening, Mr. Know-it-all?"

Remi reached for a doughnut. "Here's what I didn't quite realize about Hallmark. There are serious layers to these movies. I mean, stuff you might not pick up until the third or fourth viewing. Is this a Ridley Scott production? This is almost *A Good Year* good."

Halfway through the movie, Remi was still making his comments, and the two of them were each onto their fifth doughnut. Powdered sugar and cinnamon clung to their lips.

Remi leaned over the tray of food and kissed her. "I love being with you. Even when we're watching bad movies on questionably the worst channel on cable television."

"Oh, don't make me choose a Lifetime movie next," Margot warned. "They're *almost* as good."

Before Remi could reply, his phone rang, and he reached for it. When he looked at the screen, he turned rigid, and Margot knew exactly who had called.

She reached for the remote and paused their movie.

Putting the phone to his ear, Remi sat up and answered. "Hi, Carly. Can you hold on one second?" He covered the phone. Looking like a teenager about to give his first public speech, he asked Margot, "Can you give me a few minutes?"

"Of course," she said, but he was already exiting the bedroom. She heard him descend the stairs as his powerful voice faded away.

In the quiet, Margot realized how happy she was for him. She couldn't imagine not talking to Jasper for an extended length of time. Had she not just opened her inn, she might have considered moving to Boston just to be near him. Remi getting a second chance with his daughter was the best news in the world, and the timing was perfect. Carly was going to be Margot's stepdaughter and Jasper's stepsister. It would be so much better if Remi and Carly could work everything out before the wedding.

Then Margot's thoughts went to Amber, Remi's ex-wife, and Margot couldn't help but wonder if there would be a wedding at all. As much as Margot wanted Remi to rekindle a relationship with Carly, she wanted the exact opposite with Amber. The thought of them rekindling old love down in San Francisco terrified her. Margot had seen pictures of Amber. She was a brunette bombshell who looked like she basically lived at the gym doing CrossFit.

She heard Remi coming back up the stairs. He stopped at the doorway. "She's coming."

"Up here? That's great." *For so many reasons*, Margot thought.

He approached her. "You sure it's okay?"

"Are you kidding me? She's your daughter."

Remi put his hand on one of the columns of the bed. "I'll book her flight early next week, the day after her classes get out. When is Jasper coming home?"

"He's home on the sixteenth." Knowing that their lazy Hallmark day had come to an end, Margot turned off the television, slipped out of the bed, and began organizing what was left of the food.

"Good," he said, helping her clean up. "That will give us a couple of days with Carly by herself. Just to make sure she's comfortable. This will be a lot for her."

Margot pushed aside her fears and went to him, wrapping her arms around his waist. "Don't worry, honey. This will be great. I'm so happy for you."

He gently patted her back. "I know. I'm really happy—but also pretty nervous."

"There's nothing to be nervous about," Margot lied. Then, more truthfully, she said, "And she'll love Jasper. Everyone does."

"She'll love both of you," Remi assured her. "But I just hope she likes the mountain."

"Did she say how long she plans to stay?" Margot tried to downplay the question.

"No. I told her as long as she wants. She was accepted into UCLA, but I'm not sure she wants to go."

Margot took his hand, rubbing her thumb over his palm. "The mountain will be good for her. And we'll be one big happy family." The last words felt sticky as they left Margot's mouth.

"One big Hallmark story, right?"

Margot stood on her tippy toes and kissed him, tasting the powdered sugar clinging to his lips. "Only happy endings around here."

Remi smiled. "I'm not touching that comment."

9

CARMEN'S FIRST DAY

Brooks held an arm out the truck window as he turned onto Sunset. It was still dark out, an hour away from sunrise, and a heavy fog had set in sometime during the night. He could make out a pair of taillights a good distance ahead of him, another early bird eager to get started. This time of year, the vineyard workers came in early so they could finish before the afternoon sun cooked their skin.

As he passed Kiona, the first winery founded on the mountain, he caught a flash of silver twinkling in the fog, racing down a vineyard row parallel to the road. It had to be a coyote. He tapped the brakes to get a better look. It was very rare to see a song dog—as many called them on the mountain—and Otis had taught Brooks to always take a moment to appreciate the luck of an encounter. He scanned the area but gave up after a while.

Giving the truck some gas, he moved on again, reviewing what needed to happen today, including the work orders he needed to put in. His cellar rats often ran around aimlessly until Brooks gave them their list of chores. It was part of being the boss. No big deal.

As he remembered that his glass supplier was taking him to

lunch today, the flash of silver appeared again, this time darting across the road. With a curse, Brooks slammed on the brakes—

but it was too late. Screeching, the truck kicked sideways a few degrees and slid into the coyote, sending it tumbling across the pavement and into the ditch.

Heartbroken, Brooks watched for movement, trying not to think of the bad luck that came with hitting a coyote. The morning took on an eerie silence, and the fog seemed to instantly thicken. He put his fingertips on the car door handle, tempted to get a closer look. But coyotes could sometimes be dangerous, especially if they were wounded.

After a few more moments in the quiet, the coyote limped out of the ditch, situating itself on the shoulder of the road. A long stare-down ensued, so long that Brooks leaned his head out, wanting a better view—a deeper connection.

Very often, coyotes were skittish, quick to dash away at the sight of humans. This one was different and showed no apprehension at all. Judging by his stance and cutting, lava-red eyes, he looked more curious and confident than afraid. Reminding Brooks of Adriana, an old scar ran from the side of the coyote's eye to his ear. For a moment, Brooks forgot that he'd hit the dog, and he found himself both shocked and relieved that it at least appeared to be okay.

Brooks could see Otis in those eyes, the wisdom and anguish, and also a sense of being bound to a place. He suddenly felt like an intruder, like Custer invading Native American land. Brooks thought about something he'd heard one time, how the souls of dogs came back as humans. As Brooks peered into the eyes of this being, he considered the possibility that it had lived several human lives before returning to earth as a song dog.

"Who are you?" he asked, his voice breaking the quiet of the night.

The coyote twisted its head and lifted up its snout curiously.

"Where have I seen you before?"

Brooks felt less threatened now and cracked open his door. He wasn't exactly sure what he planned on doing, but he felt a calling to move closer.

The coyote whipped around and ran off into the vines, a flash of silver disappearing into the darkness and fog.

Brooks was touched deeply by the experience and wondered what it meant as he searched the darkness of the desert with his eyes.

~

THE COYOTE SIGHTING distracted Brooks throughout the early morning, and he barely gave a thought to Carmen and her first day until she followed Jake into his office about nine.

Brooks was on the phone trying to find a piece to fix the bottling line. "Let me call you back," he told the guy, hanging up before the other man could respond. Brooks set his cell phone down on the table and waved the power couple in.

With a body that had made her millions, Carmen was five-ten, pencil-thin, and busty. She wore hiking shoes and fancy jeans with fashionable holes above the knees. The slightest bit of cleavage peeked out from her rolled-sleeve, button-down shirt. Her shiny brown hair was pulled back into a ponytail.

Brooks imagined *Wine Enthusiast* would love to put her on the next cover. To the casual eye, she was jarringly beautiful, which reminded Brooks of how much trouble she'd caused in his own life, taking Abby from him, destroying their engagement. Having known Carmen for a long time, Brooks didn't look at her the way most people did, like a supermodel prancing about, a delight for the senses. He saw a damaged woman whose insecurities often showed themselves in the meanest of ways. To Brooks, she was the kind of person he preferred to avoid.

And yet, she was like family to him, so he tried not to embrace the revulsion he sometimes felt for her. Not only was she Jake's wife and Emilia's and Luca's mother—reason enough to give her the benefit of the doubt—but she also surprised him with a warm heart when he least expected it. She was a punch in the face and a hug around the neck at the same time. Or a poisonous concoction mixed with a dose from the fountain of youth in one tempting tumbler.

Carmen had changed a lot since getting sober, for better and worse. Brooks had seen a part of her that he really liked, a positivity and realness that had been missing for a long time. But she'd also brought new life to her already-existent, holier-than-thou attitude, and she seemed more comfortable than ever on her pulpit. Brooks didn't like to be preached to, but he had worked hard to give her the credit she was due for getting sober and trying to become a better person.

Having decided he would do his best to be nice to her, Brooks said, "Welcome to the team." He wanted to grin as he heard the words come to his mouth. Looking at this gazelle-like woman with her fiendish brown eyes, he knew her presence was the end of the one stable piece of Brooks's life—Lacoda.

Carmen shrugged her bony shoulders, then glanced at Jake, who was only barely taller. "Thanks," she said. "I'm excited to be here. Almost nervous, actually. I haven't started a new job in a long time."

Brooks brushed his hand through the air. "Oh, don't be nervous. We both know you've always pulled the strings around here."

"That's about right," Jake said, crossing his arms.

Carmen shook her head at the men.

The following few seconds felt like Brooks was falling down a cavern with no ropes and nothing else to grab onto. The three of them knew each other so well—the good *and* the bad—that words weren't always necessary, and they shared an unspoken conversation that dripped with jarring emotions.

Saving himself from splattering, Brooks reached for the lowest hanging fruit of potential conversation. "You guys must be excited to get Emilia back home." Their daughter, who been away at NYU, was coming home in eight days, and Brooks had agreed to let her apprentice under him for the summer.

"We sure are," Jake said. "It's not the same around here without her."

Brooks nodded, knowing that was true. "I'm looking forward to teaching her a few things. Something tells me she'll catch on quickly."

Carmen dropped her chin. "Where did this interest in working for Lacoda come from anyway? Em wanted nothing to do with wine last year."

Brooks was tempted to ask Carmen the same question. It wasn't until after Emilia had planned on working at Lacoda that Carmen was suddenly involved.

He put a hand on his desk. "I guess it's about the only summer job to be had, short of driving all the way into Richland." Having discussed the topic with Emilia numerous times, he knew much more than he was willing to share right now.

Carmen looked at Jake suspiciously.

"I figured it wasn't a big deal," Brooks added, hoping he'd not gotten himself into the middle of a larger family argument. He had run the idea of Emilia working at Lacoda by Jake, who was fine with it, but Brooks wasn't about to throw Jake under the bus right now.

Abruptly, Jake shifted the conversation. He took Carmen's hand. Her diamond was larger than Jake's knuckles. "Why don't we get your office sorted out? Make sure you have what you need." He said to Brooks, "Carmen's going to work on booking some more events and breathe some life into this place. We might even open another day or two of the week." Right now, they were only open on weekends.

"That's great," Brooks replied. He reached for a pack of papers and straightened them pointlessly. "Carm, let me know if you need anything."

"Thank you so much," she said in a high-pitched tone that was both too innocent and too upbeat to fit her. Brooks didn't want to judge, though. At least, she seemed to be trying.

When they'd left, Brooks pinched the bridge of his nose and said to himself, "Holy hell, this could go wrong in so many ways."

∼

IN THE HEART of New York, Emilia Forester found an empty bench near the arch in Washington Square and took a seat, setting her backpack down next to her. She wished she could bottle the beauty of Manhattan in May: the mid-seventies warmth, the colorful flowers, and even the people blooming. A smiling couple ate lunch together on the neighboring bench, thick deli sandwiches spilling out of white paper. Near the fountain, a man with red shoes played the slide guitar like he'd been born with it in his hands.

After listening for a while, Emilia drew her phone from her backpack, recorded a minute or so of the man's performance, and then texted it to Jasper, who was in Boston wrapping up his year at the Berklee School of Music.

I think you should hire him to be in your band.

Jasper texted right back. *I like his shoes.*

Emilia: *Right?*

Jasper: *How'd your first exam go? Chemistry? I miss you, by the way. Only a few more days!* They'd booked the same flight out of Boston.

Emilia: *Miss you too. Yeah, Chem. Easy.* She typed what was really on her mind. *My mom started at Lacoda today. Ugh.*

Waiting for him to respond, Emilia put her eyes back on the musician and lost herself in the notes. Eventually, her phone vibrated, and she looked at the screen.

Jasper: *At least, you don't have to go home to a new sister. Not to one-up you or anything, but I think I just crushed you.*

Emilia smiled as she typed back to him. *Red Mountain = Death Star. I'm caught in her tractor beam.*

Jasper: *It's good that we're in it together.*

10

NO TRESPASSING

L ike a man passing by a bad wreck on the highway, Otis couldn't help but turn his head toward the Drink Flamingo site every time he left his house. Every day brought a new surprise, another shovel of dirt over the coffin of Otis's vision for Red Mountain. The giant hole behind the winery was definitely going to be a pool, and it looked like the smaller hole next to it would be a hot tub. Otis could already hear the party music hurting his vines' ears. If only he could give them earplugs and blindfolds.

The most recent surprise had come when Drink Flamingo had raised a chain-link fence around the entire property. Rings of barbed wire lined the top. It now looked like Otis was a neighbor to a federal prison. *No Trespassing* signs hung every twenty feet from the fence, a sentiment against everything Red Mountain stood for. Why Otis had chosen to save Harry Bellflour from the coyotes last year was a mystery to him. Right now, he'd like to beat the moron over the head with one of those signs.

Drifting further away from Joan, Otis's days were plagued with the question of how to combat Bellflour and how to protect Till Vineyards and the rest of Red Mountain. Even when he spent time with Joan, he wasn't actually there, and he knew damn well that she could sense his lack of presence. It was as if she'd stopped trying with him, and that idea scared him even more.

A few weeks ago, had she sensed his mind racing, she would have put her hands on his cheeks and made him face her, patiently telling him, "Everything that matters is right here. Right now. Let the rest go." Joan hadn't done that lately.

He could only imagine how difficult he was to live with, and the truth of it kept him up at night. How long could Joan tolerate him? How long before he'd come home to find her bags packed in the foyer?

With a trio of chorizo tacos from a taco truck in Benton City by his side, Otis sat in his tasting room watching the men on the other side of the chain-link fence planting Drink Flamingo's cabernet sauvignon. The solution to all his life's troubles suddenly hit him. Perhaps it wasn't the best answer, but even the taste of the notion felt like a cool swallow of scotch burning down his throat, delivering a dose of peace throughout his tired body. Perhaps the answer was much simpler than he'd thought.

No, he couldn't kill Bellflour, nor could he burn the place down. But he *could* institute a much more discreet type of warfare, a grass-roots campaign against his enemy—a series of stealthy strikes that could potentially win the war in the end. David versus Goliath.

Otis knew exactly what his first strike would be. He marched with a mission toward his truck. The blue sky seemed more electric and inviting than it had for the last few days. Even the mountain had taken on a new glow. With a smirk, Otis climbed into his truck and pulled out. He took another look through the Drink Flamingo fence. One man worked a hydraulic auger, boring holes into the ground. Another man followed behind, dropping baby cabernet vines into the ground. Oh, did Otis have a surprise for them.

He rode through the heart of Benton City, the kind of one-horse town you could easily miss if you blinked. The news played on the radio—a story concerning an elementary teacher trying innovative techniques in Ellensburg—but Otis was barely listening. He was focused on his mission, working through the details while winding west along the country roads past apple and cherry orchards. He eventually reached the plant nursery where most of the wineries in eastern Washington State bought their vines.

"Otis!" the man behind the desk exclaimed as he rose from his chair. He was a short man and moved in a slow shuffle around his desk. "Haven't seen you in a long time."

Otis put up his hands. "I'm mostly planted out, Richard." After a quick handshake, he looked around nervously. "I was hoping I might look through your list of available vines, though."

Richard slanted an eyebrow. "Anything in particular you're looking for?"

Indeed, there was. But Otis needed to be inconspicuous. "Just perusing."

The man thumbed through a stack of papers and found the latest inventory report. Otis took it, found a seat by the water cooler, and reached for the reading glasses in his shirt pocket.

The list of varieties filled the left column. The available quantity was to the right. It didn't take Otis long to find what he was looking for. In fact, he couldn't believe this particular variety was on the list and had a sudden urge to raise his hands up in victory.

Otis pulled off his glasses and did his best to query the man without revealing his conniving pleasure. "Can I have thirty of the pinotage?"

Richard looked over his computer at Otis. "Pinotage? Should I even ask?"

Otis shook his head. "No, you shouldn't."

Though he wasn't one to typically despise a variety, he'd never tasted a pinotage he liked. Pinotage was the laughing stock of the wine industry. If cabernet sauvignon was the most noble of varieties —the king and queen all in one—pinotage was the diseased scum begging for food in the village. Otis had never sucked on the sole of a worn-out shoe, but he imagined the experience similar to drinking a glass of this putrid variety. Or perhaps it paralleled sipping a vile liquid that had been filtered through a dirty gym sock and then aged in the belly of a car tire. He could not imagine how South Africans had tolerated it for so long.

Pinotage was the perfect grape to infest his neighbor's vineyard.

He could tell Richard was dying to know why the hell the grape-father would plant pinotage, but Otis wasn't about to tell him the truth. Still, he figured he'd better offer him a bone before all of Washington was talking about how Otis had gone senile, tearing up his syrah and planting pinotage.

Otis racked his brain for an excuse and then spat out, "I've a friend in Lodi doing some interesting things with the variety. Thought I'd see how they grow up here. I'll probably rip them out in a couple of years."

"Worth trying, I guess," Richard said. "The only reason I have some is a man over in Sunnyside who's married to a South African asked for them."

"I'll let you know what I find. You never know."

"Would you like me to send you a bill?" To Otis's nod, he said, "You got it. Give me about ten minutes."

He shuffled out a back door, and Otis returned to his truck. He pulled down the tailgate and waited, further deliberating how to follow through with his plan. Drink Flamingo didn't have a dog, and he hadn't seen any cameras around the property, but he'd need to double-check. He could take no chances.

Richard came riding up the gravel road in an ATV, stealing Otis from his thoughts. Sliding to a stop, Richard shuffled to the back and pulled two black plastic bags out of the bed. "How's everything else going over on the mountain, Otis? I hated to sell Drink Flamingo my vines, but..."

"Don't apologize," Otis said, reminded of how small the wine world was. "If not you, they'd have found them somewhere else."

Richard slung the bags into the back of Otis's truck. "Hopefully, they'll play nice."

Otis knew better than that, but said, "I'll be there to slap their hands if they don't."

"I don't doubt it. Anyway, I hope this year won't be as hot as they're predicting."

"You and me both," Otis admitted. "Or I'll be back here begging you to find some Charbono and Tannat."

The man chuckled. "Let's just hope for a cold wave to come in and surprise us."

"Fingers crossed. Take care, Richard." Otis waved and drove away with what felt like contraband in those black bags.

~

THE RUMBLE of Margot's stomach was like cracking thunder in the silence of the waiting area in the Pasco airport. Between not eating and the agonizing anticipation of meeting Remi's daughter, Carly, Margot felt like her body was giving up on her.

She touched her stomach and said to Remi, "Sorry, I'm clearly not eating enough." She wasn't going to mention her nerves regarding Carly. Not that it was a secret. They were both terrified of how the next days would transpire.

Noticing Remi's trepidation, Margot squeezed his big hand and twisted toward him, touching his cheek. "Just be yourself. I don't know who you used to be years ago, but I know the man you are now. I think she's going to love him as much as I do."

He pressed his lips together into a small smile, which retreated into a sigh. "Thanks. I just don't know what to expect. She's grown up so much since I last saw her."

A ding leapt from Remi's phone. "That's her," he said, looking at the screen. "Touchdown."

A few minutes later, an overhead voice announced the arrival of Flight 541, and shortly after that, passengers came walking down the hall past security.

Margot watched each of the passengers round the corner, and her heart kicked and screamed. This is what it felt like to be a stepmom waiting to introduce yourself for the first time. When Carly appeared,

Margot's heart kicked even harder. The young woman was walking with her head down. A backpack hung over one shoulder. Between the resemblance to Remi and her goth attire, there was no mistaking her. Carly wore dark, faded jeans and a black leather jacket with a chain dangling from one zipper. A stripe of pink ran down the left side of her black hair. As she got closer, Margot saw a lip ring and a neck tattoo. She had no problem with piercings or tattoos, or dark clothes for that matter, but there was a dark cloud hovering over Carly that surely promised rain.

Margot hit Remi's arm. "Go."

He walked in the direction of his estranged daughter, and Margot could see the scared little boy inside a man's skin walking toward the edge of a cliff. She was glad to see them hugging but was instantly petrified by Carly's cold, lifeless face.

Summoning the love she felt for Remi, Margot headed in their direction. Remi was taking Carly's backpack from her.

Margot thrust out her hands. "Welcome, Carly! It's so good to have you."

"Hi," Carly said, offering an embrace that was so fast Margot wondered if it had even happened.

"You must be exhausted. How was the flight? Flying's not as fun as it used to be. Did they feed you? Not that the food is any good. At least there are movies." Margot stopped talking, realizing she was basically throwing up words all over her new stepdaughter.

Carly glanced at her dad, as if to ask, "*This* is what you're marrying?"

"I'm..." Margot stuttered. "I'm really nervous. But enough about me. Welcome to Washington. Have you ever been?"

"No, this is my first time," Carly answered flatly.

"C'mon," Remi said. "Let's go find your bag."

Margot nodded eagerly and walked a couple of feet behind Remi and his daughter. Maybe it was best Margot let Remi do the talking for a while. Reaching the baggage claim, the three of them stood in a triangle to wait. As Carly and Remi chatted, Margot silently stared at the baggage claim door like her life depended on it. She hoped Remi was saying the right things and that she hadn't destroyed it all. Who wants a loudmouth for a stepmom?

Once she determined that Remi and Carly could use an extra voice in their conversation, Margot said, "Those really are small planes coming from Seattle, aren't they?"

Carly barely acknowledged her. This was going to be a really long day.

As Margot searched for more interesting topics to discuss, she came up empty. She twisted her head back to the baggage claim door. If that light didn't flash soon and the door come popping up and spitting out bags, Margot was going to race over there and pry the darn thing open herself. For a second, she wished Jasper were here. He was always so good at easing tension.

With nowhere else to turn, Margot retreated to her favorite topic. "Are you a big eater, Carly? I mean...not like big. Oh, gosh. I mean, do you like food? I don't know if you heard, but it's my thing. I love to cook. Is there anything in particular I could make tonight? Or do you want to go out? We don't have any fancy restaurants, but we do have some great Mexican food. I guess you have everything in San Francisco."

Remi put a hand on Margot's shoulder, calming her. She pressed her lips together and nodded, understanding.

The three of them turned their attention to the baggage claim door.

Carly finally answered, "I'm fine with whatever."

Margot forced the most absurd smile she'd ever attempted, stretching it to her ears. "Okay, yeah. I don't know that I really cared about food at your age, either. Not that I can eat right now. I'm trying my best to lose some weight for the wedding." She shook her head, feeling her heart rate racing almost as quickly as her mouth was puking out words. "So I'm in the beginnings of a very serious diet. Not that it's working. Not yet, anyway."

Having run out of breath, Margot finally stopped talking with a long exhalation. She glanced at Remi and whispered, "Sorry."

Remi looked back at Carly. "How's your mother?"

"Don't even get me started," Carly replied.

Remi dared to ask, "Why do you say that?"

"She just doesn't get me. At. All. I don't know...she's changed lately. I just need a break."

A buzz sounded, and Margot whipped her head around to see the door finally opening. *Thank God!* She didn't care what came out, as long as something took the attention away from this debacle. She had no trouble getting on stage in front of thousands in a play, but performing for her future stepdaughter was like stepping onstage in the lead role without having been given a script.

11

THE BABY MONITOR

One big, happy family.

That's what it was supposed to be, Brooks thought. He'd spent his entire life dreaming of having days like this. Children running around, a puzzle spread out on the table, animated conversations over wine. The wonderful sense of belonging. His reunited family was almost there, but just like the puzzle, seemed to be missing a few pieces.

Eight of them were in the screened-in back porch at his parents' new home, a new-construction house situated down a long, quiet road in West Richland, only a few miles from the mountain. Beyond the porch, there was a small patch of grass and then sagebrush running all the way to a set of rolling, treeless hills in the distance.

Adriana was helping Zack find the next piece to the Harry Potter puzzle. Brooks's ex-fiancée, Abby Sinclaire, was standing behind Brooks's much younger brother, Shay, rocking *their* six-month-old son, Wyatt. After Brooks had made it clear that he had no intentions of rekindling a relationship with Abby—despite her valiant attempts—she'd moved on to his brother, proving just how small Red Mountain could be. They'd been dating for about a year and a half.

It was only two years ago that Brooks had reconnected with his biological family. He'd been essentially parentless until his father, Charles, had tracked him down. After getting over the initial shock, Brooks had welcomed both of his parents into his life. Not too long after that, he'd found Shay working as a fry cook in Portland and convinced him to move to Red Mountain, where Shay had taken a job working at Lacoda and at Margot's farm sanctuary. Their own puzzle really started coming together when their parents, who were desperate to make up for the many years they'd missed out on, moved up from California earlier in the year.

They were One. Big. Happy. Family.

Charles and Mary were telling Brooks about their first trip to Seattle. He was listening as best he could, while also taking in the crazy reality of the scene.

Now that this dream of having a normal life with family all around had been realized, it wasn't as clean and pretty as he'd hoped. Was Brooks the only one who could feel the tension? No wonder Adriana wanted to move to Florida.

Shay had just brought up Carmen working at Lacoda. Judging by the exploding curiosity and opinions rising from the table, the news had apparently struck like a drill finding a geyser in an oil field.

"It's really not that big of a deal," Brooks lied, not wanting to acknowledge the murky oil shooting hundreds of feet up into the air. "It's her winery, anyway."

"Yeah, but why?" Shay asked, raking his wild beard. "Why in the world does she want to work for Lacoda?"

Brooks wasn't sure he wanted to make guesses in front of everyone. Even among family, secrets could never be kept around here.

Abby, who was still working as Carmen's assistant, put a pacifier into Wyatt's mouth and jumped in. "Well, she wants to work with Jake —and Emilia, now that she's coming home. What else is she going to do around here? I'm not saying it's a great idea, but it's pretty obvious why she's trying it out."

"I think it'll be fine," Brooks said, hoping to quell the topic. The last thing he needed was Abby jumping in and defending Carmen. It didn't matter how long it had been since Abby had cheated on him with the woman, he could still feel the burn.

"Brother," Shay said, "you know it'll be anything but fine. She's a few months sober, surrounding herself with wine. And sober or not, she's not exactly easygoing. The whole thing's a mess."

Brooks dropped his head. "I hope you're wrong."

He reached for Adriana's thigh under the table. She glanced at him, and he wondered what the glare was in her eyes. Skepticism? Would she ever let go of the idea that Brooks still had feelings for Abby? Would Adriana ever fully trust him? Considering she might be leaving, did it matter, anyway? It felt like it was always something when they got together, and Adriana would often go long lengths of time without saying a word.

Thankfully, Charles cooled the tension by asking Shay and Abby, "Any new news on the house you're looking to buy?"

Brooks's and Shay's father had found new life in moving to Red Mountain, and he seemed to have lost some of his angry edge. He and Mary both had proved to be wonderful grandparents and life-savers for Shay and Abby, who were working all the time to save up to buy this house they'd been eyeing. Brooks felt the tension in his shoulders rush out as they moved on to a new topic.

Shay set his wine glass down. "It's still available. We're just working on the finances." Shay and Abby were currently living together in Abby's small villa on the Foresters' property, a space Brooks knew intimately.

Mary stepped in. "Why won't you let us lend you the money? It's not that big of a deal."

"We really appreciate the offer," Shay said, "but we still feel the same way. We want to do this on our own."

Brooks understood exactly what his brother meant.

Abby carefully handed Wyatt to Mary, who had found a renewed life of her own as a grandmother. Mary cradled Wyatt in her arms and said to Wyatt, "Look at your little face. I could just chew on your chinny chin chin."

Brooks remembered the day his mother had knocked on his door to introduce herself. She had looked plagued by sadness. Her depression had slowly dissipated with their move to Red Mountain and the birth of Wyatt. She'd spent the majority of her life regretting giving up Brooks for adoption, and now, she'd been given a second chance.

He looked down at his nephew, who was bursting out of a green onesie that read *Bossman* on the chest. The boy had Shay's rounded cheeks and Abby's warm eyes.

Mary tickled her grandson's nose.

Wyatt giggled, and those cheeks balled up like balloons, charming everyone at the table.

Brooks was reminded that a few great things had come from all this craziness surrounding them.

As they returned their attention to the puzzle, Abby said, "I'm so ready for our own place. You have no idea, Mary. But if this one doesn't work out, we'll find another. As long as it's on the mountain, we'll be happy."

Though there were still unbearable moments, Brooks was getting used to Abby and Shay being together, and he couldn't deny the pride he felt for Shay. His brother had gone from living on the streets to being a father and looking to buy a house. Good for him.

Brooks was glad to see everyone trying hard with Adriana and Zack too—even if Adriana was not very talkative. At one point, Mary asked, "Zack, what are your summer plans?"

"Oh, just some camps," he said through a missing tooth, as he tested a puzzle piece in the far-right corner.

"Don't forget fishing," Brooks said, putting a hand on Zack's shoulder. "We're going down to the Snake River at some point, right?" Brooks didn't know much about fishing, but it had become his and Zack's main way of spending time together.

"Totally," Zack said. "They have huge trout, like the size of...I don't know. Like the size of sharks."

"Or bigger," Brooks said. "I was thinking about putting Zack on the end of a hook to see if we can catch the Big Kahuna."

Zack rolled his eyes. "There's no such thing as the Big Kahuna."

"Oh, you wait and see."

Laughter filled the porch.

"All right, Mom," Brooks said. "Time to stop bogarting my nephew. Can I hold him?"

"I suppose I can share," Mary replied.

Brooks took Wyatt and lifted him up so that they were face-to-face. "As long as you don't throw up on me like last time, we're good. *Capisce*?"

Wyatt smacked his lips.

"I'm glad we understand each other," Brooks said. He moved in and rubbed his own nose against his nephew's. "Is that carrots I smell on your breath, bossman?" He touched noses again. "Yeah, I'd say so. You keep eating your veggies, and you'll grow up big and tall like me. Otherwise, you'll end up a little runt like your dad."

Brooks eyed Shay, and the two brothers shared a smile.

It took one more nose touch for Wyatt to come alive, and he cracked a toothless grin that nearly brought the house down.

∼

AT SEVEN-THIRTY, Abby and Mary went to put Wyatt down, and Brooks pushed away from his seat. "I'll tackle the dishes—"

"Oh, don't worry about it," Charles said, throwing out a hand. "Your mom and I can get those later."

Brooks looked at the others, who were highly focused on completing the puzzle, with only a few pieces of Hedwig and Dumbledore still missing.

"You keep the troops entertained," he said to his father. "I'll just get started."

Charles nodded and returned to the puzzle. "Now, where are this guy's eyes?"

In the kitchen, Brooks brushed the leftovers of grilled chicken and rice off each plate and into the trashcan. Charles and Mary had only bought the house two months before, but they'd done a good job of making it feel like a home. Mary was into butterflies; a fact Brooks had only just learned since they'd moved up here. Several butterfly prints hung on the wall to the right of the refrigerator. All the potholders and hand towels featured butterflies as well.

As he began loading the dishwasher, he heard Abby's voice coming from the baby monitor next to the fruit bowl on the counter. "If you'll grab the diapers, I'll clean him up." Apparently, the other end of the monitor was in the guest bedroom, which Mary had turned into a nursery for her grandchild.

While Brooks was scrubbing away on a pot, he heard Abby say, "He's got Shay's calves, doesn't he?"

"He sure does," Mary agreed. "And his cheeks, of course."

Brooks felt a little weird listening in on their conversation, but his hands were wet, and he was on a roll, so he didn't bother switching off the monitor.

The baby talk kept going as Brooks moved one plate at a time from the sink to the dishwasher. Then he started handwashing the stemless wine glasses lined up on his right.

He was wondering if he and Adriana might ever have a child of their own when something his mother said through the monitor stopped his heart.

"What do you think about Adriana?" Mary asked. "You think they'll last?"

Brooks wished so badly he'd turned off the monitor, but it was too late now. He wanted to hear Abby's answer. Holding one of the soapy, stemless glasses in his hand, he shut off the water and listened in.

Abby answered in a whisper. "I don't know. She's really nice, but I'm not sure she loves it here. That whole thing with her ex really messed things up."

"I know," Mary said. "How can anyone recover from that?"

Wyatt let out a cry. Brooks stood frozen at the sink with a glass in one hand and a hot, sudsy washcloth in the other.

"Brooks really loves her, though," Abby said. "That's what matters."

"Yeah, but that's the thing, Abby. I don't know that she feels the same way about him. Honestly, I don't see her sticking around."

Brooks felt his teeth grinding. Was this what it was like to have family? The ones who supposedly loved you talking about you behind your back?

"I think she likes him," Abby said. "She stayed here for him."

Mary whispered, "Let's face it. There are not many women like you around here, Abby. Shay's a lucky guy."

Need Brooks remind his mother that Abby had cheated on him? Nope, now that Abby had given Mary a grandson, Abby pretty much hung the moon.

"I give Adriana a year, max," Mary said. "I just don't think she's the perfect fit for him."

Brooks's hand tightened. The glass cracked. "Oh, shit!" he yelled, looking at blood.

"What happened?" someone asked.

Brooks turned to see Adriana racing toward him with a stack of dishes in her hand. "Are you okay?"

"Yeah, yeah, I'm fine."

There was a lot of blood, but that was the least of his concerns. As he reached for a paper towel and wrapped it around his hand, he wondered how long she'd been standing there.

Adriana set the dishes down. "Let me see."

Then Abby was speaking again through the monitor. "Brooks will find someone," Abby promised. "One day. Don't worry, Mary."

Even though Mary was on the other side of the house, her sigh filled the kitchen. "He's just been through so much. Not with you. That's not what I mean. Just in life. He deserves to find *the one*."

Brooks glanced at Adriana and then noticed Shay standing in the doorway.

Shay crossed the kitchen, picked up the monitor, and twisted the knob until the green light went away. "They're just talking. Ignore it."

Adriana gently unfolded the bloody paper towel, exposing the wound on Brooks's palm. "Let's get you to the urgent care. You need stitches."

"Nah, I'm fine."

"You need stitches, Brooks." He could hear the agitation in her voice, and it had nothing to do with his cut.

"Shay's right," Brooks said. "Just ignore my mom."

Shaking her head, Adriana brushed by Shay on the way to the porch. "It's time to go. I'm getting Zack."

"Yeah, okay," Brooks said, locking eyes with his brother.

This is it, Brooks thought. If he couldn't get his family behind the relationship, he had no hope of convincing her to stay. And why would she want to? For that matter, why would *he* want to? Being surrounded by family wasn't always all it was cracked up to be.

"That sucked," Shay said. "Mom likes her, you know. She's just looking out for you."

"Yeah, I know," Brooks admitted. "But try telling Adriana that."

Brooks pulled a fresh paper towel off the roll and wrapped his hand again. He put the other hand on his brother's shoulder and then walked out to the porch.

Adriana was saying her goodbyes. She'd somehow mustered a smile. "Thank you so much for having us. We need to get Zack to bed."

"It was a pleasure," Charles said.

Brooks questioned his father's sincerity. Were they being nice to her just so that she'd stay and not take Brooks to Florida?

The three of them hurried through the house, but Mary caught them at the front door. "Leaving so soon?"

Another fake smile from Adriana. "Yes, it's Zack's bedtime. Thanks so much for having us. What a lovely meal."

Mary hugged her. "We should do this more often."

Brooks felt like he was drowning in an artificial world.

As Adriana and Zack walked toward the car, Brooks kissed his mother's cheek. For a second, he wanted to chastise her, but what good would that do? Instead, he said, "We'll see you soon, Mom."

"Oh dear, what happened to your hand?" She took his arm.

Brooks looked down. Blood was soaking through again. "It's okay. Accidentally broke one of the wine glasses."

"Do you want me to bandage it up?"

He pulled his hand away. "No, thanks." In his mind, Brooks was thinking: *You've done enough.*

Mary waved as they pulled out of the driveway.

Once they were moving, Brooks said, "A, I'm so sorry."

"It's nothing."

"They're just scared I'm going to leave, that's all. It had nothing to do with you."

Adriana pointed a finger to the backseat, where Zack was yawning. She whispered, "I'm not doing this right now."

So this is what it feels like to have your family conspiring behind your back, Brooks decided.

12

PINOTAGE SABOTAGE

H oly hell, Otis's monkey mind was running wild tonight. Joan was sleeping peacefully next to him, as if she didn't have a care in the world, most likely galloping on a unicorn through a field of wildflowers, probably chasing neon-winged butterflies in the mellow glow of dawn. Every night, she'd kiss his cheek, tell him goodnight, and then drift off within seconds, leaving Otis to soak in the poison of the world, stewing over his issues like a warlock stirring his cauldron.

Otis could have—and *should have*—bought the Davidson property before Drink Flamingo had sunk its claws into it. All of this emotional toil could have been avoided. He remembered seeing the *For Sale* sign and, for a moment, thinking he'd better find a way to put the money together. But then he'd decided he couldn't buy every piece of land that went up for sale. He had to trust that things would work out.

As if! Since when did things work out?

Otis raised his hands and imagined wrapping his fingers around Bellflour's neck. He could see the man's eyes as he squeezed, the flames burning in the irises, the devil incarnate gasping for air. Oh, why in the hell hadn't Otis let the coyotes tear him apart, limb by limb? Otis tightened his grasp on Bellflour's neck, strangling the life out of him.

Back in reality, Joan stirred beside him. "I can feel you thinking," she whispered, her eyes still closed, surely still dreaming of white lilies and purple daisies as the bright yellow ball lifted high above her unicorn dreams.

Otis grunted.

She shimmied close and put a finger on the space in between his eyebrows, what she called the third eye. Though Otis had always believed in the mystical powers of grapevines, he'd not believed in the power of humans until he met her—his first relationship with a sorceress. He couldn't deny the power in her touch, no matter how hard he tried. There was an energy running through her that came from on high. And her touch at that moment made his chest rise, like she was charging him from the eternal source.

"You have a big life," she said, her eyes still closed. "It's understandable. But don't get angry at yourself. Just watch the thoughts go by."

"I know, I know. Let them move like a river past me. I've heard all of it before."

"You have to keep trying. It takes practice."

Otis processed a deep breath. "I have concerns tonight that can't be discarded. In fact, I feel like I need to get up and write them all down."

Joan placed her hand on his chest. "Think of sleep as a part of your to-do list. A very important part. Remember we went through this on our trip last year? Vacations and sleep should be high priorities for you right now."

Otis pinched the bridge of his nose. "How in God's name do you do it? How are you not worried about tomorrow? And how in bloody hell do you manage your chores without writing them down?"

"I'm not managing life the way you are. Mine's a bit simpler. I have my calendar to remind me when I need to meet my clients, but other than that, I really only have one thing on my list."

"Oh, and what is that? Save the world? Stop all wars? I feel like I'm in love with a Ted Talk."

She laughed at that one. "Not quite. I just want to shine my light a little brighter every day."

"Oh, brother. Give me a break."

"If I could add an addendum to the one item on my list, it would be to have fun. If we're not having fun, what's the point? Typically, if you are having fun, your light is shining brighter. See how that works?"

Imagining what his own light looked like, Otis let out a short, staccato laugh. "My light is quite dim at the moment."

Joan reached into the air and twisted an imaginary knob. "I've just turned up the dimmer. You should be good now."

Otis chuckled. "As if it were so easy."

"As if it weren't. The only thing standing in your way is you."

Otis put a hand behind his head. "Okay, I'll play your game of enlightenment. How would *you* stop all this thinking? And if you tell me to meditate an hour every morning, I'll roll off the bed."

"No, no, I think the grapefather requires much stronger intervention than meditation." She had a wonderful gift for making his nickname sound unbearably silly.

"At least you acknowledge the seriousness of my dilemma."

"I get it, my love. We'll need the whole toolbox to set you right." She thought for a moment. "The first order of business is to accept that you'll never complete your to-do list. You're playing life like a game of Tetris, and somewhere along the way, you've decided that the pieces would stop falling if you worked fast enough."

Otis could see a game of Tetris in his mind, and he knew she was right.

"Let me tell you two things about living the game of Tetris. The pieces never stop coming. But more importantly, if you take a break and let them keep stacking, you don't lose the game. In fact, as you take a step back and watch the pieces fall on top of each other, none of them fitting correctly, that's the spot of pure bliss. That's where you find peace."

Had he not been in such an ugly mood, he might have complimented her on her wisdom. No wonder she regularly changed people's lives. "It must be nice to know that you've already achieved enlightenment. What in God's name might you do when you come back in the next life? Twiddle your little thumbs and watch me suffer again?"

With all the seriousness in the world, she said, "I believe this is my last life."

A dark wave of sadness rushed over Otis, thinking she might not be with him forever. "How could you possibly know that?"

"I just know."

"So I'll be cast back onto this earth, forced to run around with all these looney tunes, while you disappear into the cosmos like stardust?"

Joan lay back on her pillow. "That all depends on how you choose to live this life, Otis."

"I'll probably come back as Bellflour's lap dog," he said. "If that's not hell, I don't know what is." All this talk of life and death was too much for Otis. He leaned over and put a hand on her cheek. "I'm sorry to wake you."

She kissed him and smiled. "It's okay, darling."

"I love you," he said. "With every bit of me. Now go to sleep."

Almost as easily as flipping a switch, Joan was soon fast asleep. Otis ran through their discussion in his head. Though much of it made sense, the simple truth was that he was an old dog too weary to change his life. The only legacy he would truly leave was what happened to Red Mountain, and it was looking like he'd be six feet under before the mountain realized her true potential.

At least, in his dying breaths, he would know that on a late, late night in mid-May, he'd infiltrated the Drink Flamingo compound, torn up a few of their precious, high-scoring cabernet sauvignon vines, and in their place, planted none other than the most frowned-upon variety in the industry, pinotage. No matter what happened, he would always know that Drink Flamingo would never bottle a true Red Mountain wine, only a poor attempt poisoned by a variety that had no business on this mountain, or, arguably, anywhere on earth.

Eager to take the upper hand, he slipped out of bed and found the pile of clothes he'd left in his office. All day he'd planned this mission, and an important part was making sure Joan was left in the dark. She'd never let him get away with such absurdity. Once he was dressed, he poured himself two fingers of Del Bac single malt whiskey—his favorite lately—and tossed it down his gullet.

With the smoky burn fueling him, he stepped out into the starlit night. The wild dogs were out there somewhere, howling. He crept toward his vines, hoping he'd find Jonathan before his friend unleashed a chorus of barking that could scare off the Reaper.

He heard a growl in the darkness, and Otis rushed to silence him. "Quiet there, ol' boy. It's just me."

The dog met him at the fence line, and Otis rubbed the animal's ears. "Just you and me and the night."

Otis hiked up to his winery to get the wheelbarrow carrying the pinotage vines, wire cutters, and a shovel. With the wheel cracking gravel at his feet, he pushed it up the road until the property came into view. Below the McMansion and the pool were long lines of plastic grow tubes that they'd put over the vines to protect them in their youth.

Deciding it would be best to enter from the opposite side, Otis pushed the wheelbarrow along the fence line. The *No Trespassing* signs glared back at him. Once he'd settled on the spot, he retrieved the wire cutters and went to work, starting at the bottom. *Clip, clip, clip.*

He cut two waist-high lines on both sides and pulled the fence back. He tossed the shovel and the two bags of vines in, then crawled in himself. It was the most fun he'd had in ages, and he couldn't stop the smirk playing on his lips.

Once Otis was safely on the other side, he stood and surveyed the land. An excavator was parked in between the pool and the vines with its bucket jammed into the dirt.

For a moment, he thought about checking for the keys. Forget pulling out a few vines. What about ramming a John Deere right into the bowels of the McMansion? Knowing Bellflour, he'd probably used the cheapest materials possible. Otis could probably push it over if he tried.

Returning to the mission, he looked left at the long lines of grow tubes visible in the moonlight. He'd already decided that he would sprinkle the pinotage vines in over a few rows. That way, they'd be harder to pick out. In fact, without someone deeply invested in the vines, it was possible that no one would ever know these vines had been planted. Otis could delight in the prank for a lifetime.

Sneaking down a row, he lifted off the grow tube and pulled back the black irrigation tubing, then plucked the first vine out of the ground with ease. He dug a hole eighteen inches deep into the already loose soil. Reaching into the bag like Santa Claus, he drew out the first pinotage vine and set it into the hole with a satisfied grin. He picked up the shovel and covered up the hole, admiring the small vine standing tall and proud like the most allegiant of Otis's soldiers.

He slipped the grow tube over the vine and replaced the irrigation tube. "Welcome to Red Mountain, my little friend."

Otis repeated the procedure twenty-nine more times, always saying an encouraging word at the end. Then, with a bag of cabernet sauvignon vines and a shovel, he crept back under the fence. Oh, how he wished he could tell Joan about his accomplishment. He might be losing the war, but tonight, he'd won a major battle.

Returning to his own property, he heard the coyotes calling out to him. Jonathan found him again, and Otis strolled with his dog into the night, feeling the truth of Red Mountain all around him. Sometimes, a man must cross lines to protect what he loves.

Otis looked up to the sky, past the stars and the Milky Way and into the black. Then, with everything he had, he howled.

Ahhwwoooo!

Jonathan lifted his head and howled as well.

Ahhwwoooo! Ahhwwoooo!

The coyotes up higher on the mountain called back, and for a few moments, Otis felt whole inside.

13

CARLY AND OTHER SERIOUS WOUNDS

"**T**he coyotes were loud last night," Remi said, on the couch next to Margot, flipping through television channels. It was the first day in weeks he hadn't gone out to his gentleman's farm after breakfast.

Margot pulled her eyes away from her phone. She was texting back and forth with her best friend in Vermont, Erica. "I was out cold. Didn't hear a thing."

They were pretending to be enjoying the late morning, but the unspoken apprehension regarding Carly filled the air. Margot had attempted to impress her future stepdaughter with homemade pasta the night before, but Carly'd barely touched it. Of course, because of her awful diet, neither had Margot. She'd watched Remi dig into her truffle tagliatelle while listening to Carly talk negatively about her mother and the rest of the world.

Margot had just started another text to Erica when they heard footsteps. Margot glanced at Remi. "Round two."

As they turned toward her, offering her the morning's greetings, Carly barely acknowledged them. She wore a black hoodie with a skull on the front. The hood was pulled over her head. "I'm going outside for a smoke."

Not to be deterred, Remi said lightheartedly, "If you're hungry, we left you a plate on the counter. Margot makes a mean French toast."

Carly nodded and possibly whispered a thanks. Her voice was so quiet, Margot wasn't sure. Then Carly was out the door.

Margot pushed herself up off the couch. "That went well. I'll heat up her food. Does she drink coffee?"

Remi shook his head. "I don't know."

Margot circled the kitchen island and unwrapped Carly's breakfast. "Don't worry about us," she said to Remi. "Come find us after your dentist appointment. She'll love meeting the animals."

"I hope so," Remi muttered, utterly defeated.

Margot was so famished, she guided the plate under her nose for a smell of the warm eggy carb-loaded goodness. She imagined taking a satisfying bite, and her mouth watered. Summoning ungodly restraint, she placed the plate in the microwave and moved onto making another carafe of coffee.

When Carly came back in, Margot turned from pouring hot water over her freshly ground beans. "I'm making coffee, Carly. And I heated up your food." *Kill her with kindness*, Margot thought.

With cigarette smoke clinging to her, Carly entered the kitchen area and took the warm plate of French toast. She poured a healthy dose of Vermont syrup on top.

Margot forced another smile. "I buy the syrup from a small farm in Vermont, not too far from where I used to live."

Apparently far less excited about the syrup's origin, Carly nodded and took her plate to the table by the fireplace. Remi sat down next to her, and Margot listened in on their conversation.

"Margot wants to show you around some. That okay?"

Margot didn't hear a response and could only imagine the face Carly was making. Something with a twisted expression that said, *Don't make me hang out with her.*

Setting down the gooseneck kettle, Margot turned. "If it interests you, I'd love to take you down to the sanctuary and introduce you to the animals."

Carly finished chewing. "Yeah, that's fine. Maybe after I get a shower."

Wow! Margot thought. *She speaks!* Maybe they *were* getting somewhere.

Margot could hear hope in Remi's tone as well. "This afternoon," he started, "I thought I could show you what I call my gentleman's farm." He scratched his head. "Or whatever else you want to do."

Margot served Carly a cup of coffee with a mug that read *Real mermaids smoke seaweed* and sat down on the far side of the table, a safe distance away. "Yeah, Carly, it's up to you. What do you want the next few days to look like?"

Carly sipped her drink. "I don't know. Just chill out. I'm tired."

Margot was relieved to get more words out of her. "Well, please let us know. I'm happy to stay out of the way or be your tour guide. I need to go next door and look through my bookings for the next few days. How about you text me when you're done with your shower?"

Remi answered for her. "That sounds great. I know she'll love meeting your babies."

⁓

AFTER HAVING SOAKED through another bandage in the night, Brooks finally agreed that he should see a doctor. They'd just dropped Zack off at camp and were headed to the urgent care in Kennewick to have his hand sewn up. From the moment Zack waved goodbye, Brooks and Adriana had started speaking their minds.

"My mother doesn't want you to leave," he said. "She probably just wants the same thing I want. Commitment. This relationship is starting to feel a bit one-sided. You and I are both on the same seesaw, and I'm sitting in the fucking dirt."

"Brooks," Adriana said from the driver's seat, "your mother is wrong about us. I love you, and I want us to work. But she's right. I don't see us staying here forever. Red Mountain is not the end-all-be-all for everyone. I'm so tired of hearing people talk about this place like it's the Holy Land. Maybe it saved you. Maybe it's your Mecca. But it feels like more of a stepping stone for Zack and me. I don't even like wine. What else is there out here? We have to drive almost thirty minutes just to take him to camp. More than that for soccer. Not to mention the bitter winters. I'm not sure this is the life I want to give him."

She sighed as she slowed to a stop at a traffic light. "Why is the conversation always about us staying? What about you coming to Florida? You act like that's not even an option."

He locked his eyes on the dashboard. "What would I do in Florida? Ferment oranges and grapefruit? I have nothing else going for me. Need I remind you that I don't have a college education? I have no other skills outside of winemaking. Besides, I have a duty to carry on what Otis has taught me."

Adriana nodded. "Life is about making choices. And we make those based on our loyalties. Apparently, yours are with Otis."

"And Jake. And the mountain. *And* you and Zack—"

"See where we fit into that? You just made my point."

Dammit, she could be frustrating. "I wasn't listing them in any particular order."

"There's a man who wants to harm me and my son. He knows exactly where we are. The mother inside me will not let that stand, even with Michael not getting out any time soon. I'm barely sleeping because I'm so freaking afraid, and I need out. If this mountain and making wine are more important to you than Zack and I are, then let's say goodbye now. That breaks my heart to say, but Zack is my first priority. You know that."

Brooks could never explain how impossible this choice was for him, how unfair it was to make him choose between the woman he loved and the place that had saved him.

He was relieved to pause the conversation once they arrived. They didn't say a word to each other in the waiting room. When Brooks was finally called back, the doctor gave him eight stitches, prescribed a round of antibiotics, and warned him that he'd have a scar. All

Brooks could think about was the gash that no doctor could help heal.

Adriana had just drawn a line in the sand.

∽

"You should have seen it," Margot told Carly as they walked in the noon sun along the dusty road leading to the sanctuary. "The tent was huge...like Cirque de Soleil huge. Jake and Jasper and the rest of the band sounded so good. I wish you and Remi could have been there. That was the night that launched my inn. I've been booked mostly every night during the season since."

Carly pulled on her cigarette and then exhaled smoke with a curt response. "Sounds fun."

"I think you'll like Jasper. Having his music in the house is such a delight. I'm sure you'll meet Jake soon enough. Did you ever listen to his band?"

With her eyes focused somewhere east, Carly shook her head. "Not really."

When they entered the gate to the farm sanctuary, the sight of her happy animals dragged Margot out of the mire. She and Shay had saved every one of these guys and gals from unfortunate circumstances and were trying to find them new homes. As difficult as it was to say goodbye to many of these creatures, the rehoming process allowed Shay and Margot to continue to bring in and save new animals. Sadly, at the moment, they had reached maximum capacity.

"Hi, my loves!" Margot said, clapping her hands together.

Though the pigs didn't get up from their mud bath, the four cows didn't seem to notice, and the horse kept to himself, much of her harem of animals rushed toward her.

Margot grabbed the bucket of grain hanging on the fence and said to Carly, "These are all my babies. They act like they love me, but they really just like my snacks."

Cody, the Australian shepherd, reached her first and sat on his haunches with his tail slapping the ground.

"I know," Margot said, reaching into her pocket. "You're the only one who doesn't like grain. That's why I brought you these!" She held up a salmon and sweet potato treat that she'd brought down from the house.

Cody chomped down as Margot said, "This guy is our guard dog, but he loves to break out and go visit Otis, who saved him from a really awful neighbor a couple of years ago."

Carly petted his head but didn't appear to be much of a dog person.

Margot dug her hand into the bucket of grain and fed the sheep and goats as she introduced them by name to Carly. "Last but not least is this girl here," Margot said, putting her hand on the long, furry neck of the newest addition to their family, an alpaca named Fantasia. "Look at that face. Alpacas are herd animals, so we're trying to find her a home quickly so she can have some companions. Aren't we, Fantasia? And if we can't, I'll just bring you home with me."

Carly hesitantly petted Fantasia for all of five seconds and then jammed her hands into her pockets.

Tough crowd, Margot thought. She pointed to the brown and white American paint horse that was grazing in a pen by himself on the other side of the property. "That's Elvis, who I was telling you about last night. When we got him, his blindness was almost the least of his troubles. He was beyond malnourished and thin as a rail. Shay spent a lot of time with him and brought him back to life. Now he rides him all over the mountain."

"Do you ride?" Carly asked.

Margot had to pause to appreciate that Carly actually knew how to ask questions. "I do *not* ride. I love Elvis, but I was thrown off a horse as a little girl, so it's not something I want to mess with. Shay keeps offering to teach me, though. Do you ride? If not, I know he'd be happy to teach you."

Carly shook her head. "I don't know that I'm a horse person."

"Believe me, they're very sweet. But once you've been thrown off, you like them better when your own feet are on the ground."

∼

THE VISIT TO see the animals hadn't lightened up Carly like Margot had hoped. As they returned to the house, Margot said, "All this arid land here is where Remi and I would like to plant some grapes. Once we're caught up with everything else, of course. It's project after project around here."

Carly nodded, and Margot decided she'd had about enough. "Look, Carly, let's talk. Woman to woman."

Carly let out a sigh, as if she wanted to say, "What now?"

They both watched a tumbleweed roll by in the breeze.

Margot crossed her arms and faced the girl who looked so much like Remi. Before Margot spoke, she reminded herself how much she loved him. That gave her the courage to say exactly what she needed to say.

"I get it, Carly. This probably sucks for you. I can only imagine what it's like to suddenly have a stepmom in your life. Especially when you haven't seen your dad in a long time."

Carly turned away, looking up toward Col Solare. She puffed on her cigarette.

Margot continued, "I keep trying to put myself in your shoes. Wondering what it would be like to have someone else love my dad. I'm not sure I would have liked it, especially at your age. But it's the way it is. Your father and I have something very special, and I hope you can find comfort in the fact that no woman on earth will ever love him like I do."

Margot realized what she'd said and backpedaled, throwing up her hands. "I mean, other than you and...I'm sure your mother loved him with everything she had. But that's over, and your father deserves to be loved. I didn't know him before, but he came out here to rediscover himself, and I think that's admirable. The man I know deserves all the love in the world, even from you."

Carly took one last puff of her smoke and tossed it to the ground. Stomping on the burning butt, she started to speak, then shook her head instead, as if Margot could never understand.

Margot reached down and picked up the butt. "We're family now, and we need to figure this out. Whether you like it or not, I will be your stepmom. Not that you have to call me that. You can call me Margot or Remi's wife or whatever. But there's no sense us spending a lifetime angry at one another." She sighed. "I don't want you to hate me. And maybe you don't. Maybe you're in your head for other reasons. I was a mess at seventeen. But I really feel like you walked off that plane already hating me."

Carly scoffed, still looking up toward the top of the mountain. Finally, she turned to Margot with venom in her eyes. "Good for you that you've found the love of your life. I honestly don't care. No matter what you say or do, no matter how nice you are, I'm not going to like you. You'll never be my mom, and you'll never love my father like my mother did."

Margot lost her breath, like she'd been punched in her stomach. Tears collected under her eyes, but she strained her face to fight them off. "Look here, you ungrateful shit," Margot said. "Do you know how lucky it is to find true love? I'm sorry if it gets in the way of your precious little life, but..."

No, she didn't say that. But she wanted to.

Pushing her anger aside, she said, "I get all of that. It must be impossible to like a woman who is jamming her foot into your life. But I'm not trying to replace your mom. You don't ever have to look at me like a mom. What if we were just friends? I'm just in this to love your father with every part of me."

Carly shook her head again in disgust, then reached down for a rock and cast it out over the vines. "Are we done yet? I'd like to go back."

Margot bit her tongue, knowing that she might say things that would ruin their relationship forever.

As the two women returned to the house, Margot couldn't ever recall having felt so deflated. She thought back to the lonely days before meeting Remi, wondering if she'd ever love and be loved again. And then, after braving the online dating market, she'd finally found Remi—the one, and everything would be perfect.

But life never is perfect, is it?

Once they got back, Margot marched up the stairs, pulled the cork on a bottle of merlot, and drew a hot bath. Sitting against the tub so that Carly couldn't hear her voice over the running water, Margot called Jasper.

"Mom! What's going on? I can't wait to see you."

The whole world could be at war, but the moment she got him on the phone, everything seemed to be okay. "I'm counting the days. Are you sad to leave?"

"Forget that," he said. "How's Carly? Are you two getting along?"

Margot burst into a foot-long cry, splashing tears all over the bathroom tiles. "She hates me. I don't know what to do, Jasper. I haven't even done anything to her, and she hates me."

"Oh, Mom. She doesn't hate you. Whatever she's going through has *nothing* to do with you."

Why was it that speaking with Jasper always made her feel as if she were visiting with some wise man at the top of a mountain?

"I know that, but—"

"Do you, Mom? Seriously. No one on earth hates you. What was it? Were you too nice to her? Did you cook too much good food for her? Or was her room too clean and the bed too comfortable?"

Out of all the tears rose a smile. "You're such a sweetheart."

"Seriously, it's her stuff, not yours." He paused for a moment. "Mom, I can hear the water running. Drop a citrus bath bomb in there, pour yourself a glass of wine, and let it all go. By the time you get out, you'll be a new woman."

Margot chuckled and wiped her eyes. "No one knows me like you do, honey. Thanks for the laugh."

Jasper changed the subject. "I hear you and Carmen are coming to pick Emilia and me up. Since when did you hang out with her?"

"I ran into her the other day, and she suggested it. That okay with you?"

"Totally," he said. "I'm just excited to get back to the mountain and see what kind of craziness has occurred while I've been gone."

"Oh, it's all quiet around here."

"Yeah, right. I know better. Someone should write a book about that place."

After saying goodbye, she slipped into the tub and took a long sip of her merlot. She'd forgotten about riding to the airport with Carmen. That was weird in so many ways.

14

HIDDEN AGENDAS AND EYE PATCHES

As if Brooks didn't have enough on his mind, Carmen had chosen today to show her true colors. She'd been surprisingly agreeable and even upbeat since she'd started a week ago. In fact, Brooks had settled into the reality of her working at Lacoda and didn't mind the little changes she was making in the tasting room, like new stemware, more elegant art on the walls, even the smaller touches like vases filled with flowers. And when they crossed paths, she was more than civil, sneaking past polite into outgoing territory, which was not typical for her.

After Adriana had dropped him off back at his house, he'd ridden his bike to the winery and spent the morning walking the vineyards with his assistant winemaker, Pak, focusing mostly on a few rows of sangiovese, a red Italian variety that grew surprisingly well on Red Mountain when harvested early and made in a more *saison,* or session, style.

The only issue they were still trying to work out was the grape skin's vulnerability to sunburn in the sweltering summer sun on Red Mountain. They'd first tried spraying a clay mist on the grapes, but there wasn't enough rain some years before harvest to wash the clay off the grapes. The last two years, they'd been experimenting with different canopy techniques, which presented their own challenges. Too much canopy, and they risked mildew and pest issues. Too little, and the grapes would bleach in the sun.

This year, they'd committed to testing a different idea on each row—various levels of pruning, different training techniques—and they were eager for August, when they'd be able to confirm their tests. That's all farming was, facing one challenge at a time, and Brooks had found his calling in taking on these challenges with eager resolve.

What he didn't love seeing was Carmen walking up the row. To Brooks, she looked like a raised gun in a church. As she drew closer, Brooks wondered what it felt like to live in her skin, to be so bogged down by darkness.

"Good morning," she sang with her best attempt at optimism, the new and sober Carmen trying to shake the past.

After a moment of small talk, she said, "Pak, could I steal Brooks?"

"Yeah, sure." Pak, who largely kept to himself and was happiest running numbers in the quiet of the lab, looked relieved to be set free from Carmen's web. His name was short for Pakkapong, and he'd originally moved with his family from Thailand to Seattle during his high school years. Brooks had hired him four years earlier as an intern, and Pak had worked his way to a full-time position.

Pak jammed his pruners with orange handles into the holster on his belt and sidestepped as if he'd been given a few seconds head start before the wolves were unleashed. Walking to the end of the row, he climbed onto his ATV and fired up the engine.

Brooks turned to Carmen as Pak sped down the hill back toward the winery. "What's going on?"

"I have a favor to ask of you." She looked over her shoulder, as if to make sure no one else could hear. "I'm worried Emilia might try to stay on the mountain after the summer. I think she misses it here."

This was not news to Brooks, but he feigned surprise. "And leave school? What makes you think that?"

"She's mentioned it a few times. I don't think she loves NYU *or* the East Coast. She hasn't said anything to you?"

Brooks had talked to Emilia several times about how she hadn't quite found her place in Manhattan. She was almost a sister to him, and he knew that her problem was more than just NYU, New York, and the East Coast. Brooks figured she still hadn't found her purpose, and that's what had been bugging her. Living under her parents' shadows was a burden she carried like a cross, and she so desperately wanted to be someone valued for more than the looks she'd inherited. As hard as she searched, her purpose kept eluding her.

Last time Brooks had talked to her, his almost-sister had said, "I actually feel like I'm moving further and further away from who I truly am."

When she'd asked Brooks if he had summer work for her at Lacoda, he'd instantly said yes. Anything for her.

Keeping these thoughts from Carmen, Brooks continued as if all this was new news. "She hasn't come out and said she's not going back. I know she was struggling a little at first, but she's just trying to make her way."

Carmen nodded and then dropped the truth like a boulder at Brooks's feet. "I don't want her to stay." *Oh, here we go.* The old Carmen was suddenly back, the woman full of agendas and selfishness. He could taste the bitterness in the air, and he wondered if the vines had constricted like his veins.

"Why not?" Brooks asked, sincerely perplexed. Even after knowing Carmen for so many years, he still wasn't able to guess the whys behind her actions. She played life like a chess player, and Brooks was no match for the female Magnus Carlsen of Red Mountain.

Carmen paused to think about her answer, clearly not sure whether she wanted to divulge the whole truth. "As much as I'd love to be close to her, I don't think it's good for her. After all that happened two years ago, she needs to break free and come into her own." Carmen was referring to Emilia's brief affair with one of her teachers during her last year in high school.

Though Brooks agreed that Emilia needed to break free, he wasn't about to guess how she might do that. Emilia was almost twenty. She could do whatever she wanted. And if she wanted to come home, why stop her?

Carmen clasped her hands together in front of her. "I don't even know why she'd want to stay. What is there here for a nineteen-year-old? What is there for anyone?"

Ah, the bitterness of a city woman forced to live out here in the wilderness. Brooks could only imagine how much anger Carmen had unleashed on Jake for dragging their family out here from Seattle almost four years ago.

For a moment, he felt a need to stand up for Red Mountain. Hadn't he just had this conversation with Adriana? There were many reasons why Emilia was looking forward to coming home, and perhaps even staying.

Trying not to sound patronizing, Brooks looked from left to right at the vines running in zigzags across the face of the mountain. "I guess there are worse places to be."

"My point is, Brooks, that I don't want you to do anything to coerce her into staying."

Who in the hell did Carmen think she was? For that matter, what was the real reason why she didn't want her daughter to stay?

Before Brooks could protest, she continued, "That's fine if she works for you over the summer, but I don't want you offering her a full-time position if she asks. There's more to the world than Red Mountain, and I want her to see that."

Brooks tried not to let the anger show on his face, but the cynicism in his voice gave it away. "You're the boss, Carmen."

"I'm glad we're on the same page."

Were they? Brooks had been here before, where the poison resided, where the demon yet to be exorcised housed itself. He knew exactly how she'd react if he offered some parenting advice. He looked right, avoiding her trap.

A man driving a tractor bumped along a few rows down, and he and Brooks exchanged a wave.

"I don't want you to judge me," she said.

Brooks twisted his head back toward her. "I'm not judging you." Though he kind of was.

"When you have children, you'll understand. Sometimes, you need to make their decisions for them."

Brooks inclined his head. "I see." The words he wanted to say were chambered and ready to fire, but he focused on not pulling the trigger, not giving her a reason to bite.

For the sake of Jake and Emilia and the others, he said, "I'm walking away now." With that, he pivoted and was gone.

As much as he wanted to tell Emilia what Carmen had just said, he knew he couldn't. Today had just confirmed that his worst fears were correct. No matter how sober Carmen might be, no matter how hard she tried to be a better person, she was a dry drunk and had a long way to go in terms of personal growth. In the meantime, she could—and probably would—tear Lacoda apart.

Several rows down, Brooks sat on a stack of vineyard poles. He dug his hand into the earth and pulled up a handful of Red Mountain dust. As it fell from his fingers, he closed his eyes and saw palm trees and turquoise water. The Red Mountain dust turned to powdery white sand, as if the tropics were calling him through the vibrations of the earth.

～

INFILTRATING Bellflour's property and planting the pinotage vines had given Otis a welcome boost emotionally. Though he was short on sleep, he'd attacked the day with youthful verve. Something about taking the upper hand against his enemy had given him the fuel he needed to focus back on his own life.

He and Joan ate lunch together and then went for a stroll around the property. They'd taken a moment to put fresh hay in the chicken coop and collect eggs when Joan said, "I've been thinking about our chat last night, and I have something you might try."

"I can't wait to hear this," Otis said, emptying the dirty water from the waterer.

She was filling a basket with eggs from the back hatch. "Have you ever heard of eye patching?"

"I don't believe I have." Otis could only imagine where she was going with this notion. He turned on the hose and began to fill the waterer.

"I want you to try wearing an eye patch over your right eye for a little while."

He nearly dropped the hose. "Are you kidding me?"

"As I'm sure you know, the right eye is connected to the left side of the brain, which is the more analytical side. You, my love, have an overactive left brain. By covering the right eye, I think we could simmer it down some, give you a chance to reconnect with the right brain—that's the one you need right now. That's where your love of *terroir* and your farming instincts come from."

"An eye patch?" He twisted the top back onto the waterer and lifted it up into the coop. "I know you're not serious. You want me to run around like the bloody pirate of Red Mountain?" Otis laughed from his gut. "I can't imagine the looks I'd get."

"You're nearing seventy years old," Joan said. "Do you really still care what people think of you? I'll wear one too...for solidarity."

"Oh, give me a break. Sometimes I must draw the line with all your voodoo. I'd rather have a lobotomy." He shook his head. "An eye patch..."

Having collected all the eggs, she shut the back hatch. "I'm just trying to help."

"I know you are, and I so appreciate it. You know I do. It's just...we might need to explore some other ideas."

15

MARGOT AND CARMEN GO TO THE AIRPORT

Riding in the passenger side of Carmen's new Tesla Model X, Margot felt slightly uneasy. Though Carmen had forgiven her quickly for sleeping with Jake, Margot was still trying to forgive herself. More so on her mind were the tremendous feelings of intimidation and flat-out inferiority that seemed to want to strangle her as she glanced at the supermodel next to her. Margot knew it wasn't healthy to compare herself to Carmen, or anyone else for that matter, but she couldn't stop herself.

Margot hadn't measured, but compared to herself, she was pretty sure Carmen was three feet taller. Carmen's right arm on the gear shift was about the same circumference as Margot's middle finger. Carmen's SUV was a million times cleaner than Margot's Volvo, which Margot hadn't had time to take to the car wash in more than a month. Though Carmen was older than Margot, she looked ten years younger, with skin that must have been peeled right off a child. And look at her tiny little purse compared to Margot's, which suddenly felt like a duffel bag.

As they rode by the Yakima River heading toward the highway, Carmen asked, "How are the wedding plans coming along?"

"Don't even get me started." Margot told her about the dress and Carly's arrival, and Carmen listened with apparent interest.

"You're really going through a tough time, aren't you?" Carmen asked.

"At least Carly is clean. Like, really clean. Makes her bed, does her dishes, picks up after herself. At least there's that."

Margot and Carmen were actually getting along quite well, and it had become all too obvious that these two women had not shared much—other than Jake.

As Red Mountain disappeared in the rearview mirror, Margot finally had to ask, "How in the world do you stay so fit? I need a secret or two. If I can't squeeze into that wedding dress, I don't know what I'm going to do."

Carmen smiled as if Margot were the twentieth person to ask today. And Margot felt so unoriginal. Couldn't she come up with a better conversation with a supermodel? Wasn't Carmen made of more than her slender body and gorgeous face? Still, Margot really needed to know, and she would have kicked herself if she hadn't brought it up before they reached the airport.

"It's not easy," Carmen admitted as she sped past a dually truck towing a horse trailer.

"I have less than four months to lose...let's just say a lot of weight. And I've barely eaten, and nothing's coming off. I swear, Remi can eat salads for three days and lose six or seven pounds. I can basically stop eating and *gain* weight! So please tell me, what's the secret? If I don't figure it out, I'll have to rip a sail off the mast of a sailboat in Seattle to wear down the aisle."

Carmen let out the tiniest laugh. "You crack me up. Why haven't we ever hung out?"

Margot felt a warmth creep into the car. "I don't know. We live too close not to."

Returning to Margot's question, Carmen answered, "One thing I've realized as I've gotten older is that being thin isn't all it's cracked up to be. Why are you so worried about losing weight, anyway? I think you're stunning. And I'm not the only one in my family who thinks so."

Margot's mouth fell open. Here they were again. "For once in my life, I'm speechless."

Carmen smiled a very real smile, and Margot felt like she caught a glimpse of the woman's soul. "It's true. Anyway, I'm serious. If you want to be thin, you have to strip the joy from eating. When I sit down for a meal—if I take the time to sit down—I'm not excited about the menu or the flavors. I've heard you talk so eloquently about a meal you've prepared. You have such a gift as a chef. I wish I knew what that was like. My eating experiences are so methodical. Before I even pick up my fork, I've decided how much would be the right portion to keep my figure. And before I quit drinking a few months ago, I would decide how much I could eat and still get away with a bottle or two of wine. Let me tell you, an empty stomach is not a good base for a bottle or two of wine."

Margot appreciated Carmen's honesty and added, "Especially when you barely weigh as much as one of my legs."

Without reacting, Carmen continued, "I've loved my profession, but it's exhausting. I've spent every waking minute since I was a teenager concerned about my looks. It's what everyone expected of me from a very early age." She lifted a finger. "Then you get old, and a whole new set of problems arise. Forget gaining weight. Once you're in your forties, and, God forbid, fifties, it's the wrinkles and sags that are terrifying."

"Aren't they the worst?" Margot looked past Carmen to the landscape flying by through the window. An army of sprinklers was showering an apple orchard, a beat-up truck was putting along Frontage Road, and a woman was racing across a field on a horse.

Carmen glanced in the rearview mirror and turned on her blinker. "I think you'd be surprised how gloomy it is living in this body."

"Oh, I don't think so." Then, realizing Carmen was deadly serious, Margot asked, "Really? I mean, I know you have some stuff going on, but you seem so perfect."

She smirked. "Margot, if you only knew."

A few miles later, feeling much more comfortable navigating the intimate spaces, Margot asked, "How's the whole getting sober thing? I mean...if you want to talk about it." It had occurred to Margot that Carmen had as few boundaries as Margot. Maybe they *should* be friends.

Apparently not offended at all by the question, Carmen answered, "Well, there are probably better places to be sober than a mountain where everyone lives for wine. Including my husband. I've made it six months, though. It's nice to remember what happened the night before. I like being able to eat a little bit more, now that I don't have the alcohol calories. The AA meetings can be grueling."

"Oh, gosh, you're going to meetings here?"

"The worst part is wondering if someone is taking pictures or recording me." She shrugged. "But I guess that just comes with being a public figure. My privacy is an open book." She said the last part with the humor of a seasoned veteran in the business of being in the public eye.

"I hadn't thought about that," Margot said. "Isn't there something you can do without the meetings? Or can you go to famous-people meetings in Seattle?"

Carmen shook her head. "The meetings have been great, and the people are very respectful. We're all going through the same thing. Frankly, I don't think they care who I am. We're all just trying to get sober."

"It's a noble feat, getting sober." Margot said. "You should be very proud of yourself. I know your family is."

Carmen thanked Margot and paused in thought. "I just hope it's not too late. I've done a lot of damage over the years."

"It's never too late," Margot said. "And we're never too old."

Silence filled the car as the women breathed in the idea of second and third chances.

"I hope you're right," Carmen finally said.

Thinking of her second life, the one that had started the moment

she and Jasper had driven west from Vermont, Margot put her hand on Carmen's slender arm. "I know I am."

~

A SCRATCHY VOICE from overhead kept Emilia from nodding off on Jasper's shoulder. "Ladies and gentlemen, please stow your carry-ons and bring your seats and tray tables to an upright position. We'll be landing in just a few minutes."

Emilia lifted her head and rubbed her eyes. Seeing his face—the rounded profile, the gentle curves—drew a smile. So many things about him continued to stop her in her tracks. The way he stared off into space as if pondering a mathematical mystery, like now, with his eyes trained toward the cockpit. The care he put into his attire—more for him than to impress anyone else. The way his shaggy hair seemed to always be the perfect length. And his kind, gentle gestures and facial expressions, always authentic and trusting.

She'd fallen in love with a man cut from the same cloth as her father, a musician obsessed with his craft. As much as the idea that she might always play second fiddle terrified her, she couldn't imagine it any other way. What was more attractive than someone who lived and breathed his art? And hearing him play, even if he played a tune over the phone, crept into the marrow of her soul.

"You're missing it," he said, pointing out the window.

Emilia leaned over him, pressing her hand down on his leg, and looked over the scabland cutting across eastern Washington. The topography was bursting with the vitality of late spring. The giant Columbia River came into view with its cold, blue water serving as the main artery of life east of the Cascades.

Emilia pulled away from the window. "I don't know why exactly, but I've missed this place. Haven't you?"

"I'm excited to get back, that's for sure. It'll be a great summer."

She grabbed his hand. "What if we didn't go back? I mean, I know you have to. I know school is so important. But sometimes I feel like everything I want is down there. Other than you, I mean."

He looked down toward the carpet in the aisle. "It's a really cool place, but..."

"But what?"

"Probably not the best for my career. I could play music with your dad, but if I want to find my own touring band, or establish myself as a studio musician, then I need to be where the action is."

Emilia frowned. "I know." A flash of the future zipped through her mind. She and Jasper married with children; Jasper always on tour; Emilia dragging the kids from hotel to hotel chasing him.

He drew a circle on her thigh. "What would you do out here if you stayed?"

Emilia bit her lip. "Maybe keep working for Lacoda. Or...I don't know. Your mom's kind of my hero. I'd love to learn how to garden and cook like her. Maybe I could do something similar."

"You know she'd love to teach you."

Emilia wished Jasper could be the pianist in the house band at Épiphanie, and she could be the gardener. He would never have to go on tour. He'd never have to chase his dreams. Alas, she knew as well as anyone that his talent belonged in arenas, not hotel lobbies in the middle of nowhere.

"I don't want to ever say goodbye to you again," she said.

Jasper moved in and put his cheek to Emilia's; his breath tickled her neck. Then in a whisper, he said, "I love you."

Almost like it had been waiting discreetly on the ledge, a tear escaped her eye, rappelling down her cheek like a rock climber easing down Mount Rainier.

~

THE ONLY THING more awkward than her mom being drunk and high was her mom sober. As Emilia wrapped her arms around Carmen, she could sense her mother's nerves. "I missed you, Mom." She wore a new perfume, maybe violets.

Carmen burst into a sob, and Emilia hugged her tighter, thinking

of her own tear back on the plane. *How awful it is to be afraid of what's to come,* Emilia thought.

Emilia wiped her mom's cheek. "You never cry. You're not getting soft, are you?"

"I guess so." Carmen seemed to be hyperaware of her surroundings, wondering who might be watching her.

"You look really good, Mom. Healthy."

She locked eyes with Emilia. "Thanks. It's good to have you home, honey."

"Oh, come here." Emilia pulled her in for another hug. She'd never seen her mom so vulnerable.

Once they broke away from a second hug, Carmen whispered, "I hope it's not too late, honey."

Emilia tilted her head. "For what, Mom?"

Carmen let out a slow breath. "Too late to be a mom. I'm so sorry for the past few years. I'm going to try to do better."

Emilia was just happy to see her mom trying, period. "You're a great mom. Quit beating yourself up."

They both turned to Margot and Jasper, bringing them into their circle, and after more hugs and greetings, the four of them—mother and son, mother and daughter—crossed the airport toward the baggage claim. Questions and answers about exams and roommates and dorms and college life rounded out the conversation, but Emilia's mind was elsewhere.

She looked at the happy people embracing the loved ones they hadn't seen in days or weeks or longer. People living a long way from the big city of Seattle, happy to be away from it all, dreaming more of healthy crops than tall buildings. Emilia wondered if these were her people, if she was one of them. New York City felt like a harsh spotlight shining in her face. This place was a candle twinkling in the twilight.

Would she be back here in August to board a plane? If not, what would become of her and Jasper?

∽

"IT'S NOT that big of a deal," Jasper said. They were walking from the car to the house, and Margot wanted to turn and run. She was about to introduce her angry future stepdaughter to the light of her life.

Margot was carrying his messenger bag and pulled it higher up on her shoulder. "If she's mean to you—"

"I think I can handle whatever she throws at me." He glanced back at the setting sun, which had painted rainbows across the entire sky. "Gosh, it's good to be back."

"We'll see how you feel tomorrow." Margot wondered if she needed a prescription or two to get through the next few days.

Jasper hefted his suitcase, which might have weighed more than he did, up the steps. He put a lot of effort into his style and therefore always traveled with a large wardrobe.

Margot reached for the doorknob. "Whatever happens in there, I've got your back."

He grabbed her arm. "You get her wrists, and I'll get her ankles."

She snorted out a laugh and whispered, "It's so good to have you home."

Remi and Carly were in the living area, on the couch, watching television. Remi pointed the remote and paused their show.

Before Margot could even set the backpack down, Jasper was crossing the room and opening his arms. "Hey, Remi, it's good to see you."

"Welcome back, my man."

After the two men embraced, Remi introduced Carly, who was standing awkwardly and looking sullen.

Margot had been watching all this from a safe distance but had the sudden urge to rush in and play defense.

"Hi, Carly," Jasper said. "I can't believe I have a sister now."

Carly half-smiled and stuck out her hand. "Good to meet you."

Jasper wasn't having it and stretched out his arms. "I'm a hugger."

Margot watched as Jasper wrapped his arms around his future stepsister. The two were about the same height. When he gave hugs, he leaned into them, and the sight made Carly seem all the more brittle, like her son was hugging a bundle of sticks.

"How's the mountain treating you?" Jasper asked, holding his position very close to her.

"Not bad. I've only been here a few days."

Jasper offered a warm smile. "It's a long way from San Francisco, isn't it? And I don't mean the miles."

Carly made a face that almost signified relief, as if she'd finally found someone else who understood what she was going through. "Uh, yes, a long way."

"Stick around long enough," Jasper said, "and this place will grow on you. Trust me."

With another half-smile, she said, "I hope so."

16

DON'T BREATHE THE AIR

O tis slid out from under his orange Kubota tractor, wiping the grease from his hands onto a rag. Pressing up to a stand, he noticed the leaves on the vines were dancing in the wind. It blew cool against his sweaty forehead, and he welcomed a break from this surprisingly blistering May heat. With the wind at its tail, a tumbleweed was trying to break free from one of the wires holding up a post.

Hearing another tractor kick on up near the Drink Flamingo property, he looked south. A dust cloud rose like a swarm of bees around the McMansion. He shook his head in disgust. Once again, they'd neglected to spray water over the newly cleared land, and now the neighbors would be breathing dust all day.

His eyes focused in on one of the *No Trespassing* signs, and he wondered if they'd noticed the cut in the fence. Otis had done his best to fit it back cleanly, but someone would come across it soon enough and wonder if they were missing tools or parts.

Only the truth of their vineyard has been stolen, Otis mused, thinking of the pinotage vines taking root, spoiling Bellflour's dream of making the most seductive cabernet sauvignon in the world. He hoped—oh, how wonderful it would be!—that crooked critics would

give Bellflour the scores he wanted—the high nineties or even the sacred *one hundred*—writing some absurd sales blurb like, "Red Mountain has a new king!" or "Finally, a cabernet sauvignon hedonistic enough to make you feel guilty drinking it."

If Otis heard another reference to hedonism in wine, he was going to bury the whole world in cotton candy and chocolate syrup. It was just wrong to want your wines to taste as oaky as Maker's Mark.

When the critics offered their praise, Otis could finally announce what he'd done, how their new "darling of Red Mountain" wasn't a noble cabernet sauvignon at all. It was just another factory-farmed imposter buying its way to the top with a cabernet sauvignon/pinotage blend. Otis could out everyone who'd sold their soul to the devil.

Otis figured Bellflour knew exactly how to get the scores and acclaim he wanted, practicing the nefarious art of buying and shoving his way to the top. Not that all critics had compromised their integrity, not at all. But it was no secret that there were many ways to break into the big time, and many had nothing to do with farming and producing an authentic wine true to its surroundings.

The quantity of Drink Flamingo ads was already increasing in the most influential magazines. Otis wouldn't be surprised if Bellflour was offering Seahawks season tickets or free trips to Mexico, perhaps by private plane, to anyone willing to get behind Drink Flamingo's Red Mountain wines. No doubt hiring big names to consult on the project was another ploy in the preparation to launch the brand.

Another key component in gaming the system would be their practices in the field and in the cellar. Who knew what they might spray to make sure their vines survived, even if that meant destruction of the habitat? Who cared about the meadowlarks and pintails or the honeybees? And what heinous crimes did they commit in the cellar: the artificial practices of chaptalization—adding sugar—or, God forbid, the addition of Mega Purple, a grape concentrate used to enhance color?

Even the less aggressive tactics drove Otis crazy. For a wine to compete well in a blind tasting among fifty other wines, it needed to have a certain element of power. *Power* wasn't always an attractive term in Otis's mind. He preferred the delicate nuances of a balanced wine, not the diesel-fueled, high-budget Hollywood action movies that some wineries were bottling these days.

These were the thoughts that fed Otis's nightmares.

Joan was right. Bellflour was winning. He could be miles away and still infect Otis's brain like a disease.

Knackered by his overactive monkey mind, Otis decided to give Joan's suggestion a shot. Though he wasn't about to employ an eye patch, he covered his right eye with his hand, just to get an idea of what she was talking about, this balance between left and right. A bout of dizziness rushed over him. Pulling his hand away, he blinked a few times to regain reality.

"Forget that," he said, looking down toward the house, wondering if Joan was watching him through the window with an approving nod.

Leaning against the tractor, he tried again, looking over the lines of vines leading down to the sheep. He looked beyond his flock to where the ground dipped again, eventually leading to the river. The dizziness felt more like a high, and as he settled his one eye on Mount Adams many miles west, he felt free.

"What the heck are you doing?" a voice called out behind him.

Otis ripped his hand away and turned, feeling his face flush red.

It was Brooks. "Something wrong with your eye?"

"Don't ask," Otis answered. He wasn't about to tell Brooks about Joan's newest idea.

As Brooks stopped a few feet in front of him, he glanced at the tractor and then Otis's toolbox next to the tire. "I told you a John Deere would have been a better buy."

"Oh, c'mon. I was just changing the oil." Otis stuffed the rag into his back pocket. "This Kubota will outlast both of us. Tell me something good, Brooks. I'm having a tough day. The damn Flamingo crew forgot to spray water again. I can barely see through all the dust. And my back hurts like hell."

"I wish I did have some good news," Brooks said. "Not that I have anything bad. But I'm like you, having a shitty week."

Otis looked up at the sun dominating in the blue. "Can you imagine how hot August is going to be this year? Forget tequila. I'll be raising camels and building pyramids."

"I'll help you if I'm still around in August."

"What the hell does that mean?" Otis asked, not liking Brooks's tone. "Carmen giving you more trouble?"

"Carmen, Adriana. My mother. Just about everyone seems to be conspiring to get rid of me."

The fear of losing Brooks showed itself as an ache in Otis's chest. "You're not really thinking of leaving, are you?" The pain cascaded down his spine and settled into his lower back.

Brooks looked up to the sky and closed his eyes. "I don't know. Adriana's outta here."

"Why in the world would she leave?" Otis asked—like there couldn't be a reason good enough.

"I'm not sure she feels the same way you and I do about the mountain."

"We're a rare and dying breed, Brooks. I'm sorry to hear this. I know how much you love her."

Brooks nodded. "I can't imagine saying goodbye to this place, but I can't imagine waving at her as she drives away, either."

"Jesus, Brooks. I wouldn't wish that decision on anyone. And I'll do my best to stay out of it, though you know how I feel. We need you. How about Carmen? What's she done this time?"

Brooks lowered his head. "I can't work with her...definitely can't work for her."

Otis knew something would have to change over there, or Jake would lose his head winemaker. "Talk to Jake. He'll understand. If he doesn't, you know I've always got a job for you. As does every other winery in Washington State. Or hell, anywhere in the world. Anyone would be lucky to have you."

"I appreciate that."

"You've earned it, son."

They turned to the sound of hurried footsteps sliding down the gravel drive. It was Eli, one of the only people Otis trusted with his vines. He was short in stature but tall in integrity.

"Otis," Eli said, out of breath, his eyes hiding behind mirrored sunglasses, his head covered by a worn-out trucker's hat. He could barely put his words together. "They're spraying something over at Drink Flamingo. It's blowing into our vines."

Otis turned and hissed though gritted teeth, "What are they spraying?"

"I don't know. But the guy's wearing a protective coverall and a respirator."

"You're kidding me."

Otis marched toward enemy territory in a fiery-red haze. Once neared the fence line, he saw a man in a white protective suit bumping along through the rows of green grow tubes. Otis stared for a moment, assessing the danger. As the man in white reached the end of a row, only a few feet from Otis's property, the orange hazard symbol plastered to the big, white tank on the back of the tractor reflected in the sun. Sure enough, Otis could see the mist rising and drifting through the chain-link fence and over the road into his own property.

It was perhaps the worst sight he'd ever seen.

Not thinking of Eli and Brooks somewhere behind him, Otis marched left along the fence line until he reached the wide-open gate where a group of workers sat in the shade of a young acacia tree, eating lunch. He ignored them and continued through the construction site, past the tall wooden frame that was coming along much faster than Otis had hoped, and past the pool and hot tub that would soon be full of wine-drunk idiots.

Someone called out from behind. "What are you doing?"

Otis ignored him and beelined it to the tractor, stomping through the dirt.

Staring at the mist rising into the wind, Otis wondered what the guy was spraying. Probably an herbicide. Glyphosate? Paraquat? Whatever it was, Otis could lose his own certifications if too much drifted over.

Had he not been so furious, Otis might have cried. Screw the certifications. They were killing the soil, killing the essence of Red Mountain. It felt like someone had taken his children and forced chemicals down their throats, poisoning them.

About ten rows away from the tractor, Otis began unleashing hell, his fist shaking in the wind. "What the hell are you doing up there? Cut that fucking tractor off right now!"

An angry man behind him warned Otis to get off the property.

Otis kept his eyes on the man in the white suit, who'd now noticed him—but kept spraying.

"Don't make me climb up on that tractor and throw you off!" Otis picked up a piece of granite the size of a baseball and slung it toward the tractor. The rock bounced off with a ping.

That must have gotten the driver's attention. He finally shut off the sprayer and stopped the tractor, cutting the engine. The silence stung the air. The mist of the unknown chemical still drifted in the wind.

After a stare down, the man raised his hands and said something unintelligible.

"Take off that damn mask!" Otis yelled.

The man lifted up his hands, like he couldn't understand what Otis was saying. Otis screamed louder, and the man finally pulled the hood back and his goggles up and dropped the respirator to his neck. The young man's hair was doused in sweat, the skin around his eyes red from the goggles.

Otis didn't give him a second to explain. "You have any idea what you're doing? Your chemicals are drifting! You're killing my vines— my bloody organic vines!" He heard the fury in his own voice as his victim's eyes widened.

"You might not know what you're doing, but your boss sure does. Where the hell is Bellflour? That blowhard is killing this mountain." Otis put his fist back in the air. "Both of you should know you can't spray on a windy day, and you *shouldn't* be using these chemicals, anyway! I haven't sprayed a chemical on my vines in ten years, and look at them." He pointed. "Look at them!"

Once the fool had gotten a good look, Otis said, "You're killing your soil before you even begin. It might be fine this year, but what about five years from now?" Rage, rage, rage! Otis felt it boiling up around his feet. "How old are you?"

The man was too stunned to respond.

The angry voice behind him was getting closer.

Otis didn't let up. "Don't you want your children to have the opportunity to farm? Don't you give a blue-bloody shit about the earth? You keep spraying whatever the hell is in that tank, and there will be nothing left but an apocalyptic wasteland!"

A hawk passed by, soaring proudly, and Otis pointed to it. As the man looked up, Otis asked, "See that bird? He'll be long gone. Forget about the vines. Your kids will be lucky if they can grow sagebrush! Do you understand what I'm trying to tell you?"

Otis's heart raced. He slammed a fist onto the tractor. "Do you hear me!"

Finally, the young man found the courage to speak. "*Lo siento. No hablo inglés.*"

"Oh, you must be kidding me." Otis reached for his cap and crumbled it in his hands. In broken Spanish, Otis screamed, "*No más! Estás matando las viñas. Detente, por favor!*" Repeating himself in English, he muttered, "You're killing the vines."

Exhausted in fury, he finally turned to see a crowd collecting behind him. Brooks and Eli stood with the men and women who'd abandoned their lunches, all of their eyes as big as golf balls.

Otis dropped his head and stalked past them, holding back a cry. This is what it felt like to be hanging from a cliff with one weakening hand, each finger fighting for life, each one slowly slipping.

17

AN EYE FOR DESIGN

After sitting with Otis for a while, mostly in silence, Brooks climbed back onto his Scrambler and cut through the vineyards to Lacoda. He hit the turns hard and the straightaways even harder, and dust swelled around him. As the two wheels fought the slippery terrain, Brooks wondered if they'd ever have a peaceful vintage on the mountain.

What a sad sight to see Otis so down on what he'd spent the latter part of his life building. Brooks wished he could do more, but there was only so much any of them could do. With all the attention Red Mountain was garnering—the rising land prices, the countless articles, the sold-out vintages—it was inevitable that ignorant people with greedy intentions would chase the potential of this place.

He'd hoped that would be the last of the drama for the day, but as he pulled open the door to the Lacoda tasting room, he felt a chill far colder than the air conditioning. Jake stood behind the concrete bar with his arms crossed, talking to Carmen, who was perched on a stool in front of a line of Lacoda bottles. They turned when they heard him enter, and Brooks offered a quick wave and started in the opposite direction.

"Got a sec?" Jake asked.

Brooks felt like his energy had been zapped as he stopped and pivoted. "Of course." He walked up to the bar, assuming a position on the opposite end from Carmen. He told them about the drift issues.

"Though I doubt it will go anywhere," he said, "we're bringing it up at the Alliance meeting. Otis wants the entire mountain to commit to organics."

Jake sipped water from an old army canteen. "Wouldn't that be nice?"

"One day, maybe." Brooks glanced at Carmen and the line of bottles. "Everything good here?"

Carmen looked back over at Jake, clearly letting him break the latest news.

Jake set down his canteen. "Yeah, we've been brainstorming some new ideas." He picked up the bottle closest to him and held it out for examination.

Brooks felt something catch in his throat. In the past years, Jake and Brooks had spent many long hours debating the perfect packaging to capture their project. They'd finally decided nothing in their message was more important than being understated and minimalist, the antithesis of what you might expect from a rock star. This vineyard wasn't about Jake and his music. Otherwise, they'd have put a picture of him on the label, maybe used his last name. The idea behind Lacoda was to make the project about the land, not the brand. These thoughts had led to their decision of a squat bottle, which they considered sexy and hip like a Paris street wine.

Brooks looked at the yellow capsule covering the tip of the bottle —a nod to the sun—and then down to the label. The simple Lacoda logo hovered above the words *Red Mountain*, which was printed in a thin, cursive font. Understated. Simple. Elegant. The vineyard block, vintage, and variety were printed under the appellation. Only the most necessary information.

As all three of them looked at the bottle, Brooks braced himself. Not to be an elitist, but Carmen didn't understand wine like he and Jake. He'd never seen her wander the vines or taste through the latest vintage in barrel. He'd not known her to even read a book on wine.

And he'd never seen her mesmerized by the bouquet or dazzled by a first taste. The only thing that had mattered to her in the four years since starting Lacoda seemed to be the buzz.

Of course, she'd spent a lifetime in the fashion industry, so he wasn't surprised she might have something to say about the Lacoda aesthetics. In fact, after the way she'd been transforming the estate, Brooks should have seen it coming. The cynic in him couldn't wait to hear how she was going to destroy their concepts. As he braced for impact, he realized how absurd it might seem to be so obsessed over the packaging, especially when the idea was to be understated and even humble. But the bottle was what carried the wine they'd put all their hard work into. Its appearance was a big deal.

Jake looked at Brooks with apologetic eyes. "I'd like for Carmen to have some say in the packaging. She has some good ideas." He opened his hand to her, giving her the floor.

Carmen gestured toward the bottles on the bar. "I know you don't want to hear it, Brooks, but the squat bottle just isn't working. I think we'd look much more elegant in standard bottles, Burgundy and Bordeaux shapes. I know it's hip to go alternative, but this just feels like we're trying too hard."

The only thing Brooks was feeling was a tightness in his neck. He looked over at Jake, who was still staring at the bottle, almost hiding behind it.

Breaking through the silence, Carmen continued, "It just makes the wine look fat and sloppy." She wrinkled her nose like she was smelling rotten trash. "While we're at it, the labels really need more character. No offense, but it's just so manly and out of touch. Where's the color? Where's the...I don't know...complexity? To me, this wine says, 'Drink me with a ham sandwich.'"

Brooks thought it amazing that Carmen could so easily find a way to throw insults with whatever came out of her mouth.

"I dig the packaging," Brooks finally said. "We don't want complicated. No offense, but we don't want a bottle that belongs on a catwalk."

"That's fine," Carmen replied, "but this looks like it belongs in a gas station. Is that what you want?"

Following that zinger, Brooks was reminded that taking on Carmen was never a good idea. Biting his tongue for Jake's sake, he said, "To me, what we have is perfect. It captures everything we're trying to do here. But you two are the bosses."

"Yeah," Jake agreed, "but you're a partner with us. You're a big reason why we're here. We want your opinion." He put both hands on the bar. "Hell, we need it."

Brooks knew Jake was in a tough spot. Brooks lifted his hand and then dropped it. "You've got my opinion."

Carmen shook her head, laughing to herself in an apparent attempt to belittle Brooks. "What about using a name?" she asked, moving on as if she'd already won the bottle-shape argument. "There's too much white space. And this says *Red Blend*. It needs a name. Someone like me isn't going to drink this wine."

Brooks wanted to mention that this wine wasn't for people like her, but he didn't. Nor did he point out that she was sober, either, or that someone like her would drink *any* wine that landed in her glass.

"You fellas need to think bigger," she continued. "I can see this very elaborate, almost Château Mouton-Rothschild artist series. You could keep your logo but do something with the white space. We could hire the guy who did the mural behind me. As far as names, we could do something in a big, elaborate scroll, a different, cute name for each project."

Cute? Brooks thought.

A master of dealing with his wife, Jake did the only thing he could do. Go with it. "What are you thinking, Carm? Any ideas come to mind?"

"Oh, I don't know," she said, looking at her loyal husband, her long neck craning toward him. "Something very literary, even mythical. Or..." She raised a finger as if she'd suddenly been struck with an Einstein-worthy notion. "Stay true to your roots. Use musical names."

Brooks imagined smashing his own head against the concrete bar, over and over. He wanted to scream. How dare she, a person who didn't even take wine seriously, come in here and start throwing out her ideas? She wouldn't know *terroir* if it wrote its name on her unblemished, Botoxed forehead.

Since no one else spoke up, Carmen kept going. Who would dare get in the way of a brainstorm of such Einsteinian authority? She spun the bottle around. "As far as the back label, it needs to tell a story. If you go with the musical theme, talk about how the wine matches the idea. For example, you could go with a family of names like *concerto*, *legato*, and *fugue*. The names could fit the style of the wine."

Oh God, please kill me now, Brooks thought.

He looked back at Jake, who was hiding a tsunami of frustration behind his smile. But Jake was doing what he'd always done, putting family first. Carmen was fighting to stay sober and to regain control of her life. Jake would do anything to support her, even if that meant letting her have her way at Lacoda. He'd no doubt hand over the reins entirely if that's what she wanted.

Concerto, legato, fugue.

What in all holy hell was Carmen thinking?

Jake leaned against the back wall under the hanging stemware. "What do you think, Brooks?"

Brooks pinched his chin. "I don't know what to say, guys." Feeling antsy, he picked up a wine key and opened and closed the corkscrew.

"I'm a simple man. I don't want to make some big, flowery splash on the shelf. I want our seriousness to be interpreted by the simplicity of what we do." Brooks wondered if Carmen was even listening. "I don't want the bottle to scream for attention."

"I hear you," Jake said. "I don't think anyone wants the packaging to scream. And we're not making any decisions yet. But it is hard to argue with Carmen when it comes to design." He looked at his wife. "Why don't you have some things drawn up? We're in no rush. Once you're ready, we can take a look."

Brooks wondered what it would feel like to jam the corkscrew into his own eye.

Carmen stood from her chair and said victoriously, "Sounds good."

Yeah, you won, Carmen, Brooks thought. *You'll get the label of your dreams. The tallest and heaviest bottle ever made. And a broken family and a crumbling winery to go with all your wins. And I'll run far, far away.*

"That all right with you, Brooks?" Jake asked, tearing him from his tumbling thoughts.

Brooks dropped a single affirmative nod.

"I'm sure we can find some middle ground," Jake continued. "Who knows? Emilia and Luca might like to have a say as well. Lacoda will be theirs one day."

Brooks would much rather have the Foresters' son, Luca, draw something with crayons than have an artist from Carmen's fashion circles design an elaborate portrait that had absolutely nothing to do with Red Mountain.

After this encounter with Carmen, Brooks wondered how Emilia was faring with her recently sober mother. As excited as he was for Emilia, he was starting to think she might be better served taking a job in town somewhere, maybe as a lifeguard or a server. She would no doubt learn a lot about wine this summer, but she might just learn *way* more than she wanted to about Carmen and the realities of life.

Escaping the tasting room before he blew a gasket, Brooks walked through the cellar, dodged a forklift, and checked his phone.

His mother had texted. *I'd like to come by later.*

Brooks dropped his head. He'd been so busy with work, he'd almost forgotten about the damn baby monitor from hell and his mother piling onto Adriana's reasons for leaving Red Mountain. What a hell of a day.

18

THE THINGS THAT STAND IN THE WAY

Exiting out a side door, Brooks found a spot of shade under a pine tree and called his brother, who was somewhere out in the field trying to train the sheep not to eat the canopies.

"Hey," Brooks said, "did you tell Mom about the baby monitor?"

"Yeah, I had to. Sorry. She needed to know."

That meant Abby knew too. Brooks took a long breath. He was too tired to even argue.

With a groan, Brooks hung up the phone. Taking a seat on the wall near the crush pad, he texted his mom back. *Don't worry about the other night.*

She replied: *I'd like a chance to apologize.*

Brooks felt like he was a thousand feet underwater, being crushed by the pressure. How could he possibly focus on the wine with all these distractions? He looked down at his bandaged hand and started laughing. What else was there to do but laugh? This was what he'd wanted, wasn't it? To be surrounded by friends and family, to live the so-called "normal" life.

He finally typed back: *Come by around eight, after Zack goes to sleep.*

Mary: *Okay! I'll be there.*

At four, Brooks drove the truck into town to rent a trencher for an irrigation project they were starting the next day. Once he'd dropped it back off at Lacoda, he climbed onto his bike to head home. Taking the long way, he swung a left on Antinori Road and raced up the hill to Col Solare, where he stopped for a moment to take in the view. Holding his helmet in his hands, he spun his head from left to right, looking at the flourishing canopies painting the entire slope green.

All this pain for the grapes, he thought. *All this...for the grapes.*

When he pulled into his driveway, he was debating how to tell Adriana about his mother coming over, that Mary wanted to apologize for saying those things. "I guess I just come out and say it," Brooks said to himself as he entered.

"Where's the wild man?" Brooks yelled, reaching down for an Amazon package.

Zack came barreling down the stairs. "My mom said we could play Xbox. You in?"

"Yeah, buddy. Can you give me a few minutes to cool down? Then I'd love to."

"Awesome!" Zack threw his arms around Brooks, and the problems of the world seemed to disappear momentarily.

Brooks squeezed him and patted his back. "How was camp?"

"Pretty cool." Returning to the topic of the Xbox, he said, "I figured out how to get that robot to drop the hammer."

"Oh, finally."

Zack gave him the details and then ran back upstairs. "Hurry, Brooks!"

Brooks kicked off his shoes and called for Adriana. He found her sitting on the couch. "I'm not sure there's anything better than your son running down the stairs and hugging me when I get..." He stopped when he saw her solemn face. "What's wrong?"

She turned toward him with red eyes. "Michael was in a fight. He shanked another prisoner. Almost killed him."

"What?" Brooks rushed to her side and took her hand.

Her hand tightened into a fist. "My old lawyer called. They caught the incident on camera. He said Michael may not be eligible for parole for another ten years, at least, depending on the judge."

Brooks resisted a smile. This was the ex-husband who had beaten her and thrown her into a china cabinet, giving her the scars that marked her face. The man who'd hurt Zack. He was also a man she'd once loved. Above all, he was Zack's father.

Adriana sniffled and pulled back her hand. "I don't know what to think."

"Hey, come here." Brooks pulled her close, wrapping his arm around her. "I know it's shocking, but don't you feel...free? No more hiding, Adriana. No more watching your back. You and Zack are safe now."

Adriana cried into his neck, and he wondered if she was thinking the same thing, that this news offered them a real chance to be together.

Now, nothing stood in the way.

∽

MARY KNOCKED on the door at eight. Brooks had totally forgotten she was coming. He and Adriana had put Zack to bed and were watching a documentary about penguins in the living room.

"Who could that be?" Adriana asked.

Brooks paused the television hanging on the wall and set down the remote. "I, ugh, I forgot to tell you." He pulled his feet off the coffee table and stood up from the couch. "It's my mom. Shay told her about the baby monitor thing."

"No." Adriana's cheeks hardened with anger. "I'm not dealing with her right now. Please don't let her in."

"She only wants to apologize."

Adriana sighed, letting her eyes close.

"Let's just get it over with," Brooks pleaded.

"Fine." She cast the blanket that had been covering her to the arm of the couch.

Brooks pulled open the door to find his mom, sad and small, waiting on the porch. "Hey, Mom. Come on in."

With hesitant steps, Mary opened up her arms. "I can't believe you didn't tell me."

Brooks hugged her and said into her ear, "I didn't know what to do."

"You should have told me," she whispered back. "Then I could have at least tried to make it right."

As he let her go, he said, "Some other stuff is going on too."

Mary looked at him inquisitively.

"Just come in."

Adriana turned to them as Brooks and Mary entered the living room. Not that Brooks could blame her, but Adriana didn't bother getting up.

Holding onto the silk scarf around her neck, Mary launched into what sounded like an apology she'd been rehearsing all day. "I'm just scared about losing Brooks, Adriana. The things I said...had nothing to do with you. Truly. I hope you can understand. As a mother, I'm just being protective. I was absent Brooks's entire life, and being up here feels like a second chance."

Mary sat in the chair by the window. "We've finally connected, and the idea of losing him again is just heartbreaking. But I had no right to start making assumptions. I think you're a wonderful woman and a great mother, and I know Brooks loves having you in his life." She stopped, like she'd suddenly run out of words.

Adriana sat up straighter on the couch and fingered the bandage covering Brooks's stitched wound. "I have no intention of prying him from Red Mountain if this is where he wants to be."

"You wouldn't be prying me," Brooks said. "I..." He didn't know what else to say. How absurd to think he wouldn't follow her to Florida. When it came down to it, a decision to be with the woman he loved or staying to ferment Red Mountain grapes shouldn't be a difficult choice at all.

Then why did it weigh so heavily on his shoulders?

It was a wasted thought anyway. Michael wasn't getting out of prison any time soon. Though she hadn't come out and said it yet, why would Adriana leave now? Because the winters were cold? Surely, he was more important than the outside temperature.

"Mary," Adriana said, "no offense, but you have no idea how I feel about your son. Don't put your guilt on me like I have anything to do with it."

"Whoa, honey," Brooks said. "Please, let's just..." He looked at his mom. "Adriana's ex-husband almost killed someone in prison last night."

Mary's mouth fell open. "Oh my God."

"We just found out," he said.

Mary sat up and clasped her hands together. "You should have called me. Here I was, coming over to apologize because of my big mouth..." She shook her head.

"It's okay, Mom," he said, the designation still funny on his tongue. "I forgot you were coming over."

Mary blew out a blast of air and stood. "I'll get out of your hair. Please let me know if there's anything we can do. Again, Adriana, I'm beyond sorry. You have every right to be angry with me."

Adriana didn't respond.

Mary got the message and retreated through the hall toward the front door.

Brooks followed her into the foyer. "It's just a bad time."

His mother waved him off and apologized again. "We can do this later. I'm sorry to bother you."

"Mom," he said, "she'll be fine. Just give her some time."

They shared a quick hug and then she was off.

Returning to the living room, Brooks nestled in close with Adriana and pulled the blanket over their legs.

"I'm sorry, Brooks. I'm not going to bend over and take it. She wronged me."

"I completely agree." He pushed a stray chocolate-colored hair from her eyes and held his hand on her cheek. "I love you, Adriana, and I'm forever on your side."

Though he couldn't imagine the rampant thoughts running

through her mind, he wished she'd come out and say that she would stay, that this news was the best thing in the world. Michael's violence had just breathed new life into Brooks's hopes for his own family. If she'd just stay, they could work out the kinks.

19

THE YOUNGER GENERATION

"Oh, come on, Mom," Emilia said, trying to convince her mother to go to Margot's inn for Ladies' Night. "You're the only woman on the mountain who doesn't go. Even Abby's going tonight. Margot would love to have you. Everyone would."

Emilia and her ten-year-old brother, Luca, were sitting at the white quartz counter watching their mother cook breakfast. The two women were wearing chamois microfiber robes that Carmen had been gifted recently, one cream and the other gray. With one Instagram post, her mother could put a startup on the map, so companies fought to send her free merchandise. As much as her mom's career drove her crazy, Emilia definitely couldn't complain about this perk.

Carmen turned from the stove, frying pan in hand. Sliding their egg white omelets with asparagus onto her children's plates, she said, "I know. I'm so boring. It's just...I won't feel comfortable." Emilia knew Carmen might have said more if Luca hadn't been sitting there.

Luca brushed his longish, dark hair away from his eyes and asked, "Since you're not going, do you think I could have a sleepover with Zack tonight? He hasn't been over in forever." Emilia couldn't believe how much her brother had sprouted in the past year. Before long, he'd be asking girls out on dates.

"I think a sleepover sounds like a great idea," Carmen said. "Let me get Adriana's number from Abby, and I'll ask."

"Really?" Luca said, apparently as shocked as Emilia by Carmen's offer.

Carmen leaned over the counter and met her son's eyes. With a beautiful smile, she said, "Yes, really."

Luca threw his hands in the air. "Sleepover!"

Though she was bummed that her mother always skipped Ladies' Night at Épiphanie, Emilia couldn't *believe* the words that had just come out of Carmen's mouth. She was going to text Adriana about hosting a sleepover? This was huge news on so many levels. Emilia didn't realize her mom even knew Adriana. Even more surprising, Abby was the one who typically instigated and hosted sleepovers for Luca. Carmen was always too busy with work or whatever else she'd been doing.

After Luca had eaten and excused himself, Carmen approached the counter and said to Emilia, "I just have to say this..."

"Oh God, here we go." Emilia had seen her mother's mood turn on a dime a thousand times.

"The wine business is dangerous," Carmen said. "You are so much more responsible than I am—but *please* use a spit bucket. You'll be around wine all day long, and that's fine. It's obviously the new family business. But I don't want you drinking all day."

"I know about spitting, Mom. I used to live here. And it's not like I can't get alcohol whenever I'd like at school."

"I know, it's just...We don't know what's in your genes. We don't know if you have some of the same addictive tendencies."

"Mom, *stop* worrying." Emilia returned to her omelet, cutting another bite.

"Easy for you to say."

They turned when the front door opened and closed. A few seconds later, Jake strolled into the kitchen wearing exercise clothes.

He was breathing heavily. "Good morning, my loves. Em, ready for your big day?"

"I had the talk with her," Carmen said. "About spitting."

He wiped his forehead and nodded. "Something tells me she'll be just fine."

~

MARGOT HAD experience with winning people over with kindness. For those who had known her back in Vermont, and those she'd share the stories with, they'd heard all about the year Margot tried to win her husband back. Instead of sliding divorce papers across the table when their marriage took a turn for the worse, Margot had decided to do everything she could to become his idea of a perfect wife.

Looking back, it hadn't been the healthiest year. She couldn't have been less genuine to herself. But there were invaluable lessons she'd learned. Tricks she could put to use this year. First of all was the weight loss. In becoming the perfect wife, she'd stopped eating and dropped down to the body weight that she'd always dreamed about. Though her husband hadn't whipped his head around lustfully like she'd hoped, the diet had certainly been effective. That's why she was suffering through it now—all the headaches and cravings and dizzy spells. Not eating actually worked!

So did turning the other cheek and killing a person with kindness. It had taken a while to take effect with her ex, but he'd come around. How could he not have? So many wives would have waged war, pointing out the long list of reasons their spouses sucked. Not Margot. If he forgot to put the seat down, no big deal. Didn't get around to emptying the dishwasher? No worries; he was busy. Glanced at another woman? Ah, that's fine. She *was* rather cute. Forgot a birthday or anniversary? Oh, plenty more chances to get that right. He'd eventually figure out how lucky he was, proving her efforts had worked. Fortunately, she'd also learned a lot about herself in the process and had realized that it was time for her to move on.

The tricks that had worked on her ex-husband weren't working on Carly. Even Jasper, who'd been home four days, had gotten nowhere with her. Not that Carly was always mean, but she was perpetually reserved and short on words. It had become apparent that she was much happier in her room doing whatever it was she did as opposed to spending any time developing relationships with her growing family.

Remi had tried everything he could think of too, but he'd failed to crack Carly's hard exterior. Though she'd continued to express anger with her mother, Carly had made it clear—many times—that she was also still mad at Remi for abandoning them. The regret was tearing at him, and the funny and chivalrous man Margot had fallen in love with was sinking into his own hole as well.

Today, Margot had been at it since five, unable to sleep amid all the sadness in the house. There was nothing worse than seeing the man you love hurt so inside. She'd spent most of the morning prepping for her Ladies' Night at Épiphanie get-together, but now she was checking out several of the guests at the front desk. An Etta James album played softly in the background.

"How was your stay?" Margot asked the middle-aged woman with blond hair longer than Margot's.

"It was *absolutely* perfect. You've thought of everything, haven't you?"

Margot beamed. "When I lived in Vermont, I used to lie in bed and dream of all the little details that would make my place perfect. Now I get to make them *all* come true."

"Oh, we can tell." The woman glanced at her reserved husband, who was fishing a credit card out of his wallet.

"And you enjoyed the wines?" Margot asked.

"Maybe a little too much," the woman confessed. "I think we joined...what was it, Don? Four wine clubs?"

He handed Margot his card. "Not to mention the several cases sitting in our car right now."

Margot smiled and pushed the card into the slot of her machine. "I really do hope you'll come back and see us. And if it's not too much trouble, would you mind leaving a review or two online?" She'd gotten used to asking this very important request.

"Would be happy to," the man replied.

~

As MARGOT BID farewell to her guests in the driveway, she looked at her house and saw Carly take a seat on the porch and fire up a cigarette. Her soon-to-be stepdaughter wore the same black hoodie she'd been wearing for days, and the hood was pulled over her head. Margot dreamed of making that hoodie disappear. Between the tattoos, the piercings, the chains, and the hoodie, Carly looked not only dark, but dangerous—almost criminal.

Still, Margot the perfect stepmom wouldn't be deterred. As she walked that way, an idea came to her, and a wry smile lifted the corners of her lips. What she'd failed to do so far was to connect with Carly in any meaningful way. She'd tried several different avenues, but since Carly apparently didn't have a care in the world for food or cooking, or even animals, Margot had come up dry.

But she'd learned this idea from her devious mother during her Virginia childhood, and it was bound to be a step in the right direction.

Margot walked over and put on her biggest smile of the day. "Good morning, honey."

"Morning," Carly said, her frown the yin to Margot's yang.

Though Carly hadn't decided to be nice to Margot, she wasn't quite as mean as she'd been during their first talk near the farm sanctuary, almost as though being mean took too much effort.

"Think I could bum one of those?" Margot asked as casually as possible, like she was one of the cool kids at the party. She sat on the steps facing the inn and reached out her hand. Though she'd played her role well, she felt tremendously nervous.

Just as casually, Carly opened up the pack of Marlboro Reds. "Yeah, sure."

Pulling one out, Margot set it between her lips as if she'd been smoking all her life—when, in fact, she hadn't. She'd dabbled some in high school, but that was about it. No matter. She was an actor and could pull this off. *No problemo.*

Carly reached over with a lighter. Tapping into her inner Rita Hayworth, Margot leaned the cigarette into the flame. Whatever she did, she was not going to cough. She puffed lightly at first, testing the power, but the tip wouldn't catch. She drew in harder, and as the smoke filled her lungs, the burn was too much. She burst into a coughing fit that forced her to fold over and grab her chest.

"Wow, those are strong." Margot's eyes dripped tears.

"I guess you don't smoke," Carly said, calling Margot's bluff.

Margot *actually* heard, "You're about as cool as a fanny pack." She sat up, wiped her eyes, and cleared her throat. "How could you tell?"

Carly shook her head and turned away, obviously hiding something.

"Oh, wait," Margot said. "What was that? A smile? I didn't know you did smiles."

"I don't." Carly kept looking the other way, taking another toke.

"I'll smoke the whole pack if that's what it takes to get you to smile."

Carly blew out a cloud of smoke.

Margot said, "Fine, I'll take down this whole thing. You'll have to pry me off the ground."

Having successfully returned her lips to a horizontal position, Carly finally turned to her. "It's probably not the best habit to start later in life."

"Later in life? For the record, I'm not even fifty yet. No, I'm not exactly a spring chicken, but I've got a few years left before I'm considered old." Without thinking, Margot took a puff and broke into another bout of coughing.

As she folded over again, she could hear Carly laughing. Coming back up, Margot said, "I've been trying to crack you for a week and turns out all I need to do is burn my lungs." She shook her head. "You're too easy."

Still laughing, Carly pulled her hood off her head.

"Oh, look at that. You have a whole head under there. Hair and everything."

Margot glanced at her future stepdaughter's multiple earrings climbing up her ear: a sword, a black jewel, a pagan cross, and a skeleton. Now that Margot had broken through the ice, or at least chipped away at it, she wanted to ask Carly what her deal really was. But she had a feeling she'd done enough for the day.

As one last gesture, Margot said, "Tonight, all the women of Red Mountain are coming over to the inn. We're making pizza. I'd love for you to join us. It's the most laid-back, crazy bunch of women in eastern Washington. Think book club on steroids."

Like Margot had just asked her to attend a knitting class, Carly said, "Yeah...probably not."

Margot stood and put out her own cigarette, dropping it into the bottom of the pot with the rest of the butts. "Thanks for the smoke. Hey, you might really love it here if you give it a chance. The people are one of a kind. And though you obviously don't like food, I make some of the best pizza you'll ever put in your mouth."

Carly stood and turned to go inside. "I don't hate food."

"That's good to know," Margot said.

Carly offered a very small wave and went back inside the house.

As Margot returned to the inn, she felt Carly's loneliness like a hollowness in her own chest. How difficult it was to be a teenager working your way to adulthood.

Then she found Adriana in the kitchen and was reminded that the difficulties of life weren't only reserved for teenagers.

"What's wrong with you?" Margot asked.

Adriana looked stone-faced while cracking eggs into a stainless bowl. She turned to Margot as the bright-orange yolk fell. "You don't even want to know."

"Oh, I do. Anything to take me away from my own troubles."

"Michael got in more trouble."

Margot froze. "Oh God."

Adriana picked up the next egg. "He stabbed someone in prison."

Crack.

Margot processed the news for a moment. "Wait, isn't this a good thing? Won't he get more time?" As she tried to imagine what Adriana was going through, Margot realized that this meant Adriana wouldn't be leaving. The sudden urge to pop a bottle of Champagne came over her. Then Margot scolded herself. What a selfish thought.

She approached her friend. "What are you thinking? How do you feel about this?"

Adriana dropped a shell into the compost bucket. "I'm all over the place. It's the best thing that could have ever happened to us, but it's really sad too. He is Zack's father, after all."

Margot's bottom lip pressed out, and she forced Adriana into a hug.

"Why do you smell like cigarettes?" Adriana asked. "You're not smoking, are you?"

"I just had one with Carly, trying to connect with her. Not my best idea, but I did get a smile out of her."

"That's good." Adriana went back to cracking eggs.

Margot couldn't bear seeing Adriana's pain and rubbed her back. "What can I do for you? Why are you even here?"

"I'm not going to skip work. It's fine." *Crack.* "Actually, Carmen just texted me about a sleepover with Luca tonight. That will give me some time tonight to process it."

"Carmen texted you about the boys getting together? Hmm. That's really cool, but *soooo* un-Carmenlike of her," Margot said. "Well, I hope this is the last of all your troubles. It just has to be. Maybe this is the universe closing the book on the past. It's all sunny skies from here."

"I hope you're right."

Crack.

20

MOUNTAIN WOMEN

"Ah, there she is," Brooks said, raising his eyes from his computer. "Ready for your first day, my apprentice?"

"Totally." Emilia looked so much more like her father today for some reason. Maybe it was the look of hunger and eagerness in her eyes. Brooks liked to see that in Emilia. The more Jake she had in her, the better.

He pressed up out of his chair and smacked and rubbed his hands together. "I thought we'd start where it all begins."

"Where's that?" she asked.

"In the vineyard, of course."

Brooks led Emilia down the stairs, out the back door, and up the hill. As the morning sun sprayed rays of light through the clouds, he was reminded of his walks with Otis years ago. His mentor had given Brooks a reason for living, literally dragging him off the streets of New York, flying him to Washington State, and teaching him everything he could about raising vines. The grapefather had lit a fire inside Brooks that continued to rage inside, this desperate need to grow wine and capture the essence of a place and time in a bottle. Never before his first year on Red Mountain had he felt so alive and full of purpose. Could Brooks pass along that same passion and knowledge? He sure hoped so. Was Emilia even that interested? He'd find out soon enough.

They stopped halfway to Sunset Road, and Brooks explained that the rose bushes at the end of each row were used as early indicators of irrigation or pest problems. They used red and white roses to mark the color of the grapes down each row.

Wandering down a row of very healthy-looking syrah vines, he stopped and pointed. "The trunk rises up into these two cordons that run along the wire." He pulled his clippers from their holster and made several cuts. "They were a little lazy here, but we want one cane per fist-length, and then two buds per cane. That's how we get the perfect yield and concentration."

Moving on, Brooks wondered if she would notice why he'd chosen this particular row.

Halfway through, she stopped and pointed to the gnarly vine he'd come to know well. Its trunk and cordons were twice the thickness of the others, and its canopy had already developed fully.

"Why is that one so much bigger than the others?" Emilia asked. "Looks like you're feeding it steroids."

Brooks was delighted and impressed. "She's why we're here. Your dad named her Angeline."

"After my grandmother?" Emilia asked.

Brooks nodded as he felt the energy of Angeline rise up through his feet. "She's become the heartbeat of this vineyard. We can't explain why, but all the other vines grow in her direction. We can train them anyway we like, but they'll bend and eventually grow toward her, almost like she's drawing them in. And she grows the way she wants to, no matter how we prune her."

Emilia's look alone answered the question of whether she'd find all this interesting. "Why did my dad never tell me?"

"Maybe he didn't think you were ready."

"This is one of the vineyard blocks that was here before us, right?"

"Yeah," Brooks said, "this block is one of the oldest on Red Mountain."

He bent down and took a handful of Red Mountain dust near the trunk of Angeline. As Otis had done for him, he said, "Open your hand."

Brooks slowly dropped the dust onto her palm and fingers, and some of it collected in the air like ashes. "We have one objective, and that's to capture the truth of this place. The air. The soil. The wind. The rain. The year. The people. The culture. We can't explain it, but it all intersects here with Angeline. She's the keystone." He pointed to the ground. "Take a knee."

Emilia knelt in the dust.

"Close your eyes and touch her trunk."

Emilia looked at him like he was crazy.

"I'm serious. Get to know her, and Angeline will make you believe in a higher power."

She reached out and placed her fingers on Angeline's trunk, a foot above the earth.

"There's something special here," Brooks said reverently. "Your vineyard is holy land. We think this spot is the source."

She looked at him. "Really?"

"None of us can explain it, but an energy resides here. Almost like someone was buried here a long time ago. You feel it?"

"Yeah, I feel something very powerful."

Brooks smiled. "Now you know why wine is so much different from anything else in the world. Our job is to bottle that feeling. If we're respectful to this land, and if we are minimal in our intervention and inputs, we can capture Angeline and share her with the world."

Emilia let go, and Brooks could tell she understood what he meant. Those eager eyes had lit up, and Brooks knew she felt the same way he had when he'd first walked Otis's vines. Maybe she was meant to be out here too. Maybe this was her calling, the one she'd been searching for so desperately.

"Can you believe all this is yours?" Brooks asked. "This is your family's land. You live here."

"I can't believe my dad has never taken me to Angeline."

Brooks shook his head. "It can't be a spectacle to come here. You have to earn the right. And for you to want to work at Lacoda means it's your time."

"So everyone who works here knows about Angeline?"

"Everyone who works here has knelt in this exact same spot."

Emilia smiled.

"Yeah, pretty cool, right? We're not building auto parts around here. This is serious business. We're cutting deep."

"Does my mom know about her?"

"Yeah, she does. I'm not sure she was impressed, but Jake's brought her up here before."

They dusted themselves off and stood. Emilia's eyes were still planted on Angeline. "What do you mean by minimal intervention?"

"It's hands-off winemaking. Of course, it's not completely hands-off. You have to pick the fruit and move it into fermentation tanks and guide it all the way to the bottle, but the idea is to intervene as little as possible. It's so easy in this day and age to manipulate every process in order to get what you want." Brooks shook his head. "That's not what we do here. We want a wine with specificity and vintage differentiation. How do we do that?"

Emilia looked up from Angeline. "By staying out of the way and letting nature do her magic?"

"Exactly."

~

THE LAST THING Margot had heard in her house before she left to host the ladies of Red Mountain was Remi and Carly screaming at each other upstairs. It had been so bad that Jasper left to visit Emilia after her workday. Margot had wanted to say something, anything to make them stop, but she knew she had no answers to end their bickering. If they were to reunite as father and daughter, they'd have to figure it out on their own.

She left a note for Remi next to the dinner she'd prepared for them: a healthy soup and lovely loaf of bread from her new friend, Sarah Goedhart, the head winemaker of Hedges Family Estate, who had cut a Red Mountain triangle into the crust. All Margot could do at this point was to keep loving him with everything she had.

Doing her best to keep her troubles at bay, Margot looked with a smile at the nine women surrounding her massive oak island in the industrial kitchen of Épiphanie. They each had an aperitif and a measured pile of *doppio zero* flour in front of them. Behind her were two large farm sinks and the windows overlooking her garden. Large glass containers with bulk foods lined one wall. Dried herbs dangled from the metal racks alongside beautiful copper and stainless pots and pans. Though she'd abandoned many of her cookbooks when moving, her collection was growing again, and two shelves were crammed full of new ideas just waiting to be tested.

The days were getting longer, and it was still bright outside, but she'd turned on the Edison light bulbs so they could see exactly what they were doing. Every time Margot stood here in front of the women of Red Mountain, she was reminded of how far she'd come since first driving west.

"Okay, ladies," Margot said. "I know we all have so much to catch up on, but we'd better get started if we want to eat tonight." Once the women had quieted, she continued, "This is not the easiest way of mixing dough, but it's the traditional way, and something that's not only effective but really fun once you get the hang of it. We *could* mix everything, including the flour, in a mixing bowl with a wooden spoon. Or we could cheat with a mixer. But we want to be as Italian as possible tonight."

Demonstrating as she talked, she said, "I want you to carve out a hole in the middle of the flour, like you're making a little volcano. Then take your mixture of water, yeast, salt, and honey, and pour just a little bit into the hole, forming a lake of goodness. Then work them together like so. You have to be very careful here, making sure your walls stay intact, or the liquid will escape and run right off the table."

Once they were all kneading, an army of Red Mountain women pressing and pulling their dough, Margot said, "Since we'd all be drunk as skunks if we waited for the dough to rise, I've already made enough to use tonight. You can take these home and either cook them in the next day or so, or throw it in your freezer for later."

Margot answered questions about shelf life and thawing the dough after freezing, then they moved onto the current gossip of Red Mountain. When Margot had first started these nights, it had occurred to her that these women had not had a place to gather and share. They came for the cooking lessons but stayed for the camaraderie.

Sarah Goedhart asked Emilia about her first year in New York, and Emilia replied, "New York is fine. I had a lot of fun, and it was nice being so close to Jasper. But honestly, I'm having more fun tonight. I missed everyone."

"We missed *you*," Joan said, standing next to Emilia. "At least we get you back every summer."

"It might be more than that," Emilia admitted. "I'm not sure I want to leave again. Anyway, how are you and Otis?"

All eyes went to Joan, who stopped kneading. "We're fine. Everything's good."

"Oh, c'mon," Margot said, knowing there was more to the story. "We're all friends here. Tell the truth."

Joan glanced around the room and caved. "Well, this Drink Flamingo thing is tearing Otis up. And for some reason, I'm letting it get to me too." The ladies worked their dough in silence, which forced Joan to continue. "I keep internalizing everything he's going through, and I can't help but try to fix him, which is exactly what I should *not* be doing. I find myself preaching at him all the time, and he's getting tired of it." She started kneading again. "I'm even grating my own nerves."

"I'm so sorry," Emilia said.

A woman named Ivy, who was a newcomer to the mountain, jumped in. "Relationships in general just aren't easy. I don't know whether to divorce my husband or strangle him and bury him in the backyard."

Everyone smiled, but Margot started to think Ivy was serious.

"After work," Ivy continued, "he plops his lazy butt down on the chair in front of the television and waits for me to bring him a beer and dinner. As if I'm a fembot who's supposed to switch on the moment he walks in the door. He can go eat a bag of Fritos for all I care. I'm done putting in all the work."

Having endured a brutal first marriage herself, Margot totally understood where Ivy was coming from. "And this," Margot said, "is why we come here. We need a place to vent."

~

AFTER TEACHING the class how to make the perfect pizza sauce, Margot led them outside, where carafes of red and white wine waited under strings of lights on the patio a few feet away from her pizza oven, which sent a nice warmth into the brisk evening. The sun was bobbing on the horizon now, and the temperature was falling. Margot peeked inside the oven and saw the flames of the burning applewood licking the brick above. As the women laughed with each other, she fired her infrared temperature gun onto the bottom tiles of the oven. "Brava! We're ready to go."

Margot asked everyone to gather around as she stood in front of the outdoor counter and took her first ball of dough. Talking as she went, Margot worked the dough ball into a disc and then began stretching it. "Throwing pizza in the air is fun but not necessary at all. The secret to forming a circle is starting with a perfect ball. And if you've nailed the elasticity, and if the dough is the perfect temperature, it won't break on you."

Once she'd reached the desired thickness, Margot flung a handful of semolina onto the pizza peel and then set the pizza carefully on top. She painted the dough with her uncooked sauce and finished with slices of fresh mozzarella.

The women clapped as Margot slung the pizza into the oven with ease.

As they broke up into smaller groups, Emilia appeared with a handful of fresh basil from the garden. "Is this enough?"

"Oh, you're a dear. That should do it." Margot set the handful of basil on the cutting board and retrieved one sprig. As she began to tear off the leaves, she asked Emilia, "You couldn't talk your mom into coming?"

Emilia shook her head. "I tried. She appreciates the invite but isn't quite ready to venture out."

"I totally understand."

"She says she liked you a lot."

"That's sweet of her."

Emilia looked into the oven. "How are things with Carly? Jasper was afraid to go back home."

Margot frowned. "It's been challenging." She glanced at the pizza and saw the edges closest to the fire blackening a bit. She rotated the pizza with the peel. "Another minute or so, and we'll have our first pie."

"Let me know if there's anything I can do for Carly," Emilia said. "Jasper and I have asked her to hang out, but I don't think she's interested."

Margot thanked her. "We'll get through it. As you and I both know, being a teenager isn't easy."

"No, it's not."

Addressing everyone on the patio, Margot said, "Okay, first one is done. Let's see how we did."

They broke away from their side conversations to watch Margot pull the pizza out. *Oohs* and *ahhs* rose up into the night as she slid the steaming pie onto a wooden board. Margot arranged the basil leaves across the surface and then brushed the beautifully bubbly crust with Tuscan olive oil and sprinkled it with sea salt. Taking her long pizza cutter, she rocked the blade back and forth, slicing the pie into eight pieces.

"Who wants to be the guinea pig?" Margot asked, holding up the cutting board and trying to ignore the tempting scents.

"The chef has to do the honors," one woman said.

Margot shook her head. "Sadly, I'm on a strict diet. No pizza for me tonight."

The ladies sighed collectively in disappointment.

"Hey," another woman said. "We're all on diets. Tonight is about breaking the rules."

Margot's eyes bulged as she shook her head. "If you only saw the dress I need to fit into in September, you'd know there is no cheating."

"Oh, let it go, Margot," another said.

"Easy for you to say."

That same woman broke into a chant. "Margot, Margot, Margot..."

To Margot's dismay, everyone joined in. "Margot, Margot..."

How could she get out of this one? "Oh, you guys, give me a break."

They ignored her and kept chanting.

"Okay, fine." Margot took a slice and raised it up in the air. "You win, everyone."

With that, she tested the temperature with her tongue. It was cool enough to eat. She took a proper bite, and it was a pizza dreams were made of.

Everyone cheered.

21

A GENTLEMAN'S WAR

Two days after the bastards at Drink Flamingo poisoned Otis's vines, Otis decided it was time to strike back. He'd been watching to see if anyone had noticed the pinotage taking root; his sabotage had apparently gone unnoticed. The first sign of a poor farmer is one who doesn't walk his vines. Unless they were spraying chemicals, it seemed Bellflour and his team never set foot down the rows.

Still, his little prank wasn't enough to satisfy his need to beat Bellflour. Though Otis hadn't seen any damage to his own vines from the spray drift, the chemicals had seeped into the soil and tarnished the land he'd tended with great care for many years. His virgin soil had been spoiled by the chemicals of lazy farmers. Otis could only hope that his land was strong enough to fight off this and future attacks.

And that's what it had been, a full-on attack. Otis wouldn't have been surprised if Bellflour had demanded that the man spray on a windy day. Anyone certified to spray chemicals knew about drift. Surely Bellflour knew too. And as much of an idiot as Bellflour was, nothing he did was without calculation.

The same went for Otis. If Bellflour wanted war, then by God, Otis was ready to do battle. Creeping out of bed again well past midnight, he tiptoed out of the house and rushed under a fingernail moon to find Jonathan before any heavy barking broke into the night. Once his dog was happy, Otis hiked up to the winery. It was an eerily quiet night, and the big, inky sky was so vast it looked like it might swallow the earth at any minute like a hungry black hole. Otis found the great star Spica and made out the rest of the Virgo constellation —his sign, his arrangement up in the heavens.

Working his way past the vines, he reached the gravel road leading to the back of the winery, where he'd left the wheelbarrow full of the equipment needed for his next strike. He pushed the wheelbarrow up the hill. He stopped when he reached the chain-link fence marked *No Trespassing.* Drink Flamingo had recently put up deterrent lights that shined brightly over the growing McMansion, the future pool, and the vines. When Otis looked up, he could no longer see the stars.

What a perfectly awful omen for the future, he thought. *Drink Flamingo and snuff out the light.*

With a flashlight shining at his feet, he watched for animal holes as he pushed the wheelbarrow off the road and along the fence line, circling the property. A lone coyote howled in the silence. When he reached the section where he'd broken in last time, he was happy to see the door he had made in the fence was still there. Waging war on these people was too easy when they weren't even paying attention.

Tugging on the square of fence he'd cut, he peeled it back. One by one, he tossed the contents of the wheelbarrow through the hole: a shovel, a pipe saw, a bag of irrigation parts, a smart valve, and PVC primer and glue. Looking around to make sure no one was watching, he crawled under the fence.

He avoided the spotlights as best he could as he snuck to the edge of the vineyard and then up ten more feet toward the pool. He could see they were working on an outdoor kitchen to feed the drunks spilling out of the hot tubs, of which he now knew there were three. Three effing hot tubs! It was hard not to think Bellflour was doing all this just to piss Otis off.

Otis had been watching the vineyard workers for weeks and had

seen them dig other holes where he had to assume the main irrigation line ran west from Sunset Road. From what he could tell, the line
feeding the vineyard broke off the main line near where the tractor
was resting and ran directly under where he was currently standing.

Pulling on his leather gloves, he thrust the shovel into the soil,
carefully moving it into a nearby pile to be reused later. Though he
could feel his age, he could have dug all night. Add all the feet he'd
dug as a wine farmer together, and it might be enough to break
through to the other side of the globe.

His research paid off quickly. The shovel hit something with a
ping, and he saw the white of the pipe flash in the light. "Only three
feet, you lazy shits. You should have gone deeper."

To his delight, he saw that he'd guessed the correct width of the
pipe. Everything was going as planned. He widened the hole, still
careful to save all the soil he was extracting. When he was finished,
the hole was about four feet by four feet, and he'd dug enough under
and around the white pipe to easily manipulate it. Dropping down,
his knees falling into the dust, he grabbed his saw and cut through
the pipes slowly and methodically. He was in no rush. Having infiltrated the enemy's camp, he needed to revel in the victory.

Once the line was prepared, he primed and glued the necessary
surfaces and then lowered the smart valve down and fitted it to the
pipes. He had to pull both pipes up some, bending them, but once he
had it where he wanted it, the valve snapped into place. He held the
valve upright for a few seconds as the glue dried. The last thing he
did was take a rag and wipe down any possible fingerprints.

Connected to the smart valve was a wire leading to a small,
circular antenna the size of a hockey puck. It was through this
antenna that Otis would send signals to the solenoid, telling it to
open and close the valve, controlling the amount of water going to
the vines. He could kill the vines if he wanted to, but for now, he was
thinking he'd just make them weak. Every wine farmer knew that
baby vines needed an excess of water the first year or two in order for
them to produce good fruit and to thrive for years to come. Otis had
learned the hard way that if the young vines didn't get water in the

early years, they would often produce overly tannic, nearly undrink-able grapes for the remainder of their years.

Stretching out the wire, he set the antenna to the side and filled the hole. The only questionable part of this particular mission was that the hockey puck antenna had to be above ground so that it could communicate with Otis's phone. But Otis was confident in their laziness.

Feeling a surge of pride, he let out a little howl, not loud enough to draw attention, but a call of victory out into the night.

This might be the greatest thing I've ever done for this mountain.

~

HARRY BELLFLOUR COULDN'T SLEEP. He tugged open the refrigerator door and searched for something in the sparsely covered shelves to occupy his mind. Nothing interested him. A jug of low-pulp orange juice. A stick of salted butter. A dozen jumbo eggs. He definitely didn't feel like cooking. Smoked fish spread. A box of leftover pizza. Thai leftovers from the place in West Richland. Four bottles of white wine. Time to get more. Coke Zero. Why was he still drinking that stuff? No matter what he did, his damn belly wasn't going away.

He pulled out a bottle of wine and the box of pizza and headed for the back door. He'd been so hot lately, barely able to sleep. If he went back to the doctor, the know-it-all would just tell him stop drinking and eating so much, to exercise more. Oh, screw it. Under the fingernail moon, he took his midnight snack out to the deck that overlooked Red Mountain. Dropping into the Adirondack chair, he poured himself a glass of wine and took a long sip.

If it wasn't the heat, it was the loneliness that kept him up. He'd never married, but he'd fallen in love and fallen hard. This view over Red Mountain would be so much more beautiful if his ex, Charlotte, were sitting next to him, but she'd chosen to end their relationship instead of following him from California to Washington State last year. He reached for a slice of sausage and onion pizza and shook his head. Was he that difficult to live with? Yes, he worked too much, and he had issues controlling his temper, but he'd tried his best. If only he didn't have so much of his father in him.

Harry had promised himself his whole life that he'd do anything not to be like the man, who had never hit him but might as well have. If Harry had a dime for every time his father had called him a disappointment, he could buy the whole damned mountain. Emotional abuse often cut deeper.

"Look at these grades," the old man used to say with frustration that cut like a chainsaw. "You're a disappointment!"

There was ten cents.

"What's wrong with you, Harry? I find it hard to believe you're my son."

"Harry, I've never been so disappointed."

A few more dimes.

Why was the man's angry voice still in his head? It was probably why Bellflour worked so damn hard, still trying to please he who'd been dead for twenty years. He wished his father could see him now. He'd helped build an empire. Maybe he owed his father for that. There were probably better ways to raise a child, but if he'd done nothing else, Harry's father had given him the drive to work his ass off.

There was always action on the highway, cars and trucks whizzing by. Bellflour looked at the property he'd once owned on his side of the highway, a perfect plateau that would have been Drink Flamingo's biggest project yet. How many nights had he sat up here, imagining the thousands of cars filling the lot with eager tourists whipping out their wallets? No, it wouldn't have been the classiest establishment, but that's not what Drink Flamingo was meant to be. Forget all the bozos on the mountain who had a problem with the idea. All he was trying to do was bring the foot traffic needed to make good money. Why was it so hard for people to understand how business worked?

It still hurt his heart to think about how he'd dropped the ball and let the project fall through. Not that it had been his fault. That bastard hydrologist had screwed up the analysis. Bellflour had tried to sue him and had lost quickly. But if Bellflour ever ran into that boy again, he'd kick him up and down the mountain and throw him off the overpass.

Looking over the highway, he could barely make out the silhouette of the mountain—but it was there, a jagged, horizontal line halfway up the sky. Not many lights out there. One flashing red light at the tip of the tower on top. Col Solare down the slope, lit up like a spaceship. Down lower, Margot Pierce's inn. He shook his head, thinking of the woman with long, blond hair whom he'd once fancied. "What a tiger she is," he said to the night. He recalled the night she'd rejected him and kicked him out. Some women were so easily offended.

After another long sip, he twisted his head to the left in order to face his own project. Knowing they weren't the most popular winery on the mountain, he'd installed spotlights so no one was tempted to sabotage the project. Besides, he'd heard of people stealing tools and materials. Bellflour couldn't afford any setbacks.

October first was the date he'd promised the board, and there was no way in hell he'd miss it.

Last year's failure was still heavy on his mind, but he could see the light of redemption ahead. All the board members who had doubted him would now eat their words. The media would backpedal and offer their praise to one of the most important men in wine. And perhaps, most importantly, the people of Red Mountain would see that Harry Bellflour was not a man to laugh at.

At first, he had tossed around the idea of a Pacific Northwest-style building with giant timbers and sharp angles. He would call it White Hawk. It would have been a far cry from what they'd done in the past and almost the direct opposite of the wild theme park they'd been working on by the highway, but he felt like it would be a strong image boost and counterpoint to Drink Flamingo's reputation as a bulk-juice, boxed-wine factory. Though Bellflour knew as well as anyone that one was judged by their lowest-priced product, at least they could provide an alternative view as to what Drink Flamingo stood for.

But on the way to present his idea to the board in Lodi, as he'd sipped a Jack and Coke Zero and thumbed through the ads in the in-flight magazine on the ascent, he'd had an epiphany. Why was he pushing to build something they, as a company, were not? Why did they have to create yet another stuffy winery? Drink Flamingo was about fun, and that's what he'd ultimately started with as he opened his presentation. "Let's be the brightest light on the mountain," he'd said. "Hell, let's be the brightest light in eastern Washington. I don't want to be a stop on the wine trail. I want to be *the* stop."

The great orator that he was, he'd painted an entirely different picture than the one he'd intended the day before, but he could see it so vividly now. And that's why he considered himself a master of business development. He knew how to be flexible and make fast decisions. What he'd painted in the minds of the board members had been nothing short of brilliant. By the time he'd rested his case, his dazzled board members' eyes had sparkled with dollar signs.

Squinting toward his property, he let images of the future come alive. He could see it all so clearly. His most ambitious project to date, perhaps his legacy. "You want to be rich," he'd told his colleagues, jabbing his pointer at them, "I'll make you filthy rich."

He let the bright lights and loud noises exploding in his imagination drown the incessant laughter and doubt of the feeble-minded shits who would rather see him fail.

"It's my mountain now," he said, smacking his lips. He poured another glass, filling it to the brim. "My mountain."

Casting his eyes back to the property that would soon be his legacy, he noticed a light that didn't belong. Was someone out there? Was that a flashlight bouncing up and down on the outskirts of the property? It was too far away to be sure. He set down his glass and pushed out of his chair.

With nothing better to do, he decided to go check it out.

22

SOMEONE IS BOUND TO GET HURT

S till standing over the hole he'd mostly filled, Otis saw taillights creeping up Sunset Road. With an uneasy feeling, he looked down. Even if the vineyard workers weren't paying attention, the loose dirt might give him away, but he didn't have time to hide the hole properly. He patted down the hockey puck antenna so that it was flat against the dirt, and then began to move his equipment to the fence and toss it back under. It took him three fast trips as he watched the car moving his way. *It could be anyone*, he thought. After tossing over the shovel, he crawled out of the hole and through the cutout in the fence. But as he started to stand, the door he'd cut out dropped and caught his pants.

"Ah, dammit to hell."

Otis reached for the snag but couldn't free himself. He looked up the road. Was that Bellflour's gold Lexus? He cursed as it turned into the drive.

Scrambling now, he tugged at the snag as his adrenalin pumped. He couldn't be caught right now. Bellflour would press charges for breaking and entering, trespassing, vandalism, and who knew what else if they found the smart valve he'd installed.

With complete frustration, Otis gave up trying to untangle

himself, and he pushed up and pulled away from the fence. His trousers tore down his leg with a loud rip, and Otis collapsed onto his side.

The headlights shone over the vines and the fence line, very close to Otis. He pressed himself hard against the earth, tasting the dust. He glanced at the wheelbarrow.

A car door shut.

Otis stayed down and listened.

Footsteps.

Fifty feet away.

~

BELLFLOUR STEPPED out of his Lexus and opened the gate to the front entrance. He stared at the unfinished building, the one he'd promised would be open by the end of September. Making a mental note to once again jump all over his contractor in the morning, he looked left and right, wondering if someone was out there.

He listened for any movement. Nothing but the sounds of the desert. The far-off cry of a wild dog. The rustling of the leaves in the night breeze.

Climbing onto a stack of concrete blocks, he lifted himself up and slipped in between the framing of the building. He climbed the steps to the second floor and worked his way past the future offices and wine club space to the back of the building, where he could see over the pool to his vineyard. Putting a hand on the frame, staying a few feet back so as not to fall, he ran his eyes from fence to fence. It looked quiet out there.

Damn it, he wished he could fast-forward and get these vines bearing fruit. The sooner, the better. That was one big problem with the wine industry. Nothing happened quickly. If you wanted to make a change to the business plan, you'd have to project what would happen a year or two down the line. There was all that wasted time waiting for the vines to bear fruit, the wine to ferment, and then for it to age in barrel and bottle.

Firing up a cigar, he looked down to the pool area and let his imagination come alive. He could see himself next summer on a bright-pink float—a perfect tan, an aged Cuban cigar, and a shit-eating grin—surrounded by a harem of scantily clad women drinking his Fro-grias. Dollar bills would fall from the sky as the women danced to house music that shook the entire mountain.

Bellflour looked up from this lovely Vegas dream and fixed his eyes on Till Vineyards. In his imagination, he could see Otis Till with his stupid tweed cap standing in the middle of a very elaborate gold chessboard. Bellflour flicked the night air and watched the grumpy bastard tumble off the board.

"Who's the grapefather now?" Bellflour whispered.

～

As QUIETLY AS HE COULD, Otis pressed up to his knees and moved the shovel, the bag of parts, and the other items into the wheelbarrow.

Another sound—boots on wood. Bellflour was walking through the McMansion that still didn't have walls. What the hell was he doing there this time of night?

Otis saw him standing, perhaps swaying, on the second floor, looking out over the vines. He dropped back down to the ground.

Bellflour's watch and gold bracelet shone brightly in the spotlights, and he spent a long time watching over the property.

When his nemesis finally turned away, Otis stood and grabbed the handles of the wheelbarrow. His heart was still kicking at his chest. Praying Bellflour wouldn't hear him, he pushed the wheelbarrow as quickly as he could through the sagebrush of the neighboring property, disappearing into the safety of the desert.

He moved so quickly that he lost control of the wheelbarrow when it hit a root, and he and the wheelbarrow tumbled onto the ground with a loud thud and metal clang. The contents spilled out in the darkness. Otis stayed low and peered up to the winery. Surely Bellflour had heard him. Otis didn't see him, though.

Once he'd caught his breath, Otis searched through the black to find his belongings and return them to the wheelbarrow. After glancing up the hill, he moved at a much slower pace south, only cutting back to his property at the westernmost point. His dog met him as he slipped into the gate. Otis was sweating like a madman, and he sat on the ground and coughed for a while. Jonathan rested his head in his owner's lap.

"I'm way too old for these games, ol' boy," he said, petting him. "That might be the last time I ever run."

Jonathan licked his hand.

Before going back inside his house, Otis gave one last long look toward the Drink Flamingo property. Up on the second floor, he could see Bellflour's silhouette and the red glow of the man's cigar. An unbearable tension rose in his jaws. Never had he despised a man more in his life.

Otis quietly opened the door of his house and stepped inside. To avoid getting in trouble with Joan, his plan was to sleep in the recliner in the office—something he'd done many times in the past. In fact, he'd slept in that recliner for years after his wife passed. When Joan asked in the morning, he'd just tell her he hadn't been able to sleep and hadn't wanted to wake her with his tossing and turning.

In the foyer, he stripped down to his boxers. He winced at the sound of the hardwoods creaking. Though he loved his little cottage, it was too small for such midnight shenanigans.

As he passed the living room, a light came on, and he jerked his head left. Joan sat in a chair by a glowing lamp.

"You scared the heck out of me," Otis told her. "Why aren't you asleep?"

"I should ask you the same question, shouldn't I? What in the world are you doing out there at this hour?"

Otis had told some tall tales in his day, but he'd never been able to get away with them with Joan. She was so good at reading him that, even if he tried to bend the truth just a hair, his hesitation, his shaky hands, or his shifting eyes would betray him.

"My love, some things are better not discussed."

"What does that mean? Don't tell me this has something to do with your neighbor. I don't like all this late-night running around."

Otis drew in a long breath. "It's best you not know what goes on out there."

Joan shook her head, and once again, he could see her frustration with him.

"Look, Joan. Please don't ask. It's nothing, really. Just old-man games between me and Bellflour."

Joan put her hand on the knob of the lamp. "You're acting like a child. And these games...if they continue, someone is bound to get hurt." With that, she switched off the light.

23

TEENAGE BLISS

The ups and downs with Carly went on for another week, and almost every time Margot and Remi thought they were getting somewhere, Carly would fall back to her old routine, the gloomy life of a lost teenager. Margot had been doing everything she could to take it on the chin, but it was no easy task. Her ex-husband had been a much easier target to manipulate.

Tonight was truly perfect, though. Margot had asked the Foresters to dinner and spent all day cooking. They'd gathered in the lobby of the inn with six of her guests for an impromptu jam session between Jasper and Jake. Jasper sat at his piano with a huge smile on his face, listening intently to Jake, who was expertly strumming his acoustic guitar. Margot and Remi had carried chairs in from the dining room, and everyone sat quietly, nodding their heads and tapping their feet. When Jasper and Jake sang in harmony, Margot's spine tingled.

She delighted in seeing the two musicians play. What made her happiest of all was seeing how much Jake enjoyed playing with her son. It had never once been about Jake trying to help Jasper. They'd always been on the same musical plane, both exceptional at their craft, and as they played tonight, it felt as if they had always been destined to unite.

When they finished their session, everyone beamed, knowing the rest of the mountain would have killed to have been there. Then off they went to Margot's house across the way for dinner, where Margot had everything prepared.

Opposite Carly at the table, Jasper and Emilia were doing their best to make conversation with her. Luca was "working on a new invention." Remi sat across from Jake, and they seemed to be getting along well. And Carmen helped Margot bring the dishes to the elaborately set table, which was covered with fresh flowers and her finest china.

"What are we having, Margot?" Emilia asked. "This looks amazing."

"Oh, let's see. A radicchio salad; a fava bean puree; fried Brussels sprouts with shaved ricotta salata; and pasta with a celery leaf and parsley pistachio pesto. Lots of green tonight. I hope that's okay."

"I'm moving in," Emilia joked.

Though Carly wasn't speaking much, the conversation bounced around comfortably as the platters of food quickly emptied. Jake and Jasper talked about writing songs for a new album. Remi told everyone about the many trials and tribulations of learning to farm down at his property by the river.

"How about you, Emilia?" Margot asked, sprinkling sea salt on her small serving of Brussels. "How's your new job?"

"Kind of amazing, actually. Brooks is a great teacher."

"I can only imagine," Margot said, noticing Carmen stiffen.

Remi, who had aged quite a bit in the two weeks since his daughter had arrived, asked, "Do we have a budding winemaker on our hands?"

"Maybe so," Emilia said, obviously enchanted by her new job. "It's a lot of fun. I could totally do this for a living."

Carmen tapped her fingers on the table. "Yeah, but honey, you never know what you're going to do for a living after your freshman year of college. Don't even try to make that decision now. Just keep taking as many classes as you can, and you'll figure it out. You're not exactly *winemaker* material." She said *winemaker* like it was an occupation punishable by death.

Emilia shrugged and breathed through her mom's words. It was obvious she was already tired of her mother's not-so-subtle steering. "Anyway, I'm loving it so far."

"That's great," Margot said, thinking she'd better not push it.

"How about you, Carly?" Jake asked, leaning back and sniffing his red wine. "What are your plans for the summer?"

Carly looked up from her plate like someone had doused ice water on her, and Margot wondered if Carly was starstruck. As normal and kind as Jake was, he could be intimidating.

"I don't really know," Carly said, dropping her eyes again.

The entire room felt so cold all of a sudden, and all the anger Margot had felt toward Carly vanished for a moment. She'd been so preoccupied with herself—wishing the wicked stepdaughter away—that she'd forgotten Carly was just a young girl trying to get by. How sad it was that she could open her mouth for one second and strip all the light from a room. Margot wanted to get up and hug her and tell her she was sorry for being such a selfish bitch.

In the silence, forks pinged the plates, and the stemware rose to everyone's mouths as if the glasses were oxygen masks.

The gem that she was, Emilia broke the silence. "Carly, I'd love to show you around. That is, if you're interested. I remember being the new kid around here. It took a while to figure things out."

Carly whispered a thanks and then dropped her eyes back to her plate.

"That's so nice of you, Emilia," Margot said, once again, finding the sound of her own voice terribly annoying. Why did she talk so much when she was nervous? And why was her voice so high-pitched all of a sudden, like she'd tapped into Julia Child. *That's so nice of you, Emilia.*

Apparently, Margot wasn't the only one who was annoyed.

Carly dropped her fork. "Oh my God. I just can't do this." Without any further explanation, she pushed away from the table and stomped up the stairs.

As Carly's footfalls faded away, Margot looked at Remi. He pressed his lips together and inclined a shoulder.

"I'm sorry, honey. I didn't mean to—" Margot started.

"You didn't do anything." Remi looked at their guests. "She's having a rough go at life right now, as you can see. Please forgive her."

"We've all been there," Jake admitted.

"Should I go talk to her?" Margot asked Remi.

"No, no. Let her cool down. Let's enjoy your beautiful dinner. You've worked hard all day, and everything is absolutely wonderful."

Right. Everything was absolutely wonderful.

~

A WEEK INTO THEIR LESSONS, Emilia rode with Brooks into Benton City to get lunch. "Can you really taste the difference between, you know, like factory wine and wine farmed consciously? How do you know it's better?"

Her questions were getting more intelligent, and he knew the wine bug had bitten her. "Now that's a good question, Em. The answer is, of course, complicated. If you blind tasted me on five wines, one of which was made in a less invasive style, I'd like to think I could pick out the right one. *But*, if the two wines were picked on the same day, grown on the same slope, I might be stumped."

"Wait," Emilia said. "So you really can't tell which wine is better?"

"Now, hold on. I can tell which vineyard is healthier if I walk the vines. But the resulting wine...I could be fooled. That's why blind tasting can be dangerous. It's like shaking a person's hand and trying to assess his integrity. Give me a chance to get to know the wine over the course of dinner, and I'll have a much better chance of guessing. To me, poor farming leads to wines that lack depth. If you raise vines the right way, the wines change in the bottle and in the glass. They're as alive as you and I are."

Crossing the bridge over the Yakima River, Brooks said, "This is why context matters. You *know* that it's better. Or, sorry, *better* is not the right word. Wine is subjective. Like any other art form, there is no better or worse. If you like it, you like it. There's no set standard to judge by. The critics who like scores want you to think there's a standard. For example, if a critic rates a wine one hundred points, then they are essentially saying the wine is perfect and all wines should be like that. But that's their opinion, nothing more. No one can say a wine is better, but we can certainly argue that a wine is honest. Am I losing you?"

Brooks slowed to let a man on a black horse cross the road.

"I kind of get it," Emilia admitted. "It's a lot of extra work for something you might not be able to taste."

"But you'll know in your heart that the wine is true."

Emilia stared out the windshield, pondering his words.

"Let's take this to the art world." Brooks said. "Think of the most perfect reproduction of a Van Gogh—one that fools both of us. Why doesn't it have the same magic as the original?"

"Because it's not the original?"

"It's not the original," Brooks repeated. "It doesn't come from the hands of a man so emotionally charged that he cut off his own ear. It's not the canvas that his hands touched. It's not the paints a genius mixed. It's a copy—a giclée. That's context. I don't want a fake on my wall *or* in my bottle. It doesn't matter whether you can see or taste the differences. The greatness of art is in the context. I want the original."

As they wound the curve and downtown Benton City came into view, he asked, "What would you like for lunch? Mexican or...Mexican?"

"If I have to choose, I'm thinking Mexican." Returning to their discussion, she asked, "Do you have any books that talk about all these ideas?"

"I have a shelf full of them."

"Can I borrow a couple?"

Brooks smiled to himself. "I thought you'd never ask. It's cool to think about, right? This idea of capturing *terroir*."

"Yeah, it's more about philosophy than anything else."

"And yet, it's a vine—essentially a weed—that grows out of the ground."

Emilia looked out the window. "I can see why people devote their lives to it."

"Yeah," Brooks said. "It is kind of cool, isn't it?"

~

AFTER RETURNING TO THE WINERY, Brooks led her down toward her house to another block of syrah. "So I was thinking," he said, "you need your own project for the summer." He pointed. "These vines are yours. Starting here and twenty rows down, all the way to the tree. You're in charge until you go back to school. How does that sound?"

"Are you serious?" She looked like he'd given her keys to a new car. "I get my own vines?"

He took a moment to admire Emilia in her western wear, her jeans and boots and clippers dangling from her belt. She belonged out here. They both knew it. And that's why he'd chosen to give her this gift.

"These are your babies, and you're in charge of them all the way to the bottle. You can even decide when to pick and how you want me to make the wine."

"But I'll be back at school," she said.

"I'll send you the numbers. You can be a virtual winemaker."

A smile plastered her face. "You know this means I won't go back, right?"

Brooks raised his hand halfway. "Hold up. That's not the intention here. You have your whole life to make wine if that's what you want to do. Coming from a guy who didn't go to college, I highly recommend you finish. These vines aren't going anywhere."

Emilia nodded, but they both knew the truth. There was no way she was leaving the mountain again. Once the wine life got you, it was a hard thing to shake.

She ran a hand through the young leaves of one of the vines. "Thanks for this. I won't let you down."

"Just don't get me in trouble by dropping out of school."

"I'm happy to take responsibility for whatever decisions I make."

Brooks had to hold back from laughing. He knew exactly where this was all going. Somehow, Emilia had fallen in love with Red Mountain while she was in New York.

24

THE WHITE KNIGHT OF JUNE

The heat of June came racing to Red Mountain like an angry bull breaking free of a pen. As the temperatures skyrocketed, everyone suspected it would be one of the hottest years on record.

Emilia visited her vines five or six times a day, studying the minute changes in her little microclimate. Brooks had told her that the best fertilizer was a farmer's footsteps, meaning a great farmer spent abundant time walking his crops, watching for changes in the soil, the leaves, and the irrigation. That idea had resonated deep within Emilia, as if farming were rooted far back in her genes.

The appeal of wine hit her from every angle. She loved the idea of capturing "a year in the life," as Brooks had said. She imagined how many other families across the world were similar to hers, living among the vines, working the land, coming together in celebration at the end of each harvest.

There was a sophistication that was also terribly attractive. Some people could study farming and wine their entire lives and never truly grasp it. Though some snobs could get annoying and pretentious when it came to wine, she loved the men and women she'd met over the years who'd become a part of the wine tribe, people who'd also been bitten by the bug, who'd sought out wine regions like Red Mountain to experience the different *terroirs*. Emilia had suddenly wanted to become one of them. She wanted to go back to Europe immediately and visit all the great wine regions, to understand the different methods, and perhaps to even bring some of their techniques home.

She felt kind of sorry for having spent all of the previous summer in Europe without visiting even *one* wine region. That young girl seemed so far away from who she was now, a young woman craving the intellectual stimulation that the wine life offered. Having her own babies heightened her feeling of belonging.

Emilia was waking before her dad in the mornings, which was clearly blowing his mind. She'd barely take time to eat a protein bar before she was out the door, running up the hill to her little vineyard block. There were never any monumental changes, but she felt she needed to be there, to be on the lookout for threats.

She loved seeing how the leaves reacted to the sun and how the vines changed during the watering days. Most of all, she loved sitting on the ground in between the rows, listening to the sounds of the desert, imagining that she, herself, was a vine.

After more pruning lessons from Brooks, she'd gone in with her clippers to make sure there were no more than two buds per spur and that the canopies weren't too thick.

When she had questions, she'd rush to Brooks. "I feel like I'm watering too much. Will you come take a look?" Or, "Some of my leaves are being eaten up. What do you think? Leafhoppers?"

Back in the cellar and in the lab, she couldn't get enough of the wine talk. Discussions about the coming vintage were more interesting than any Red Mountain gossip. The arguments over American versus French oak, or even Hungarian, or which white variety was best suited for the mountain, or who was growing the best wines in eastern Washington—all were ear candy to Emilia.

When she wasn't working her vines or soaking up knowledge from everyone at Lacoda, she read books by wine geeks like Kermit Lynch, Kevin Zraly, Karen MacNeil, Alice Feiring, and Lawrence

Osborne, and the content was much more interesting than anything she'd studied in school.

It was the magic of growing vines and the chemistry of fermentation and the concept of vine-to-bottle that enraptured her. How had she been living here for so long among the vines and not noticed the beauty? It was almost like someone had recently yanked a covering off the mountain, revealing its wonders.

One day during lunch, she took Jasper to her vines, excitedly tugging him by the hand. "Aren't they beautiful?" she asked.

"These are your babies, huh?"

"Twenty rows of syrah. Brooks is letting me do whatever I want with them. And I basically get to make the wine—" She stopped.

Jasper had put on the smile he used when he wasn't entirely happy.

"What is it?" she asked.

He took her hand. "You're not going back to school, are you?"

Emilia frowned, imagining how difficult it would be to let him go back without her. They were a foot away from each other, standing among her vines, and she loved him so much and hated the idea of saying goodbye. But she wasn't sure she had a choice.

"I keep thinking about this place as my legacy," Emilia said. "I know my mom wants me to go back to college and do something else, but what if my future is supposed to be here?" She wanted to tell him about Angeline but held back. It wasn't her place.

"What does your dad say?"

"You probably know better than I do," Emilia said.

"Are you kidding me? I try not to bring you up when we're playing. It still feels weird."

Emilia shrugged. "I haven't officially brought it up with him, but I know he's happy for me. I just wish my mom would back off. If it's not her worrying about me drinking, it's her going on endlessly about how I need to see the world. I backpacked Europe, and I've lived in Seattle and Manhattan. At some point, we all have to decide what we want to do for a living." She looked at her vines. "I could see myself here." And then, "If only I could talk you into staying."

Jasper put his hand on her waist. "You know I have to go back."

Emilia leaned into him, pressing her cheek against his. "I know."

"But as far as you and I are concerned, I'm not going anywhere. I don't care how far away we are from each other."

"I feel the same way," Emilia admitted. She shrugged. "Maybe I'm being stupid. What if I mess up by dropping out of NYU?"

"You have to go with your heart. College will always be there if you ever want to finish."

She nodded. "I can go to WSU here. They have a great viticulture program." She stopped and searched his eyes. "Would you ever come back? After Berklee, I mean?"

"I don't want to make any promises, Em." He scratched his head. "I love it here too, but it's not easy to do what I do out here. I love playing with your dad, but he's already done his thing. I've always been the best player in the room. That all changed at Berklee. I like not being the best. I like learning from people. So who knows what happens after school? I want to find a band of my own. Can I do that from here? I don't know."

Emilia understood what he was saying more than she wanted to. Having grown up the daughter of a musician, she knew exactly what Jasper meant. She knew that to love such a man was to accept a second love in the relationship.

It was so sad to think about not being with Jasper forever. And at the *idea* of maybe even falling in love with someone else, she could feel her bottom lip quivering.

Just when everything seems right, you realize it never actually is.

They didn't talk much more about it, and once Jasper had left, she tried to stay busy. Too much dwelling on losing him would just kill her. She couldn't imagine loving anyone more. Plenty of guys had asked her out in New York, and she'd rejected them without hesitation. Jasper was the only guy she'd ever really wanted.

∾

THE NEXT MORNING, Emilia rode with Brooks and Otis to the Red

Mountain AVA Alliance meeting in downtown Richland. Though the fear of losing Jasper had kept her up most of the night, riding with these two men stirred her soul. They were talking to her like she was one of them—a true guardian of the *terroir*—and she could barely hide her excitement.

She'd known Otis for several years now, but she'd never had much meaningful conversation with him. He'd been nice enough, but they hadn't had a lot in common. She'd been a young girl with little interest in wine. He was the grapefather. Now that she was falling in love with the art of wine, the topics of conversation seemed endless.

"She's got the bug, Otis," Brooks said, slowing to a stop at an intersection. He flipped up his blinker, and it ticked rhythmically. "You can see it all over her."

Otis was sitting shotgun. "Emilia, I remember Brooks's first year on the mountain. It took me a little while, but once I broke through to him, I could see little grape clusters dangling from his eyes. The wine bug has a vicious and intoxicating bite, doesn't it?"

Was Otis really taking her that seriously? To compare Brooks to her in any way was so freaking crazy. This had to be what it felt like to belong.

Otis turned back to her. "You're in good hands with Brooks. I've met very few men and women in my days of farming who grasp the deeper meanings in wine. He's certainly one of them. And I imagine he's a wonderful teacher."

"Better than the PhDs at my school," Emilia said.

With his eyes focused on the road, Brooks thanked her and said, "Otis, I'm hoping you'll share a few things with her too, from time to time."

"I'm happy to contribute to this budding winemaker's education. And I may still have a trick or two up my sleeve."

Had Otis just called her a winemaker?

Otis turned his head to the backseat again. "Why don't you come spend a few hours with me every week, Emilia?"

"Are you serious? That would be incredible."

"Take down my cell."

Emilia had never reached for her phone so quickly in her life. Her fingers trembled as she entered the digits. *This is really happening*, she thought. If she wanted this life, it was here for the taking.

In place of Otis's name, she typed: *The Grapefather.*

Brooks pulled into the parking lot of the hotel where the meetings were held. When they climbed out of the truck, Emilia felt a sense of pride that was almost too much. She was having a hard time not strutting as she walked in between Brooks and Otis, this entourage focused on preserving their homeland. She was beginning to understand the meaning of the Guardians of Red Mountain. Was she becoming one of them?

Her nerves ignited as they entered the large conference room with white walls where twentyish other winemakers from Red Mountain had gathered. She felt like the new kid in town, and everyone was extremely kind to her as she took her seat next to Brooks. Looking around, she knew most of the faces, including Harry Bellflour sitting directly across from her.

Emilia had never met the man but knew of him. Who didn't know about his attempts to wedge his way onto Red Mountain? He looked terribly unhappy and lonely, she thought. Everyone else seemed to be friends, catching up as they waited for the meeting to begin. Bellflour sat hunched over, staring at his phone.

She found herself feeling sorry for him. As awful as he supposedly was, she wondered what led a man to be that way, to be so greedy and angry. At least that's what she'd heard about him. Emilia glanced at his hand. No wedding ring. She wondered if he might be divorced. Did he have children? Had anyone ever loved him? He looked tremendously unhealthy, like he ate and drank way too often.

The meeting was soon underway, and the woman at the end of the table ran through a list of announcements. Then they went over lighter topics like recycling, an upcoming consumer event, and a new stop sign on Antinori Road. Emilia was surprised to see how heated things were, even for the seemingly inconsequential topics. She could only imagine what would happen when Otis took the floor to bring up organics.

After discussing a potential Red Mountain tasting in Denver, Otis finally got his chance.

"I know I've sat here before and said the same thing, but I want to revisit this topic. There was an incident recently where my vineyards were exposed to chemical drift. Thankfully, I was able to stop the violator, but I feel compelled to stand before you today and plead my case."

Emilia noticed he had not once looked at Bellflour. Otis dropped a soft fist onto the table. "I believe we should become the first certified organic appellation in the United States. Can you imagine the power we'd have? Can you imagine the grapes we'd raise?"

Emilia loved the idea of "raising" grapes. Just like children. She could listen to Otis talk all day, every day.

He carried on. "Those of us practicing regenerative farming are fighting an uphill battle when our neighbors choose to spray whatever they'd like. We can't think in terms of vineyard blocks. We need to think of ourselves as stewards of the same farm. If we're not working together, then we're not tapping the true potential of our AVA."

Bellflour made a show of shaking his head and grinning.

A winemaker named Mark Wallace interrupted. He had a long, brown beard that was graying at the ends. "Otis, not all of us are selling out of our wines. We can't take the risk of committing to organics. Not when we're still trying to get some good scores and build a following. No offense, Otis, but I don't think forcing people to farm your way is the purpose of this group."

"It's not my way at all, Mark." Otis paused. "It's the proven way to sustain a growing area for the long term. If we could somehow get past all the opposing views in this room and agree that taking care of our land is paramount, then our wines will garner the attention they deserve."

The two men went back and forth for a while, and then others jumped in. Emilia was starting to feel uncomfortable. She couldn't believe how differing their opinions could be. She was no expert by any means, but she found herself easily siding with Otis and Brooks. Maybe she was biased, but everything they said made sense.

Bellflour eventually spoke, having to tap the table to grab everyone's attention. He looked directly at Otis. "Your idea is very nice, but we're not communists, Otis. It's like Mark said. You can't tell people how to farm their land. You worry about your property. Not mine."

Otis looked like he was about to jump across the table. "You and I both know that the choices you make on your property can and do affect mine."

Bellflour sat back and crossed his arms. "My guy messed up and sprayed on a windy day. A few droplets drifted your way. You're making too big of a deal out of it."

"It *is* a big deal, Bellflour. Those vines are my life." Otis drew in a long breath and looked around the room. "Sometimes, I think we aren't looking at our mountain from a global perspective. Not only is farming organically the right thing to do—and the easiest once you get the hang of it—but it's what the world wants. It's where we're going. You people are worried about selling your wines. Instead of begging for wine club members with discounts and free parties, let's make them come to us." He put a finger on his temple. "Let's think bigger. Imagine a purely organic AVA. Imagine Red Mountain lingering on the tips of every wine drinker's tongue. You're worried about making money, making a living. *This* is the answer."

He hit the table. "We must think and move as a collective. We must heed the call from the planet. How do we make wines that can compete on the global stage? By making them as true as possible! By farming them to express Red Mountain. You can't do that by killing all the living things. They each have a purpose."

Bellflour started laughing. "Otis, are you growing wine or weed down there? All I hear are the words of a washed-up British hippie."

The rest around the table laughed nervously.

Emilia could see Otis struggling to find his words. "We don't always see eye to eye on the mountain, but at some point, if we're to excel, if we're to have a region that people in Burgundy talk about, then we need to elevate our game. That means some of us must compromise."

"Or bend to your will," Bellflour jabbed. "Some of us think it's time you accept a little technology and innovation."

Otis pleaded with the rest of the group. "Is that the mentality we want? To do whatever is easiest?" He shook his head. "I am getting old, but I've learned a few things in my day. It's not about conforming to my ideas; it's about working together to take care of our mountain. And if we do, she'll give us her finest bounty. You won't be worrying about paying the bills. You'll be free to make a wine you believe in, and the people will come out in droves to support you."

The moderator at the end of the table said, "We can't let this topic take up the entire meeting. It's apparent we're not even ready to take a vote on the matter. We'll table this for later discussion. On to the next point on the agenda." She glanced down at the piece of paper before her, and the rest of the meeting was spent going over what seemed like more trivial issues.

After it was over, they climbed back into the truck, and Otis was eerily silent. Only once they were driving did Brooks say something. He patted Otis's knee. "We're not going to give up. They didn't build Burgundy in a day, you know?"

Otis sighed. "I hope to be here to see our little mountain realize her full potential."

"Come on, Otis. You're still young."

"Young? I'm young like the mountain is young. But my body is catching up with me. I can't keep fighting this fight forever."

"That's what I'm here for," Brooks said.

Emilia had been afraid to speak but couldn't stop herself. "And me too." She wanted to say more but knew it wasn't necessary. She had just made a tremendous promise to the grapefather.

He turned back to her. "Thanks, dear."

25

A GUESSING GAME

O tis sipped the honey-colored juice in his glass—a barrel sample of marsanne that Brooks had brought from Lacoda. "Astoundingly vibrant. A nice expression, Brooks. What's the pH?"

"Three-point-two, I think. Give or take."

Otis sniffed again. "Yeah, quite crunchy."

"What does *crunchy* mean?" Emilia asked, loving Otis's seemingly never-ending list of wine adjectives.

"Think of biting into a crisp apple," Otis answered. "A crunchy wine has a snap to it."

They'd taken seats under an umbrella on the deck of a restaurant that overlooked the Columbia River. An empty barge crept by in the distance.

Emilia emulated Otis, spinning the glass in the air, sniffing the wine. She thought of all the white-wine descriptors she'd been studying. Apricot, banana, mango, citrus. Which ones could she detect in this glass?

She took a sip and breathed in some air to activate the flavors. Was it melon? Or maybe...honeysuckle? She reached across the table for the dump bucket and spat the contents against the side. Though she'd been nervous to spit in front of them, she'd been practicing in the shower and was proud of her effort.

"What do you think?" Brooks asked her.

Emilia blushed. "Please don't make me talk about the wine."

"Oh, c'mon, young lady," Otis said. "Brooks has invented more absurd wine descriptors than anyone in Washington. And half the time he's been right! Give it a go."

Emilia nodded, thinking back to her last sip. "Okay, well, I did like the brightness. I think I smelled...fried green tomatoes? And definitely some honeysuckle. I liked it a lot."

"Fried green tomatoes," Otis said. "I think you're spot on with quite an original thought. Well done." Otis pointed at the brown bag Brooks held. "And what's this?"

Emilia was glad to be off the hook and felt her shoulders lower and release.

Brooks drew the bottle out of the bag. It had no label, which Emilia had learned was called a shiner. This one had a beer cap as opposed to a cork. "You remember we used to talk about making a Red Mountain piquette?"

Otis smiled proudly. "Oh, bloody hell. Well done, sir."

"Seven-point-eight percent alcohol, from malbec and merlot pommus. Twenty cases made. I call it Red Mountain Light."

"What's a piquette?" Emilia asked, thinking nothing was cooler in the world than these geeky projects that they were sharing.

"A wine for peasants," Otis said.

"Yep," Brooks agreed, popping the top and pouring the fizzy, light-red wine into three glasses. "You know what pommus is, right? The leftovers from the grapes after pressing. So the skins, stems, seeds, and pulp. The scraps, really. Vineyard workers for hundreds, or maybe thousands of years, have been making this little delight. I used some Red Mountain honey just before bottling to get that fizz. Or as Otis calls it, *petulance*."

The three of them tasted Brooks's creation and shared their opinions, and Emilia found herself eager for harvest when she could finally make her own wine. They eventually fell into more casual wine conversation as they waited for their food to come. Otis and Brooks were sipping more than spitting, and the mood lightened. She thought both of them were quite funny after a bit of wine, and she hoped there would be many more lunches like this one.

Otis smacked his lips after a big long sip. "I feel compelled to share something I've done recently, but I must hold you to secrecy. You must promise me. This stays between us."

Brooks and Emilia both promised. Emilia couldn't imagine what great secret he was about to divulge. Maybe that he'd started a new project? Or that he'd proposed to Joan?

Otis looked around and whispered, "I've infiltrated the Drink Flamingo compound."

"What?" Brooks said, his eyes blowing up.

The grapefather grinned. "I ripped out some of their cabernet and replaced it with a less noble variety. Only a few vines, nothing terribly harmful."

Emilia and Brooks looked at each other in surprise.

"Are you serious?" Brooks asked. "How'd you get inside?"

"With wire cutters, of course. Care to take a guess at the variety I chose?"

This was quite possibly the most interesting piece of news Emilia had ever heard, and she couldn't wait to hear what variety he'd planted. *Nothing like this happens in New York*, she thought.

In the silence, Otis sipped his wine. "I'm serious now, both of you. You must take this secret to your graves. I feel slightly guilty clueing you in on my crime, but I couldn't keep it to myself any longer."

"Muscadine?" Brooks asked.

Otis shook his head with a devious grin.

Brooks tapped the table. "Something like Petit Verdot?"

"Oh, c'mon. You can do better than that."

Emilia searched her memory, revisiting the pages of the books she'd been reading. There were so many varieties out there. "Dornfelder? Or Mouvedre?"

Brooks lit up. "Look at this girl. I don't even know what Dornfelder is."

"A good guess, indeed," Otis said, "but I'm afraid she's not quite there. Let's see if we can get it out of her. Emilia, it's new world. It's prevalent in only one region. And it's been the butt of wine jokes for as long as I've been alive."

Emilia wanted to say shiraz, but she was pretty sure that was the same as syrah, which couldn't be the answer. Brooks and Otis were deep believers in the greatness of syrah on Red Mountain. *New world*, she thought. *South America. North America. Australia. New Zealand, but that's mostly pinot noir. Oh, South Africa,* she thought. "Is South Africa new world?"

Otis smiled. "It is."

Emilia had the variety on the tip of her tongue. "It's starts with a *P*, right?"

"Someone's been studying," Brooks said.

"Pinotage!" Emilia almost shouted.

Otis clapped. "There are now thirty pinotage vines sprinkled in Bellflour's precious little vineyard."

The three of them burst into the kind of laughter you might hear among thieves after a successful robbery.

Brooks eventually asked, "Where in the world did you find pinotage?"

"At the nursery in Prosser. Leftovers from a South African woman trying to get a little taste of home."

Otis told them the dirty details of his mission, and Emilia couldn't stop smiling at the idea of him sneaking out of bed and trespassing while Joan slept peacefully through the night.

Once the food came, Otis and Brooks regaled Emilia with war stories from the different harvests over the years. The cold, the hot, the wet, and the dry—each presenting new issues. Emilia couldn't wait to get a few harvests under her belt.

∾

FOR MARGOT AND REMI, the days with Carly ticked off like slashes of a blade. What made it all the worse were the moments when Carly would seem to be coming around, like the day she'd laughed at Margot smoking. Then Carly would come back twice as vicious.

Remi had, for the most part, done a good job of holding back his anger in the two weeks since Carly had arrived. But no one could keep his emotions bottled forever, and he'd occasionally snapped. Hearing Remi and Carly yelling at each other was the saddest symphony of sounds Margot had ever heard. Carly could be ruthless, and her tone grew deeper when she yelled, revealing her teenage fury at its most animalistic. Remi's voice was so deep at normal levels that when the yelling came, he roared.

Today was one of the worst fights Margot had heard yet, and she was tempted to go upstairs and intervene. If Remi and Carly yelled at each other any louder, the guests at the inn might hear them. Thank goodness Jasper was spending most of his time hanging out with Emilia and playing music with Jake.

Finally, Margot heard Remi coming down the stairs; his footsteps were easy to discern. He plopped down onto the couch next to her and rubbed his temples. "I'm just about at the end of my rope."

Margot put her hand on his upper arm. "I'm sorry."

He sat back and sighed. "Apparently, I'm the least of two evils between her mother and me, which is why she's up here. This guy Amber's been dating for a few months sounds pretty awful, and Carly says Amber always takes his side."

"Well, that sheds a lot of light on things. Both her parents are being pulled away from her."

Remi nodded. "Poor girl."

Margot took his hand and patted it. "This isn't forever, Remi. She'll come around."

"I just hate bringing you and Jasper into this."

"Don't even think like that," Margot said. "I am happily marrying *you* and *everything* that comes with you. We will get through this together."

He glanced at her. "I told her I'd buy her a car if she'd just get a job. I think she has too much time to sit around and think."

"How did she respond?"

"Nothing interests her." He shook his head. "This is what money does to kids. I think her mom's been spoiling her. Now she's acting entitled. It's exactly what Amber and I used to fight about." He choked up. "I'm afraid I've screwed up so badly with her."

Margot's heart sank. Nestling next to him, she said, "You didn't abandon her. Amber took Carly away. You had your own growing up to do. No one is perfect, Remi."

His big chest heaved. "What do I do?"

It all came down to love, Margot thought. "The only thing *we* can do. Be patient and loving. And lead by example."

"I think she needs a job."

"What she needs, Remi, is a reason to leave her room. A reason to smile. Let's give her the space she needs to find it. Don't worry about a job right now."

He choked up again and dropped his head. The tears rolled down his cheeks, and he reached for them. "I'm desperate for another chance to be her father."

"You'll get there. I promise you." Margot wondered what she could do, how she could be a better stepmother. For two weeks, she'd spritzed around in a ditzy fog, pretending like everything was just fine. How absurd that felt now.

She could hear her silly high-pitched voice. "Oh, Carly, good morning! So good to see you." Or, "I know you didn't mean to be a jerk, Carly. Would you like to go to lunch?"

Bottom line, Margot had turned into a pitiful bobblehead and wasn't doing anything effective to help the situation.

26

FALLING BACK IN LOVE

Once a week, Adriana taught English to her fellow Mexicans in the dining room of Épiphanie. Though it was her way of making a little extra money, it was also her way of giving back and taking some of the focus off her own life. To that end, her students weren't required to pay, but donations were welcome.

It had been wonderful to reconnect with teaching English again, something she hadn't done since leaving California. Helping others get a leg up in the world was so fulfilling. This class was one of the things she would miss most if she left.

If she left.

Today, nine students were looking back at her, most of them still dirty from working with the vines. She knew how much they appreciated her help, and there were few things better than teaching students who were eager to learn. These people could obtain much better paying jobs and live better lives if they learned English. Sadly, even some of the young men and women in their twenties hadn't learned.

A man with a mustache raised his hand at the end of the long table.

Adriana pointed to him. "Yes, Jorge?"

"*Cual es la diferencia—*"

"No, no, no. English, please."

He smiled nervously and tried his best. "Okay. What. Is. Div...diff?"

"*Diff,*" Adriana said.

"What is difference...?"

She helped him work through a question about the use of *a* versus *an*.

As she finished her point, Brooks entered the dining room and waved. He took a seat by the fireplace. Adriana tried to concentrate as she continued with her lesson, but all she could think about was how she'd met Brooks last year while he was sitting in that same chair. He'd looked at her like she was the most beautiful woman in the world, and she remembered her heart fluttering as she returned to the kitchen that night.

He was looking at her the same way now as he had back then. It was like he'd never even noticed her scars. He was such a handsome and kind man. How was she so lucky? How had *he* been crazy enough to stick with her through everything? Sometimes she didn't feel worthy of being loved, but he was somehow blind to her flaws. All that, and he was an excellent role model for Zack.

Now that Michael wouldn't be a threat any time soon, she'd considered staying on the mountain. Moving could be hard on Zack. And there were other reasons to leave. But she'd suddenly found a renewed sense of hope here on Red Mountain. With that hope came the reminder of how much she loved Brooks. She'd buried her own feelings to focus on Zack, but now that Michael wasn't a problem, she'd realized how wonderful it was to have Brooks in their lives.

A voice cut through her thoughts. Jorge was asking another question.

"Sorry," she said, "I was daydreaming."

She answered his question and worked through the rest of the lesson. After class, Adriana crossed the room and said hello.

"You're a pretty great teacher," Brooks said. "Can I start taking your class?"

She rolled her eyes and kissed him. "Tell me something."

"What's that?"

"How do you put up with me?" she asked.

"Put up with you? What do you mean?"

Adriana sat in the chair next to him. "I know I've been awful to live with. I just want to say thanks for sticking by me."

"Don't you see I'm stuck on you, A? I don't have a choice." He reached for her hand. "You've had a long couple of years. Forget about it."

"That's no excuse. I will try harder. I promise."

∾

BROOKS LOVED the mystery that was Adriana. Had she just insinuated that she was staying on the mountain? Even though Brooks had seen a change in her, he'd avoided bringing up this topic that meant so much to him.

Carmen had taken such a toll on his happiness lately, but feeling Adriana's love at this moment made Carmen and her little agendas seem insignificant. This is why he'd stayed with Adriana and fought off all the doubt. Because he knew who she was as a person, and he knew how much she really loved him. Even when everyone around him, including his mother, felt like he'd be better off on his own, he was sure he just had to stay the course until she came around.

"Let's do something fun tonight," Brooks said.

"Like what?"

"Why don't we both pick up Zack and see what he wants to do?"

"Oh, I think we know what he'll say. He'll want to go back to the mall and eat ice cream and play video games."

Brooks raised his hands, palms up. "That makes two of us."

∾

FOR THE NEXT WEEK, Brooks and Adriana repaired their relationship, and they found connection in all sorts of ways. They laughed together and held hands. They listened to each other as they shared the things on their minds. They also found a wonderful connection in parenting.

Every day, they rode together to pick up Zack from camp and went to the mall, the bowling alley, and the driving range. They fished and hiked together. When they were home, they played checkers, built paper airplanes, and cooked Mexican recipes.

Brooks was amazed at the transformation he was seeing with Adriana, but it was one particular phone call that blew his mind.

"I just left your mother's house," Adriana said, catching him while he was changing a propane tank.

Brooks froze. "Oh God."

"No, it was a great visit," Adriana assured him. "I told her not to worry about what she'd said and that I totally understood."

"Wait," he said, holding the phone in front of him and glancing at the screen. "Is this Adriana Hernandez? I don't think I'm speaking to the right person."

She laughed. "Oh, hush. I'm not that bad. Your mom and I are fine. In fact, she and your father are going to watch Zack so that we can go on a date."

"A date? What's that?" Convincing Adriana to let *anyone* watch Zack was a tremendous task, and this giant step she'd taken was not lost on him.

It was during this date two nights later, while sitting across from each other in an intimate French restaurant in Walla Walla, that she finally brought up staying. "I guess I'm realizing that I can't run away from my problems. And if you're willing to stick by me, then I definitely don't want to run away from you."

Brooks nearly choked on a mussel. Knowing they finally had a chance filled his cup in a wonderful way.

She stabbed a fork into her *salade Niçoise*. "Zack loves you too, and he needs you in his life."

"I need him," Brooks admitted. "I need *both* of you in mine."

Like he'd discovered the secret to life, Brooks found himself dancing through the following days. He was more carefree about the goings on at Lacoda and more confident about his place on the mountain. Finally, he was getting the break he needed.

27

DON'T FALL HARD

Agravel drive and a chain-link fence divided Till Vineyards from Drink Flamingo. Otis looked at it more like twenty feet of purgatory, the line between heaven and hell. Standing a few rows into his own vineyards, he marveled at the differences. Comparing the two properties might be the perfect study in wild farming versus the less earth-conscious path.

Thankfully, he hadn't found any damage from the spray drift. All his vines looked healthy—in a more real sense of the word. His vineyard had always had a wildness to it, with grasses and weeds that he rarely mowed and grape clusters that looked far from uniform. To an untrained eye, Till Vineyards looked like it was cared for by an unkempt hippie living off the grid. But when standing there in the quiet, as Otis was now, one noticed the grasshoppers bouncing through the tall grass and the butterflies dancing through the canopies where robins had made their nests. Otis's idea of farming was to manipulate as little as possible, planting the vines and letting them settle into the natural habitat.

And then twenty feet away...

Otis peeked over his last rows and through the fence. The division couldn't have been more pronounced. Trying not to gag at the sight of the McMansion that now had walls and was being prepped for stucco, he looked at the bright, almost neon-green grass that had risen from the cleared soil. Synthetic fertilizers had a way of making things look so perfect on the outside while ripping the insides apart.

A ring of brown circled the trunks of the vines and trees, the evidence of spraying glyphosate, the primary ingredient of Roundup. It was such an easy and lazy way to deal with weeds. So much easier than hand hoeing or running a weed eater.

Otis wasn't close enough to see, but he could guarantee there were no grasshoppers or butterflies making their homes over there. And there were certainly no robins' nests with their beautiful blue eggs hidden in the leaves.

He knew exactly what those chemicals would do to the vines. They'd seep into the soil, potentially settling in for decades. The roots of the vines would soak up these chemicals and be clogged by them, which would prevent them from taking in the essence of the place. Though they might look like they were thriving, the vines would end up pushing out homogenized, lifeless berries. Grapes that tasted like every other lifeless fruit across the world.

That wasn't the Drink Flamingo vines' biggest issue, though. While the chemicals worked to stunt their vitality, Otis was keeping them dangerously thirsty. On watering days, he'd wait until one of their guys had done a pass to check the irrigation, and then he'd pull out his phone like he was taking out his sword. He'd navigate to the irrigation app and swipe down, closing the smart valve. He wasn't tech savvy at all, but most farmers on Red Mountain these days were using technology to control their irrigation process. Not to his surprise, his neighbors hadn't noticed the water deficiency. This is what happened when you hired a vineyard manager who didn't live in the state. It served them right.

The only problem was that Otis might have been a little trigger-happy. The vines had barely grown out of their grow tubes, and he wondered if some had failed to take root at all.

"Better ease up for a while," Otis said to himself, slinking back down into the row.

After taking a moment to appreciate a ladybug inching down a vine, he looked at the time. He'd agreed rather reluctantly to join Joan for a bicycle ride around the mountain. Didn't she understand how much work he had to do? Who had time to go lallygagging around the mountain? He burned his calories with a shovel and an axe, not a bloody two-wheeled Mary Poppins machine.

Still, he'd been deep in the doghouse and knew he needed to shape up. There was a time when he couldn't imagine the two of them ever having problems. It seemed like she'd put up with him forever. But apparently, the honeymoon was over. Now, she was expecting him to actually become a better person. Ugh, who had time for such things? Wasn't it enough to make fine wine?

◆

OTIS HAD to knock the cobwebs off his bike, and he felt like a damn idiot prancing around in his shorts and silly tennis shoes. It didn't help when Joan, in her tights and T-shirt, burst into laughter upon seeing him in the driveway.

"You redefine a farmer's tan," she said, gawking at his legs. She had pulled their bikes out of the garage, and they were waiting behind her.

"I'm glad you're having fun with this whole thing."

"I'm proud of you. And I think you look adorable."

Otis growled. "You know how I feel about looking adorable." He wrapped a leg over his bike. "Apparently, you've forgotten how small this mountain is and how the only sport is talking about the other inhabitants."

Joan climbed onto her bike. "I'm a misfit and don't care who knows it."

"Easy for you to say. Let's get on with it before I change my mind."

"Otis Till, take a moment to appreciate what you're doing. If hanging out with me is a nuisance, I'm happy to find someone else who will spend the morning with me. Besides, your ticker could use a bit of cardio. Don't give me that 'my farm is my gym' routine. Your blood pressure readings don't justify your argument."

Knowing he wouldn't win this one, he resisted challenging her. "I'm very happy to spend some time with you."

For about three minutes, as he dug in and pushed himself up the hill, he let go of most of his thoughts. It wasn't that he achieved Zen, which was most likely where Joan was at the moment, but the required physical exertion prevented him from thinking anything other than, *Well, this bloody sucks!*

As he passed by Drink Flamingo's McMansion, however, his mind returned to his war with Bellflour and a notion he'd recently been tossing around. What about a wall? What if he built a huge concrete wall that would at least protect him from looking at Drink Flamingo every time he walked his own vines? *How tall would it need to be?* he wondered, eyeing the purgatorial gravel road. To do it right, he thought eight feet would be best. Expensive, but well worth it. He wasn't sure he could do another vintage with that damn eyesore lingering. A wall would also block any further drift incidents.

Otis planned the process as he and Joan cut along Sunset Road and swung right onto Van Giesen. Thankfully, seconds before his heart exploded and his lungs gave out, they reached the downhill stretch to the river. He stopped pedaling as the bike accelerated and his hair blew back in the wind. Though he wasn't prepared to admit it to Joan, it was a wonderful feeling to be out of breath and sweating and having earned the downhill run.

Hanging a right, he followed her along the river on Demoss Road. Remi Valentine's property came into view on the left. *What a piece of land that is,* Otis thought. Four stunning acres of superb farmland planted with just about every fruit and vegetable growable on this side of the Cascades. For a novice and a one-man show, Remi was doing a darn good job of taking care of it. Looking down the hill, Otis saw the overhead sprinklers spraying river water over the garden. Otis thought Remi would be wise to switch over to drip irrigation to keep the weeds down.

As that thought passed, Remi poked his head up from the bank of the river, where it looked like he was working on the pump. Joan and Otis waved back as they sped by.

Winding around several more curves, they passed Brooks's house and the many gentlemen's farms with horses, goats, and sheep grazing in the pastures. Once they hit a flat stretch, Otis took a break from pedaling, and his mind returned to the wall. He was thinking about how long it might take to build when Joan slowed down to let him catch up.

"What are you thinking about?" She looked like she'd barely ridden anywhere, and here he was feeling the burn of his sweat in his eyes.

"Oh, just a little of this and that," he replied.

Their bikes were moving at the same pace, only a few feet from each other.

"I certainly don't want to be a nag," she said, "but if we are to spend time together, we need to spend time together. I not only want your body on the bike next to me, I want your mind and your heart too."

"I know, I know. I'm trying, Joan. This has just been one hell of a year. I was thinking about the wall again. Something has to be done, or I'm not going to make it to another vintage."

A car came up behind them, so they broke away for a moment. Once they'd realigned, he said, "You would think I'd get a break from time to time. I just feel so tired."

"This *is* your break. Look around you." With that, she sped up and raced ahead.

"If it were only so easy." He pedaled as hard as he could and caught up with her. "Don't give up on me, Joan. I know I'm a pain in the arse, but don't give up on me."

"I'm not giving up on you."

As they reached the back side of Red Mountain, Otis's mind wandered again. He thought about climate change and how the grapes might be affected. He wondered if any varieties could be planted on the dark side of Red Mountain, which only enjoyed the morning sun.

His mind was all over the place when a bump jarred him, and he realized he'd run off the road. Another bump knocked him off balance, and his tire jerked right, throwing him toward the ground. His shoulder hit first, and he winced as something sharp stabbed his upper thigh. Rolling several times, he tumbled to a stop in a ditch.

Joan jumped off her bike and rushed to him. "Are you all right?"

Otis sat up, wincing in pain as he reached for a bad scrape on his leg. "Yeah, yeah, I'm okay. At least, I think so."

"What in the world happened?" Joan asked, negotiating the slope of the ditch.

Otis was assessing the damage. The stab he'd felt hadn't punctured the skin, but he was bleeding from his arms and legs. "Just thinking too much. But I'm okay. Nothing's broken. Holy hell, I'm having a day."

Joan lowered to him. "You're torturing yourself. No one else is doing this to you. It's all in between your ears."

"Not all of us are cruising through life on a glider." He could taste the venom on his tongue but didn't give a damn. "Some of us have *real* issues to deal with."

He hadn't seen her angry in a long time, but she flashed a pair of terribly angry eyes at him as she rose and stood over him. "I'll see you back home."

"What about my bike?" he asked her as she climbed out of the ditch and left him. "I don't even know if it works."

"I'm not sure I care," she spat back. "Maybe you can overthink yourself back."

As he pressed up to a stand, he watched her pedal away. The fear of losing her settled uneasily in his stomach and chest.

28

A TASTE OF THE REAL WORLD

Emilia watched Otis lift the steel top off the amphora in front of him. He had scabs on his arms from a bike accident several days earlier. On the other side of the cellar, Eli was moving empty barrels out the large door for cleaning.

Otis dipped his barrel thief into the red juice and let it fill. Emilia had seen these same clay pots in Lacoda's cellar and was excited to learn more about them. Otis had told her that amphorae had been used since the Stone Age and that he was exploring the differences in textures given to the wine by testing both clay pots and concrete.

He drew out a sample and filled both of their glasses. "We've just blended this—both an early and late pick of syrah from the last vintage. It will take a little longer for the two wines to meld together, but you'll get the idea. Syrah is one of the few varieties that can handle being picked so much later without the risk of losing its identity. If you allow cab to hang too long, you get riper fruit in a sad cascade of homogeny—a big purple explosion that belongs on sourdough toast. With syrah, there are, of course, the obvious darker and riper fruits, but you also tap into the smokier, meatier flavors. A savorier and even earthier experience. I'm rather fond of the flavors."

Emilia stuck her nose in, and a foray of heavenly smells rose up. "And how about from the earlier pick?"

"Notice the brighter fruits, like raspberry and bing cherry." He sniffed. "A bit of orange peel as well. Then in the tertiary dimensions, we find pencil lead shavings and herbal notes. It's a lot to take in, but they blend nicely once the two picks have had a chance to settle."

Emilia had always considered him a slightly grumpy man, but as he tasted and talked about wine, he morphed into a possessed young man. He was nearly giddy during the experience.

Otis spun his glass and took a long sip. After letting it rest in his mouth for a moment, he spat into the drain on the floor. Emilia mimicked him and tried to catalog the experience. It was overwhelming to try to think of the wine's body, the acidity, *and* the level of alcohol, while *also* searching for specific flavors and aromas. However, it was more intriguing than daunting.

He put the top back on, pressing it against a putty-like material that snaked around the rim. As they moved to the next amphora, she said, "You and Brooks talk a lot about the picking date. Is it that important?"

"Yes, my dear girl." He lowered the glass to his waist. "The moment one chooses to pick their grapes is of *paramount* importance." He held up his hand, as if showing a graph. "Imagine a grape ripening each day—each hour, for that matter. In the early stages, we have these hard, green berries that accumulate acid and tannins. Absolutely deplorable to taste. In late July or early August, depending on the year, we begin to see *veraison*, the wonderful time of year when the berries soften and turn purple." He lifted his hand farther. "It's about that time that the sugars accumulate and acids fall to more appealing levels. The berries reveal their varietal attributes as well. In the following weeks after *veraison*, the grapes ripen rapidly, and we must make the decision of when to stop the process. If we pick too early, we risk a lack of phenolic ripeness and could end up with a wine that tastes like green peppers and olives. The juice might be too bitter and astringent. The acids could be over the top."

Otis raised his hand above his head. "Too late, and we'll have lost the acid and any sense of place. The sugars will have skyrocketed, which will have led to higher alcohol content. There are some, like my neighbor, who want high-octane Hollywood wines. Imagine a two-hour action scene with car chases and endless explosions...but at the dinner table. I prefer to pick much earlier in development and end up with a wine that makes for a more interesting dinner guest. When a grape is picked on the earlier side, you get the exact balance you need. With that balance comes the specificity of the vineyard. You can taste that my syrah came from the block my wife and I first planted. Just like with your vineyards, you can quite easily discern which grapes came from Angeline's block."

"You know about Angeline?" Emilia couldn't believe he'd just brought up a vine from Lacoda.

"Of course, I do. It's one of the magical mysteries of the mountain."

Otis held his hands out in a teepee formation. "Every moment past the optimal picking time, the wines start to race toward homogeny, meaning they lose their character and start to taste like every other blasted wine on a shelf. When you pick at the optimum time as I define it—the earlier side, your acid is high and your pH is low, which creates a very safe environment for your wine to vinify. Bacteria doesn't grow well in low-pH environments, so you're essentially making it easier on yourself."

He crossed his arms, spinning his glass in the air by rote. "Think about it. By picking at the perfect time, you capture the essence of your vineyard, *and* you give yourself juice that safeguards itself. You don't have to throw a bunch of sulfur at it to keep the yuckies out. This is where the late-picking bozos get themselves in trouble. They pick late for this modern, high-scoring style but quickly realize how unstable and susceptible their juice is to unwanted growth. So what do they do? They have to douse it with chemicals to prevent the wines from going even further south. I don't know about you, but I don't want chemicals in my soil *or* in my wines."

Otis took a long sip and spat it to the drain. "Brooks told me he's given you a few rows to make wine with this year."

"Yes, he has," Emilia beamed.

Otis wagged a finger. "Make sure you walk the vines every day. Taste the berries. When it comes to picking, run the numbers for sure, but in the end, it's about tasting. Find the balance. Find the voice in your vines."

Emilia wanted to shout from the top of the mountain that she was talking wine with Otis Till. She wanted desperately to tell her mother how much fun she was having, but she was terrified to even bring up the experience at any point in the near future.

Bubbling over with excitement, she said, "And Brooks just told me that he and my dad are letting me participate in the blending trials next month."

"Oh, wow," Otis said. "What a high honor that is. And I'm sure it's no doubt earned. I remember when Brooks and I started that same tradition down here."

Every year, Brooks, Pak, and her dad collected to decide on the varietal percentages for Lacoda's main red blend. Each person came up with his own blend, and the decision was made through a competitive blind tasting.

Otis drifted off for a moment and then said, "When done right, a bottle of wine is a liquid journal, an entire vintage of entries—intimate, unedited, and raw. That's what we want to pour into people's glasses. Tell *your* story of the mountain."

Emilia smiled, thinking of something she'd heard. "Brooks told me about the year you picked cabernet in July. Is that really true?"

Otis dipped his chin. "Guilty as charged. It was more to prove a point than anything else. People call me a hardhead now, but I was much worse in my youth. That was a hot year in California, but I went a tad overboard." He raised an eyebrow. "That being said, the wine wasn't awful. A bit stemmy and green, but it held its own. Would you like to try it?"

Emilia attempted to act cool. "Um, yes. I would love to."

"Tell you what. Why don't we break for lunch, and I'll pull a few fun bottles?"

They agreed to meet in the tasting room in an hour, and Emilia raced home to tell her father what she'd been doing.

~

SINCE OPENING, Margot had never turned down a request for a late checkout, but her generosity was biting her in the derriere today. It just so happened that every one of her guests were leaving today, and five of the six parties had asked for late checkouts. *And* every one of the rooms was spoken for tonight.

But that wasn't half of it! She'd promised several guests a bagged lunch; she was hosting a gender reveal luncheon at one; and worst of all, like an anvil that had just dropped on her head, the air conditioning had gone out on the hottest day of the year so far. Her guests had been complaining all morning, and while trying to find a heating and air company that would come out immediately, she'd been begging her guests' forgiveness with free mimosas and bloody marys.

Her habit of pulling at her long hair was in full effect today as Margot the Chia Pet answered her cell phone with her best attempt at cheeriness. "Hi, this is Margot at Épiphanie. How may I help you?" As she did often, she'd forwarded the inn's calls to her cell.

"Margot, this is Alexander." He was the dad who'd arranged the gender reveal.

"Hi, Alexander. I'm just about to pop into the kitchen to finish prepping for you."

"I'm glad I caught you then." He sounded out of breath. "The word got out that we were having a party, and now my in-laws have invited half the world. Is there any way we can up the count from twenty to forty?"

Margot felt like a juggler who'd just been thrown four more flaming sticks. But she wouldn't dare reveal her hesitation, so in the cheeriest voice she'd used since Broadway, she said, "The more, the merrier. No problem. We can do that!"

"Oh, thank you so much, Margot. I love my in-laws, but sometimes they drive me nuts."

"It's my pleasure." She was already thinking of what else she had in the freezer and fridge. As long as Adriana could take care of flipping the rooms, Margot could handle the luncheon and be done in time to start checking in the next round of guests, who wouldn't be arriving until three.

Her phone rang again, and she was terrified to answer this time. "Épiphanie. This is Margot."

"Hi," said a woman in a tired voice. "We're checking in today and got an early head start from Seattle. Is there any way we could... maybe...get into our room a little earlier? There's a club event this afternoon at Cooper, and I'd love to wash my hair."

If Margot had been at the end of her rope, she might have said, "Didn't you read the email? Three o'clock check-in. Are numbers hard for you? Three. Not two. Not one."

She didn't say that, though, because Margot enjoyed the pressure. Once you'd run an inn for a while, you got used to the surprises. And if you wanted to be a fine innkeeper, you had to embrace them.

So with the spirit of the finest innkeeper on the mountain, Margot nearly sang, "We can't have dirty hair, can we? By all means, we'll find a room for you. Guests are just starting to check out, but I'll make sure your room is ready first. What's your last name?"

Once she hung up, she jogged into the kitchen where Adriana was helping prep for the gender reveal. "Would you like the bad news? The really bad news? Or the devastating news?"

Adriana cracked a smile and looked up from the mixer. It had livened up the inn to have her friend back in good spirits. Selfishly, because of the news regarding Michael, Margot suspected Adriana was no longer planning on leaving. Margot couldn't bear to think of running the inn without her.

"Let's start with the best of the bad news," Adriana said, "and get worse from there."

Margot counted the problems on her hand. "I've just gotten off the phone with the Dykhuis party, and they've requested an early check-in."

"Oh, *díos*," Adriana said animatedly. "Not like we have anything else going on around here."

"I know," Margot agreed. "As if we always have clean rooms waiting for the arrival of our guests, no matter the hour."

"Let me guess," Adriana said, pulling the bowl from the mixer. "You told her we'd be happy to accommodate."

"Of course, I did. So the rest of the problems"—she went back to counting on her hand—"in ascending order of severity. I can't find anyone to come out today to work on the air conditioning. It's officially the hottest day on record in June. Five of our six rooms have yet to check out. And," Margot said matter-of-factly, "the gender reveal is now forty people."

"Forty? I thought it was twenty."

"It was."

Adriana dropped the mixing bowl into the sink and turned back to Margot. "Okay, okay, *no problemo*."

Margot put a hand on her chest and fluttered her eyes. "Oh, how I love having someone willing to suffer with me. You're a gem."

Adriana dried off her hands on a towel hanging from a rack by the sink. "What would you like me to do first?" she asked, then deadpanned, "Should we order pizza?"

"I know you're joking, but I would actually consider the idea. However, there's one small problem. Not even Domino's delivers out here." She held out her hands. "Twenty...forty. It's only double. If you'll start working on the rooms, I'll focus on the food. The moment the guests check out of number four, please drop what you're doing and get it cleaned. We must allow Ms. Dykhuis time to wash her hair before the club event."

As Adriana passed by, Margot gave her a high five. "We've got this."

"Never a dull moment at Épiphanie," Adriana said, pushing through the swinging doors.

29

THE LAST RESORT

What *a brutal day to lose A/C*, Adriana thought. June was off to a blistering start. She'd only just started cleaning the first room, and sweat dripped down her chest like she'd gone for a run.

As she snapped open a second garbage bag, her phone rang. Fishing it out of her pocket, she glanced at the screen as if she were screening calls, but the absurdity of her action almost drew a laugh. Like Adriana, the queen of overprotective parenting, wasn't going to answer. As if there were something on the screen that might deter her. How many spam callers had succeeded in reaching her because she refused to miss a call, no matter the area code? A phone couldn't ring without triggering Adriana's apprehension.

That being said, at least she'd become aware of becoming a helicopter parent. That's what marrying an abusive psychopath would do to you. These thoughts ran in fast-forward as she pressed the green button and put the phone to her ear.

"This is Adriana."

"Hi, it's Kelly over here at the church..."

Adriana's pulse quickened. "Yes? Everything okay?"

"Zack's fine, but he's been involved in a fight. Actually, he hurt another boy." Adriana's overprotective nature came rushing in. Zack had never hurt anyone in his life. The apparently misinformed woman asked, "Could you come get him? He's sitting in the office."

Adriana looked at the filthy room and thought of the others that hadn't been cleaned, the ones the guests with their late checkouts were still inside dirtying. Margot would kill her, but she had no choice.

"Um, yeah, yes. Either Brooks or I will be there in a few minutes." She had to add, "I'm finding it difficult to believe Zack would hurt someone."

"I know," the woman agreed placatingly. "He's such a sweetheart. But we've definitely seen a little change with his disposition lately."

Adriana slumped. "What kind of change?"

"Let's talk in person."

"Yes...sure. One of us will be there as quickly as possible. If I can't be the one who picks up Zack, I'll call later to set up an appointment with you so we can discuss this."

Adriana terminated the call and tried Brooks on his cell. She left a message on his voicemail. "I was calling to see if you could pick up Zack." She briefly explained what had happened as she rushed down the stairs.

Adriana found Margot pacing the kitchen floor with her phone to her ear. "I can't wait until tomorrow for an appointment," Margot said to the person on the other end. "My guests will be miserable in this heat. Is there anything you can do? I'm happy to pay overtime."

She muted the phone against her chest and looked at Adriana. "Worst day ever." Back to the phone, she said, "Okay, okay. Let me call around. But please hold that first appointment in the morning."

Once Margot hung up, Adriana bit her lip. She hated to do this to her boss, but she had no choice. "The church just called. Zack was in a fight, and I have to pick him up. I'm so sorry."

Margot's mouth fell open. "Is he hurt?"

Adriana shook her head. "No, he's fine. Please forgive me. I'll come right back—if you're okay with him hanging around the inn. I know this is the worst day..."

Her boss pointed to the door. "This is all little stuff. I can take care of it. Do what you need to do with Zack."

"Are you sure?" Adriana had never loved working for Margot more.

"Go take care of your son."

Adriana put her hands up in prayer. "Thank you. I'll be right back."

She felt awful as she drove away from the mountain, but Margot was right. What mattered more than her child? Even if Brooks could have picked up Zack, she needed to be there. She wanted to talk to the counselors and maybe the other child's parents to understand exactly what had happened. Zack had never been in a fight in his life.

Parking as close as she could, Adriana marched briskly toward the office. She and Zack had been attending this church ever since they'd moved up from California, and all the other members, including the preacher, had gone out of their way to welcome them to town.

A woman at reception led Adriana to a back office, where she found Zack sitting in the corner, drawing. "Hi, honey," she said, rushing to him.

Zack looked up. "Hi, Mom."

She dropped her knees to the carpet. "What happened, sweetie?"

He shook his head in shame.

She could barely stand seeing him this way. "Why were you fighting?"

"He started it," Zack said with an attitude.

Kelly, the head of summer camp, stood from her desk. "Hi, Ms. Hernandez."

Adriana turned from her red-faced son and faked a smile. "Hi."

A headband held back Kelly's shoulder-length brown hair. With her calm demeanor, she evoked a sense of authority and experience. "The other student called Zack a name."

"Yeah," Zack said. "He called me a beaner."

Adriana gritted her teeth at the derogatory term she knew from her youth in Los Angeles. The name originated from the amount of beans in Mexican cuisine. Adriana's first instinct was to yell that the boy deserved a beating. Was the camp condoning racism? Surely, the boy had been kicked out for good.

"We do not allow such language at the camp," Kelly assured her, "and the other boy has been sent home. Neither do we condone fighting in any capacity. Why don't you both have a seat, and we can talk about it?"

Adriana nodded and looked at her son. "Come sit down, Zack."

"I'm fine here." His tone was both angry and defensive.

Adriana snapped her fingers. "Right now, Zack. Next to me. Let's go."

He popped up and plopped down next to her.

Adriana looked around for the first time, noticing a wooden cross hanging next to pictures of Kelly's family on the wall.

Kelly sat down and smiled at Zack. "You've been disrupting camp lately, and it's time we talk to your mom about it." Adriana appreciated Kelly including him in the conversation. "You're preventing other students from learning."

Adriana lifted a hand. "Why is this the first I'm hearing about it?" She could hear the fire in her voice and reminded herself that Kelly was probably a very nice person and didn't deserve the bark Adriana was capable of unleashing.

Kelly answered like she'd said this a thousand times before. "We try to address the issues in the classroom and don't bring in the parents unless absolutely necessary. Obviously, today is that day. Zack punched the boy in the face."

Adriana's head snapped back. "What?" She side-eyed her son. "Why would you let him upset you like that? Words are just words, *mi amor*."

Zack seemed to slink into his chair. "He's a jerk, mom. Nobody likes him."

"That doesn't give you reason to hit him." Looking back at Kelly, she asked, "What else has he done?"

"It's nothing huge, but it's adding up. Interrupting during reading sessions, saying bad words, not following directions."

The truth of his behavior hit Adriana hard. As much as she'd like to blame it on Michael having shown up last year, it was more likely Zack feeding off her own depression. How could she expect him to excel when she, herself, wasn't giving him the happy home life he needed?

~

PANIC HAD SET IN. Margot's feeling of conquering the world as the hostess with the mostest quickly dissipated as she watched Adriana pull away from Épiphanie. She'd been sincere in telling Adriana that Zack mattered way more than these petty obstacles, but Margot needed to figure out how to get through the rest of the day. She needed help.

She tried Remi and Jasper, neither of whom answered.

Tears welled up in her eyes as she thought about all the potentially bad future reviews from guests who couldn't sleep in because it was too hot or because they couldn't check in earlier, or worst of all, that the food was terrible.

"C'mon, Margot," she said to herself. "You've dealt with worse before."

And then...

An idea came to her. A terrible idea. It was perhaps the worst idea she'd ever had, but she had no choice. She barely acknowledged her hens scouring the dirt for bugs as she crossed over to her house on a mission to recruit help.

Carly was curled up on the couch. The black hoodie with a skull on it was pulled over her head like usual.

"I need you," Margot said. "Adriana had to leave, and I'm hosting a party in a little while and have a full house tonight. I know you probably don't feel like it, but would you please help me?" She added, "I'll pay you."

Carly pulled earbuds from her ears. "What are you saying?"

Margot tried not to show her frustration and put on her ditzy stepmom costume, saying in a high-pitched tone, "I have a ton of fires going on at the inn and could really use your help today. Could you please give me a few hours of your time? I'll pay you well. Please."

Carly dropped her head backward and looked at the ceiling.

Margot wanted to scream at her. *Get your ass off the couch for once! Stop thinking about yourself! While you're at it, take off that wretched hoodie! You smell like an ashtray.* Though that would have been an authentic reaction, it wouldn't help their relationship or the issues at hand. She went back to not being herself.

Margot sat on a chair facing her. "Believe me, I hate asking you. I know you don't like me. But please, I'll make it up to you."

"I guess I don't have a choice."

Carly was right about that, but Margot didn't say as much. Carly pulled the black hoodie off her head, acting as if she'd been terribly put out. "What do you need me to do?"

Margot smiled through her anger. She almost suggested that Carly change clothes, but maybe that was asking too much. She'd take whatever she could get at this point. "Clean some rooms, answer phone calls. Maybe help in the kitchen too. Seriously, I'm really sorry to ask."

"It's fine. I'm tired of sitting around, anyway."

30

THE LOST VINTAGE

"Not many people have been down here," Otis said, slipping a giant iron key into a lock dangling from a chain. He reminded her of a wizard in a fantasy novel, leading someone through a secret chamber. Emilia hadn't noticed the arched wooden door when she'd gone from the cellar into the tasting room earlier.

A musty odor wafted out as Otis pulled open the door. Emilia peeked around him, wondering what in the world lay in store for her this afternoon. Stepping through, he retrieved a lantern from the wall and switched it on. A narrow set of stairs descending into the earth showed itself. The brick walls formed into an arched ceiling. She followed him down, feeling the drop in temperature as they descended.

When the two of them reached the last steps, her eyes feasted on one of the most incredible wine cellars she'd ever seen. Having toured with her father in Europe, she'd visited many of the greatest wineries in the world, and this one was on par. She cringed as she recalled her lack of interest in wine back in those days. Her face had been glued to her phone as they'd navigated the Gallo-Roman chalk mines that made up Taittinger's wine cellar in Champagne.

Now, she couldn't think of anything more interesting and intriguing than a lifetime of bottled memories from vintages the world over. So many souls and their stories trapped in bottles, waiting for their corks to be pulled.

"This is so cool. Has my dad been down here?"

"A time or two." Their voices echoed.

Otis set the lantern down and turned a dimmer knob. Sconces along the brick walls lit up in a soft orange, revealing this truly marvelous feat in architecture. Large brick columns held up the arched ceilings. Thousands of bottles lined the walls, and Emilia suddenly wanted to get lost in the passageways. After being down here and also meeting Angeline, she wondered how many secrets this mountain had been keeping from her.

They walked further into the space, circling a column to an opening. A small wooden table stood in the middle with four chairs around it. Several candles protruded from empty wine bottles caked in wax drippings.

Emilia approached one of the walls of wine. The shelves were made of concrete, and each section held a couple of cases. There were chalk marks indicating vintages and regions, places she recognized in the Rhone Valley. From the south, Châteauneuf-du-Pape, Gigondas, Lirac. And from the north, Hermitage, Cornas, Côte-Rôtie. She ran her fingers along the dusty bottles. Some of the labels were peeling off.

"How long have you been collecting bottles?"

"Much of this I brought up from Sonoma. Rebecca and I started buying wines in our twenties. So forty years. Some of these wines date back beyond my days, though."

"Prewar?"

"A few. You're in France now. In the next room are the more obscure regions. A bit of Georgia and Greece. Past that, you'll encounter my riesling problem. If you've not had a chance to wrap your head around riesling, it's the wine of the gods. I'm not sure any other white ages with such grace."

Her eyes glazed as she touched the dusty bottles with faded

labels, and Otis narrated her tour through time. She felt like she'd fallen into a storybook, each bottle a different mystical chapter.

After the tour, Otis said, "Look around if you like. I'll retrieve a couple of bottles and meet you at the table." He disappeared past a column.

Emilia lost herself in the endless bottles, feeling the energies of winemakers who'd struggled through vintages long before her time. The idea of stories captured in a bottle was nearly overwhelming, and she wanted to laugh and cry at the same time, utterly exposed to the raw beauty of humanity, a world where such an endeavor was possible.

A chair scraped the concrete floor, and she peeked around a column. Otis had set two bottles down on the table and was taking a seat.

Joining him, she said, "I'm honored that you'd share your cellar and these wines with me. My mind is exploding." She shook her head, thinking she might tear up. "I could stay down here forever."

"I feel the same way." He dragged a match along the table until it burst into flame. As he lit the candles, she took a seat opposite him and eyed the bottles, dying to know what they were about to taste. One was from his vineyard here. She didn't recognize the other one, but it was much older. She could barely make out on the fading label that it was Californian.

"Does Joan like coming down here? I imagine she does."

Otis reached for the first bottle and pushed the corkscrew into the cork. "We haven't been down here for a long time together. I'm afraid my love of wine—or, as she might call it, *obsession*—is beginning to grate on her nerves. I can't blame her. She's tired of hearing me talk about Drink Flamingo."

"It's a pretty big deal, them being there. Especially for you, as their neighbor."

"No question. But she claims I'm overthinking it all." He tilted his head. "She tells me not to let the things I can't control control me."

Emilia was touched that he was being so honest with her, but this cellar had a sacred feeling and seemed to demand nothing but honesty. "You're very lucky to have her. She helped me so much when I was going through all my issues two years ago."

He nodded as he sniffed the cork he'd extracted from the bottle. "She's saving all of us, one at a time." Setting the cork down, he continued, "She may have met her match with me, though."

"I don't believe it."

Arching his eyebrow, he said, "I fear I might be losing her."

She felt his pain in her heart. "Why would you say that? You two are meant to be together."

He poured the wine into two gorgeous crystal glasses, and Emilia could see from the light-brown edges that it was an older vintage. "She deserves much more than me." He watched the candle for a while as the wine breathed.

Emilia didn't dare speak, and an incredible silence ensued...too powerful to be awkward. The candles flickered between them. For a moment, she caught herself considering the possibility that they weren't alone down there, almost like dead winemakers were surrounding the table, hoping their bottles might be next in line.

Finally, Otis broke into the quiet like he'd lit a match in the dark. "Though I would like to say I could choose to walk away and into the sunset with Joan, I'm not sure I'd survive. Last time I left for any length of time, I felt like I'd lost everything. I fear I'm bound to this place, for better or worse." He waved a hand in the air. "I don't mean to get gloomy. Let's taste some wine."

Emilia felt a deep connection with Otis at that moment. She knew exactly what he meant and felt his pain. "Something tells me you and Joan are just beginning your life together."

"I hope you're right." He turned up one corner of his mouth, lightening the mood. "She wants me to wear an eye patch."

Emilia covered her mouth, stifling a laugh. "Why in the world?"

"Something about my overactive left brain. If I wear an eye patch over my right eye, I can supposedly quiet the left brain for a while. You know Joan and all her wizardry."

"I love her wizardry."

"As do I, but there are limits. An eye patch, for God's sake?" He shook his head and slid one of the two glasses past the flickering flame to Emilia. He lifted his own glass and held it out to her as a toast.

"This is the one from California when I picked in July. Not even Brooks has tried it, but I thought you'd appreciate it."

No one had ever treated her so much like an adult, an equal. She lifted her glass and stared at the ruby-red wine with brown edges. It felt wonderful to hold a wine of such power. Once again, tears pricked her eyes. What a legendary wine. "Thank you for sharing."

"That's what wine is all about." He stuck his nose into the glass.

Emilia did the same and nearly tumbled inside. It wasn't about the faint notes of cigar box and raisins, though she did detect those scents at first sniff. She could sense the tartness, which she'd expected from this early picked vintage.

But all those thoughts seemed so unimportant...so...inconsequential. With her eyes closed, Emilia took a sip and leapt past all the flavors she'd studied and recognized and fell into another world. She was in California, and she could see Otis as a young man, still wearing his tweed cap. But this time, he was clean-shaven, and he beamed with the love of Rebecca filling his heart. She could see a younger Rebecca too, and Emilia thought about the two of them falling in love on a bus from San Francisco to Woodstock in the sixties. The pain she felt for him ran away as chill bumps fired on her arms. Her spine tingled, and she nearly lost her breath, and—

"What do you think?" His voice seemed distant, like he'd taken his own mental trip.

Coming back to reality, she looked at him. A tear dripped from her cheek.

They shared a smile, and she felt like she'd just seen his whole beautiful life in a glance. Did he know what she was experiencing?

Another silence followed. Very comfortable and knowing.

Something occurred to her. "I forgot to spit."

Otis grinned. "I've been forgetting to spit for many, many years." He pushed up and retrieved a steel spit bucket from a shelf. Setting it on the table between them, he said, "Just so we can stay sharp."

They spent ten minutes discussing the wine. Otis recalled his methods and the specific vintage, one that the critics had loved. Emilia was excited that she'd been able to get past the initial thoughts of a wine and dive deeper as Brooks had been teaching her. That's where the beauty was, well beyond the five senses. Somewhere deep into the ethereal was the truth in wine.

Otis opened up the wine from Red Mountain. "This," he said, "we don't spit. The trade calls this *The Lost Vintage*. Do you know of it?"

"Yes, sir." Emilia knew exactly what it was. Everyone on the mountain knew about the day two years ago when Henry Davidson had broken in and dumped out Otis's wine.

"Not much of this one left, but I think you deserve to taste it. You were a part of it, after all."

"Thank you," she said, wondering how she'd missed the wonders of wine while living here, like two ships passing in the night.

Otis took her glass, dumped the rest of her California vintage into the spit bucket, and poured her some of the new one. "It really was a wonderful year. Hotter than I would have liked, but I always say that. It was easy farming. By the time I reached the cellar, most of the wine had gone down the drain. We collected everything that was left and blended it together. Varieties from all over the property."

Emilia lifted it to her nose. Such a different experience from the previous wine. This one was far from hedonistic, but it was much fruitier and tantalizing. It begged to be sipped. The cinnamon and cherry notes were dazzling.

She took a long sip with her eyes closed.

It was perfection. Nothing she could or cared to put into words other than, "So freaking delicious."

Otis wasn't paying attention. She looked past the flickering candle and saw his eyes closed, his body still, his fist wrapped around the stem.

Knowing he was paying reverence to the wine, she did the same, returning to it fully. As the juice danced on her palate, she felt like she was melting into the earth, becoming one with the land. Beyond the taste descriptors that only seemed to oversimplify things, she found that this wine tasted like Red Mountain. The marrow of it. She'd not had much experience tasting wines from around the world, but she knew, without a doubt, that she could have identified this wine from hundreds of others. This bottle had come from where she lived. From her home. The pride of that fact rose from the ground and up her legs.

She looked back at Otis, wanting to share all these erupting thoughts and feelings.

His eyes were still closed. This man had done it. He'd mastered his craft by taking himself out of it, by paying homage to his land and bottling the truest sense of it.

Emilia wondered if she'd ever get there. One thing was for sure, though. She wanted to try. She wanted to learn how to farm a wine with this much life, the absolute essence of it.

By the time they climbed back up the stairs, she was not only 100 percent positive that she was not returning to school, but she also knew beyond all doubt that she would work with wine the rest of her life.

THANK GOD FOR CASSEROLES

Margot couldn't believe she'd pulled off the gender reveal without a hitch. As she stood there at the door to the patio, watching this group of forty having so much fun, she reminded herself that she could do anything—with the help of frozen casseroles, that is.

Thank God for casseroles.

A handsome man clapped his hands and drew everyone's attention to the beautifully wrapped box in the grass. The crowd circled around it dutifully. A little girl with bright-green shoes reached to pull the bow. Margot looked at the mother with her bulging tummy and the father with his proud smile.

This was what life was all about. It was so easy to get caught up in the trivial things. Why worry so much about losing A/C or early and late checkouts? For that matter, why worry about a future step-daughter who didn't like her? Life could be worse! She reminded herself to stop sweating the small stuff and remember that she was living her dream and would soon be marrying the man she'd hoped to find since she was a high-school romantic.

The girl with a bow in her hair pulled back the ribbon on the box, and a lone blue balloon rose up into the air. She thrust up her hands and turned to her mom and dad. "I'm going to have a little brother!"

Margot joined the crowd in enthusiastic applause. Moments like these were exactly why she'd created Épiphanie.

Knowing she'd better check on Adriana and the crew, Margot slipped into the dining room, crossed into the lobby, and climbed the stairs. As she looked down the hall, she heard a little boy's laughter. Was that Zack? She followed the noise and found the cleaning cart holding open the door to one of the rooms.

It was definitely Zack's laughter. But someone else's too. That wasn't Carly, was it? Margot passed the cleaning cart and entered the hallway. Adriana was in the bathroom to the left, polishing the claw-foot tub.

"How's it going up here?" Margot asked her.

Adriana turned and then pointed toward the bedroom with a smile. "See for yourself."

Margot crept farther down the hallway and came around the corner quietly. Adriana followed her.

Carly was showing Zack how to make the bed. "Pull that side up, stinker. Not that high. Yep. Nope. Ah, there you go. Now see if you can straighten it some. See those creases?"

Zack straightened the sheet. "Did you know that my mom and Brooks never make their bed? I always make mine, but they don't do theirs."

Margot and Adriana smiled at each other but didn't dare interrupt the moment.

"Maybe you need to remind them," Carly said. "Or better yet, what if you made their bed every morning?"

Zack's jaw fell. "Are you crazy? No way, José. I'm the kid in the house."

Carly laughed as she made one last adjustment to the bed. "You know what I think? Grown-ups still have a lot to learn, don't they?"

Zack crossed his arms and nodded. "Got that right." The phrase had to be something he'd learned off a television show, and it was the

most adorable thing Margot had ever heard. She nearly fell to her knees watching this exchange. She wanted to freeze this moment and go grab Remi. He needed to see his daughter right now. Was this the real Carly?

Margot finally stepped into the room. "What's going on in here?"

Adriana was right behind her. "Zack Hernandez, did you just tell someone that I don't make my bed?"

The kids both grinned.

Carly set two pillows on the bed to finish up. "Actually, Zack just promised he'd make your bed every morning until he goes to college."

Zack whipped his head around. "I did not say that!"

"Just kidding." She threw a pillow at him.

He picked it up and threw it back. "Pillow fight!"

"No, no, Zack," Adriana said. "This is not your bedroom."

On just about any other day, Margot would have agreed with her. But today was different. She reached for one of the other pillows from the chair and swung it at Adriana, hitting her in the arm.

Adriana put her fists to her waist. "Okay, if that's how we're playing it. It's on."

All four of them erupted into laughter, and quite possibly the first pillow fight in the history of Épiphanie ensued.

∼

SEVERAL HOURS after his tasting with Emilia, as he and Joan moved the sheep to a new patch of grass, Otis noticed he had an extra kick in his step. The wine might have had something to do with it, but his elation was more about the hope he felt for Red Mountain's future. He'd seen a bit of his younger self in Emilia today, and he felt like the mountain might just be in safe hands after all.

The sheep had once again eaten everything down to the nubs in their current location, so it was time for a move. In order to keep their wooly friends occupied, Joan had dropped a fresh stack of hay down, and the sheep fought over it as she and Otis scrambled to set up the next perimeter.

"You know, Joan, I am a wild dog at heart, so I'm no stranger to the doghouse. But at some point, I would appreciate a proper chance at redemption."

It had been six days since the bike accident, and Joan was still angry with him despite his daily apologies and even a box of chocolates and a bouquet of long-stemmed yellow roses.

Several feet ahead of him, Joan plucked a section of portable fencing out of the ground and carefully guided the netting and poles to his open arm. "You know, I can't just turn my emotions off and on. You're difficult to live with sometimes."

No one knew that more than he did. "What if we went out to dinner tonight?"

She fed him the next section and broke into a smile. "You mean spend time together doing something other than farm chores? I'd love to. I'd like to go back to that sushi place. What's it called?"

"Ah, yes, Aki. What a wonderful idea. I'll even iron my shirt."

She flashed a smile. "*This* is the Otis I've been missing."

He showed his teeth. "I'm like a bowl of Padrón peppers. Every once in a while, you get a deliciously spicy one. But you must suffer through the others to find it."

"Well, my little bowl of Padróns, I'd be honored to go on a date with you."

"The honor would be mine."

Once they'd collected the fencing, Otis walked up to the corner of his land that backed up to Drink Flamingo. It had been weeks since the chemical drift incident, and he thankfully saw no evidence of spray damage. They'd had two good rains, so he felt confident that the sheep were now safe to mow this part of the property, which was terribly overgrown.

He glanced over to the construction site. How much longer must he endure the awful sound of nail guns and saws, the instruments of his enemy's growth?

He drew in a big breath and blew it out like he was extinguishing a wildfire.

Let it go, Otis. Let it go.

He went to work setting up the new perimeter while Joan moved the solar energizer and water containers. As she propped up the energizer with a rock to face the sun, she said, "I'm sorry I missed Emilia. How did she do today?"

Otis perked up. "She's got it, Joan. Not even old enough to drink, but you can see the fire in her eyes. I like how she talks about wine. No matter what happens here, it's lovely to know that Lacoda is in good hands."

"You see, Otis? It's not only you and the mountain."

"I know. I know. I'm a slow learner, but I get it. There will be others to pick up the flag."

"Yes, exactly."

Once everything had been set up, Otis stood by the opening he'd made in the fence, and Joan went to where the sheep were finishing up their hay. "Let's go, everyone," she said. "Time for a new piece of land. Lots of goodies up there to eat."

The sheep looked up as they chewed.

Otis had told Joan she should use a bell to train them to follow her, but she'd insisted they would follow her voice. And she was right.

"Up the hill we go, ladies and gentleman. Let's go."

Apparently trusting Joan, one brave sheep left his hay. Another sheep broke away and then they were all trotting after her.

Otis beamed. "Look at you," he whispered. "My girl."

Joan ran through the gap in the portable fencing, and the fifteen sheep followed. As the last of the animals entered their new setup, Otis closed off the fence. Once Joan climbed out, he turned on the energizer, electrifying the fence. The barrier wasn't as much to keep the sheep in as it was to keep the predators out.

If only Otis could fence in the whole mountain. He glanced over to his enemy's lair again. A man on the far side of Drink Flamingo was inspecting the fence exactly where Otis had cut out his door. The man pulled back the cut fencing. Otis was busted.

He cursed to himself, wishing he'd snuck back over there and ripped the antenna out of the ground, eliminating the above-ground evidence of the smart valve he'd installed.

Let it go, Otis. Let it go.

~

THAT EVENING, they gathered in the living area, and Margot and Carly told Remi and Jasper about their day.

"I'm sorry I didn't hear the phone ring," Jasper said. "I was playing music with Jake."

Remi had already apologized for not answering, either. He'd been on the tractor mowing.

"We didn't need you two," Margot said. "Carly and I had it under control. Right?"

Carly nodded from the chair to Margot's left. "Yeah, it wasn't so bad."

Margot wasn't sure what had happened, but it seemed that Carly had found a little happiness through being needed. Who didn't need to feel needed?

As Margot pulled the cork out of a bottle of Aqualini cabernet sauvignon, she said to Remi, "I think the kids deserve a glass of wine tonight. How does that sound?"

"I totally agree," Remi said. "Heck, they can have two as far as I'm concerned. Sounds like you dodged a bullet today."

He hadn't been so chipper since Carly's arrival. "We really did. I've had some challenges in the past couple of years, but this one ranks at the top."

Margot filled four glasses and divvied them out. Raising her glass to Carly, she offered a toast. "To being there for family. I really appreciate your help."

Carly smiled.

The following clink of crystal was a sound that had needed to be heard so badly in the house. It wasn't just a toast. It was a sound that rang the bell of unity, a sound that marked the true beginning of this family of four.

What brought it all home was the look on Remi's face as they each sipped their wine. Sitting in front of her was the exact man she'd fallen in love with—and he was on his way back from the dead.

32

GOT A LIGHT?

L ater, Margot sat with Remi on the couch, watching a *Hallmark* movie. His protective arm was around her, and she felt like she was exactly where she should be. Philippe and Henri were curled up next to each other on the rug. Jasper had gone to Emilia's house, and Carly was upstairs watching television in her room.

"Is this one up for an Oscar?" Remi asked. "What's it called again?"

"*King of Hearts.*"

"That's right. I'm surprised they couldn't get Leonardo DiCaprio or Zac Efron. What a well-written script. Was this the guy who wrote *The English Patient*?"

Margot turned to Remi. His pearly whites shined back. She asked, "Is this going to happen every time we watch a Hallmark movie together?"

"Only if you continue to pick such winners. This wasn't made for TV, was it? It would have crushed in the box office."

They shared a smile and a kiss. It felt wonderful to be joking around again after weeks of gloom. All they'd needed was a little sign of hope to bring back the feelings of the old days.

She poked him. "By the way, your daughter is a really funny and sweet girl. I don't know why she hides it. I so wish you could have seen her with Zack today."

"Me, too," he admitted. "Well, maybe she's coming around."

"If today is any indication, I'd say she is."

They went back to watching the show, and Remi hopped back into making fun of her movie. What Margot might never admit was that her Hallmark movies were a million times more fun to watch when he was pulling his *Mystery Science Theater 3000* routine.

"What's so funny?" Carly asked after coming down the stairs.

Margot paused the movie. "Your dad loves to make fun of Hallmark. Come join us if you'd like. He's almost as entertaining as the movie."

"Carly understands my humor more than anyone," Remi said. "Isn't that right?"

She pulled the cellophane off a new pack of smokes. "I appreciate your effort. Let's put it that way."

Remi acted like he'd been stabbed in the chest. "Ouch, that hurts."

Carly flashed a sinister smile and glanced at Margot. "I'm watching something upstairs, but thanks. I'm just grabbing a smoke."

As Carly left, Margot turned to Remi. "That almost felt like normal family behavior."

"It did, didn't it? I just don't understand. Is it really that simple? One good day and everything's better?"

"I'm not sure anything is that simple, but maybe today was a turning point." Margot started to get up. "Would you mind if I go chat with her a second? I just want to thank her again and...I don't know. Something's telling me to pop my head out and see if she feels like talking."

"Please do. I will stare at this frozen screen and ruminate over the various themes being explored by this masterpiece of a film."

Margot dipped her chin. "That's enough. Feel free to put on *SportsCenter* if you'd like."

He reached for the remote like it was an EpiPen and he was the victim of a deadly allergic reaction. "I might just check a few scores."

"Right..." She blew him a kiss. "I'll be right back."

Poking her head out the door, Margot asked Carly, "Can I turn a light on for you?"

Carly turned from her seat on the steps. "No, I like to look at the stars."

Margot raised her head to the big sky night. "They are wonderful, aren't they? Can't get this view in a big city."

"Nope."

Margot felt slightly nervous but didn't want to miss a moment to connect. "Mind if I join you?"

"I'm not sure you're cut out for smoking," Carly said.

"No, no. I think I proved how uncool I was the last time." Margot sat down on the same brick step but several feet away. The inn was lit up and gorgeous on the other side of the property. Thankfully, it also blocked any view of the new Drink Flamingo site.

"I just wanted to thank you again," Margot said.

"It's really not that big of a deal. I feel like I'm starting to drown in your thanks."

"That would be a good way to go, wouldn't it? To drown in thanks?" Margot didn't wait to see if her joke hit home. She said, "It is a big deal, Carly. It means a lot to me and your dad that you'd step in to help."

Margot had heard that the Japanese were very comfortable sitting in silence and that they believed you should speak only if you have something important to say. Margot tapped into their culture as she breathed in a full minute of silence.

It was in the quiet that an authentic curiosity arose. "Have you talked to your mom lately?"

Carly shook her head. "Not in a few days. Why do you ask?"

Margot straightened. "Can I admit something to you?"

"I guess so."

Here goes, Margot thought. *No turning back now.* "It's always been in the back of my mind that Remi might fall in love with her again.

Or go back to her. And I sometimes punish him for it for no reason at all."

Carly blew out a puff of smoke with a snide chuckle. "I don't think you have anything to worry about. I tried for a long time to get them back together, and it just kept getting worse. I'm not sure they were ever a good match."

Though she felt bad for Carly, Margot was pleased to hear her take. "She's really beautiful, but what's she like? Are you more like Remi or your mom?"

"I guess more like my dad. Well...I can be a bitch, like my mom."

"You hide it so well, though," Margot said, letting the words slip out before she could stop herself. "I would have never known."

Carly turned to Margot. "I don't mean to be that way to you. It's just..." She stopped and took a puff.

"It's just what?"

Carly met her eyes again. "Nothing."

"Oh, no, Carly. I'm not letting you off the hook. This is a safe space. You can say whatever you want. It's just me and a billion stars."

Her future stepdaughter flicked an ash. "You just seem, like, kind of fake half the time."

"Okay, this just got real," Margot said, breathing through the comment. At least, they were getting somewhere. "Tell me what you mean by that."

"Well, let's see. Is there anything more important to you than losing weight and fitting into that stupid dress and having the *perfect* wedding?"

Margot felt the sting of that one. "Maybe I do need a cigarette."

As Carly reached for the pack, Margot waved her off. "Just kidding."

She thought about what she might say next and then, "Yes, there are a lot more important things to me than getting into that dress and having a wonderful wedding. Jasper. You and Remi and your relationship. All the animals down in the sanctuary. The inn. It just so happens that fitting into the dress seems like the biggest challenge of all of those other things."

"Why does it even matter? Who cares? And why go around acting like everything is all right all the time?"

"Is that what it seems like?" Margot asked.

"Totally. You're living in la-la land."

The gloves were off. Margot intended to tread carefully, but if they were going to build some sort of foundation with honesty, she had things to say. "Okay, fair enough. You make some good points. Let me ask you. Why do you go around hiding in that hoodie? You act like the whole world has done you wrong. Guess what? You're not the only one whose parents got a divorce and found new love. In fact, last time I heard, more than half of marriages end in divorce. Look at Jasper. He's not moping around like some sort of victim."

Carly stared at her own feet.

Margot caught herself from going on, knowing she was pushing this teen really hard, and said, "Sorry. I obviously have had some stuff penned up inside that needed to get out. I guess we both did."

"I'm just surprised to hear you say something meaningful," Carly admitted.

"I've come a long way from the woman I used to be,' Margot said, realizing that maybe Carly did best with tough love. "But I'm still a work in progress. No one knows that more than I do." Margot thought back to the woman she had been in Vermont.

Carly put out her cigarette. "You need to get over the weight thing. Who cares?"

"Easy for you to say. I've been struggling with my weight all my life."

"If you need things to worry about, there is way worse shit out there to get hung up on."

"Fair enough. So you hate me because I want to be skinny on the day that I marry your father? That's all this is?"

Carly thought about it. "I don't hate you, but you definitely drive me crazy sometimes."

"I get it," Margot said. "My dad died when I was in my twenties, while I was living and acting in New York. And my mom wasted no time in dating again. I was so angry about it. She even had the nerve to bring…"

"That's what it is," Carly said, a light bulb apparently going off. "I guess it just occurred to me. You're an actor, and you haven't stopped acting. I feel like my dad doesn't even know who he's marrying. I *definitely* don't know who you are."

Margot couldn't remember being so beat up in many years. At the same time, it felt like she needed a little tough love too. "I guess it just comes down to my trying to make you like me—an effort that's obviously not working."

"I don't like fake."

"Maybe not, but you're a pretty good actor yourself, hiding behind all your problems, acting like the world is against you. I think your problem is that you're worried your mom and dad are moving on without you."

"That might be part of it, but it's not that simple."

"Explain it to me then."

Carly took a moment to consider her response. "It's not that I think my mom is moving on. It's just that the person she is with…her boyfriend…just sucks. He walks all over her, and she doesn't even realize it. I don't want to be around that. And then look at you guys and your perfect life up here. You and your cooking, and your inn, and the gardening. What do you not do?" She rolled her eyes. "And of course, you have the perfect son. I don't exactly fit in here. I don't fit in anywhere."

Margot scooted toward Carly. "Who paid you to call me the perfect wife and mom? I'll double it if you'll whisper that into my ear every morning."

Carly slowly rolled the wheel on her lighter, making a series of clicking sounds.

"First of all, I'm so far from perfect, and I'm not talking about my body. More importantly, you are a part of this family. How much you participate is up to you, but you will be my daughter, and I'm going to love you as such. You do fit in. That's the great thing about everyone on this mountain. We all fit in. And believe me: we like having you here."

"Yeah, right. My dad wants me to go to school. I think that's his way of getting rid of me."

"Let me tell you something about your father. He loves you more than anyone else in the world. Even more than me."

Carly suddenly burst into tears, and Margot felt like the stars were dropping around her. She moved closer and wrapped an arm around her. To Margot's surprise, Carly didn't push her away.

"I'm never going to replace your mom," Margot said. "I just want to love your dad—and you too, if you'll let me. My choice to marry Remi was also a choice to have you in my life. In fact, he was very specific in saying that he would not stop trying to get you back. And when he did, I'd have to accept you as my own."

"He said that?"

"He said exactly that." Though this was one of the hardest conversations Margot had ever had, she felt more clear-headed and present than she'd been in a long time.

"I'll make a deal with you," Margot said.

Carly wiped her eyes. "What's that?"

"I'll stop obsessing over my weight and try to be more real if you'll try a little harder to be a part of this family and give your dad a fair shot. Look, I want you to like me, but I can't force you to, but it's time to give your dad another chance. You don't want to spend the rest of your life regretting how you're treating him. Or your mom, for that matter. Life's too short."

Carly lit up another cigarette.

"Even shorter if you don't quit smoking those things, but that's for another time."

Carly smirked. "Smoking does help you lose weight."

Margot shook her head. "I'd like to think there are better ways to get in shape."

"Possibly. So does this mean I won't have to suffer through your dieting any longer?"

That was a big promise, and Margot wouldn't make it unless she meant it. She took a moment to imagine her wedding day in another dress.

Carly said, "Yeah, I didn't think so."

Margot sliced her hand through the air. "Oh, don't you challenge me. I'll rip that dress out of the closet and set it on fire."

"Yeah, right."

"You don't think I would?"

Carly flicked another ash. "Not a chance."

Margot crossed her arms and straightened. She thought about how much work she'd already put into squeezing into it. Then she thought about how stupid the entire idea was, a woman in her forties hanging her happiness on a number on a scale. Who was she losing weight for anyway? Why did it even matter? The last few weeks of not eating had been awful—and for what? How many times had Remi told her he liked her just the way she was?

Enough of these thoughts!

"I'll up the ante," Margot said. "I'll burn my dress right this instant if you'll burn your hoodie."

Carly looked down at her black hoodie. "I know you're not serious."

"Test me."

A smile played at Carly's lips as she produced her lighter. "I have a light."

33

ARE YOU SURE ABOUT THIS?

Remi turned from his sports show. "You were out there a long time. Everything okay?"

"It's better than okay," Margot admitted. "We're having a little girl time. I'm going back out in just a minute."

With incredible determination, Margot ran up the stairs and into her room. As she pulled open the closet, the antique white dress made of French lace seemed to stare back at her, almost taunting her.

You wouldn't dare...

"Oh, wouldn't I?" Margot said, reaching for the hanger. "You can take your size eight and shove it up my curvy, beautiful butt."

Holding up the dress, she admired it one last time. The form-fitting elegance, the tasteful plunging neckline of lace flowers. She'd imagined wearing a crown of woven wildflowers to match. Letting go of what she'd envisioned, she said, "It would have been nice, but it wouldn't have been me." Carly was right.

Folding up the size eight in her arms, she went back down the steps. Finding a small tin of lighter fuel in the pantry, she snuck past Remi toward the door. This was a girls' moment. "Don't mind us," she said as she slipped out.

Carly was still sitting on the porch. "I didn't think you'd actually bring it down."

"Oh, I'm full of surprises. I would have looked gorgeous in this thing, but you're right. It wouldn't have been me." She held up the dress and tossed it onto the driveway. "Do you know how much this useless piece of fabric has tormented me?"

She pointed at Carly's hoodie. "Almost as much as that hoodie. Let's go. I'm desperate to see that thing go up in flames."

Carly snickered as she pulled it off.

"You have such a great laugh," Margot said. "Today was the first time I heard it. Now give me a light."

Carly tossed her hoodie on top of the wedding dress and handed Margot the lighter. "I'll let you do the honors."

Margot doused the pile with lighter fluid. "It's just amazing how much value we women put on clothes and what we look like in them. I'm done. Enough worrying about what other people think. Don't get me wrong, I'm still going to shop every chance I get. But I'm done. No more trying to look like women on television. I'm so done faking it. I'll wear polka dots to my wedding if I want to."

Margot looked at Carly. "Do you have anything to add?"

Carly blushed. "This feels kind of stupid, doesn't it?"

"Not at all. Let's go. What do you have to say?" Margot was on a mission and couldn't wait to see that darn dress on fire.

"I promise I'll try harder," Carly finally said.

Margot lifted up the lighter. "That's all any of us can do, right?" She lit the flame and bent down toward the dress. "Your father is going to kill me."

"I think he'll be all right."

This ritual was about so much more than the dress; it was a cleansing.

"Mother Earth," Margot started, "please forgive me. I'll plant a hundred trees to make up for it."

She lit the edge, and the dress ignited, burning much faster than she'd expected. The hoodie caught next, and within several seconds, a huge flame rose up into the air as the materials curled into ashes.

Margot couldn't recall ever feeling more fulfilled. She glanced over at Carly, who looked possessed with life. They nodded at each other and turned back to the flames.

Remi's voice came from behind them. "What in the world are you two doing?"

Margot pulled Carly in and put an arm around her. As they both turned to face Remi, she said, "We're burning all the bullshit."

He looked back at the fire and smiled. "I don't know what that means, but I think I like it."

~

MARGOT WAS SITTING by the unlit fireplace when Remi came down the next morning in his robe and slippers. One of her favorite brown hens sat in her lap. She'd named her Elphaba from the character in *Wicked*. Cannonball Adderley was playing from the speakers in the ceiling.

Philippe and Henri, who had been staring at Elphaba jealously from the floor, raced to Remi's side.

"House chickens," he said, petting the dogs. "We have house chickens now. Fellas, I think she's finally lost it."

Margot stroked the chicken's back. "She wanted to come spend some time with her mama."

"That is one lucky bird." He looked at her coffee cup. "Can I get you a refill?"

"Sure." As he turned to the kitchen, she called out, "I have something I want to read to you."

"Oh, yeah, what's that?"

"You'll see."

Once he'd topped off her coffee, he sat in the seat beside her. "That's good coffee this morning."

"I put a little extra love into it." Still stroking her hen, she set down her coffee and picked up a piece of paper she'd printed out. "I want you to know, Remi, that I've been a little lost lately. Maybe for a long time. That ends today, though. I'm not going to joke about Margot 2.0 and 3.0. It's not like that; it's much more than a new me. It's the real me. Everything seems so clear now."

Remi grunted. "Dare I say you've had an...*epiphany*?"

Margot hit him. "Why didn't I think of that? That's exactly it." She reached for the piece of paper on the table. "So I woke up and raced down to see if I could find this little bit of writing. Do you mind if I read the whole thing?"

He rested his mug down on his thigh. "Please."

She straightened the paper and read, "I don't know what kind of woman I'm looking for. All that I do know is she's out there. I've spent my life looking for love in all the wrong places. I've spent most of my life misunderstanding love. Not the love that I have for my daughter. I do understand that love. I mean the kind of love that you share between partners. After a lifetime of doing it wrong, I finally know what love means. Love is something we do as an offering, expecting nothing in return. Love requires trust. Love takes everything you have. Love is *not* a lusty affair. Love is a commitment beyond any others, an action that takes every ounce of effort you have. I'm looking for a woman who will allow me to love her with everything I have."

Margot looked at the man she'd chosen to love for the rest of her life. "Do you know who wrote that?"

"I did. That was my *Match.com* profile."

"Yeah." She reached for his hand. "From this moment forward, I'm going to be that woman. I don't know why I've been so afraid to let myself go, and I don't know why I've ever doubted you...but no more. You have all of me." She looked down at her body and smirked. "And I mean all of me."

"You don't think I know that, Margot? I've never doubted you for a moment, and I definitely never gave up on you."

She let go of his hand. "Thank you."

They sipped their coffee together and laughed and fell back into being the couple they used to be.

When Jasper came down, he sat at his Steinway and filled the house with beautiful sounds. Margot loved that he could say more with his music than anyone could say with words, and each note seemed to tickle her soul.

Carly followed shortly after. "Good morning, everyone." She approached her father and kissed his head. Margot couldn't help noticing Carly's head was free of the hoodie and any other material. Her long brown hair even appeared to be washed.

"You're up early," he said.

She knelt down to say hi to the dogs. "If I'm not too late, I thought I'd cook breakfast for everyone."

"Not too late at all," Remi said in shock.

Margot tried not to make a big deal out of the offer and said casually, "Yeah, I'm starved. Haven't eaten in weeks."

As her future stepdaughter turned to the kitchen, Margot realized how similar they were. Carly wanted her dad back in her life and to know that she never wanted to feel abandoned by him again. In Margot's case, all she'd wanted was to know that Remi wasn't too good to be true and that she hadn't made up this fairy tale in her head. In these past hours of self-clarity, it had become evident that Margot's lack of faith in him was her own insecurities coming to life. He wasn't returning to his ex-wife, nor did he have any skeletons in the closet.

Like Carly, all Margot wanted was to know he would hold her tight and never let her go.

Looking back at the man she loved so intensely, she took his hand. Why had she ever doubted him? He was one of the good ones, and for some wild reason, he'd decided that Margot was his soul mate.

Carly's obvious change of heart had hit him hard. He was fighting tears. Margot wanted to tell him to let them fall. He'd just gotten his daughter back. There still might be some bumps along the way, but he'd been given a second chance. What could be better than that?

Forget the past. Forget the fear of the unknown. Forget the fear of what she looked like. Margot's old self was as much in ashes as the gown and hoodie in the driveway.

With her love spilling over for her new family, she thought a good unwavering hug was all any of them needed, and Margot decided right then and there that she'd never let any of them go.

34

WE NEED TO TALK

One month later, Joan told Otis, "We need to talk."

It was July 15, and Otis's mind was focused on the coming harvest. The berries would change colors soon, and before he knew it, he'd be making the rounds, testing and sampling the ripening grapes, working to choose the perfect day and hour to harvest. The fall would go by in a flash as fermentations filled his cellar, and he needed to prepare for the frenzy.

As he heard her words, however, harvest lost its prominence.

Joan had made him breakfast, as if breakups were best served with a healthy meal. More specifically, the worst breakup of his life served with a quinoa-crusted quiche with broccoli, peppers, and onions.

It was a great quiche. It could have used some bacon, but nevertheless, much more appetizing than the four words she whispered across the table.

We need to talk.

Otis pulled the fork out of his mouth and nearly spat the quiche back onto his plate. Were it possible to frown with his whole body, that's what he did. His shoulders collapsed, his lips fell, and his chin dropped. What kind of fool would let a woman like Joan go?

He'd seen it a mile away, too. As those four words seemed to paralyze his body, he scolded himself for not taking her subtle threats seriously. Like watching a meteor head toward earth from a million miles away, he'd known his world was coming to an end. He'd watched her pull away from him. He'd listened to her as she kindly urged him to give her more attention, to stop biting down like a bulldog on his problems—many of which he couldn't affect anyway.

He pulled off his reading glasses and set them on the table next to the newspaper he'd been working his way through. Nothing he'd read mattered now. The only headline in his world was: *Otis Till is a damn idiot.*

Like a tsunami that came out of nowhere, a sadness rose high and crashed over him. The world had given him a second chance after Rebecca. Never had he thought he would love again after losing her. Joan had come in and given him the special gift of breathing life back into an old man's crusty body. He'd found a reason to live again, a much stronger one than those damn vines out there that seemed to be more trouble than they were worth.

He finally turned to her. "I hate myself for not loving you the way you deserve to be loved."

She looked away, thinking about his words. Then, locking eyes with him, she said, "Don't say that. This isn't just about you. You're obsessed with Harry Bellflour and his project. I've become obsessed over your obsession. We're dragging each other down."

"You're not dragging me down."

"I am, Otis. Listen to the way I speak to you. I've somehow turned into your mother, and that's not fair."

"I'm sure I deserve it. I'm acting like a child."

"I'm worried about you," she said. "Your blood pressure is through the roof. You look ten years older. You're sneaking out in the middle of the night to do things that I suspect are against the law. And if you're not careful, your wines will start to suffer."

Otis dropped his head. "I'm trying. I swear to you."

"I know you are, and I am too. But I think being together might keep us both from getting healthy. I'm not pointing fingers. Please know that."

Nodding, he looked at a picture of his two boys in front of him on the wall. They would have loved Joan, and they would have been beyond disappointed in him for so many reasons. Even Rebecca would shake her head.

The idea that losing Joan might be because of Harry Bellflour and Drink Flamingo crushed him. He only knew of one thing to do. "I'll put the vineyard up for sale tomorrow. We'll leave this place and never come back."

Joan shook her head ever so slightly. "I would never ask that of you, and running away isn't the answer. It's like I've told you before. Even if Drink Flamingo didn't exist, you'd find another obstacle to occupy your mind. That's how you deal with the pain that's eating you up inside. And I'm clearly dealing with my own pain by trying to solve your problems for you."

"Tell me what to do then. I'm out of answers."

"That's just it. I don't need to be telling you what to do. I can't help you."

"Of course, you can."

As if she had no fight left, she said, "You know what I think it is? We need to address what's troubling us deep down. For me, it's not your actions. It's my inability to accept them. For you, it's not Harry Bellflour and his cabernet."

And his pinotage, Otis thought but chose not to say it out loud. Now was not a good time for humor.

"It wasn't even Henry Davidson that was the real problem," she said, referring to the man who'd shot her.

"Then what is it?"

"You fear losing the people and things you love."

Otis thought about her assertion. "Well, I'm certainly afraid of losing you."

"I think it's the mountain you're afraid of losing right now."

~

BROOKS REACHED for the top button of Adriana's lavender housekeeping uniform. She drew in a breath as he undid it, revealing more of her soft dark skin. Another button and her uniform began to separate.

He looked up into her brown eyes. "I don't want to wait this long again."

"Then don't," she murmured.

He couldn't remember the last time they'd slept together, but it had been weeks for sure.

When she was eager for him, she showed it well, and at this very moment, he knew she wanted him as badly as he wanted her. He touched and kissed her scars and ever so gently kissed her neck. She gave in to him, opening up and letting go.

Zack was at the Foresters' for a sleepover with Luca, and they had the house to themselves. Brooks had planned a candlelit dinner and maybe a bottle of wine if she'd been interested, but the moment she'd walked in from work, everything had fallen into slow motion. He'd reached for her hand and led her up the stairs. There weren't many moments like these with a seven-year-old in the house. Knowing Zack would be gone, Brooks had been thinking all day about having Adriana to himself.

Unable to contain himself any longer, he untied the knot of her belt, and her dress fell completely open. His heart raced, and he wanted to lift her up and set her on the bed, but he didn't want to lose these precious minutes. Something about her standing there was the most tempting sight he'd ever seen.

Ever so slowly, he pulled the uniform from her shoulders, and she shimmied out. As the uniform fell to the floor, he slowly moved his eyes from her face down her neck and to the delicate white lace.

The rest of her clothes fell to the floor, and she took over, undressing him just as slowly, moaning in his ear as she reached between his legs.

They stood naked, pressing against each other, and Brooks felt like their bodies were made to fit together. He lifted her up by her thighs and set her onto the bed and made love to her, a playful sort of love with whispers and laughter.

Afterward, he cuddled up behind her and put his hand on her naked thigh. "Where did you learn to do that thing with your teeth?"

She nudged into him. "You liked it?"

"That would be an understatement. Same time tomorrow?"

She took his hand and placed it on her breast. "If you're lucky."

He pressed into her and softly kissed her back.

As much as he loved being here with her, as much as his libido erupted, something was still missing. It was almost too perfect that her back was to him at this moment. In a way, it felt like her back was always to him, like she was constantly walking away.

~

ADRIANA LOVED his arm around her. She loved the way he touched her. As much as she could feel a part of her pushing him away, she wanted nothing more than to be close to him. The problem was that she'd set out to confess that she'd made the decision to move to Florida. She'd ended up sleeping with him instead.

Perhaps she knew deep down that he'd never leave Red Mountain, so she was putting off what was effectively the end of their relationship. She hated how awful she'd been to him lately and wouldn't blame him for staying. What she wanted to tell him—no matter how weak it sounded—was that she couldn't help the way she felt inside. Her anxiety was off the charts. Between the nightmares and the fear of being a terrible mother and the *fact* of being a terrible girlfriend, Adriana felt like she was suffocating.

Was it any wonder that Zack was acting up? Children can sense when their parents are struggling—even when their parents go out of their way to pretend that things are fine. This is why they had to go to Florida. She had to get farther away from Michael. She wasn't a fool. In this day and age, it was almost impossible to hide from someone, but at least he wouldn't know exactly where they were. Besides, Adriana didn't like driving up to Épiphanie every day and seeing

Margot's house, where Michael had attacked them. A fresh start might be the only thing that could heal her. Maybe there would be no nightmares in Florida.

But how could she possibly ask Brooks to move with them? She didn't want to put that burden on him. He had enough on his plate with work right now. Who could possibly want to be with her right now anyway? Adriana hated being in her own skin and could only imagine how miserable she was to be around. She truly loved Brooks, but she was feeling increasingly incapable of reciprocating. Maybe Mary was right when she'd said those words through the baby monitor.

Adriana held Brooks's hand on her breast and wiggled her bottom into him, as if that were the same as telling him the truth.

35

THE FLAGSHIP TAKES A NAME

Harry Bellflour woke up with a terrible headache. He'd suffered through yet another sleepless night of tossing and turning and sweating. Was it the wine? He'd only had a couple of bottles. Pushing himself up, he limped to the bathroom, feeling a tightness in his legs. As he relieved himself, he ran over the speech he would be giving later as he announced the name of Drink Flamingo's flagship winery and pulled back the tarp on their new sign.

His idea of the social media campaign to find a name was nothing short of genius. Not only had it garnered some wonderful media and consumer exposure, but the campaign had landed the perfect name. He smirked as he saw the sign in his mind's eye. The name was just controversial enough to cause a stir, and Bellflour was *all* about causing a stir.

Descending the stairs in his boxers, he saw the coffeemaker timer hadn't worked. Cursing, he pushed the button. It was supposed to be ready for him by seven. He switched on the news, pulled a bottle of orange juice out of the fridge, and sat at the kitchen counter. As the coffee brewed and the kitchen filled with the aroma of the morning, Bellflour sipped his orange juice and scrolled through his emails.

"Bastards," he said, seeing a note from one of the board members. They wanted more updates on the project. He'd been sending them weekly. Wasn't that enough? Hadn't he earned their trust by now?

Another swig of OJ. More emails asking things of him. Was he the only one in the company who got anything done? He was glad to see his supplier had found some very nice pink umbrellas for the pool. He approved them and kept going, working through all the details that only he knew how to do. Everyone in the company loved having meetings, setting action items to follow up on later. Bellflour was a fucking action item!

He drank his coffee as he read the latest wine news on his iPad. A winemaker in Napa had been arrested for tax evasion. A worker had been injured in a tractor accident in Dundee, Oregon. A new AVA had been approved in Paso Robles. He worked his way to the national news. The president. More taxes.

Bellflour slowly enjoyed the last sips of coffee as he knew what he had to do next. Once he'd put his mug in the dishwasher, he sat down on the living room rug to follow his new routine. Thirty push-ups and thirty sit-ups. He made it to ten push-ups before he had to drop to his knees. At thirty, his arms burned. But he made it. Bellflour wasn't the kind of man who made a promise that he didn't keep, especially to himself. He rolled to his back and knocked out the sit-ups. The last ones barely counted, but at least, he'd gone through the motions. That counted for something.

Standing, he walked to the windows overlooking the highway and Red Mountain beyond. What a long two years it had been, and he was finally there. Something about announcing the name today felt like a major milestone. An endcap.

Nothing could stop him now.

∾

Two days since she'd had her talk with Otis, and Joan was still there. He'd been working hard to be a better partner, and he sure as hell didn't want to let her go. In fact, he'd quit at three o'clock the day

before and cooked dinner. A healthy dinner to boot. They'd sat
together listening to the London Symphony Orchestra and talking
about another trip—a redo, as Otis liked to call it. Their trip around
the world last year had barely counted as a vacation at all, as he'd
spent the entire time worrying about Harry Bellflour's initial vision
for Drink Flamingo by the highway.

Otis liked the idea of a redo and had brought up the idea again in
the morning while Joan was doing her morning stretches. They were
on the back deck looking west toward Mount Adams. Having
declined her invitation to stretch, Otis sat in a chair with his legs
crossed. That's about as limber as he desired to be.

As she leaned down and reached well beyond her toes, he said,
"You've just about recovered from the bullet, haven't you? I wonder if
you could kiss your feet."

She smiled from down on the mat. "I'm not quite there."

When she sat back up, she twisted left and looked up at him. "You
always talk about going to Europe for a vacation. There are other
places in the world."

"I've had enough of Asia for a while," he said. "It was fine, but I
want to be closer to the vineyards."

"Otis, your *only* idea of a vacation is to eat and drink your way
through Europe."

"What's wrong with that?" He noticed he'd made his coffee particularly strong this morning.

Going for another stretch, she said, "Believe me: I enjoy France
and Italy just as much as you do, but there is more to the world than
vines and wines."

"Here we go again," he said, trying not to think about the Drink
Flamingo press conference today. He couldn't dare let his mind
wander in that direction, or she'd know it in an instant. "Please tell
me. What would be more fun than a couple of weeks in Beaune
exploring menus and Grand Crus?"

"As much fun as that would be, I can think of a few things. What
about joining a research boat to Antarctica? Or bungee jumping in
Australia?"

Otis scoffed. "Are you mad? You want to know what I would look like bungee jumping?"

"Desperately."

"Well, I can tell you. Picture an old man dropping from the sky with a rubber band dangling from his leg."

She closed her eyes. "I see your tweed cap preceding you. Okay."

"Now watch as the rubber band tightens." Otis could see it himself. "Yep, there I went, broken to pieces. See my legs go back up in the air and the rest of me still falling?"

They both laughed at the image.

She turned to him. "I see a big fat smile on your grumpy face. Who cares where the rest of you went?"

Otis had an idea. "How about we go back to South Africa? I've been attracted to pinotage lately."

She looked at him strangely. "I seem to remember you saying you wouldn't urinate on a pinotage vineyard."

He shrugged. "I suppose things change. I've taken to the variety. Besides, while we're down there, we could surf giant waves among great white sharks. Shoot, we could even stop by North Africa so you could take a few poachers to justice while we're at it."

Joan rolled over and lifted her legs in the air. Then she pressed up into a handstand.

"Look at you, woman. That's incredible."

"Wanna try?"

"Will you quit trying to push your ballistic holistics on me? You know darn well I can't pull off that nonsense."

"You know what I really want to do?" she asked, still upside down.

"I'm dying to hear. Sail around the world on a twenty-foot skiff? Scuba dive down to the abyss? Fly over the Bermuda Triangle?"

"You're being absurd."

"Only because it's called for, my dear."

She lowered herself down with ease. "We Americans always forget our own country. We just so happen to have some of the most wonderful sites in the world right here at home. People from other countries actually come to see what we have to offer. What if we bought an RV and visited every single state?"

Oh, here she goes. Somehow, she'd just escalated a little two-week jaunt into an entire year of traveling.

"And what about my wine?" He hated to bring up wine again, but it was a real concern. Winemakers can't take a year off.

"It must be so frustrating to be tied to a piece of land for eight months out of the year," she said. "Take a year off. Let's see what happens. You can travel with a little bonsai tree on the dash of your RV. Just to keep farming close to you."

"Is that what you think I do? You can't bottle bonsai juice."

No matter how hard Otis focused on the conversation at hand, he still couldn't shake the idea of journalists surrounding Bellflour as he pulled back the tarp on the sign. He'd decided to have Eli record the conference, so Otis wouldn't have to attend in person.

~

Harry Bellflour loved the spotlight. He stood on one side of the ten-foot-long sign that was covered with a large black tarp. He was wearing a crisp pink button-down and khaki pants. His sleeves were rolled up, showing his watch and gold bracelet. He'd even had his neck cleaned up by the barber the day before.

A crowd of maybe fifty people were gathered around him, including journalists from as far away as Seattle. He had a cracker-jack PR team that had a keen ability to get the media interested in their goings-on. Ten microphones dangled in front of him, and three video cameras pointed at him.

Looking down Otis Till's driveway, Bellflour was disappointed not to see the old grump stopping by for the announcement. He would have loved to have seen Otis's shocked face as he looked at the sign for the first time. Bellflour was sure both the sign and the name would be Otis's worst nightmare.

"Why don't we get started?" he said, flashing a smile he'd practiced earlier in the mirror. He waited until everyone was quiet to continue.

Rubbing his hands together, he said, "As many of you know, we've wanted to be a part of this mountain for a long time. As admittedly frustrated as I was by last year's struggles, it seems there were much bigger plans in store. We've spent a long time deliberating as to what we wanted to bring to Red Mountain, what we could offer and how we could put our best foot forward. Otis Till and the rest of the visionaries have done something very special with this place, and they've brought great acclaim to the wines. What we want to do is bring a little fun."

There it was. Fun. Stick to the message, Bellflour thought.

"When we started Drink Flamingo and first broke onto the national stage with our box wine, the idea was to bring wine to the people. I've never liked the stuffiness that came with wine. You all know what I'm talking about. The pretentious intimidation that scares off good people. We're not that. The entire vibe of a flamingo is good times. Yes, the wines we will make on Red Mountain in this beautiful facility that you see rising up behind me will be serious. They will be high-scoring modern masterpieces. But that doesn't mean we can't have a little fun while enjoying them. That's why you can expect a flamboyance of flamingos and lots of pink!"

He pulled at his shirt. "Real men wear pink, right?"

As always, the crowd laughed at his terrible cliché of a joke that he'd been using for years.

He waved a hand in the air as his vision came alive in his mind's eye. "We'll have huge parties, and I mean parties they'll hear about in Las Vegas. We'll have the best wine club you've ever seen, and our members will have access to our entire property: the pool, the cabanas, three hot tubs. We'll bring in live DJs from all the big cities. You will not want to miss it." He eyed one of the cameras directly and added, "Don't delay in visiting our website if you want to join our club. We have a finite number of spots, and the interest has been overwhelming."

Bellflour looked again to see if Otis might be popping his head up over the vines. He so wished he could be here. Gesturing behind him, Bellflour said, "Let's pull back this tarp and celebrate the most exciting winery to ever hit eastern Washington. We're not a stop on the wine trail. We're the end destination."

He reached for one side of the tarp. "Ladies and gentleman, I give you..."

The gasps and the click of cameras were music to his ears.

He tugged on the tarp until it broke free, revealing the sign. LED lights flashed pink and yellow.

As if he were announcing the next president of the United States, Bellflour exclaimed, "Château Smooth!"

$\sim$

"Château Smooth?"

Otis said the words like he'd just bitten into a rotten apple. He'd gone down into the cellar to listen to the announcement Eli had recorded.

"Château Smooth," he said again. He dropped his elbows to the old wooden table and buried his face in his hands. Still reeling from the name alone, He hadn't even pushed play yet.

Otis poured himself a neat glass of Del Bac whiskey and pushed the cork back into the bottle. He took a long breath, staring at his phone. Eli had warned him of the contents. The name was only the beginning. Taking a long swig, he pressed play.

Bellflour's voice sounded so damn proud and confident as he painted a picture of what was coming. Otis could hear the terrifying screams of the mountain. It was worse than he'd imagined. His heart ached with exhaustion and sadness as Bellflour detailed what sounded like a new property on South Beach.

Taking his glass of whiskey, Otis slung it to his side, and it shattered against the brick. This was it. Bellflour had won.

36

CHÂTEAU SMOOTH AND THE SMART VALVE

Now that the name of the project was on the tip of everyone's tongue, it was time to put some color down. Bellflour was sitting in the air conditioning of his Lexus a few hours after the press conference when the concrete mixers pulled up. Standing by a long line of orange tape that had cordoned off the area for paving, he waved the drivers down.

Everyone had doubted that he could pull off dyeing the driveway gold, but doubt was fuel to Bellflour. As it turned out, the idea wasn't that difficult to execute. After a few phone calls, he'd found someone who was eager to take his money, promising him that a gold-oxide dye and white Portland cement would do the trick. Expensive, but not impossible.

A few cheaper material choices elsewhere would make up for it. He'd learned a long time ago that any framing could be done with two-by-fours, and he'd angrily throw a finger at any contractor who demanded two-by-sixes. He wasn't trying to make a building that would stand a thousand years. One hundred or so would be fine.

"Wait till they get a load of this," Bellflour said, chewing on his cigar, looking at the mixers spinning the gold concrete.

One of the drivers pulled up beside him. "Good afternoon," he yelled over the sound of the big truck. "You're sure about this, right? No turning back once we get started."

Bellflour smiled. "It'll be the most beautiful driveway you've ever seen."

"Suit yourself."

Bellflour glanced at the gravel making up the U-driveway. By tomorrow, it would be a glittery gold. No, it wasn't going to be gaudy at all. Far beyond gaudy. That's why it would work. Just like the name Château Smooth, it was so over the damn top.

Bellflour walked around back. They'd finally finished up with the polycarbonate tile pool liner. It wouldn't be long before he'd be sitting his fat ass on a Pink Flamingo float with a Fro-gria in his hand and about twenty-five babes, or Flaminglets, sitting around him.

"Harry," someone called from down toward the vines. It was Steve, who was in charge of his wines when Andy, the Napa consultant, wasn't around. "Come take a look at this!"

"What you got?"

Harry pulled on his cigar and moved toward the vineyard. The vines were starting to pop out of the grow tubes. One or two more years, and they'd be the most famous vines in eastern Washington.

"What is it?"

Steve and another guy were both on their knees with a saw and shovel. "You know anything about putting in a smart valve? We found this antenna sticking out of the ground. I called Andy, and he didn't know anything about it."

Bellflour looked down at the valve a couple of feet into the hole. "I don't either. Why the hell would it be there?"

"Somebody could be messing with you. That's the only thing we can figure. I ran this irrigation myself just a few weeks ago. I've got all my controls up near the pool."

Steve didn't need to say another word. Bellflour looked across the property and through the fence to Otis Till's winery.

It just so happened that Otis was pulling out of his driveway in his truck.

Bellflour pointed. "I bet that son of a bitch is behind it."

~

OTIS KNEW he'd have to see it sooner or later, that damn sign. He was pulling out of his driveway and riding toward Sunset Road when he saw Bellflour pointing at him from the Drink Flamingo vineyard.

"Oh, dear God," he said, wishing he'd already built the wall. "Will I have to see his smug face every time I drive by?"

He extended his middle finger in a neighborly gesture and then reached for the radio knob, turning up the classical music on NPR.

As he drove past the McMansion, he saw two mixers pouring concrete along the U-driveway. Men were following the pours with hand trowels, smoothing it out. Otis wouldn't have thought much of it as he'd been watching this construction site for months now, but the color of the concrete caught his eye as he drew closer.

"That's not gold, is it?" Otis said to himself.

It sure as hell was.

Then he saw the sign everyone was talking about. Hanging a right on Sunset Road, he passed right by it, and the hideous pink-and-black sign wasn't as Eli had described. It was infinitely worse. It was as if Bellflour had plucked it right off the Vegas strip. Flashing pink-and-yellow lights lit up in a wave around the border. In huge pink letters, it read: *Welcome to Château Smooth.* Above the words was their new logo, a pink flamingo smoking a cigar.

A fury filled Otis, and he suddenly had an urge to find a bat and smash the thing to pieces. He might have been having a bit of fun with the smart valve and the pinotage, but this sign was a direct attack on Red Mountain. Wondering if he had a big enough tool in his truck to tear the sign apart, he slid to a stop and switched off the radio.

Not in his wildest dreams could he have come up with something less appealing, something that would insult this mountain more. The idea of the theme park by the highway with the lazy river and the RVs and the putt-putt—that all seemed like nothing compared to this travesty.

He imagined one of the journalists from *The World of Fine Wine* or

Decanter coming to taste the wines of Red Mountain to bear witness. They'd drive down Sunset Road, perhaps ready to taste Otis's new vintage, knowing that some of the finest wines in the new world came from this place. Then they'd see Château Smooth, and all they'd do was laugh.

Laugh themselves silly. Still wiping their smiles, they'd drive as fast they could to Walla Walla, giving up on Red Mountain entirely, saying something like, "It was an appellation with extraordinary potential. Such a shame."

Another would say, "Red Mountain is no longer red. It's pink! Bahahahha!"

Otis slammed his fist onto the steering wheel, and just as he considered driving right through the sign, he saw Bellflour marching toward him with something in his right hand.

Ah, the smart valve.

Otis didn't care. What he mostly saw as he watched Bellflour marching his way was a man who'd destroyed everything for which Otis had worked his entire life.

Pink Mountain.

Otis flung his door open and stepped onto the gravel. "You proud of yourself, Bellflour? You finally ruined it for all of us."

Bellflour held up the smart valve. "This is your idea of funny, you son of a bitch?"

No use denying it, Otis thought. "I should have done a lot worse!" he yelled, heading Bellflour's way.

They met on the side of the property, fifteen feet from the driveway wet with gold concrete.

Otis raised a fist. "I should have done this a long time ago, you son of a bitch."

Bellflour belted out a laugh. "Come and get me, you geriatric. I'll throw you in the hospital before you can blink."

Otis threw the first punch and was surprised when Bellflour showed the reflexes to stop it. Bellflour's big forearm came up and barely budged in the air as he blocked Otis's arm.

Having boxed some when he was younger, Otis wasn't afraid of using his left and struck Bellflour in his fat gut.

The man lost his breath and folded over, but not for long.

Bellflour swung back, a big right that Otis barely dodged. He figured he'd better take the big man to the ground. Otis raised his boot and hammered down on Bellflour's leg. His knee buckled, but he grabbed Otis by the shirt and pulled him down with him. Otis jammed an elbow into Bellflour's face, and the first blood of the match was drawn.

They wrestled for a while, and at one point, Otis felt the hard ground give way. It took him a moment to realize they'd rolled into the newly poured gold concrete. With the concrete splashing up all over them, the men rolled back and forth, scrambling to get their best punches in.

Otis's lower back burned unbearably from lifting that damn wine barrel a couple of years ago, but nothing was going to slow him down. He kept swinging and throwing elbows like his life depended on it. He wasn't only defending his honor but the mountain as well.

Finally, Bellflour started to wear down, and he covered his sweat- and concrete-soaked face with his arms as he gasped for air. Almost every part of him was gold.

With a fury of a man protecting his mountain, Otis didn't stop. He couldn't. Though he didn't connect them all, he unleashed several powerful blows to make sure he'd ended the fight.

Bellflour folded in and sunk lower into the concrete, groaning in pain.

Otis finally pressed up and wiped his eyes. He could feel the concrete running down his body, burning his skin.

His enemy wiped the gold from his eyes. "I'll sue you for everything you have."

"Oh, fuck off!"

Otis turned and stomped to the new sign. With Bellflour screaming at him from the gold ground, Otis kicked the first of the lights, and it blacked out. Then another. And another. Fifty or so to go and he wasn't stopping until it was done.

After several more lights shattered to black, he glanced back at his property. Something didn't feel right. Standing at the dividing line between the two properties was Joan with her arms crossed.

His anger turned to shame in an instant, and he could barely look at her. He glanced at Bellflour, glittering in gold and nearly dead, and Otis realized he was no better than that bastard.

A far more painful realization followed.

He'd just lost Joan forever.

37

THE POLITICS OF A TASTING

"Château Smooth," Brooks said, saying it out loud for the first time. "It's like someone is playing a cruel joke on our AVA."

He sat with Jake, Carmen, Emilia, and Pak at the gorgeous solid-slab walnut table in the kitchen of Lacoda. Like the tasting room, the kitchen was modern and almost industrial with exposed concrete and steel. Several large windows looked out over the courtyard, the sheep pasture, and vineyards to the north.

Though they hadn't walked down to attend the press conference, they'd seen it on the local news.

"It does seem impossible, doesn't it?" Jake said. "After all we've done to defend this place."

Brooks ran a hand through his hair. "It's definitely getting harder and harder not to be an elitist. We should have drawn up plans to require approval before a winery could buy land in the AVA."

"Probably should have worried about that before we pushed for organized organics," Pak said, adjusting his visor.

"Or even the same bottle shape," Brooks admitted. "I just never could have imagined this." He thought about the details Bellflour had mentioned, the word *pink* really sticking out. Brooks had tried to call Otis to see how he was taking the news, but Otis hadn't picked up his phone. Brooks, however, was beyond sure that his mentor wouldn't be taking the news well at all.

Ready to move on to better things, Brooks reached for one of the many glass containers full of wine sitting in the middle of the table. This one read: SY-oi-ANG. He unscrewed the small black cap and poured a small amount of wine into one of his polished crystal glasses, then passed it around.

"This is the Angeline block. Thought it would be a good place to start."

So it began. As was typical, all who participated in a tasting were supposed to keep a poker face and not reveal their feelings on the wines until it was time to share. The power of suggestion was too strong otherwise. If Brooks looked up and said he smelled cranberries, the others might smell cranberries. That's why it was suddenly as quiet as a library in the kitchen.

They'd come together to make the decision on the varietal percentages for their red blend. Though they often bottled single varieties as well, it was their red blend that captured the entire essence of Lacoda. The forty or so glass containers held wine lots from all the varying fermentations from the different red grape blocks, and it was their job today to figure out how to best express the property.

These bottles contained the results of all their hard work for not just the previous vintage, but from all the years of Lacoda that had led to this moment.

And yet...

There was Carmen. Thankfully, she wasn't partaking in the tasting, but her presence felt like a corkscrew twisting into Brooks's side. Yes, it was her winery, and she was the boss, but did she need to sit there and peck at her computer while the rest of them tried to concentrate on the wines?

Finally breaking free of Carmen's poisonous tentacles, he put his full focus on the wine before him. He'd found that the Angeline block gave a brilliant window into the entire vintage. He couldn't explain why, only that he knew with one sip what kind of wines they'd be working with throughout the property. Angeline was the mystery that kept Brooks coming back year after year. Even with all the science Otis and others had taught him, he couldn't explain this enigma.

He stuck his nose into the glass, and a bouquet of flavors that might not even have names delighted him. The vibrancy and liveliness was exquisite, and he knew he'd made a wine that was alive and ever changing.

Taking in the first sip, he was pleased with the evident roundness. There was certainly crunch, but there was a sexiness, too, this kind of velvety blanket that coated the tongue. Holy hell, this was a good wine. He picked up the red Solo cup in front of him, spat into it, and then wrote a few notes in his notepad. A few minutes passed, and he saw that the others had set down their pens and were ready to talk.

Jake went first. "This is why we're here. I think it's exactly as it should be. Well done, Brooks."

"Well done to all," Brooks said. He looked to his right. "What about you, Emilia? What's the new kid on the block have to say?"

Emilia blushed. "You love to put me on the spot lately."

"Otis used to do the same thing to me. Don't worry. No judging here. Besides, you've already proven yourself. I love the way you speak about wine. Let's have it."

"No pressure." Emilia said, sniffing the wine again. "This is the heart of the vineyard, right? I think it's incredible. I mean, I don't really have tons of tasting experience, but it's very different from the other wines I've tasted from Red Mountain. Or anywhere else for that matter." She looked at her dad. "I really think I would know this wine anywhere."

"This is your home, Em," Jake said.

Emilia opened her mouth but chose not to speak. Instead, she smiled and stuck her nose back into the glass.

"Okay," Carmen said, looking up from her computer. "Let's not get all metaphysical. You guys and your wine talk can get a little ridiculous."

Brooks nearly snapped. How dare she intervene right now?

"Mom," Emilia said. "Have you seen Angeline? Something crazy is going on up there."

"Of course, I've seen it." Carmen shook her head with disgust. "Your father tries to drag me up there all the time."

Emilia glanced at Brooks and then back at her mom. "Well, I think that vine is something to be taken seriously. And since when was metaphysical a bad thing?"

"Honey, you've been working at the winery what? A couple of months? Let's not pretend you're an expert. It's a beverage. Sometimes the men in this room get a little carried away."

"I think Emilia knows exactly what she's talking about," Jake said.

Carmen scoffed. "Oh God, Jake. This is getting absurd."

"Carmen..." Jake pressed his mouth together, holding back a temper. After an uncomfortable stare down, he said, "You don't have to be here if you don't want to. Why don't you take a walk?"

She didn't like that and hissed, "This is just as much my winery as it is yours."

With finality, he said, "Don't belittle my daughter. She's earned a right to sit at this table."

Everyone but Carmen and Jake suppressed smiles.

Carmen crossed her arms in disgust and nearly lasered two holes in the table with her eyes.

After a long uncomfortable pause, Jake said, "Moving on..."

Brooks took the hint. "So here's the deal. Angeline is the heart of the vineyard. Using her as a base, how do we make her sing even more?" He turned to Emilia. "As natural winemakers, we can't and don't want to add any acid or water, or anything else for that matter. So we have only one way. That's blending."

Brooks pointed to the samples. "All these lots and varieties are our spice rack. Merlot for roundness. Petit verdot for color. Cabernet sauvignon for spine. The earliest-picked sangiovese for acidity and texture." He clapped his hands. "Now comes the fun part. Time to create our blends. Then we'll see who comes out on top."

In the hour that followed, they worked on their own, tasting through every lot, playing around with percentages of the different varieties and testing different theories. Brooks was trying not to dwell on Carmen coming in and out of the room as he dove into the experience.

Eventually, he felt that he'd found the perfect blend. He'd tried quite a few different ideas, but in the end, he'd settled on a sixty-percent syrah, twenty-three percent cabernet sauvignon, ten percent merlot, and then a smattering of other varieties for enhancement. There were so many things to consider in this blend. Balance and flavor, of course, but also age-ability. He and Jake wanted their wines to live for decades, while at the same time being approachable earlier on for those who didn't have the means to cellar wine.

Pak collected everyone's final blend and took them into the next room to prepare for the blind tasting. Brooks and Emilia grabbed a rack of clean glasses and set four down in front of each person.

"I'd like glasses too," Carmen said, shocking everyone. "Don't worry. I just want to smell them."

Emilia got another set for her mom, and they all took their seats.

Pak returned and began pouring. "From left to right, A, B, C, D."

As the final tasting commenced, Brooks decided to first eliminate any outsiders. *A* seemed to stand out in a less than appealing way. The others all had wonderful Red Mountain character, and the choice was almost impossible. But as he went back and forth sniffing, and then sipping and spitting, *D* began to stand out.

If there was one thing Otis had impressed upon him more than any other, it was to let the science go, and listen. To put your ear to the ground and let Red Mountain speak.

Brooks smiled, knowing *D* was his blend, and it spoke even louder once he leaned into its quiet whisper. There was something so savage and alive about this wine. Brooks wrote his choice down, hoping he'd defeat Jake, who'd won last year.

He waited until everyone else was done. "Who wants to go first?"

"I'm *D* all day long," Pak said, showing what he'd written down, reminding Brooks why he liked having Pak on board.

Brooks held a poker face as Carmen said, "I like *A*."

Jake made a show of looking around the room. Smiling, he toyed with them, reaching for each glass and then stopping.

"C'mon, Dad, which one did you pick?"

With a final grin, Jake picked up his piece of paper showing a big fat *D*. Brooks tried not to gloat but couldn't wipe the grin off his face.

Jake turned to his daughter. "Em?"

She held up a *D* as well.

Brooks laughed and showed a *D*. "Almost unanimous." He looked to Pak. "Whose was it? Sure does taste like mine."

Brooks was about to smile in victory when Pak glanced at his notes and announced, "*D* is Emilia's blend."

Brooks twisted his head to the four other astonished faces, including Emilia herself. He patted her back. "Look at you. The princess of Red Mountain has spoken. What an incredible blend."

He'd never seen Emilia happier. She was trying not to cry as she shrugged it off, but it was nearly overwhelming. "I thought it was pretty good," she said nonchalantly.

"Well done, Em," her dad said. "You get the crown. The blend is yours this year."

She was too shocked and excited to say another word.

Brooks noticed Emilia look at Carmen for a second, perhaps searching for approval. Carmen gave her no such thing. Her mother was staring past her at the wall with an angry look on her face. Or was it jealousy?

Just like a scene in a movie where all the Navy SEALs' phones rang at the same time, the phones in everyone's pockets dinged and buzzed. It was a funny coincidence, and they all looked at each other curiously.

"What the heck is this?" Emilia asked, staring at her screen.

Brooks was not surprised to see the youngest had beat everyone to their phones.

"What's going on?" Jake asked.

"Otis and Harry Bellflour just got into a big fight," she told them.

Brooks wasted no time running out the door. He climbed onto his motorcycle in the back lot and sped up the hill to Sunset Road. Once he was on pavement, he rode as fast as his Scrambler would go until he reached the turn to Otis's house.

Two mixers were pouring gold concrete in the Drink Flamingo driveway a little farther down Sunset. He made a mental note to process that vision as he swung right toward Otis's house. There was a police car in the driveway. Looking past it, he saw two policemen escorting Otis down the steps.

38

JAILBIRD

It wasn't Otis's first night in a cell, and judging by the way things were going, it wouldn't be the last. Though he tried to sleep, he was up most of the night, his monkey mind racing like a caffeinated hamster on a wheel. Other than the occasional door opening and closing somewhere down the hall, it was quiet, and the quiet made his thinking so much noisier. Not having a clock was torture enough. He had no idea how long he'd been there, and at one point during the madness of his captivity, he thought he might have been there for several days.

The vision that most plagued him was Joan and her crossed arms, watching him lose his mind. He could still feel the anger running through him as he'd pushed up from the gold concrete and smashed the lights on the sign, then, turning and seeing her and knowing that he'd lost more than his mind.

Was there anything worse than having Joan angry with him? He didn't think so. He thought about the way she'd walked with him back to the house before the policemen had shown up. How she'd hosed him off, treated the concrete burns, and dressed his wounds, all without saying a word. No, when you've upset Joan, you know you've done wrong.

He'd called her from the jail, asking her to come pick him up. She'd said it would be good for him to stay the night and that she'd find him in the morning. He'd attempted to apologize, but his words felt wasted.

Finally, as Otis paced in his windowless cell, hating himself for the things he'd done, he heard a noise in the hallway. The clang of metal, the sounds of other inmates. It had to be morning. A guard escorted him and a line of other prisoners to the cafeteria where he ate a dry and stale bagel. Still, all he could think about was her.

Back in his cell, he returned to pacing. Where was Joan?

The wretched coffee still lingered in his mouth when the same guard came to get him. "Playtime's over."

Otis glanced at the guard's night stick, wondering if he'd ever used it. *Oh, the places your mind goes when you've been cooped up in a cell.* He stood from the cot, thankful he wouldn't have to spend another night here. They returned his clothes and the contents of his wallet, and he changed in a separate room. Then the long walk to freedom, the sun shocking his eyes. Joan stood in the lobby, her arms crossed as if she'd slept that way.

He was hesitant to hug her. As loving as she could be, he didn't feel much love coming from her at the moment. Stopping a few feet short, he said, "Thank you. I'm sorry you had to come up here."

"Let's get you home." Her matter-of-fact tone was the kind that arises when she was trying to hide her fury.

They climbed into her electric car, and she pulled out of the parking lot and worked her way through the busy intersection and past the mall toward Red Mountain. He was reminded of being in trouble in England as a child. His mother's silent treatment was the toughest punishment of all.

Otis glanced over at Joan and wondered if she might stay silent the entire twenty-minute ride home. He wished the darn electric car would make a little noise. Something to break the unbearable quiet.

Once they hit the highway, Joan said, "I've packed my things."

Though he'd expected as much, dreaded it really, he wasn't prepared for the wave of agony that overcame him. What was he to do, though? He had no business with this woman. Everyone had joked that he was the luckiest man on earth to have found her, and they were all correct. What they should have said was that she was the unluckiest woman on earth. They would have been right about that too.

To love Otis was to lash yourself to a sinking ship.

He knew he needed to say something, and he searched for the words. He felt a heaviness inside and thought he might burst into tears. With his eyes on the dashboard, he said, "I'm so ashamed of myself, Joan. More than anything, I hate that I've brought you into my world." He glanced at her. "I'm going mad, and I'm sorry you've had to see it."

A beat went by. "As I've said before, we're bringing each other down. I'm just the one pointing it out."

"I don't want you taking the blame," he said. "This is all me."

"It's not all you, honey. It's me too. I'm just as guilty. Instead of loving you just the way you are, I've been trying to change you. And that's not okay."

"Well, I do need changing."

Joan shook her head and moved on. "Don't think for one moment this is an easy decision for me." She choked up, and Otis wanted to touch her, but he didn't want to invade her space. Instead, he let her sadness stab him like a dagger.

"I'd sell my land in an instant to be with you."

"Oh, c'mon. Then what? We'd go live in Richland at my place? You'd give up on Red Mountain? What would you do with your life? I will not be the reason you leave the wine world."

He wanted to argue further, but the truth was that he loved her so much that he *wanted* her to leave him, to find some peace and maybe another lover. He didn't want to be the one who kept dragging her down. Though he'd like to think he would come around, he wasn't so sure.

Even the sight of Red Mountain off to the right as they sped down the highway was unnerving. He looked at the shape of the mountain, at the face of her, almost as if she were a woman looking back at him.

He was losing it all for *her*. Joan had once rightly called her "the other woman."

Back home, Otis pushed open the door to find Joan's three bags and yoga mat lined up in the foyer. A hollowness opened up behind his ribs, and a deep sadness rose up his throat, making it hard to breathe. What had he done? The best thing to ever happen to him, and he'd not stepped up and loved her the way he should have. As much as he did want to set her free, it still wasn't an easy pill to swallow.

"If you'll get my things," she said, "I'm going to say goodbye to Jonathan."

Otis nodded and reached for the first bag. "You sorry sack," he said to himself. "What have you done?"

He carried the first two bags down and set them in the trunk of her car. When he turned, he saw her standing at the fence line pressing her face against Jonathan's muzzle.

Unable to hold it another moment, a sob rushed out of him, and he let his head drop. "What have you done?" he asked himself again.

Never before had he felt so lonely. He'd been given another chance at life, and he'd squandered it. Loss and loneliness drowned him as he climbed the steps to retrieve the final bag. Coming back down, he put it in the back seat and shut the door. By then, she was standing on the driver's side.

Tears fell down her cheeks as she stared at him.

"I still believe in you," she whispered.

He removed his cap and put it to his heart. "Goodbye, Joan."

She offered a faint smile and was off, riding back to her home on the Columbia River thirty minutes away, escaping the constant black clouds that seemed to hover over Till Vineyards and its lonely owner.

Otis sat on the front porch for a long time, stewing in the loss. Sometime later, the phone rang. He wouldn't have answered it but was expecting a call from his lawyer, Theo, who was a fan of Till Vineyards and always happy to trade his services for wine.

"Otis, you're one lucky guy," Theo said. "I just talked to Bellflour's lawyer, and he's not pressing charges. For the assault *or* the alleged damage to vines with the smart valve."

"That's good to hear." Otis wasn't sure he cared. He was in prison whether he was behind bars or not.

Theo cleared his throat. "I get the feeling he's trying to make friends on the mountain. That's probably why he let you off the hook."

More than anything, Otis just hoped all this would go away. He could only imagine what the wine world was saying about this YouTube video of him and Bellflour fighting in the gold concrete. The wine media seemed to eat up stories about his life.

"I appreciate your work, Theo, and I'll send you a few bottles for your time. Just do me a favor. Don't let the whole smart-valve thing get out. It's honestly embarrassing."

"Gosh, who could blame you, Otis. That's why we all love your wines. Your dedication is unparalleled. Just keep it in between the lines from now on."

"Yeah, I'll do that." Otis ended the call and tossed his phone off the porch.

∾

EMILIA CLIMBED the steps to Brooks's office and knocked. Once he'd invited her in, she took a seat opposite his desk and listened to him type the last of an email. Her heart pounded.

When he looked up from the computer, he said, "I'm assuming you came to gloat about your winning blend?"

Emilia smiled, and his comment distracted her for a moment. "That was one of the topics."

"You have every right to, Em. You made me proud yesterday."

"Just a little beginner's luck."

"I think it was a little more than that." He closed his laptop and reached for an aluminum water bottle. "So, what's up?"

Emilia clasped her hands together on her lap. "I'm not going back to school."

"How did I know this was happening? Let me guess...you want a job?"

Emilia nodded. "I'm going to transfer to WSU, into the vinicultural program, but I'd like to stay here too. Study under you." She noticed Brooks wasn't as excited as she hoped he'd be. "Why do you look like you think I'm making a bad decision?"

Brooks held up his hands defensively. "Look, Em. I have to stay neutral on this. By no means do I think it's a bad idea. It's really not my say either way. But I'll tell you this. You need to ask your parents. They're the bosses. I appreciate your coming to me, and you know I'd give you a job. It's their call, though."

Emilia glanced back to the door, like someone might be listening. "My mom doesn't want me to stay."

Brooks nodded. "I know."

"She told you?"

"Don't get me in trouble, Em, but yes, she told me she'd like you to go back to New York."

Emilia's jaw tightened. "What the hell does she know? She comes back from rehab and thinks she's...a saint. Whose life am I living? Mine or hers?"

Brooks held up a hand again. "Seriously, Em. I can't get involved."

"I've seen the way she treats you. The way she treats everyone here. It's like we're all living in her world—like we have the *privilege* of living in her world." Emilia could hear herself unleashing but couldn't stop it. "She has no business working here. I just wish she had something else to do."

He tapped the table. "I know she loves you, Em. She might not know what's best for you, but she *wants* what's best for you."

"I dare her to try and keep me away."

"Well, you're right. It's your life. Your choices."

Emilia simmered down and asked, "What do you think? Am I being an idiot by staying here? Maybe I wouldn't even make a good winemaker."

"I think you have wonderful potential, but I also think you'll be great at whatever you do."

Emilia sat back and let her leg shake. "Spoken like a politician." She understood why Brooks had to be neutral. This mountain was so small, and the winery was even smaller. Taking sides was dangerous.

"Thanks, Brooks. So if my parents say yes, you'll give me a job and teach me?"

Brooks screwed the cap back onto his water bottle. "Absolutely."

Emilia thanked him again and jogged down the steps back toward the tasting room.

Her mom was meeting with someone at one of the tables. "Emilia, this is Sandy. She'll be helping out on weekends."

Emilia shook the woman's hand. "Great to meet you."

After a quick chat about life on Red Mountain, Emilia turned to her mother. "You're coming home for lunch, right?"

Carmen nodded. "Yep."

"Okay, cool. I'd like to talk to you about something."

~

BROOKS COULD ONLY IMAGINE how bad things were about to get with the Foresters, and he'd found himself right in the middle of it.

Though he wished he could hide in his office, he had work to do. He'd put an older vintage of chenin blanc in the fridge downstairs to taste how it was faring. As he descended the stairs and walked by the wine tanks in the cellar to retrieve it, he navigated each turn like he was creeping through a minefield, hoping he wouldn't round the corner to find Emilia and Carmen in a throw down.

When he entered the tasting room, he was relieved to find Carmen in a meeting with one of the new tasting-room employees. After a quick hello, he rounded the concrete bar and opened up the fridge where he'd left the bottle.

The chenin blanc he'd pulled from the cellar was missing.

Popping back up, he said, "Excuse me, Carm."

Carmen looked up from the discussion, making it very clear how annoyed she was.

"Do you know if someone might have taken that bottle of older chenin in here? The tasting room staff wouldn't have sold it, would they?"

Even more frustrated now, Carmen said, "Keeping inventory is a nightmare here. None of you mark down when you're pulling bottles. I can't help you."

Brooks raised his hands in surrender. "Just asking, sorry."

Carmen shook her head, and it looked like she'd whispered something not so nice to the new employee.

He wanted to shout, "Don't take the job!"

Instead, as he passed by the two women, he said to the woman who had no idea what she was getting into, "Welcome to the team!"

39

WOMEN RULE THE WORLD

Emilia stopped by her vines on the short walk home. She could see over the remaining canopies down to her house, where a potential battle with her parents would be had at lunch. Her dad had always been the wise one of her two parents, and like Brooks, he'd always encouraged her to make her own decisions. Look at her dad now. He was one of the happiest people she'd ever met. Why was her mom the one playing puppeteer?

Leaving all that behind, she strolled down one of the rows, inspecting each vine from trunk to berry. The sheep had recently mowed, and the cover crops were low. Kneeling down, she reached for a handful of soil near the trunk and rolled it in her fingers. There was just the right amount of moisture. She was pleased to see the grape clusters looking healthier than ever. She'd learned that tight clusters like she might see in a grocery store were harbingers for mildew and rot. She wanted looser bunches that allowed air to pass through, keeping the berries dry.

She took one of the green clusters in her hand and lifted it up gently. How amazing that this fruit had been filling vessels and accompanying meals for thousands of years. An entire industry had formed around the fermentation of grapes, and people around the world had dedicated their lives to it.

Twisting the cluster, she saw a few of the berries had turned purple. "No way."

Pulling out her phone, she snapped a shot and sent it to Brooks. *Veraison?*

A minute later, he texted back, *Looks like it!*

She felt silly being so excited, but everyone at the winery talked about *veraison* as the point of no return, the change in colors marking the downhill run to harvest. It was only a matter of time until these little berries would demand eighty- and ninety-hour-weeks from the entire crew until every last one of the grapes had been picked and ushered toward fermentation.

What an incredible way to spend the fall, and no one, not even her mother, would take this opportunity away from her. Red Mountain was on the brink of an explosion, the next Napa Valley as some said, and Emilia wanted to be right in the middle of it.

~

SHE FOUND her dad at the dining room table. As he did almost every day, he'd prepared lunch and was waiting for his two ladies to join him. His bare feet were propped up on the chair beside him, and he held a Kindle in his hands. Though he was no stranger to the vines, Jasper had clearly lit a fire under him musically, and Jake was spending his mornings in the studio with his guitar in his hand.

"Daddy, my grapes are turning purple."

"You're kidding. This early?"

She showed him the pictures with her phone.

"Incredible," he said. "It's going to be an early harvest. Can we take a peek after lunch?"

"Yeah, I'd love to."

He looked at her and shook his head, like he was thinking, *I should have known.*

"What?" she asked, putting her phone on the table and sitting down next to him.

A slight grin rose on his face. "Oh, boy, do you have the bug."

Emilia held out her hands. "You created this."

"I did, didn't I?"

She glanced at his Kindle. "What are you reading?"

"Shakespeare. *All's Well that Ends Well.*"

"No, you're not."

He looked offended. "I am indeed. Thou shall not doubt my interest in the great bard. What did you expect me to say?"

Emilia rolled her eyes. "I don't know. John Grisham or something. Stuff old dads read."

"I should have you thrown in jail for saying such a thing. I haven't even reached my peak yet."

"You might want to get started then. Sixty is around the corner."

He brushed the idea off. "Sixty is the new thirty."

They smiled at each other, and for a few moments, she forgot that she was about to drop a pretty big bomb. Through the window, she saw her mom pull up in her new SUV, and Emilia was brought right back to the dread of sharing her decision. She was so proud of her mother for being sober, but sometimes she wanted drunk Carmen, the one who wasn't quite as bitter and was more easily swayed.

She heard her mother's bitterness in her own voice when she asked Jake, "Why does mom drive to the winery? It's like a hundred yards away."

Jake pulled the Saran Wrap off a giant salad. "To each her own, honey."

Carmen came in with much to say. "Jake, I don't know how anything gets done up there. You really need to spend more time managing."

Emilia thought she saw her dad take a moment of calm before answering. "Thankfully, that's why Brooks is up there. I was never one for managing."

Emilia hated how Carmen spoke to her father lately. Sometimes, she wondered why he hadn't just left her. She loved her mom, but the woman needed a swift kick in the butt.

"I'm not going back to New York." Emilia blurted her announcement out like she'd just confessed to killing someone.

Her parents swung their heads around and looked at her in the manner a surprise murder confession might require.

"I've talked to Brooks, and he said he'd give me a job. Don't worry. I'm not dropping out of college. I'll transfer to WSU."

"First of all," Carmen said, "it's not Brooks's place to offer you a job at *our* winery."

"Settle down, Carm," Jake said. "Let's hear her out." He pushed the salad toward Emilia. She might have complimented the gorgeous red and yellow tomatoes if her mother hadn't shattered any hope for a nice family lunch with her close-mindedness and bad attitude.

"It's not like this is some big surprise, Mom."

Her mother looked like her head was about to explode. "You're all over the place. One day it's Europe, the next New York or Seattle... and now this? A winemaker? Don't you know what your father and I can do for you in New York? We could get you hired almost anywhere. C'mon."

"Oh, please. Let me work in the fashion industry. Or no, shall I work in the record business? Why don't you just decide, Mom? I'm like your little doll that you had growing up. Just point me in a direction, and I'll go."

"That's not fair."

"C'mon, guys," Jake said. "Let's not—"

"Fair?" Emilia interrupted. Her father was trying to settle them both down, but Emilia had things to say. "Who is the one trying to control everything? Just because you're finally getting a grip on your life doesn't mean you need to try and pull everyone else's strings. We did perfectly well without you for years."

"Em, that's enough." Jake's stern voice was borderline angry, a card he rarely played.

When he did, though, Emilia knew she'd crossed a line. Trying to find some compassion for the woman who had given birth to her, she said, "That was too much. I'm sorry. What I'm trying to tell you is that nothing has ever interested me as much as the work I've been doing this summer. I'm actually happy."

"Life is not always about being happy!" Carmen spat.

Emilia looked at her mom like Carmen had just thrown a knife at her. "Tell me why you have a problem with me staying here. Let's get down to it. What's wrong with me going into the family business?"

Carmen side-eyed her. "I can give you a thousand reasons. You're better than this place. You have a brighter future than being stuck in the middle of nowhere playing farmer girl with a mountain of eccentric hippies."

"Oh, should I be a model like you?" Flapping her hand, she said, "Should I paint my face and stop eating and let people take pictures of me half naked? What a wonderfully noble profession." She dropped her hand to the table. "Where's the closest catwalk? Sign me up."

"Why don't we talk about this later?" Jake interrupted. "We all need some time to process the idea."

Carmen shut him out with a flinging hand. "Emilia, you're eighteen years old. You don't know shit. What if you spend the next few years studying wine and then find out my genes have poisoned you? Alcoholism passes down, you know."

"It might, Mom, but I've never had a problem with drinking in my life. It's not like I haven't been around it. Don't put you and your issues on me."

"I'm not putting them on you. I'm looking *out* for you." Carmen turned to Jake for help. "Tell her, Jake. I know you don't want her staying here either."

Emilia had never heard that and felt sick inside. "Is that true, Dad?"

"No, it's not."

"I didn't think so."

Carmen eyed Jake like he'd betrayed her.

Emilia found herself hating what she'd said to her mom. It had felt right coming out, but as she now looked upon the woman who undoubtedly loved her, Emilia realized that she needed to show some respect.

She grabbed Carmen's frozen hand. "Mom, I love you, but this is not your call. For the first time in my life, I have direction. I'm sorry it's not what you dreamed for me, but this is my life."

With a powerful voice of finality, Jake said, "We are going to talk about this later. This conversation is over."

Carmen's bottom lip quivered as she pressed her eyes together. As if she couldn't stand it another moment, she stood and stomped into the other room.

40

VEGGIE CHIPS

"Joan Tobey, is this really what your idea of a breakup depression looks like?" Margot didn't know whether to give her friend another hug or burst into laughter.

Knowing Joan had just broken up with Otis that morning, Margot had come bearing white lilies and a bottle of Canvasback cabernet sauvignon. After putting the flowers into a vase, Margot had followed Joan to the back of her riverfront home.

The large deck looked over her lawn and garden to the vast Columbia River, where a paddle-wheel steamboat was chugging by. Since moving in with Otis, Joan had replaced the vegetables and fruits in her garden with flowers.

Margot pointed at the scene on the deck hosting Joan's heartache. A turquoise beach towel was stretched over a lounge chair, which was arranged perfectly under an umbrella. Joni Mitchell sang through a wireless speaker on the nearby table that also happened to host the most absurd prop of them all.

"Veggie chips and a glass of ice water and lemon?" Margot asked. "I collapse into *pommes frites* and Champagne, and this is what you do? I have so much to learn."

Joan wore a one-piece swimsuit with a sarong wrapped around

her waist. She sat back in her chair. "When I get down, I need to be outside with Joni."

Margot sat in the other lounge chair and adjusted her sundress before crossing her legs. Letting go of the jokes, Margot said, "I'm so sorry, my friend."

Joan lay back on her beach towel and frowned. "Thanks. Things didn't go the way I'd hoped."

Trying not to focus on Joan's red eyes, Margot thought back to when she'd first met this extraordinary woman. Margot had thought she was bulletproof. When Henry Davidson had shot her in the neck, not only had Margot learned that Joan wasn't bulletproof, but she'd also been reminded that Joan was human and could hurt emotionally like everyone else. Even though Joan had fought back from her injury, Margot always tried to remember that her friend had vulnerabilities. It was actually a wonderful lesson Margot had learned, that even the most enlightened humans are still human.

"What can I do for you?" Margot asked.

"Oh, Margot, it's just nice to have a friend here."

"I'm surprised your house is not full of friends."

Joan shook her head. "I haven't been answering my phone. Only for you."

Margot felt so lucky to have a friend like her. "That's really sweet of you to say. Isn't it *my* turn to be there for you, anyway? Not that we're keeping score, but if we were, I'd say you're safely in the lead."

"Oh, c'mon. Friends don't keep score."

Margot glanced at the steamboat fighting the current. "Do you want to talk about it?"

Apparently needing to talk about it, Joan turned to her side. "The tough part of my line of work is hoping we can change people. We can point people in the right direction, but we *can't* change anyone. I love Otis for so many reasons, but he's hurting inside. I knew it that first night when Morgan introduced us." Joan smiled at the memory. "He was so far from my type but just what I wanted at the time. I knew within minutes that we'd have a future together."

She dipped her chin. "I also knew because of the way he suffers so from the past that there would be a long road ahead. I thought I could love him so much that he'd break through all of his loss. In hindsight, my hopes for him were our downfall."

Joan sat back and looked at the river with a long breath. "I can't fix people. That's not what I'm here for." Joan took another long breath. "I think I became more of a nuisance than anything else. These past few months, I've driven both of us crazy, nagging him, but I couldn't help it. I was watching him kill himself. He's gone unhinged with this Drink Flamingo thing, and I don't know if he'll survive it."

Along with the rest of the wine world, Margot had seen the footage on YouTube of Otis's fight. "As much as I can't stand Harry Bellflour, I felt very sad watching that video."

"I had to witness it firsthand. All those people egg him on. He hears the way they talk about him, and it pushes him into living in a dream world where he has to be the grapefather. He's become a caricature of himself. There was nothing I could do."

Joan raised a finger. "I take that back. I guess I realized that the best thing I could do for him was to set him free. Let him fight his own battle. So here I am, heartbroken and hoping that he'll be okay."

Margot sat next to Joan and took her friend's hand. "If anything will wake a man up, it's losing a good woman. I bet he's kicking himself right about now."

"Maybe. But he's got one eye on Harry Bellflour, and that's the problem. I'm telling you, Margot. When I first met him, his devotion to the mountain was adorable. I'd never met a man so committed to something. This year, he let his dedication get out of hand."

"You think it's over for good between you two?"

Joan inclined a shoulder. "It's a very real possibility. I refuse to endure any more of the suffering he's putting on himself. I...I can't be around it. I'm an empath, and when he's going through his stuff, I feel it almost as much as he does."

"You did the right thing. He was pulling you down with him."

"Ugh. I hate to think that I'm abandoning a drowning man, but there's nothing else I can do for him."

"You're not abandoning him. I've seen his changes too. Everyone on the whole mountain has. Part of me gets it. We've seen our share of disasters and challenges around here. But...in the end, it's just a mountain, right?"

Joan rubbed her eyes and nodded. "Anyway, let's not go down the wormhole of my heartache all afternoon. What about you?"

"No, no, no," Margot said. "I'm not letting you off the hook that easily."

"Yes, you are. I want to talk about Margot Pierce. You look wonderful."

Margot let Joan win and smiled. "Thank you."

"I see lots of changes in you. What's going on?"

"Oh, things are really good. For once, you don't need to worry about me."

"I want to hear all about it. I could use some good news."

Margot pushed up from the deck and reclaimed her seat. Like a woman sitting for her first confession, she whispered, "Burning that dress might have been the best thing I've ever done. Otis was *drowning* you. The darn dress was *strangling* me. What was that? Like a month ago? I feel so much better."

Joan's smile rose slowly like the sun in the morning. "You *look* so much better."

"It's like everything I've been working on for years all came together at the same time. It was like I ripped tape off my eyes and could finally see. I've been trying to be someone I'm not and don't know why. Who am I living for? It's so funny that Carly was the one who pushed me over the edge."

Joan tapped her own thigh. "It's not that surprising. It's our toughest challenges that see us through to the other side."

"I guess that's true. What I realized was that my weight issues...all the crap I've put myself through since I was a teenager...it was really a larger issue screaming at me. I needed to learn to love myself for who I am. Our bodies are really just our 'earth suits.' Our *real* selves are what's inside." Margot stopped. "Sounds like something you'd say, right?"

Joan let another smile lift out of her heartache. "We can't take our bodies when we go. That's for sure."

"No, we can't, but that doesn't mean I will let myself go. It's just that I will love my body the way it is. I will *rock* this body. It's what I was given, and I'm not going to starve it as a way to make myself look like Carmen or the rest of the Red Mountain beauties with their skinny little waists and torpedo boobs." Margot shook her head, feeling wonderful as she spoke. "Remi loves the way I look, and that's all that matters."

"As I've told you from day one," Joan said, "I'd love to have your curves."

"Thank you. I still do want to get in shape though, but in a healthier way. Shay's promised to teach me to ride Elvis."

Joan made a face showing she hadn't seen that one coming. "Oh, that's a great idea. Hold on. Didn't you tell me you were afraid of riding?"

"I was thrown off when I was a girl, but it's time to get over it."

"Good for you. Your whole new thing is nothing short of inspirational for this sad sack of bones—speaking of earth suits." Changing the subject, she asked, "Is Carly still doing better?"

"Every day," Margot said. "She and her dad are spending all their time down at his place taking care of his farm. I think Carly has a bit of a green thumb. You wouldn't believe the baskets of fruit and vegetables they bring up to the inn. The guests are in heaven."

"I bet."

"And she quit smoking and is talking to her mom again," Margot added. "Remi's just beside himself."

"I couldn't be happier for you all."

"I couldn't have gotten here without you. That's for sure. So what can we do to make you feel a little better? More veggie crisps? Maybe a Coke Zero? Dare I suggest celery and a reduced-calorie ranch dip?"

As Joan broke into a laugh, Margot said, "You really could learn a thing or two about breakdowns. Joni Mitchell is great and all, but we can make it much more pitiful around here if you'd like."

Joan drew in a huge breath, the kind a woman takes when she's caught in the middle of a cry and a laugh "It might be time for that bottle of wine."

"Now, you're talking."

41

NIGHTMARES

Brooks woke to a woman screaming, and it took him a minute to come to his senses. Peeling his eyes open, he saw Adriana, lying on her stomach, striking the bed like she was fighting off an attack. Her next gut-wrenching scream jolted him to reality.

He reached for her. "Hey, baby. It's a nightmare. That's all. It's just another nightmare."

Adriana struck the bed again with her fists, screaming, "Let go!"

Brooks shook her shoulder forcefully. "Adriana! Everything's okay. You're having a bad dream."

She came out of it like someone had slapped her face.

As she made her own journey back to consciousness, Brooks rolled over and put his hand on her cheek.

She pushed him away. "I'm okay."

Once she was fully awake, he said, "You really need to talk to someone, A. This has been happening for months now. It's not healthy."

Ignoring him as usual when it came to her seeking help, she asked, "What time is it?"

He turned to the digital clock on the nightstand. "Three."

She sighed, threw her legs off the bed, and mumbled something about getting a drink of water.

Returning his head to the pillow, he listened to her movements in the bathroom, wondering what he could do. He didn't like how she buried her feelings. It was like these nightmares were the only time she allowed herself to feel at all.

When she slipped back into bed, she said, "We can talk about it later, okay?" She kissed his forehead. "Go to sleep."

"But we won't talk about it," Brooks said. "You never want to talk about it, especially if Zack is anywhere in the house. I'm serious. You need to see someone."

He braced for her to scold him for the suggestion, wondering why she was so strongly opposed to seeing a therapist.

"I'm dealing with it my own way," she said.

"That might not be enough, A. You were in an abusive relationship for a long time. Before that, it was your father. I'm not sure waiting for these feelings to go away is the right answer. No offense, but I don't see you dealing with it at all."

"I appreciate you worrying about me, Brooks, but this is my fight."

"That's always the way it is with you. Your fight. Never *our* fight. You know who I'm really worried about? Zack. He can sense all this stuff going on inside you. That's why he's been a handful lately. He's just mirroring everything going on at home." Brooks felt like he'd just pulled back the string on a bow and loaded the arrow for her.

She popped up, ready to shoot. "Don't you think I know that about Zack? And can't you see I'm doing the best I can?"

"I do see that," he admitted, "and I think you're an incredible mother. What I wish is that sometimes you'd accept a little help. Let's do the best *we* can to get past your life with Michael and to give Zack the leg up he needs."

Adriana turned away from him, shaking her head. After a long pause, she turned back. "I'm doing my best."

"Lean on me a little bit, Adriana. Stop taking on the world by yourself."

~

AT LACODA, Brooks was still thinking about Adriana when Carmen burst into his office without a knock. "What the hell have you done?"

He whipped his head toward her like she'd bitten his arm. "What?"

"You told Emilia you'd give her a job?"

"Now, hold on. I told her to talk to you and Jake."

"You told her you'd give her a job." Carmen could win awards for the way she delivered her accusations.

Anger Brooks wasn't aware he had rose up from inside and settled on his tongue. "I told her I'd give her a job if you guys approved."

Carmen shook her head. "All you've done is encourage her to stay. You and Otis both, putting Emilia under your trance, ignoring what I told you. She wants to give up her entire potential to be a farmer."

"First of all, you told me not to offer her a job. I can't control Emilia's decisions. She's not a little girl anymore." He could so easily raise his voice but didn't want to. Not for Carmen's sake but for Jake's and Emilia's. "She's got talent. Can't you see that? She's falling in love with the art of wine farming. You said the word *farmer* like she's learning to be a thief."

"You don't get it, do you?"

"I really don't, Carmen. Please enlighten me, I beg of you."

She welcomed the opportunity. "Wine might be everything to you and Jake and that crazy old man down there, but Emilia can do so much better. She's meant for bigger and better things. I don't want her throwing away her twenties living in the desert of eastern Washington learning how to drive a tractor."

"Just because you hate it here doesn't mean she doesn't belong."

"This is my husband's stupid project, and for some reason, I went along with it. If we hadn't moved here, Emilia wouldn't be settling for a life out in the middle of nowhere."

"Settling? Have you not seen the transformation I've seen? Your daughter has found what she's meant to do. Do you know how rare that is? Most people search their whole lives and never find it. She's nineteen and knows what she wants to do with the rest of her life. You make her go to New York, and you might as well clip her wings."

"I'm not sure you're qualified to give parental advice."

Brooks was getting closer and closer to blowing a gasket. "I've been around Zack long enough to know that you can't smother their dreams."

"I'm not going to waste my time arguing with you," she said.

"Why the hell did you come up here in the first place?"

"Because I apparently needed to remind you that I'm your boss— just as Jake is. I told you that Emilia is leaving this mountain at the end of the summer and that you were not to sway her decision."

He wanted to pull his hair out. "Have you once considered that *you're* the one who doesn't belong here? Maybe you're projecting all your own issues? Have you even once walked down to her vines? Do you know how much this vintage means to her?"

"They're grapes," Carmen snapped, and Brooks was starting to wonder if maybe she'd gone back to the bottle. No sober person could be so mean.

He chose not to explore that idea and said, "They're more than grapes. Until you understand that fact, you'll never get what we're doing here. I can appreciate that you and alcohol have a problem, but that doesn't mean it's a bad thing."

Carmen shook her head in disgust. "Maybe it's *you* who doesn't get what we're doing here. This winery is Jake's and mine, not yours. Don't you ever forget that. We're the ones signing the checks. Somehow in the last few years, Jake has misled you into thinking otherwise."

"I guess he has."

They both stared at each other. Brooks was done talking. There was nothing he could say to get through to her. They were two very different people.

∿

ONCE SHE'D LEFT, Brooks called Jake. "Can we chat for a few minutes?"

"I'm in the studio with Jasper," Jake said, "but he's about to take off. Can you give me fifteen?"

"See you then."

Hoping he didn't run into Carmen again, Brooks snuck out a side door and meandered through the vines. When he reached Emilia's rows, he saw Jasper leaving and waved. Passing through the open gate, Brooks circled around the house toward the studio, hearing Jake still playing his guitar.

As Brooks passed the pool, he heard a voice from the main house cut through Jake's blaring guitar work. Abby poked her head out the door. "What are you doing here?"

"Oh, hey." He met her near the house so that they could speak over the dark chords Jake was hammering out fifty feet away. "I thought you were taking time off to be with Wyatt," he said, referring to his nephew.

"There's no time off around here. Now that Carmen's working at the winery, I feel like I have a million more things to do. She has me cleaning out cabinets today. I welcome the money, though. Shay and I are closing on the house in three days and have next to nothing to furnish it with."

Making a joke he knew she'd get, he said, "I can't believe you don't want to stay here forever." She and Shay were still living in her villa on the other side of the Forester property.

Abby made a show of looking around and whispered back, "I want out." Returning to regular volume, she said, "Anyway, I've turned into Luca's professional driver. Tennis. Music. Sailing. Well, not that I mind, of course. Well, not that much. Can you believe he's ten now?"

"It's shocking," Brooks said. "He told me the other day that he didn't have any imaginary friends anymore. He says he's too old."

"I know. How sad it that? Growing up is just the worst."

Brooks chuckled from his core. "It sure can be." He asked about Wyatt, and Abby shared a few new photos.

"What's new at your house?" she asked, shoving the phone back into her pocket. "You and Adriana doing well?"

"Yeah, we're good. Everybody's good."

"You never were a good liar, Brooks. What's going on?"

Brooks had an urge to tell her everything. It would be nice to tell someone what he'd been going through. "I think she's giving up on going to Florida, but it's been a tough road. She's still having nightmares."

Abby nodded. "She's still mad at your mom too, I gather?"

"Probably. We don't talk about it."

Abby looked at him, almost into him. "I hope she realizes what she has. You deserve to be loved."

"I appreciate that." His little detour was over, and he found himself thinking of Carmen and his future with Lacoda again. "Anyway, good chatting. I really do want to spend more time with you guys. Sing Wyatt the 'Beans, Beans, the Musical Fruit' song for me."

She smiled beautifully. "I'll be sure to do that."

Offering a wave, he said, "You gotta teach 'em early, you know?"

He watched her walk back into the Foresters' house, thinking about what would have happened if he'd forgiven her for sleeping with Carmen. They might have been good together.

Pivoting, he headed into Jake's man cave. Sounds poured out when he passed through the hall and opened the thick door into the studio. Jake was standing on an oriental rug beside a drum set with a Les Paul in his hands. The wall behind him displayed a row of black-and-white photographs taken of his band, Folkwhore, performing during their prime. Jake used to have longer hair back then and would often take the stage shirtless.

Though Brooks had not seen many movies growing up, and he'd certainly not seen any concerts, music had saved his life more than once. He remembered breaking into a car and stealing a portable CD player and book of CDs full of Seattle grunge music shortly after he'd run away from his last foster home. That's when he'd discovered Folkwhore for the first time, and it was always funny to wonder what that young teenage Brooks would have said if someone had told him he'd grow grapes with the lead singer one day.

Jake hadn't heard Brooks come in and was working through a Grateful Dead tune.

"Hey!" Brooks yelled.

Jake spun around and turned the volume knob down on the guitar. The room went silent. "What's going on?" He rested his hands on the guitar.

"You a Deadhead now?" Brooks asked. "Was that Jerry Garcia on your Les Paul?"

"He did play a Les Paul back in the day, before he went custom. I've been listening to them more and more lately. Jasper and I were toying with a tune. The Dead is like natural wine. They were so tuned in. Even when they were singing out of tune, they were more in tune than any other band of their era. I caught a few shows years ago and really liked what I heard, but as I get older, they're making more sense. Jerry was brilliant. Anyway, what's going on?"

Brooks knew how impossible it was to have a serious conversation with Jake while he held his guitar and didn't want to relive the experience as they talked about his wife. "You might want to put your guitar down for this one."

Jake pulled the Les Paul off his shoulder and set it down in the rack next to six other guitars. "You're not breaking up with me, are you?"

Brooks crossed his arms. "I'm not sure."

Jake pointed toward the other side of the studio, past the pool table to the bar. "Why don't we sit down?"

Brooks sat on a red stool and swiveled it to face the man who'd given him a real shot years ago. Though he had the credentials of being Otis's understudy, Brooks had nothing else on his resume. Jake had trusted Otis's word and given Brooks a job he never could have imagined landing.

"This isn't a conversation I want to have, Jake. But I don't have a choice."

His boss nodded, and Brooks could tell he knew what was coming.

"It's Carmen," Brooks said.

"Yeah, I know."

"I can't do it, man. I care about her because she's your wife and the kids' mom, but we just don't mesh, and it's getting in the way of my job."

Jake raised his arms above his head and stretched. "I don't know what to do. I dragged her out here, and she's lonely. I can talk to her, though. Make sure she stays out of your way."

"That's not going to work, and you know it. I hate to say it. This breaks my heart, but it's me or her."

Jake shook his head. "Nah."

"I have no choice," Brooks said.

Like so often when they were together, the silence said it all. Brooks didn't feel he needed to elaborate on what Carmen had done. Jake was no fool. He understood.

Jake took on a frustrated tone. "What would you do if you left Lacoda? You're not thinking of leaving the mountain, are you?"

"I have no idea."

"Don't walk away from what we've created here. You know Carmen. She'll come around. She just has these bad stretches. Let's figure out a way to make it work."

Brooks shook his head. "It's me or her..."

42

ELVIS AND ADIÓS

A couple of days after visiting Joan, Margot walked the path to the farm sanctuary to have her first lesson with Shay and Elvis. She had exactly one hour before she needed to get back to the inn.

As always, her animals came rushing toward her looking for treats. Cody was especially excited today and nearly knocked her over with a jumping kiss to the face.

"I missed you too, Cody," she said, playfully squeezing his ears.

She was glad to see the turkey come waddling up with her tail feathers spread. "Look at you, Precious. Back on two feet already." A week earlier, she'd held Precious down as Shay cut out a bumblefoot infection with a scalpel. It wasn't the prettiest procedure, but Margot had grown tougher since moving out to Washington State.

When she saw Shay come out of the red barn, she said, "Precious looks better."

He pulled the straw hat from his head. "Yeah, I think we got all of it."

"How's Fantasia?" Margot asked, referring to one of their now *four* alpacas currently grazing on the other side of the field. A month earlier, Fantasia had stepped in a gopher hole and broken her leg.

"She's still limping but seems much happier."

Margot turned her eyes to Elvis, who was swatting at flies with his tail in the corral. "And Elvis? I hope he's in an extra-good mood?"

Shay shook his head and turned back. "Don't worry. You're in good hands."

"As long as he doesn't throw me fourteen hands down into the dust, I'll be happy."

"He's a sweetheart. Don't worry about it."

Passing through a round of gates, they approached Elvis, who was now chewing on a mouthful of hay. Due to his blindness, they'd learned to approach him carefully, always announcing their presence. "Here we come," she said.

Margot put her hand on the white spot on his nose. "I haven't ridden a horse in a long time, Elvis." She broke into the chorus of one of her favorite Elvis songs, "Don't Be Cruel."

"Just remember," Shay said. "You're the one in control. Make sure he knows that, and you'll be fine."

"How do I show him I'm the one in control?" Margot was starting to wonder what she'd signed up for.

"With the reins. He goes where you want to go, always. Don't let him push you around."

Margot felt her heart kick as she recalled that fateful day when a horse named Serenity went wild with Margot on her back, racing across a field and then tossing her like a ragdoll into the dirt. There was nothing serene about Serenity, and Margot hadn't climbed on a horse since.

Shay spat tobacco juice to the ground. "I thought I'd show you how to saddle him first, and then we'll get you up and going."

"Sounds great," Margot said, her fear escalating.

They walked Elvis to the red barn and stopped at a fence where the saddle waited. Shay took a brush from a pail and handed it to her. Though she couldn't ride, she'd spent plenty of time brushing Elvis. While she worked out a patch of dirt from his wiry hair, she said, "Are you still closing on your house tomorrow?"

"Yep, nine a.m."

"I'm really happy for you."

Shay nodded and spat again. "It's the first house I've ever owned. It's a big step for us both."

Once Elvis's back was clean, Shay handed her the pads. "Now set these on him. There you go." He lifted up the saddle, and they swung it up onto Elvis. Shay showed her how to cinch the straps. "I think he's ready for you."

She looked at Elvis's face and then the saddle, and then Shay. "I'm nervous."

"Don't be. We saved his life. He knows to be gentle."

Knowing it would be best to get on with it before overthinking, she put her foot in the stirrup and pressed up. Shay gave her a boost as she threw her leg around. He handed her the reins. "Margot, you have the conn."

"Thanks, Captain Kirk." She made a clicking sound and sang the opening lines of the chorus for "It's Now or Never."

Shay always rewarded her with a laugh when she referenced Elvis songs. He said, "You're his eyes, Margot. Earn his trust, and he'll be the best-riding horse in Benton City. I've let him gallop me home in the dark more than once."

"Baby steps, Shay. I just want to survive the corral."

～

WHEN ADRIANA TOLD Brooks she still wanted to go to Florida, he wasn't surprised. Knowing Michael would be locked up for a longer period of time hadn't done much in the way of bringing her out of the gloom. Almost in parallel, Zack was still misbehaving at camp and at home.

"I guess it all makes sense," Brooks said, wondering why he was even trying anymore.

They were standing in the kitchen. Zack was playing video games upstairs while they talked. "This was never about Michael, was it?" Brooks said. "It was about you and me. I'm not sure you ever really loved me."

"I've loved you a long time. My life is complicated, Brooks. Haven't we been over this? It doesn't exactly matter what I feel. My son comes first. This life is not for him. It's not for either of us. I can't shake what happened last year, but it's more than that. It's the living so far from everything. It's raising my son hundreds of miles away from the life I had in Los Angeles. It's being stuck in a culture that doesn't always support Mexicans. I have a million reasons to leave and only one to stay."

She looked around the living room before locking eyes with him. "You."

Brooks nodded slowly.

"I want you to come with us," she said.

Whoa, did those words stop Brooks in his tracks. "Do you? Are you sure about that?" He was tired of always being the one advocating for their relationship. Her excuses could only go so far.

"Brooks, I love you, and I want to keep seeing you. It just can't be here. What's keeping you on Red Mountain anyway? You're leaving Lacoda."

"Leaving Lacoda is different than leaving Red Mountain and the West Coast."

"The choice is yours, Brooks. Zack and I are going to Florida. We want you to come." She touched her heart. "I want you to come."

Brooks thought it weird he'd just given an ultimatum to Jake, and now, here she was giving Brooks a taste of his own medicine. He turned away from her and sat at the dining room table.

She followed him and put her hands on his shoulders. "Come with us," she whispered. "We could build a brand-new life."

"What about my family? Don't tell me this has to do with my mom. Are you *still* holding a grudge?"

"I'm not holding a grudge. I just know the truth. She won't like me whether I stay or go. But this decision is much larger than my relationship with your mom."

Brooks dropped his head. He imagined what it would be like to drive away from this place, to have a packed car and ride across the country with grapevines in his rearview mirror. Once again, he pictured himself riding his bike past white-sand beaches and palm trees. He wondered what their life would look like and what he'd do for a living.

He'd never once thought of how signing up to be a winemaker limited a person for the rest of his life. Unlike many other professions, a winemaker couldn't pick up and go wherever he chose. Unless you wanted to truck in someone else's harvest, you needed to be in an area that could grow exceptional grapes.

"What would I do, A? It's the same old question."

"Do you know how many breweries are there?" Adriana asked. "People would kill to have your skills."

He'd thought about beer too. He'd even researched some of the breweries. Was that a life he could live? Being out in the fields was what gave him the greatest joy. They didn't grow world-class grapes or hops in Florida. He wasn't sure if the art of fermentation was enough to satisfy him.

"Come with us," she said again, kissing his cheek. Here she was, hot and cold again, and dammit if he didn't suddenly remember how much he liked being with her when she was in a good place. That had always been the way with Adriana. Her good days in their time together made up for the bad.

Brooks thought of Otis, and that's when the answer truly hit him. He thought of how his lonely mentor was toiling away on a wall right now, still fighting a war that might never end. Otis had all but lost his mind. Was that all this wine world would lead to? A lonely existence fruitlessly fighting for a piece of land?

Brooks patted Adriana's hand and turned to her. "Can we wait until harvest is done?"

"Of course, we can." Adriana smiled. He hadn't seen her so excited in a long time. "Are you really coming?"

"I don't want to lose you," Brooks said, tasting the tropical salt air on his tongue. The idea was suddenly thrilling.

Adriana grabbed his cheeks and kissed him like she hadn't in months. "I love you."

"Me too," he whispered, thinking of his first warm winter in years.

43

PALM TREES AND TURQUOISE WATERS

I t was their little secret. Brooks wasn't ready to break the news of their move to anyone, so he and Adriana spent the next two weeks holding their plans close to their chests. They didn't even tell Zack, who wasn't the best at keeping secrets.

Not sharing burned, though. He wanted to rub his departure in Carmen's face but did no such thing. He settled into a positive attitude and focused on his job. Jake was the only one who knew that he was about to lose his head winemaker. Brooks would break the news to everyone, including Emilia, soon, but he wanted to tell his family and Otis first, which wouldn't be easy. Perhaps he was stalling over those two weeks, but whatever it was, he and Adriana were having a ball planning their new life, and she'd had a long string of good days, which made it all the better.

One morning, Adriana rolled over in bed and threw her legs over Brooks. "Are you really coming with us?"

"I'm strongly considering it, though I'm taking offers from a few other women begging me to follow them to exotic locales."

"How dare they attempt to steal my man?" She'd lowered down and bit his lip. "You're all mine," she whispered. Wonderful things transpired from there.

Though he'd been skeptical of her intentions at first, wondering if she really wanted him to go, these exact moments assured him that their East Coast future was bright.

The move began to take shape. They met with a real estate agent who provided a seller's report for Brooks's house. To his great delight, he would make good money, which meant he could take his time securing a new job in Florida.

The next order of business was picking out where to live in the Sunshine State. They'd already decided they'd rent for a while, just to test their decision. Having grown up in L.A., she wanted Zack to have access to a big city. That meant either Jacksonville, Ft. Lauderdale, or Miami on the east coast; or the Tampa/St. Pete area on the west coast.

After Zack would go to bed, they'd sit on the couch next to each other scouring the internet for articles on the quality of life, the schools, the culture, the breweries. The more they read about East Coast hurricanes, the West Coast started to win out for both of them.

"The Tampa area never gets hit," Brooks said, during one of their searches. "It just seems like a safer bet, especially if we want to eventually buy something."

"Give me an earthquake over a hurricane any day," Adriana agreed. "I don't care if you have warning or not. I think I'm out on Miami."

"Is Sarasota too far away from Tampa?" Brooks asked.

"Yes, I don't want to live that far away. Plus, from what I'm reading, Sarasota is too much of a retirement community. It says here St. Petersburg's median age is thirty-eight. I think that's perfect. The schools aren't great, but we could send Zack to private school. Think of the breweries. St. Pete is covered in them. Not to mention, look at these beaches." Adriana held up a picture of Pass-A-Grille Beach.

Brooks imagined days under the umbrella, the two of them watching Zack build sand castles. "I want to be there."

"I know!"

St. Pete won out, and they started looking for places to live. They connected with a real estate agent down there, who'd suggested they wanted to be as close to downtown as possible. Sealing the deal, one of the agents said, "Oh, yeah, St. Pete is so West Coast. We call it the San Francisco of Florida." Brooks and Adriana had both loved the idea of holding onto a little of the West Coast on their move east.

Whenever Brooks felt the mountain calling, he'd reminded himself of the one thing he knew. Love came first. No way he was going to let them go without him, even if it meant he'd have to say goodbye to his biological family to do so.

At the end of the two-week deliberation, they accepted an invitation to a housewarming at Shay and Abby's new place, and Brooks and Adriana decided it was a good time to break the news.

Before leaving, they called Zack over. He jumped up in between Brooks and Adriana on the couch.

"What would you think about moving?" Adriana asked.

His little eyebrow rose. "Moving where?"

"A place with a football team and a baseball team," she said. "Can you guess?"

"Denver?"

"No. Think warmer. Like really warm."

"The Big Easy?"

Brooks poked him. "What do you know about the Big Easy?"

"I know a lot of things."

Adriana showed him the picture on her iPad of a long white-sand beach with transparent blue water. "Where do you think this is?"

"Hawaii?"

Brooks and Adriana both smiled. She pointed to the word *Florida* under the photo, and he stumbled through the pronunciation until he got it. "Florida!"

"What do you think?" Adriana asked. "It would take us a few days to drive there, but this could be your new home. We'd get a condo with a swimming pool. We could go to the beach, go out on boats, scuba dive."

"A pool? Um, I'm totally in!" He jumped off the couch and did the happy dance, singing, "I'm getting a pool! I'm getting a pool!"

～

Bumping along roads that mostly catered to tractors, they drove to Shay and Abby's new home on the eastern side of Red Mountain. Judging by the way Zack was bouncing even higher than the truck, the young boy wasn't apparently bothered by the idea of leaving this life behind. Life at seven years old was so much less complicated, Brooks thought, pondering the lengthy list of less glamorous chores he'd need to do as an adult to move across the country.

As Zack gyrated with childish innocence in the back, Adriana and Brooks were both behaving as if they'd taken the lead in a funeral procession.

"How do you think she'll take it?" Adriana asked, obviously referring to Brooks's mother.

"I'm imagining the worst." To lighten up the mood, he said, "If you get out of there alive, you'll have defied the odds."

"Funny, Brooks. You know she's going to blame me."

"What do you do, A? We all have choices to make. If she wants to follow us to Florida, then that'll be just fine."

He could only imagine the face Adriana made before saying, "Let's not offer that suggestion."

Brooks put his free hand on her knee. "I'm just kidding. Hey, this is life. We're doing what's best for us. We'll pull the Band-Aid off here in a minute, and then it's easy sailing."

"I still have to tell Margot. Once I get that over with, then I'll get back to being excited."

Shay and Abby's new house came into view. It was situated on about five acres of flat land a half-mile east of Épiphanie, which glowed in the distance.

As they climbed out of the truck, Zack went running toward the house. Taking Brooks's hand, Adriana shook her head and let out a long sigh.

"We're moving to Florida!" Zack screamed to whoever opened the door.

Brooks suddenly felt like he was falling without a parachute. "That's not how I'd planned it."

By the time, they entered, Zack was standing in the living room announcing that he was getting a swimming pool and that everyone was invited to Florida for the winter.

"Hi, guys," Brooks said, entering first, terrified to look at his mother's face.

Abby and Shay were the first to greet them.

Wishing he could pivot and run, Brooks offered a hearty, "Hello."

"Love your house," Adriana said as a round of hugs and kisses ensued.

Abby thanked her. "We've got a long way to go, but not bad for only being here a week."

"I see lots of room to plant grapes," Brooks said, delaying the talk of Florida.

Abby nodded slowly to Shay. "One thing at a time, but yeah, we've talked about it. We hoped you might help us put some vines in the ground next year, but what's this about moving to Florida?"

Brooks grabbed Adriana's waist like he was lost at sea and had suddenly come upon a bobbing buoy. "I guess the cat's out of the bag. Yeah, we're moving after harvest."

"Good for you guys," Abby said. "I know it's been on your mind."

Shay looked at Brooks. "That's a big decision."

Brooks dug his fingers into Adriana's side and asked his brother, "You think you can handle things without me?"

Shay's face flattened. "I have to admit I'm bummed. Things were almost getting normal around here."

"That's about the time I need to pull up anchor." Brooks turned to the living room and recognized Abby's vibrant art, which she'd moved up from her villa.

Zack was regaling Charles and Mary with a vivid account of what their life in Florida would look like. "...and when you come down, we'll take you on our, like, seven-thousand-foot boat."

Mary, who held Wyatt to her chest, said, "That's a big boat, Zack. Will you be the captain?"

He took her question seriously. "Yes, probably. I mean, I don't know how to drive a boat yet, but I'll have it down by the time you get there."

Charles let out a bold, and possibly concocted, laugh. "I just hope you can put me onto a school of tarpon."

Zack looked puzzled.

Brooks pulled Adriana's hand, half-assuming he might have to drag her. "Hi, guys," he said, opening his arms to his biological parents. He lightly pinched little Wyatt's cheek. "Hey, bossman."

Wyatt smirked, which made Brooks laugh despite the situation. He was sad to think about being so far away from his nephew, but Wyatt would have lots of family around him growing up. Brooks wanted to be there for Zack, who wasn't as lucky. And Brooks hoped that he and Adriana would have a child soon so that they could grow their little Floridian family.

Once they were done with the pleasantries, Charles asked, "You're really leaving us?"

Still feeling waterlogged, Brooks put his arm back around Adriana's waist. "After harvest," as if that key fact snuffed out the flame.

He noticed his mother was rocking Wyatt as if she were shaking a martini. "How are you, Mom?"

"Considering I've just found out you're leaving us, I'm just great."

Brooks frowned and went back to digging into Adriana's side. "I know it's tough news."

Mary stopped rocking Wyatt and said to Adriana, "I hope this isn't because of me." Her voice cracked halfway through.

Brooks was suddenly thirsty for a martini. In fact, this entire conversation would be much easier if he could toss back a couple.

Adriana placed a hand on Mary's arm, which was wrapped around Wyatt. "This has *nothing* to do with you. You were right in saying I wouldn't last here. And I'm sad this means you won't see your son as much as you'd like, but I'll take care of him. Trust me."

Mary's bottom lip pushed out as she nodded.

Adriana flashed a smile and let go of Mary. "Just think...you can be snowbirds now." Adriana included the rest of them with her eyes. "I fully expect all of you to visit for Christmas."

44

THE BLIND HORSE

The dining room in Épiphanie was hopping this morning. Popping out of bed at 4:00 a.m., Margot had woken with an urge to get into the kitchen. With Etta James's voice brightening the morning, Margot had set out to make a breakfast worthy of kings and queens. It was the first day of August, and that was plenty of reason to celebrate.

Typically, she served the guests family style, and she and Adriana would usher out trays of food to the tables. This morning, she'd decided to set out an entire buffet. It didn't matter if she had to take the leftovers all over the mountain, she wanted to cook everything that came to mind. Besides, with Carly and Remi's latest bounty, she had more than enough ingredients to work with.

"Good morning," Margot sang to Adriana as her favorite coworker entered the dining room a few minutes before eight.

"What in the world?" Adriana said, looking at the display on the back wall.

"I went a little crazy, didn't I? You don't want to see the kitchen. It looks like one big Jackson Pollack painting."

Adriana approached the buffet and feasted her eyes. Margot joined her in a moment of appreciation. Starting from the left, a basket featured homemade raspberry scones with raspberries from Remi's garden. She'd also made croissants, because why not? She'd squeezed a few gallons of fresh grapefruit and orange juice, and then, deciding that wasn't enough, juiced a few carrots with parsley as well. Next stood three different quiches, including her favorite: wild garlic and kale. One of her most beautiful china dishes displayed her ripest Cherokee purple and gold medal tomatoes garnished with fresh basil and olive oil. She surprised even herself with the elaborate cheeseboard she'd created. She'd made little signs noting the name and origins of each selection. Some of the dishes, like the escarole and white beans, might have been better suited for dinner, but she'd been unable to stop cooking this morning. What was better than seeing her waking guests come downstairs to this wonderful surprise?

"We might have to invite the rest of Benton City for breakfast," Adriana said unconvincingly.

Margot detected an off note in her tone.

"Oh, I know it's ridiculous. What do you do?" Never one to hold back, Margot asked, "What's got your panties in a bunch?"

Adriana looked away.

"Out with it," Margot said. "What's going on, my friend?"

Adriana looked behind her, obviously checking to see if any of the guests had come down yet. "We've decided to move to Florida."

"Again? I thought we were past that."

Though Adriana had offered the announcement rather calmly, Margot heard banging pots and pans. Her right-hand woman was leaving? As awful as the news was, however, Margot didn't let all the banging in her head consume her.

The pre-epiphany (and pre-Épiphanie) Margot might have dropped to her knees and clutched Adriana's ankles. "Say it ain't so, Adriana. You're not leaving me. What about my honeymoon to Paris? Oh God, I'll never be able to leave this place."

Well, that pre-epiphany Margot Pierce, the outdated 2.0, as she had referred to her past self more than once, wasn't in the dining room today. Filling out Margot's wonderfully supple earth suit was the real Margot Pierce, the one who could handle the twists and turns of life.

Though she felt a second of resistance from that outdated 2.0 hag, Margot quickly caught herself. Challenges in life were simply opportunities for growth. That thought was superseded by a more important one. One of her best friends on the mountain, a woman she'd been through hell and high water with, had just told her that she was moving to Florida.

Forget Margot. This was a big deal for Adriana. Swallowing all these wild thoughts in an instant, she belted out, "Well, holey Ms. Moley, Florida. I know who I'll be visiting this winter."

"Don't worry," Adriana said. "I won't leave until you're back from your honeymoon."

"Honeymoon, schmoneymoon. Don't worry about me. This is about you. Tell me all about it."

Adriana dropped her chin. "How are you taking this so well? Have you been drinking?"

"Not at all. You're happy, aren't you? About the move?"

"I'm the happiest I've been in years," Adriana said, "but I feel like I'm abandoning you."

Margot brushed the air. "Nonsense. You have to do what's right for you. I'm happy for you. How's Brooks taking it?"

A smile found Adriana's lips. "He's coming with me."

Margot opened her mouth wide. "How wonderful!"

"Are you really not mad?" Adriana asked.

"On the contrary...I'm thrilled for you."

~

AFTER BREAKFAST HAD BEEN SERVED to the delight of her guests, they tackled the mess in the kitchen, and then Margot raced down to the sanctuary to take Elvis out for their daily walk. She'd come to trust him and was committed to riding her farthest yet, all the way down to Remi's property by the river.

As they clumped along, she allowed herself a moment to think of life without Adriana. She'd done her best to make her friend feel good about the decision, but Margot was well aware of the obstacles that lay ahead. Finding someone to replace her would be almost impossible.

Just as she'd overcome her fear of riding horses, Margot could figure it out.

She. Margot Pierce. Could figure. It out.

They cut through the Kiona vineyards, and she took a moment to recognize the oldest vines on the mountain, the ones that had started it all. She removed her cowgirl hat and held it to her heart in reverence. Where in the world would she be if the pioneers of Red Mountain hadn't paved the way? Perhaps she'd still be back in Vermont grasping to save her marriage.

Moving on, she found herself completely and utterly in the moment, her body gently moving to the cadence of Elvis's walk. Forget the shocking news of the morning; forget what shocking news was sure to come in the future.

Right now, she was riding a rescued horse through some of the most iconic vines in the new world. The sun was shining from a shimmering blue sky over the mountain that she proudly called home.

Elvis couldn't see a thing but was trucking along just fine, trusting that Margot's tugs on the reins would lead him exactly where he was supposed to be. She could get used to this bouncing rhythm. She could even get lost in it. For a moment, she wondered who was tugging her reins. Whomever and whatever it was, she'd learned lately to trust the direction.

"What is your favorite Elvis song, Elvis?" she asked him, listening closely for his response.

Though he didn't say anything, his body was creating music. The clopping hooves and creaking saddle carried a nice steady beat.

Internalizing the slow groove, a tune came to her, and she broke into song. It was just her and Elvis and the vines, but she wouldn't have cared if the whole mountain were listening. With the heart and timbre of Patsy Cline, she sang "Blue Moon of Kentucky" as they ambled west.

She and Elvis dropped down the slope to Demoss Road and eased their way along the river to Remi's place. She was still singing when Remi and Carly poked their heads up from the garden.

Remi dusted off his jeans and came for her. "You're looking and sounding more like a cowgirl every day."

She leaned down for a kiss. "He likes it when I sing to him."

"That makes two of us." He eyed Elvis and joked, "I shouldn't be worried about you two, should I?"

"Maybe a little."

Carly approached with a harvest basket in her hand. Margot was still getting used to seeing her without her hoodie. "Hi, Margot."

"Hey there. What are you guys picking today?"

"Tomatoes, tomatoes, tomatoes," Carly answered. "My dad thought it wise to plant forty tomato plants."

"Forty-three," Remi corrected her. "They seemed so small back in the spring."

Margot glanced over to the long line of tomato vines growing up the trellises they'd built. "I see a lot of pizza sauce and sun-dried tomatoes in our future."

Carly petted Elvis. "Do you want me to find something you can eat?" She turned and went back into the garden.

Margot mouthed to Remi, "She's so happy."

He stroked her thigh and offered a big and wonderful smile.

After giving the moment its due, she said, "Adriana just told me she's leaving."

Remi's eyes inflated. "Noooo."

"It's okay," Margot assured him.

"How is that okay? You must be beside yourself."

"It's good for her. We'll be fine." Then, "Carly's been a big help. Maybe she could take on some more responsibility." Carly had been working part time at the inn. "Either way, it's all part of owning a business. If it were easy, everyone would do it."

"Who are you?" Remi asked. "You're nothing short of inspiring to be around. Should we get married today, before the rest of the world realizes how lucky I am?"

Margot winked at him and held up her flashy diamond. "I'm not going anywhere."

Carly came walking back up with several stalks of Swiss chard. "Do you think Elvis likes chard?"

"Try him."

Carly stuck a stalk toward his face, and Elvis twisted toward her and flashed his giant front teeth before chomping down.

She giggled. "I'd say so."

~

MARGOT RODE A MORE southerly route on the way back, and once they'd reached a plateau, she said, "Elvis, how about we push the pedal down for a minute?"

As Shay had taught her, she clicked with her tongue and gave the horse a light squeeze with her legs. Elvis responded and broke into a trot.

Margot let out a yelp as they let loose through the vines. Her heart soared, and she wondered how she'd gone this long without this exhilarating feeling in her life. The smile that painted her face was so powerful she felt like the flowers and vines were standing taller, perhaps even saluting her, as she passed.

She gave Elvis another squeeze, and he sped up. Margot nearly lost her balance but fell back into the rhythm, completely focused on the cadence. Once she settled in, it was as if she were floating on air. Even at a full-on gallop, she felt stable and free.

What a life lesson this was, the idea of finding peace by letting go, even at the breakneck speed of life. When she heard Elvis pant, she pulled back, and he slowed down to a trot and then a walk.

Margot imagined this is what it felt like to reach the ground after a skydive. "Was that as good for you as it was for me?" she asked, patting his neck.

Elvis snorted satisfaction. She thought back to the shape he'd been in when he'd first arrived. His blindness had been the least of his issues. He'd walked with a limp, and his skin had sagged.

"Look at you, Elvis. May we all live life with such grace."

She removed her hat and let her head drop back, letting the sun bathe her face. She closed her eyes and let Elvis steer for a little while, knowing he didn't need his eyes to find the way home. *This was the life indeed*, Margot thought.

Riding up the next hill, she realized she'd come upon Till Vineyards. Otis's cottage stood on a gentle slope to the right, his back deck facing her. She suddenly heard the *bahs* of his sheep as they came into view. Up the hill and to the right past the sheep and cottage, she could see his winery. Nowhere else on the mountain looked more European. It was as if she were riding Elvis through Priorat in Spain.

It was impossible not to think about all that Otis and Joan had been through. She thought of her friend in Richland still on the deck watching the river run, letting Joni Mitchell ease her troubles.

Riding farther toward Sunset Road, Château Smooth came into view. Every time she left her house to go into town, Margot passed by it, and she'd watched as the gold driveway had dried and as they'd painted the stucco a hot pink. The winery stuck out like a cartoon character in a bar, and Margot could understand Otis's frustrations. From what she could tell, Château Smooth wasn't too far from opening its doors.

It really was a shame, Margot thought. But what do you do? So far, Château Smooth didn't seem to be affecting her business. The wines on the mountain were still just as good. It's just that people saw this incredibly tacky hot-pink palace as one of the first sights upon entering Red Mountain.

"It's another thing for the people to talk about," she said to Elvis. "I guess that's what it comes down to. We'd all get bored if we didn't have all these surprises popping up."

Margot was about to turn left and ride home when she noticed the beginnings of a wall rising in between Till Vineyards and Château Smooth. Riding closer, she saw several pallets of concrete block, and then she saw Otis. He lifted one of the blocks off a pallet and, hunched over, carried it toward the wall. Fitting it over a piece of rebar, he lowered it down and then aligned it with the others.

Even from this far away, she could see the sadness of him, almost like he was withering away. Thinking of all he'd been through, she tugged on the reins and went in his direction.

45

ONE-EYED OTIS

T he rising wall ran the entire border between the two properties. Once she got close, Otis turned. He was only a few inches taller than the highest part of the wall. He was shirtless and sunburned, and he looked skinnier than she'd ever seen him, unhealthily so. His stomach was caving in, and his ribs were showing. He wore tan pants and heavy-looking work boots that were covered in dirt and lime.

Otis limped toward her and wiped his brow. His entire body was painted with heartache. It had been two weeks since Joan had left him, and it looked like about that long since he'd eaten. The only sign of life he showed was the well-developed muscles of his arms, which told tales of many long days lifting those blocks and building this wall.

She pulled back the reins to slow down and wanted to cry when she saw him up close. He looked emaciated and broken. Gray whiskers rose from his face and neck. His gray hair ran in every direction like a wild animal.

"Otis, I'd tell ya you look good, but you don't."

He cracked a grin, and it was like a crack appearing in a clay pot. "No, I don't imagine I look too good."

"What can I do for you?"

He waved a hand in the air. "Oh, don't worry about me." He sounded even gruffer than normal, his throat straining to make sounds.

"How can I not? You don't look healthy."

He glanced back at his wall. "This has proved to be more work than I thought."

"You're doing it yourself?"

A nod. "Thought it might help me take my mind off things."

Elvis stomped the dirt, and Margot patted him. "How high are you going?"

"I'd like to get to eight feet. That should do it."

Margot let her imagination stack another few feet of concrete blocks onto what he'd built. "That will be a daunting wall."

"I have no doubt." He removed his cap. "How's Joan?"

She didn't feel it was her place to get in between them. "She's okay." Margot was fighting off tears. Never would she have imagined this sight. Otis was dying, right before her eyes.

"How about you, young lady? I've never seen you ride before."

"This is new. I'm just learning."

"Well, you look like you belong up there. And you look good. Like a big splash of light up there coming down on me. I need it." He approached the horse and put his hand on the horse's muzzle. "Elvis looks as happy as you are. He must love the attention."

Margot thought he sounded starved for conversation, like he'd been walking the desert without contact for years. "We're having fun out here," she said. "What a beautiful day."

He nodded, but she wasn't sure he was appreciating the same beauty. "What's it like riding a horse that can't see?" he asked.

"You'd never know it," Margot answered. "Honestly, I think not having eyes makes him see even better. His other senses are heightened to make up for it. I think he's got a map of the mountain in his mind."

"That's an interesting notion. He *has* become our mascot, hasn't he? What an inspiration. And you too, Margot. Seriously. I don't know exactly how to say it, but seeing you right now reminds me of the first time I met Joan. It's like all my troubles seem to melt away."

Margot had no idea how to respond, so she said the only words that made sense. "Thank you. How incredibly kind."

"I mean it. What a treasure you are."

She thanked him again. "I'm worried about you. Is there anything I can do?"

"You keep riding that horse. That's what you can do for me. Keep doing everything you're doing. You're the breath of fresh air this mountain needs." He glanced behind him. "Anyhow, I'd better get back to this wall. The neighbors are opening next month, and I'm hoping it will all seem like a bad dream once this thing's done." Otis put his cap back on his head. "Will you give my best to Joan?"

"Why don't you reach out to her, Otis?"

His lips flattened. "I'm afraid that would do more harm than good."

"Why's that?"

"I can't love her the way she deserves."

"It's none of my business, but I don't believe that for a second."

"I'm an old dog, Margot."

Never had she seen someone so broken, but she could also still see the faint light of love in his eyes. "It's never too late," she told him. "Look at Elvis. Try and tell him it's too late."

"Thanks for stopping by. It was timely. But I'd better get back to it."

"You know where to find us if you need anything. If you'll allow me to impart one last bit of advice, you might want to try eating a little something."

He looked down to his skeletal body. "Yeah."

"I'm serious, Otis. Can I bring something by? I happened to have cooked entirely too much food this morning at the inn."

"Oh, that's nice of you, but I'm all right."

"Suit yourself." Margot tipped her hat and gave the horse a light squeeze. "Let's go, Elvis."

As they left him, Margot felt like she'd taken a piece of his pain

with her, and was overwhelmed with sadness. Whether he'd eat it or
not, she would be returning with a feast shortly.

~

WITH A BLOCK IN HIS HAND, Otis watched her ride away. He supposed
it took someone seeing him in this state to make him aware of it. She
was right. He did need to eat. He needed to do a lot of things.

With each block he'd stacked in the past two weeks, he'd carried
the weight of knowing he'd failed Joan. But it was the knowing that
she was better off without him that gave him the strength to carry on.
It didn't matter that he loved her with everything that he had. It didn't
matter that he wanted to spend the rest of his life with her and that
life seemed worthless without her.

What mattered was that Joan be set free to live to her true potential, and the only way that could happen was if Otis wasn't a rusty
shackle to her ankle.

Not reaching out to her was hard, though. Especially after
discussing her with Margot. He looked at Elvis and her one last time
as they crossed over Sunset Road. He'd seen a lot of Joan in Margot
just now, and maybe that had made it hard too.

He carried the block to the wall, slipped it over the vertical cut of
rebar, and set it down. *Still a lot of work to do*, he thought. *A lot of guilt
to carry.* His eyes went over the wall to Château Smooth. The
McMansion was now flamingo pink, and the area around the pool
had been developed. A line of white cabanas ran along one side all
the way to a beach bar with a thatched roof. Though he couldn't see
the pool from his vantage point, he could see the top of a pink water
slide.

The anger he'd felt for longer than he could remember faded into
a maniacal laugh that echoed off his wall. He folded over, thinking of
how wonderful a prank the good Lord above had played on him.
Surely this was a dream. There couldn't actually be a place called
Château Smooth opening next door to the property he'd been

farming for a good part of his life. It had to be a terrible, terrible dream.

Once he'd let out all the laughter, he went back to stacking concrete. As he worked, he thought more about his encounter with Margot. Thinking of Elvis, he could still see quite clearly the sown-up scars that had once been Elvis's eyes.

What was it Margot had said? he mused.

Not having eyes makes him see even better.

Otis knew there were lessons to be learned from Margot's visit, almost as if she were meant to have come by on that horse. It didn't take him long to link the blindness to Joan's ludicrous idea of an eye patch, and then he found himself laughing again. This round wasn't quite as maniacal, and the laughing morphed into crying, and before he knew it, he'd dropped down to the Red Mountain dust.

46

BACK TO THE BOTTLE

Brooks was returning from Irrigation Specialists in Pasco when he thought he'd swing by to see Adriana. He wanted to see how her conversation with Margot had gone, but there was something even more important on his mind.

Pulling into Épiphanie, he did a double take when he saw Margot riding Elvis along the road to the sanctuary. *Good for her*, he thought.

He parked out front and entered through the large wooden doors. Passing through the lobby, he found Adriana at one of the dining room tables folding linens.

"What are you doing here?" she asked, offering a smile.

"Had to run out for a little bit and thought I'd swing by to say hello. Was that Margot I just saw riding Elvis?"

"Yeah, she's riding him every day now. Your brother's been teaching her."

"That's great. So she's okay with you leaving?"

"She didn't freak out, that's for sure. Maybe she saw it coming." Adriana went back to folding napkins.

"Can I help?" he asked, reaching for a napkin.

She showed him her method and then, "When will you tell Otis?"

Once he'd figured out the folding, he said, "I'm putting it off as long as possible. I want to be there for him, but I can't lie about us leaving. I'm afraid, if I tell him, he'll go off the deep end."

"That's really sad." After a moment, she asked, "He's still building the wall?"

"By himself, yeah."

"It must be really hard to see a man you care so much about go through this."

"It's freaking unbearable. I wish there were something I could do, but I've known him a long time. The only thing any of us can do is let him fight his way through it. I swear...as much as I love this mountain and everyone here, it will be nice to be three thousand miles away. It can be exhausting. The last thing I want is to follow in his footsteps."

Adriana added another folded napkin to her stack. She was moving three times as quickly as Brooks. "Don't stay away from him for long. He needs you."

"I won't, but I need to choose the right time to break our news to him. Trust me: he's not ready for it right now."

But Brooks was ready to bring up the reason he'd really come. He took Adriana's hand. "I've been thinking about something. Ever since we decided to move."

She faced him. "Yeah?"

His pulse pounded in his wrists. He let his nerves calm and then said, "I think we should start trying to have a baby." Just the idea of it made Brooks smile, his fatherly instincts coming alive, and he looked at her, hoping she'd feel the same way. "Even if you got pregnant immediately, we'd still have time to get settled in Florida before the baby came."

To his surprise, her face went flat, and her eyes shifted away from him. For a second, he sensed a very bitter rejection and even repulsion. She quickly recovered, though, and twisted toward him with a smile. "I want to have a baby with you," she said, "but I'm not quite ready."

The last thing he wanted to do was push her. "Yeah, I get it."

Adriana squeezed his hand. "Seriously. I do. Just not yet."

Brooks nodded and whispered, "It's fine."

Dammit, he wished she would just wake up from her nightmare. Was Florida really the secret ingredient to her happiness?

~

SHORTLY AFTERWARD, Brooks walked into a bloodbath in the tasting room of Lacoda. Carmen looked like she was on the wrong end of a firing squad facing Jake and Emilia.

As much as Brooks wanted to duck back out, he asked, "What's going on?"

The three Foresters turned as if he'd just slung a grenade at their feet.

"My mom's drinking again," Emilia said. "We found a bunch of empty wine bottles in her office."

Though his body froze, Brooks's eyes slid toward Carmen. She was looking down at the bar, hunched over in shame.

"I can't believe you, Mom," Emilia said. "You made it months."

With her eyes fixed on something below her, Carmen said, "I'm sorry. I'm so sorry."

"It's my fault," Jake said. "I never should have agreed to let you work here."

"I'm just gonna..." Brooks turned.

Jake whipped around. "Brooks, you're family too. Please come join the discussion."

Brooks cautiously approached the bar. He might be family, but he didn't feel like he had anything to contribute at the moment. He'd already suspected Carmen might be drinking again, but figured it was none of his business.

"Carmen will be resigning her position as of today," Jake said. "The official story will be that she's looking into starting a new clothing line. I don't want the drinking thing to leave this room. We all know how that will play out in the media."

"Now do you see why I don't want you here?" Carmen asked her daughter, mopping her face. "Because this happens. Alcohol tears people apart. Can't you see that now?"

"Carmen," Jake snapped. "Enough. We'll get you back to rehab, and we'll get through this."

Emilia had gone behind the bar and torn a paper towel off a roll. She handed it to her mother. "He's right. We'll get through this."

Carmen took the paper towel and wiped her face. "I will not go back to rehab."

"Yes, you will, Mom. You're *definitely* going back."

"A lot of good it did," Carmen muttered. "There's no way I'm going back there."

Jake lost his temper. "We're not going to talk about it another minute. Not until you're sober."

Carmen found Brooks with her serpentine eyes. "Hope you're happy now."

Brooks raised his hands.

She pointed at him. "This is exactly what you wanted, isn't it?"

He wasn't close enough to smell her breath, but it was certainly obvious she was at least a bottle deep. "Not at all," Brooks whispered.

"All right, Carmen," Jake said. "Let's head home."

Carmen brushed past all of them and held up a middle finger, saying, "Fuck off," as she burst out the front door.

Jake looked at Brooks. "Don't suppose you want to stay now, do you?"

"Where are you going?" Emilia asked in confusion.

Jake realized what he'd done and dropped his head. "Brooks is leaving us after harvest. Or at least that's the plan. Is it still the case?"

Brooks looked at Emilia. "I'm sorry I haven't told you yet. No one really knows. I haven't even told Otis yet."

Emilia looked even sadder, if that was possible. "Where are you going?"

"To Florida...with Adriana and Zack."

Emilia pointed to the door through which Carmen had just left. "Because of her?"

Brooks found it impossible to lie to her, so he chose not to speak.

"Of course, it is." Emilia frowned. Turning to her father, she said, "She ruins everything."

Brooks didn't want her to think that way. "There are a lot of reasons why I'm leaving, Em. Sometimes, we outgrow a place."

"That's bullshit, Brooks, and you know it."

∼

THE DAYS after they'd caught her mom were the hardest in Emilia's life. She wanted to enjoy the exciting lead up to harvest. Along with the tangy smell of ripening grapes, there was a wild and nervous energy in the air, almost like soldiers waiting for war, and Emilia wanted to begin preparations.

Instead, her world was full of goodbyes.

Emilia, Luca, and Abby watched from the driveway as Jake left with Carmen to return to rehab in Seattle.

Once they'd gone, Luca said, "Is Mom sick? I know she's not going to work. Why is everyone lying to me?" They'd done their best to sugarcoat Carmen's departure for the young boy with the vibrant imagination.

Emilia put her arm around her brother. "She's a little sick but almost has it beat."

"Has what beat?"

"You know how we don't say the enemy's name in Harry Potter?" When her brother nodded, she said, "Let's not name Mom's, either."

A few days after that, Emilia had to say goodbye to Jasper. Trying to spend as much time as he could with her, he'd pushed his flight back as far as possible. On August ninth, the day before he left, they met in the morning to hike to the top of Red Mountain, which stood about fourteen hundred feet above sea level. Hand in hand, they strolled through the vines toward the trailhead above the last vineyard block on the eastern side.

As they started the steeper slope, Jasper asked "Have you talked to your mom?" She'd been gone one week to the day.

"Yeah, actually. We Facetimed with her last night. She seems really good. Not nearly as pissed as she was last time."

"That's good to hear."

"Yeah. I'm kind of glad I'll be around to help out while she's gone. There's only so much Abby can do. I want to be there for my dad."

"I have to give it to him," Jasper said. "He's the most patient man in the world."

"Totally."

"I can hear it in his playing, you know. When he's down, I mean. He channels all his pain into his music, and it's pretty wild to be in the same room."

"I'm starting to wonder who you'll miss more," Emilia said. "Him or me."

"That's a tough call." Jasper jokingly placed a finger on his chin. "But I think you win out."

After a few beats of silence, he said soberly, "Wait for me, Em."

She stopped and looked at him. They were both breathing heavier because of the ascent. "What makes you think I wouldn't wait for you?"

"Maybe I'm just afraid of losing you."

She hated to hear the sadness in his voice and grabbed his arm. "You're stuck with me, punk. Do *I* need to worry about you hooking up with one of your groupies? I've seen the way girls look at you when you're onstage."

Jasper scoffed. "All I see is you when I'm onstage."

Emilia's heart danced.

When they reached the top of the mountain, where the winds blew hard, Jasper took her hand and they spun around, taking in the 360-degree view. They could see for miles and miles over the treeless mountains and hills and the rich farmland. Emilia felt a world of opportunity looking back at her. Feeling his hand in hers made all that possibility seem achievable, and she was filled with a certainty that they'd take on the world together.

They stopped spinning and looked down over the vineyard blocks that were densely planted across the entirety of the southwest-facing slope. She searched for a moment and could barely make out Lacoda, with its sand-colored stone and minimalist architecture. Looking just above the winery, she surveyed their vineyards for the vine they called Angeline. She was too far away to see her, but she fixed her eyes on the general area and saw a cloud of healthy green leaves a few rows down from Sunset Road. From up there on high, she could feel the pulse of the vineyard she'd one day inherit.

Emilia wrapped her arm around Jasper's waist. "When you're done doing what you need to do, come back here and put a ring on my finger. I'll wait for you as long as it takes."

Jasper turned and kissed her for a long time, and Emilia knew she'd never want anyone else. He stepped back and reached down. She licked her lips and watched as he ripped a blade of cheat grass from the ground.

Jasper wound it into a band, took her hand, and slipped the circle around her finger. "I'm yours forever. Every note I ever play. Every song I ever write...is yours. I'll be back, I swear to you."

Not many men could say those words with such sincerity. No one else could have said such a thing to Emilia without losing her to laughter. When he said them, though, she lost herself in his wonderful world of poetry. She kissed him again and felt a wave of sadness coming.

Sensing it, he said, "Your place is here. We both know that. But you know what I believe?" He pushed a stray hair away from her eyes. "Nothing can stand in our way."

Emilia felt her heart thumping, and she loved him more than she ever had.

Jasper put his hand on her neck, and they kissed and spun around again—the king and queen of their world—and Jasper whispered, "This is what it's like to be standing on top of the world."

"Let's never forget right now," she said.

He shook his head. "Never, ever, ever, ever..."

47

TILL I SEE YOU AGAIN

Eighteen Days Later

Otis had been driving trucks all his life, but this darn thing was big. He supposed he'd get used to it after a day or two of driving, which was much more than he could say for the sound of the RV's horn. Some knucklehead had installed a custom beep that played "La Cucaracha" every time you pushed the soft spot in the center of the wheel.

Though Otis had acted grumpy about it when he'd heard the sound for the first time, there was a ring of truth in it, and he'd known he was on the right track with buying this RV and going after his woman.

He swung a hard right into Joan's long driveway and parked near the house. It had been one month since he'd spoken with her. Heck, one month since he'd spoken with much of anyone. Thankfully, other than his own employees, Margot and Brooks were the only ones to catch a glimpse of his recent collapse.

And what a collapse it had been. In those first two weeks post-Joan, he'd managed to let his body and house go to hell. It was a good thing Eli and the other gents had picked up his slack, for even the wines and vines had fallen from his purview. All Otis had done was stack blocks for a wall that was still incomplete.

The bad days were in the past, though. Sometime shortly after Otis had been visited by Margot and Elvis, he'd had some sort of breakthrough. When she'd returned with a giant basket of leftovers, Margot had told him about her own epiphany. Otis thought that was a good word for it.

His own awakening had struck him in the chest like a mallet. And it all started with a blind horse, a cowgirl, and an eye patch.

The day after Margot and Elvis had visited, Otis found an old leather bag and had taken it into his shop at the winery. After thirty minutes, he'd created a sharp-looking eye patch—as far as eye patches go—with a light-brown patch and a black band. He'd walked out of the shop with the attitude that people were welcome to laugh at him. He didn't care anymore. He'd woken from his daydream and realized he wanted one thing and one thing only: Joan Tobey.

Sure enough, when Chaco and Esteban saw him and determined that he hadn't sustained an eye injury, they laughed and called him *La Pirata de la Montaña Roja*. Eli laughed even harder, asking him where he'd left his parrot. Otis smirked back. "Yo ho ho, you bozos. Laugh all you want."

Four mornings into his eye-patch therapy, a funny thing happened. Still wet from a shower, he stood in front of the mirror with a towel wrapped around his waist and hacked away the grisly beard that had taken over his face.

After pulling the eye patch back over his eye, Otis found himself looking eye-to-eye, quite literally, with the Otis Till of his youth. In place of the old grump who'd busied himself with a million tasks and worries in order to soften the pain of losing his wife and two sons, he saw the young man who'd fallen in love with Rebecca on the way to those three wet and wonderful days at Woodstock. He saw the dare-he-say strapping young Otis who had partnered with this woman to realize their dream: to buy a farm of their own in Sonoma. He remembered how hard they'd worked to save enough money to buy their first several acres, and Otis smiled at the memory of the day when he and Rebecca had climbed out of the truck and realized what they'd committed to. Neither one of them knew anything about growing grapes, but they'd jumped in and figured it out.

That man looked deep into Otis's one eye and wordlessly said that he wasn't done living. There were still adventures to be had. Standing there in his towel, Otis had lifted up his arms and flexed his muscles and howled like a blooming idiot until he'd lost his voice.

As the days passed, he came to embrace the eccentricity of his eye patch, and he found that, for the first time in many moons, he didn't give a rip what people thought about him. Another wonderful realization had struck him as he'd walked up to the winery one day. He'd stopped looking over the wall at the neighbor's property. Whether it was the eye patch or just the sheer rawness of hitting rock bottom, Otis had broken through to the other side, and the weight of things that didn't matter had drifted away.

The only thing that didn't feel right was the hole in his heart. What was all this for if he didn't have the woman he loved?

Thirty days after Joan had left him, he decided that he was the biggest idiot this side of the Cascades. There was nothing in the world—including Red Mountain—that held a candle to Joan Tobey, and he became intent on sharing his revelation with her. He didn't know if she'd moved on or if he had a chance, but he'd spent thirty days of ups and downs working toward one big choice.

He'd give it all away if he could get her back.

What was the value of even the finest vintage if he couldn't share it with her?

The answer to that question is what had led him to a used-RV lot, where he'd found a Class C Winnebago that blew "La Cucaracha."

He'd also put a good deal of effort into looking good for her too. Not only had he hacked away his grisly beard, but he'd driven into Benton City to visit the barber, where they'd given him hell for his "pirate patch" as they trimmed him back to handsome. He'd laughed with them, knowing there was no better medicine in the world than the kind of laugh that nearly splits the corners of your mouth.

Sitting in his Winnebago in his best khaki pants and ironed shirt,

Otis glanced at the mirror and straightened his eye patch and tweed cap. He thought he saw the younger Otis wink back at him. Then with a big fat smile on his face, he pressed down on the horn, and "La Cucaracha" rang through Joan's neighborhood.

The sound was so absurd that Otis found himself chuckling yet again, and he realized his sides were sore from laughing so much lately. When she didn't appear, he pressed the horn again, letting the melody of the Mexican folk song fill the air.

The door finally popped open, and Joan poked her head out.

Unable to resist, he pressed the horn again and, like the conductor of a symphony, bounced his hand to the melody.

When she allowed herself to smile, it was as if the grandest fireworks display on earth had just begun. Otis was roaring and could barely get the window rolled down on the passenger side.

"*What* in the *world*?" Joan asked as the music died down.

"Hop up here. Let me show you."

Joan pulled open the door and stepped up onto the rail. "I don't know what to ask about first. The eye patch or the RV."

"I would have started with the blasted horn!"

She shook her head and fixed her eyes on the steering wheel. "I don't even know how to touch that."

Then she noticed the bonsai tree attached to the dash. Otis had thought of that little touch at the last moment and had luckily found one at a nursery near her house.

"Look at that," she said. "You're full of surprises, aren't you?"

"I'm pulling out all the stops today." He took in the beauty of her, and he told himself he'd never let her slip away again. "Wanna go for a ride?"

She dipped her chin, and he could tell she was questioning him.

"Now hold on," he said. "I'm not asking for any big commitments. I just want to take a girl for a ride in my new RV. Just a spin or two around the neighborhood."

"How could I say no?" she asked. He could tell she was holding back a grin, and she took her seat and pulled on the seatbelt. "What's gotten into you, Otis Till?"

He twisted the key and the motor cranked up. A Berlioz symphony filled the cab. He reached for the map in the visor. "It occurred to me I haven't seen all there is to see of this great country, and I thought I'd go on an adventure."

"Is that right?" she asked skeptically.

"I do need to finish this vintage, but I've decided it will be my last harvest on Red Mountain. Making wine is a young person's game. It's time I go see the sights. Of course, I need a copilot, *if*, by chance, you know of someone."

Joan turned down the music and took a serious tone. "Otis, I am not going to be the reason you leave wine. I've already told you this."

He shook his head. "You have nothing to do with—" He stopped himself. "That's not true. You have a little bit to do with it, but not how you think. I've decided to sell Till Vineyards, because it's what's best for me. I think you're right. I've been hiding behind my profession as if it defined me. The truth is, I'm not even having fun anymore. Why work my tail off if it's not fun?" Otis met the seriousness of the mood head-on. "I don't like the man I was turning into, and I think it's time to retire. It's a word I never thought I'd say, but then again, I never thought I'd meet you."

Otis reached for her hand. "I don't know what conclusions you've come to *or* if you'd consider giving me another chance, but the one thing I've decided is that I'm leaving the mountain, and I'm going to do like all the young kids do and go find myself. So I'm going with or without you, but I tell you, babe...I'd rather go with you."

"Who will you sell your winery to?"

"Well, I'd like Brooks to take it over. He's been having some troubles at Lacoda, and I think it'd be a good change for him. He doesn't have the money, but I'll help him out. Lord knows, Morgan left me enough. Brooks deserves his own spot on the mountain."

"But Brooks is going with Adriana to Florida," Joan told him.

"What?" Otis hadn't heard this news. "What are you talking about?"

"I guess he hasn't gotten around to telling you, but Adriana's told Margot as much."

Otis felt a knot in the pit of his stomach. He'd been so excited to offer Brooks a chance to own the winery, but maybe this was best. "If that's what he's chosen to do, then he's wiser than I was at his age. You know, Joan, it doesn't quite matter what I do with the property. I know it can be sold, and that's what I'll do."

He meant every word he said, but Otis couldn't deny the impact this news of Brooks's departure had on him. He wondered if he should tell Brooks what he'd planned.

Pushing past it, he said, "I just want one last vintage to go out on. Judging by how hot it is, I'll be done early. I've always said I'd rather go out on a cool vintage, but the time is now."

"You can always pick in July," Joan joked.

"It wouldn't be the first time, would it? So what do you say? Would you give me another chance, Joan? I'm a changed man. I don't think it was this blasted eye patch, but that was part of it. An eye patch. A broken heart. A blind horse. And that Margot and whatever's gotten into her. I'm a changed man, and I want to spend the rest of my life proving it to you."

As she sometimes did, Joan closed her eyes and breathed for a moment. He wondered what she saw when she closed her eyes, and he imagined a vast multiverse of color and light.

He couldn't take the waiting. "You don't have another man in there, do you? I don't mean in between your ears," he said, smiling. "I mean in your house. I'm not too late, am I?"

Joan opened her eyes. "No, Otis. I don't have a man in there." She sighed. "I'm not sure what to think. I love what I hear and see, especially the sound of the horn. You still need to put on some weight, but you look happy. I can feel it. But you can't just pull up with an eye patch and an RV and blow 'La Cucaracha' and expect me to throw myself at you."

Otis worked hard to hold his head up. He'd hoped for more but understood her stance.

"Tell you what," she said. "Why don't you take me for a spin in this beauty? That would be a good place to start."

It wasn't what he'd hoped, but it was more than he deserved. His grin came back, and he reached under his seat, extracting a costume pirate hat. Handing it to her, he said, "Would you do me the honor?"

She took the silly blue hat with both hands and set it on her head. In a pirate accent that challenged Otis's finest efforts, she said, "Shiver me timbers. Let's see how this old gal sails."

Otis put his hand on the gear knob and took one last look at Joan before putting his eye on the road. He'd made a lot of mistakes over his lifetime, but how could he regret any of them if they'd led him to this exact spot on the treasure map?

～

DOWN BY THE YAKIMA RIVER, as the falling sun reflected off the water, Margot sat with Remi and Carly on the concrete pad outside of his Airstream. Veggie burgers sizzled on the charcoal grill nearby. Philippe and Henri were tugging on a stick that was twice their size.

"We have something we thought we'd run by you, Carly," Remi said, drumming his fingers on the armrests.

"What's that?" Carly had been talking about some new ideas for weed control in the garden, but Margot and Remi were bursting at the seams to share their idea.

"We want you to stay on the mountain," Remi said.

Margot could barely wait to get a word in. "I'd like to offer you a full-time job at Épiphanie. If that interests you. With Adriana leaving, the timing could be perfect."

"And I thought you might like to stay in the Airstream," Remi said. "Not that we're kicking you out. You're welcome to stay with us too. But I know how nice it would be to have your own space."

Carly's eyes had gone wide as she took in all this information. She eventually looked at Margot, and a giant tear slid down her cheek.

"Oh, sweetie," Margot said, reaching for her hand. "Don't cry. You're going to make me..."

Margot broke into a sob as well and looked over at Remi, who was worse than either of them. There weren't enough tissues in Benton County to wipe their tears.

Margot stood and opened her arms to her big hunk of a man and said to her future stepdaughter, "Get in here, Carly."

Carly pressed up from her chair and joined them in a big hug.

"I don't know what I did to deserve you two," Remi said, "but I'm the happiest and luckiest man alive." He wiped his tears and asked, "What do you say, Carly? Will you stay with us for a while? Or is this mountain too small and crazy for you?"

"This mountain is just small and crazy enough to make me feel like I fit in. And I'd love to work full-time for you, Margot. If you're really serious?"

"Of course, I am."

Margot looked at her fiancé and thought about their wedding next month, and it occurred to her that happy endings didn't only happen on *Hallmark*. If you worked at it, happily-ever-afters were possible in real life too.

48

THE DAY BEFORE THE WEDDING

"**Y**ou're wearing polka dots to your wedding?"

Margot's best friend, Erica, stared at Margot like she was crazy. She'd flown in from Vermont late the night before. It was 8:00 a.m., and they were upstairs in Margot's bedroom.

"I'm not just wearing polka dots." Margot held up her dress. "I'm owning polka dots tomorrow."

"It's not even a wedding dress."

"I know. It was just something I had in my closet. It's what makes me feel good inside. That's *all* that matters."

Erica looked at her like she'd gone mad. "I...guess...I approve." Erica was quite a bit older than Margot but dressed like she was still thirty. She'd never been afraid to get a little work done, tightening up the loose spots and such, so she did look deceptively young for her age. Margot had missed her best friend. They'd raised their kids together and stood by each other's sides as both of their first marriages fell apart.

"I wore an expensive sequined thing for my first wedding," Margot said, "and look how that turned out. No, no, no. Not this time."

"It's not what I'd choose," Erica said, "but I'm not Margot Pierce. I'm sure you'll look lovely. I'm assuming Remi has approved?"

"That's just one of the reasons why I love him. He said I could walk down the aisle in my muumuu if I wanted to."

Erica circled a finger in the air. "Tell me we're at least going to do something with your hair."

Margot blew out a blast of air. "I'm not a savage. Of course, I'm doing something with my hair. I have an appointment at ten a.m. tomorrow with Johnny, who is the best in the Tri-Cities. And Joan is making me a crown of wildflowers."

Erica looked at her again. "Polka dots and wildflowers?"

Margot crossed her arms and nodded proudly. "It's my party, and I can do what I want to."

"Well, that's you in a nutshell. I'll give you that."

"All right," Margot said. "Shall we go next door and see how things are coming along?"

"Absolutely."

Descending the stairs, they found Remi sitting by the fireplace, sipping coffee, and looking at his iPad.

He turned. "I was just reading about the Château Smooth grand opening tonight. I can't believe it's really happening."

Margot kissed him. "Don't remind me. On the eve of our wedding day, no less. Let's hope that's not a bad omen."

"Remi," Erica said, "you are aware she's wearing polka dots, right? I just want to be sure we're all on the same page here."

"I love Margot in polka dots."

"Oh, that's right," Erica said. "Marijuana *is* legal here, isn't it?"

The three of them laughed.

"We're walking next door to check on things," Margot said. "You have your list of things to do, right, honey?"

"As soon as I finish this cup of coffee, I will be at your service the rest of the day."

"Oh, my gosh!" Erica exclaimed. "You have him trained well. Can we clone him?"

"I'm not sharing," Margot said, "that's for sure."

Erica asked Remi, "No bachelor party plans tonight?"

He set down his iPad. "Some of the fellas are getting together."

Margot whispered, "They call themselves the Guardians of Red Mountain."

Erica's mouth widened. "Oh, how adorable."

"Isn't it? And he'll be sleeping in the Airstream tonight and isn't allowed to see me until the wedding."

Erica looked surprised. "Then you haven't let go of all the traditions."

"Of course not. He's not allowed to see me in my polka dots until I strut down the aisle."

"How wonderfully superstitious."

Remi sat back and waved them off. "Stay out of trouble, you two."

As the women exited the house, Margot nearly dropped her coffee. They'd been working so crazily to prepare for the past few days that she hadn't realized how well things had come together. Though it hadn't rained for months, the air smelled clean. The grass and roses around the inn looked more alive than ever. Thank goodness for irrigation. Enrique had done a marvelous job with the landscaping, and she felt for a moment like she was living in Downton Abbey.

"You really have it made, haven't you?" Erica said. "Everything you talked about back in Burlington. I'm so proud of you for chasing your dream. You did it, my friend."

"Thank you."

~

"COME MEET MY IN-LAWS," Margot said to Erica, seeing Remi's parents eating breakfast in the dining room. They'd arrived yesterday as well.

After stopping for a couple of hellos to other guests along the way, Margot asked her future in-laws, "How did you two sleep?"

Remi's father, Marcus, looked up from his breakfast. A strange amount of gray hair protruded from his ears, and Margot had wondered why Remi's mother, Alyssa, had never suggested a trim. All grooming issues aside, Marcus was a lovely man.

"Absolutely wonderful," he said. "We just adore staying here. You are a world-class innkeeper."

Margot smiled. "We love having you. Meet my best friend, Erica. She just flew in last night."

Erica waved her hands in the air. "Please don't get up. It's lovely to meet you."

When Erica took Alyssa's hand, she said, "I just love your ruby ring."

Alyssa beamed. "Marcus just gave it to me. We celebrated our fortieth year together last month."

"Way to defy the odds," Erica said, glancing at Margot.

"I know," Margot agreed. "I've lucked out with two amazing in-laws." She looked at Alyssa. "If only my parents could have lived long enough to meet you two."

Margot made the rounds, introducing Erica to everyone, and then they walked outside to where the ceremony was to be held. Jasper and Jake would play in the lobby as people arrived and then move to the patio for a second set later in the evening after the ceremony. To keep everyone out of the sun, they'd set up a small tent in the grass just past the pizza oven and patio. Rows of chairs, forty in all, faced the altar, which waited for flowers. Beyond the tent was Margot's garden and then the neighbor's vines, which were nearly sagging with beautiful purple clusters.

Breathing in the ripening grapes, Margot said, "Someone pinch me now."

"Hey, Margot," a woman said.

Margot turned to find Carmen standing there. She was wearing black skinny jeans and a denim shirt knotted in the front, and she carried a giant white gift box with an ivory ribbon under her arm and a basket of smaller gifts in the other.

Margot's mouth fell open. "You're home? I didn't think you'd be able to make the wedding."

"There's a rumor going around that you're getting married in polka dots," Carmen said. "I broke out of rehab to come save you from such a *terrible* mistake."

"Oh my God," Margot said, stepping toward her. "Did you really break out?"

"No, not exactly, but I came home early to deliver this dress. I had a friend of mine in Paris design it just for you. It arrived yesterday."

Margot's eyes watered. "You had a dress designed for me in Paris?" Margot could only imagine the connections Carmen had.

She smiled. "You don't *have* to wear it, but I thought I'd give you the option in case you got cold feet with the polka dots." She held up the basket. "And I picked out some shoes and a little jewelry too."

Margot was nearly shaking, she was so touched. It occurred to her that Erica had never met Carmen, so she introduced them.

Erica approached her. "Thank God you're saving her from this absurd polka-dot thing. I don't know what she was thinking...or smoking."

"I get it," Margot confessed. "The polka dots were a stretch. Why don't we walk over to my house, so we can lay the dress out on the couch?" Margot wanted to see that dress!

While catching up on what Carmen had missed in the six weeks she'd been gone, the three of them circled around Épiphanie and walked through the garden to Margot's house.

Inside, Remi stood to say hello to Carmen. "Was she surprised?" he asked, offering her a kiss on the cheek.

"Wait a minute," Margot said to him. "You knew?"

"I needed your shoe size," Carmen admitted.

Margot hit Remi on the arm. "You said you loved polka dots."

He shrugged. "I love everything you wear."

"Okay, enough chitchat," Erica said. "Let's open that box."

Moving to the living area, Margot set the box down on the couch. Everyone gathered around. She pulled the ivory ribbon and then lifted off the top, revealing layers of tissue and a note in a beautiful scroll.

Margot read it out loud. "From Paris with love." Margot smiled at Carmen, then carefully broke the seal and pulled open the tissue.

The dress was winter white and made of silk, and Margot knew without even holding it up that it would be the most beautiful dress she'd ever seen. She lifted up the bodice, and Carmen helped her stretch it out over the couch. Cut on the bias, the silk dress featured bell sleeves and an ornate trim at the neckline. Margot could instantly see herself in it and couldn't have imagined a more perfect choice.

"I think it will look absolutely stunning on you," Carmen said. "I've been working with Alfonse for almost ten years. Everyone wants his wedding dresses right now."

"I can see why." Margot wrapped her arms around her and thanked her. "This means more than you know. You're an angel."

Carmen squeezed her. "Thanks for being a friend. And judging how things are going between our kids, I have a feeling we'll be family one day."

"Wouldn't that be wonderful?" Margot said.

～

HAVING SPENT a few years on the mountain, Emilia was no stranger to harvest. She recognized the smell of ripe fruit in the fall, and she'd picked and stomped grapes for four years now, but today was different.

After sleepless nights and nearly endless deliberation, she was pretty sure it was time to harvest her vines. Though a vein of doubt ran through her, a louder voice was telling her to trust her instincts.

First thing that morning, she had run the numbers, and the levels were acceptable, but as she'd been taught, the numbers only told part of the story.

When she asked Brooks for his opinion, he wasn't much help. They'd finished picking the white grapes, and he was busy managing their fermentations, as well as prepping for the coming red fruit.

"Will you just tell me if I'm off track?" Emilia begged. "You wouldn't let me pick too early, would you?"

"These are your vines. I have plenty of decisions to make." He tasted the sample from her vines again. "Don't base your decisions on when we picked last year or the year before. This is the hottest and driest year that I can remember. All you can do is pick off taste now."

"But how can I be sure what it will taste like when it's fermented? I can't taste the future."

"I think you *can* taste the future."

"But I don't want my first wine to taste like olive and green pepper juice."

"I wouldn't either."

She furrowed her brow in frustration. "You're really not going to help me decide?"

"You're attending the Otis school of trial by fire. These are your grapes. I know it's not easy, but I believe in you. This is your project." He seemed to drift away for a moment. "And when you nail the timing, Em, it's the best feeling in the world."

She'd tasted the juice so many times that she was almost out of her sample. Leaving Brooks, she ran back down to her vines with a Ziploc bag and walked the rows, plucking a grape or two from every other vine. Once she'd bagged enough fruit for a good representation, she drove a Lacoda truck over to Otis's winery. Maybe he'd help.

Standing in his lab off the main cellar, he crushed the grapes in a small container and poured the juice into two wine glasses. He tossed the contents into his mouth and made a chewing motion, before swallowing.

Once again, Emilia could see the little boy in Otis coming out, as his face filled with excitement. "It's a lovely syrah."

"Yeah, but is it ready? Have you picked any of your reds? Isn't September too early? Especially for syrah?"

He seemed amused by her questions. "It's absolutely too early. If it was last year. Or the year before. Don't live in the past. What are the grapes telling you now?" He whispered, "Listen to the vines."

"I appreciate the idea," Emilia said, "but vines don't really talk."

Otis scoffed and put his finger to his ear. "Mine do."

"Please just tell me if I'm crazy to pick today."

Otis chuckled to himself and feigned zipping his mouth shut.

"You and Brooks are conspiring against me," she said with a smile of embracing a challenge.

⤳

WHEN SHE RETURNED to her babies, she sat in the dust and closed her eyes. She could hear tractors and footsteps from other rows and music coming up from her dad's studio. To her ear, the vines were not talking.

She pressed up and plucked a grape from a cluster. Sitting cross-legged, she closed her eyes and stuck the berry into her mouth. As it burst in between her teeth, the juice hit her tongue in an eruption of flavor. Giving in to the *terroir*, she lowered down onto her back and put all her focus on the taste. She could feel the ground beneath her, almost like it was trembling.

Once she'd swallowed the juice, she chewed on the skin and gave in to the tannins as they gripped her mouth. Something kept telling her it wasn't too early. She needn't be scared. Spitting the seeds and skins to the ground, she lay there, still and listening.

The flavors of the Red Mountain syrah juice lingered for a long time, and she imagined the journey these grapes would take, all the way to the bottle. She imagined this exact flavor profile transforming during fermentation and then finding its way to a wine glass. That's when it hit her.

Today was the day. She could suddenly taste exactly what the wine would taste like six months from now. It wasn't bitter or too vegetal. Nor was it sappy and unbalanced. All the doubt and fear and anxiety that had clawed at her washed away.

She called Brooks, and within thirty minutes, they were picking her fruit. Four of them marched up and down the rows with clippers, filling small buckets and transferring them to two larger bins resting in the back of the truck. A little over two hours later, her vines were naked, and the bins were full.

Driving the truck back up to the winery, she parked near the crush pad. She pulled up one of the garage doors leading into the cellar, then climbed onto a forklift. As Brooks watched with crossed arms, she unloaded the two bins and set them down gently onto the crush pad.

Hopping off the forklift, he asked, "What's next?"

"We stomp?"

"That we do."

Brooks rolled down the truck windows and cranked up some vintage rock 'n' roll. They removed their boots and rolled up their jeans. Emilia climbed into her bin first, and a burst of pleasure hit her as her feet sank into the pillow of grapes.

Brooks swung a leg over the wall of his bin. "Too late to turn back now."

"Did I make the right call?" she asked, lifting her legs and walking in place. The grapes exploded under her feet, and she thought there might not be a better feeling in the world.

"There is no right or wrong. You know that."

She sighed. "I mean, did I screw it up? I understand that the correct picking date is subjective."

Brooks stopped stomping. "For what it's worth, I'm picking the Angeline block later today."

Emilia's arms tingled. Her eyes watered. "Are you serious?"

"You did good, kid."

She raised her hands in victory. There might not be a right or wrong day to pick, but she was proud to know she and Brooks were on the same page. With a feeling of immense satisfaction and fulfillment, Emilia went back to stomping the grapes of her first true vintage on Red Mountain.

49

THE GUARDIANS OF RED MOUNTAIN

T he Guardians of Red Mountain sat on Otis's back deck looking west toward Seattle. A full moon rose over their little get-together for Remi on the last night of his single life. It also happened to be the grand opening for Château Smooth, and a low rumbling bass thumped from a DJ's speakers off in the distance.

Though they still hadn't enjoyed a fall rain yet, the nights were getting cooler, and Otis had just pulled on a brown cardigan. He was doing his best to make peace with the loud music and hoped that this wouldn't be a regular occurrence. Even if it were, Otis only had a few more weeks before he'd be saying his goodbyes anyway. Perhaps the music wouldn't bother the new owner of Till Vineyards at all.

The man of honor held a saber in one hand and a bottle of Champagne sans the cage in the other. Since it was Remi's first time to saber a bottle of bubbly, Brooks stood next to him and offered a few helpful suggestions.

"Don't chop the glass, or we'll be taking you to the hospital. Let the pressure in the bottle do all the work. All you have to do is run the saber along the seam."

"Hold the bottle away from your body too," Jake chimed in. "I've made that mistake before."

Remi held the Champagne bottle out in front of him and placed the saber's sharp edge on the shoulder. "Tell Margot I loved her."

"Oh, you'll survive," Brooks said. "Just think more ballerina and less Bruce Lee. No chopping. You're just guiding the saber toward the tip."

"Brooks, you can have my motorcycles," Remi said, continuing his joke.

"Should I get that in writing?"

"Nah, Margot will be glad to get rid of them." Remi turned one last time toward Otis, Brooks, and Jake. "Nice knowin' you, fellas."

He took a step toward the end of the deck and held the bottle at a forty-five-degree angle over the vineyards. He paused, and Otis could tell he was running over the checklist Brooks had given him.

The night seemed to go quiet as Red Mountain waited for Remi's first sabering. He committed to the act, and the steel of the blade slid across the glass. They all clapped and cheered as the cork and the severed glass tip sailed up into the air.

Remi turned with bubbles fizzing out of the cleanly cut neck.

The other guardians surrounded him with their glasses, and Remi filled them, one at a time.

Making a toast, Brooks said, "To the newest member of the Guardians of Red Mountain. Let the hazing begin."

They moved through the Champagne in a matter of minutes, and as Jake pulled the cork on an older Barolo, Otis said to him, "You should be very proud of your daughter. I know you guys are going through a lot with Carmen, but I hope you don't overlook what Emilia has done this summer. As we were tasting her syrah today, I was reminded of Brooks's first year on the mountain. She shows great promise."

The cork slid out of the Italian wine with a light pop. "I am proud of her, Otis, and appreciative of what you two have done for her. And I'm excited to know that Lacoda is in good hands. When Brooks first told me he was leaving, I strongly considered selling, but Emilia has convinced me otherwise."

"No, no," Otis said. "We can't all abandon the mountain. I have a feeling Lacoda is the future here."

Jake smelled the cork. "Have you decided what you'll do with your property?"

Otis still hadn't mentioned what he'd hoped would have happened. Though he didn't want to mess with Brooks's mind, he felt a sudden need to tell his student the truth.

He answered Jake. "Brooks doesn't know this, but I'd planned on selling it to him." He glanced over at Brooks and added, "Before...of course, I heard your own good news about Florida."

"What?" Brooks said. "You wanted me to take over Till? Like I could afford it anyway."

Otis shook his head. "How many years did you work for me?"

"Eight or so, I guess."

"I'd say you've earned it."

Brooks broke their eye contact. "Sorry to disappoint you."

Otis wished he hadn't said anything. "Not a chance, son. We both must follow our hearts. I'll find a good buyer, someone who will carry on our traditions. Someone crazy enough to deal with that bozo next door."

Otis poured himself a glass of the Barolo as it was passed around. He could see he'd jarred Brooks with his confession and was relieved when Remi asked, "Do you think you'll ever come back, Otis? The mountain won't be the same without you."

"I'm not sure I could ever say goodbye for good. In the meantime, I'll be counting on you gentlemen to send me bottles so I can keep up with the vintages. I'll surely be watching Emilia from wherever I am."

Otis turned to Brooks and felt a wave of sadness. "I suppose I'll see Brooks before any of you. Joan wants to reach Florida for New Year's. She says she wants to cure me of my farmer's tan."

"I'll have a beer waiting for you," Brooks said.

"I'm assuming you'll brew something with Red Mountain hops, right?"

"No question. You know I can't shake Red Mountain entirely."

"No," Otis said, shaking his head. "I don't think any of us can."

The music from Château Smooth increased in volume, and though they couldn't see the neighbor from the back deck, they all turned. An idea came to Otis in the same way his mother had first delivered a bite of asparagus to him as a child. He knew the green vegetable was healthy for him, but it had no appeal. Still, just as that boy had eventually taken his first bite of asparagus, Otis knew his idea had great merit.

Before he could second-guess his thought, he said, "Perhaps we should walk over there, gents. I have some unfinished business with Bellflour."

"Oh, c'mon," Brooks said. "I thought you were done fighting. Joan will kill you."

"I am done," Otis assured him. "It's just time I apologize. No matter how different our visions for Red Mountain are, I've come to realize that it takes a great deal of effort and a tremendous emotional toll to start a winery. I need to at least recognize what Bellflour has done. I'm not sure I have a quiver full of kind words to say about the man, but he is as relentless as they come."

Otis saw a quick flashback of the day he'd pounded Bellflour into the gold concrete. "I suppose I owe him more than an apology. Perhaps all of us, the Guardians of Red Mountain, owe him a welcome."

Jake slapped his hands onto the armrests of his chair. "I think it's a great idea."

Remi lifted the saber off the table and held it high. "Then to Château Smooth we go."

The four men walked through the house and out the front door. The electronic beats grew louder as the Guardians of Red Mountain hiked up the road. Though the white-stucco wall blocked the view of the pink McMansion, flashing neon lights shot up over it and seemed to dance with the music.

"That's one hell of a wall," Remi said as they drew near. "How tall is it?"

"Eight feet," Otis said, thinking of the immense amount of effort he'd put into completing his vision, and it wasn't only physical. With every block he'd stacked in the five weeks since pulling into Joan's driveway in the Winnebago, he'd reminded himself of how lucky he was to have lived such a rich life.

Otis would have loved more time with Rebecca and their sons, but he was lucky for all the wonderful moments they had shared. And though his time working the vines might nearly be over, he was fortunate to have enjoyed so many lovely vintages. But the idea he ruminated on more than any other was that *he* was the luckiest man alive to get a second chance with Joan Tobey. There was no way in hell he'd jeopardize their love again, and he'd spend the rest of his life showing her how much she meant to him. Growing honest wine was a pretty good reason to live, but to love a woman with all that you had was what life was really about.

"You put it all up yourself?" Jake asked.

"Every damn block," Otis said proudly, knowing that wall symbolized his entire journey as a man.

Brooks jumped in. "I figured Joan would have made you tear it down."

"Even Joan has her limits, as I've learned this year. I don't think she likes looking at the Flamingo McMansion any more than I do. The pink starts to hurt your senses."

They shielded their eyes as they came around the side of Otis's wall and Château Smooth appeared. Though Otis didn't dwell on the notion, he wondered how much the power company would be dinging his neighbors every month. He'd never seen more lighting in his life. The gold concrete upon which he'd nearly killed Bellflour seemed to glitter, and the palm trees they'd brought in were each lit up like statues. There must have been thirty powerful spotlights shining up toward the hot-pink McMansion. This was no Caribbean pastel pink. This pink was the same pink they use to make the pink-flamingo lawn ornaments, and he knew that fact because there were several giant ones lining the gold driveway.

Otis was okay with it, though. At the end of the day, all he could do was worry about his own property. To each his own. Wasn't that the entire idea of this country? And wasn't Red Mountain an essential piece of America?

He braced himself as he led the men through the white doors of the McMansion to join the packed crowd of fifty or so in the tasting room. The lights had been dimmed. Half the people swayed to the music coming from the open back doors, and the other half were straining over the sound to talk to each other.

Through the crowd, Otis saw a line of pretty women in pink T-shirts serving at the bar. What caught his eye more than anything, though, was the sheer amount of drywall that had been used in this place. He was a man of stone and concrete, and the sight of drywall made him fear for the future—a time when plastic and drywall and other cheap materials might rule the earth.

A voice in his head told him to lighten up, and he was reminded why he was here. As they moved through the crowd to the bar, he reached into his pocket and dug out his eye patch. Once he'd put it on, he turned back to his comrades. He didn't care if they laughed at him. He didn't care if anyone did.

Finding himself in the center of the tasting room, he raised his fists to his chest and fell into the rhythm of a pounding kick drum and a spacey synthesizer. A woman with a particularly sultry voice sang about the bitter taste of love, and Otis went with it, letting his entire body groove in ways he'd not known were possible. If only Joan could see him now.

Once they'd procured glasses of Drink Flamingo's finest, they made their way out the back door toward the source of the music and flashing lights. It was a pool scene straight out of Las Vegas, and not the Vegas Otis remembered from his youth. This was the Vegas he'd heard about from the younger generations. The DJ stood behind two turntables on an elevated stage to the right of a very crowded tiki bar. He held one hand to a giant pair of glowing earphones while his other hand twisted a knob on his board. The pool spilled over with young people in skimpy bathing suits sipping adult beverages and dancing among neon pink and green strobe lights.

Otis lost the others as he searched for Bellflour. He passed by a line of cabanas and worked his way to the tiki bar. Several slushy machines spun frozen red and pink drinks.

A woman with a shirt that read *Flaminglet* asked him something, but he couldn't make out her words.

"Would I like a what?" Otis asked, nearly dizzy from the sensory overload. He leaned in.

"A Fro-gria," she repeated louder. "It's all Red Mountain fruit."

Otis chuckled. "Well, if it's all Red Mountain, I'll take you up on it."

She filled his cup from one of the machines.

He dropped a five into a bucket of tips. Finding a small area of space near the pool, he took a sip. All Red Mountain fruit. At least there was that.

Muttering to himself, he said, "If I can make it through tonight, I can handle anything."

On a light-blue float in the center of the pool, Otis found Bellflour. He was surrounded by a group of young women, and judging by their laughs, must have been telling a very funny story. Otis watched him for a while, and in those few moments, the man tossed back two pink Solo cups of whatever he was drinking.

Bellflour eventually looked Otis's way, and a stare-down ensued. His nemesis hopped off the float and waded toward him. His tanned belly hung over a ridiculously bright hot-pink Speedo. Two thin gold chains hung from his neck and wrist.

Otis met him on the side of the pool, and he felt his knees crack as he knelt down. "I came to apologize," he said loudly.

Bellflour's face tightened.

Nearly yelling over the music, Otis continued, "It wasn't right of me to fight you...or to install that smart valve, and I hope you'll accept my apology. I was wrong. And I'm glad to see your vines are okay."

After a long debate, Bellflour grinned. "Apology accepted."

Otis stuck out his hand, and Bellflour's hand rose out of the water to meet it. "For an old man, you sure as hell can throw a punch."

Otis's fists had been sore for a week after their bout. Squeezing down hard on the Bellflour's hand, he said, "Congratulations on the opening. Welcome to Red Mountain."

Bellflour seemed to match Otis's effort with a punishing grip. "I appreciate that."

For the first time ever, Otis looked at Bellflour like he was actually human. Maybe the guy wasn't all bad. He might be drunk and certainly lacking in vision, but maybe he was just another guy trying to survive the sometimes harsh world.

Otis realized there was a crime he'd not yet confessed to: planting the pinotage vines. He looked around at the wild scene that Bellflour had concocted, and he decided he wasn't ready to divulge this last bit of information. Otis needed to carry with him one small victory.

"How do you like my Fro-gria?" Bellflour asked, stealing Otis back from his thoughts.

"I'd say you've got a winner."

Bellflour circled his thumb over his fingers. "Money, money, money."

"Now that you're done here, what's next on the Drink Flamingo agenda?" Otis asked.

"That's a good question. We've got our eyes on a property in Burgundy that might just be perfect."

Otis felt a murmur in his heart and had a sudden urge to race back home to find his blood pressure medicine. "Burgundy, huh?"

Bellflour broke into a grin. "Nah, just kidding. I think I'm done for a while. I'm tired, Otis. So damn tired."

"Yeah, that makes two of us. The wine business is not for the faint of heart, is it?"

"No, it's not."

~

SOMETIME PAST MIDNIGHT, Bellflour was still in the pool. Only the real party animals remained, and he was glad to see he was the oldest of them. He still had a few tricks up his sleeve and a few late nights in his future.

Damned if his bladder wasn't pushing, though, and he wasn't about to pee in the pool. Not after all the work he'd put into this place. He did hate to leave the women hovering around him, though. He liked watching them dance as he sipped on Fro-grias and thought about all the people he'd proved wrong.

Hopping off his float, he slid it to a pretty brunette. "Will you hold onto this for me, honey?"

"You got it," she said, shaking her shoulders to the beat.

He used the rail to climb the steps out of the pool, but as he lost the water's support, he felt his legs buckle. Catching himself before tumbling backwards, he shook it off and grabbed the towel from his lounge chair. After slipping into his leather sandals, he slowly stumbled to the tiki bar and snagged the attention of one of his Flaminglets.

"Hey, sweetie, can I get one of those Nicaraguans?"

"You got it, Harry." She must have been the last sober one left.

He, on the other hand, was mumbling, but who cared? It was his fucking party.

She clipped the cigar for him and handed it over with a box of matches. "Enjoy, boss."

Turning back toward the pool, he leaned against the bar and lit his cigar. The music was getting a little annoying, but he was beyond pleased at the turn out. Wendall, the Drink Flamingo CEO, hadn't been able to make the party, but Bellflour was sure he'd hear all about it. Not one person on the board would ever doubt him again. He'd beat his deadline and done more in one year than many could do in two or three. As if that weren't enough, their wine club was already beyond full, and the waiting list was thousands of sign-ups long.

Even his father would be proud.

"Harry," he might say, "I'm sorry I ever doubted you."

Bellflour felt his bladder swelling again. He didn't feel like dealing with all the drunks pissing all over his toilets, so he stumbled toward the back and exited through a gate in the fence.

Looking down at his army of vines, he raised his hands in the air. "Who is the king of this fucking mountain now?"

He turned right to the wall Otis had built. He appreciated that Otis had said his apologies, but Bellflour preferred to think of it as a surrender. The old man had finally met his match. By accepting Otis's apology, Bellflour had proved he was the better man.

Thinking he'd have the last word of the night, Bellflour stumbled the fifty feet to the end of his property and approached Otis's wall, which was two feet taller than he was. He pulled down the front of his Speedo and pulled out what he liked to call the Grand Flamingo.

As he relieved himself, a wave of nausea hit him. He'd had about eight or nine too many, and it was catching up with him. The stream of yellow splashed onto Otis's lime-washed wall as Bellflour took another drag of his cigar.

When the smoke filled his lungs, the nausea worsened, and he felt his legs go wobbly and give way. Thinking that tomorrow would hurt badly, he began to fall backward, one hand holding the Grand Flamingo, the other holding the cigar.

As his back slammed the earth, his vision blurred. Tasting alcohol and acid creeping up his esophagus, he curled up and closed his eyes. He thought he heard a coyote call out, but he had no idea where he was anymore. After a few minutes in the haze, he smelled smoke.

Cracking one eye open, he saw that a patch of cheat grass had caught on fire around his cigar and was spreading like spilled oil.

"Oh, shit," he said, feeling a dose of clarity hit him. He pressed up to an uncertain stand but couldn't hold his balance and fell back down to the desert floor. Pressing up a second time, he saw that the wind was pushing the spreading fire toward the Château. The fear of losing everything he'd worked on gave him the strength to find a small degree of balance, and he attempted to stomp out the fire with his sandals.

Ashes rose into the air and burned his legs as he clumsily danced over the reddening ground. But the fire was already too big and moving too quickly. He looked back to the pool area and the Château above.

"Fire," he mumbled, as if announcing it to himself.

Nearly naked and fully drunk, Bellflour started running back but tripped and tumbled down to the earth. Rolling to his back, he fought to find his voice. "Fire!" he yelled. "There's a fire!"

50

LIT UP LIKE TIMES SQUARE

T he howling woke Otis. His eyes snapped open like a robot that had been switched on from its control board. Gathering his bearings, he realized he'd fallen asleep in the recliner in his study. An unsteady lowball glass of Scotch bobbed in his hand. He fought through the haze of too many drinks to read the time on the antique wall clock. It was one-thirty in the morning, and he assumed Joan had made it home from her jaunt with the bride-to-be and was currently dreaming of never-ending fields of wildflowers in the bedroom.

As he set the glass on the side table, the coyotes howled again.

Sitting up, he looked through the window in front of him, finding that the full moon had lit up his front vineyard block in a silver and purple glow. He'd often seen one of the song dogs hovering there in the dark hours, as if it liked to watch Otis sleep. There were no animals out there tonight.

On the other side of Sunset Road, he could see a few wineries on higher ground that always left their lights on at night. More than two miles away, red lights from antennas on top of the mountain flashed rhythmically, warning off any low-flying aircraft.

When the coyotes howled again, he perked up. He'd never heard

songs like these in his life. Typically, he could hear the low howls of
the elders rumble like a double bass in an orchestra. The younger
pups would call out in much higher octaves with staccato yelps that
seemed to offer a melody to their savage symphonies. Tonight, the
calls sounded like a fleet of British police cars rushing across London,
the now foreign tones evoking Otis's childhood.

It took a moment for his old bones to get moving, especially
considering the various forms of alcohol he'd indulged in. A night
that starts with Champagne and ends with Fro-grias was sure to
come with great pains in the morning. He pulled on his boots and
cardigan and slipped out into the night.

The moon was huge in the black sky, almost like a planet drifting
toward earth. Another alarming round of coyote sirens rose up from
the desert, and Otis knew something was wrong. He surveyed his
property, looking for disturbances.

Jonathan must have heard him and ran to the pasture fence and
jumped up, resting his paws on the top. His giant wooly white tail
wasn't wagging like usual, and there was an urgency to his cries.

Otis was relieved to hear that the DJ at Château Smooth had
apparently played his last set, as the thundering bass that had been
shaking the mountain since sunset had finally quieted. The neon
lights were still flashing above the wall, though, and he could hear a
few drunk voices, so he figured a few stragglers were splashing about
in the pool.

Looking again at the neon lights, he realized the pink and green
had been replaced by yellows, reds, and oranges. He didn't spend
much time pondering the mystery before a wave of acrid smoke hit
his nostrils.

Taking off in the fastest run his body would allow, he raced
toward the fire. After 100 yards, he confirmed that the lights flashing
above the wall were actually red and orange flames licking the air.
The drunken voices he thought he'd heard sounded more like
screams now, and his fears were confirmed when he heard the sound
of fire trucks off in the distance.

Otis felt a shot of adrenalin fill his veins as thick smoke filled his lungs. Rounding the wall, his eyes went to the front doors of Château Smooth, where people were piling out with a cloud of smoke. He ran across the grass and along the gold driveway and raced up through the crowd.

As terrified people pushed past him, Otis entered the tasting room and saw a wall of fire rising from the back door.

Grabbing the last person to leave, a young man with a UW hat, Otis asked, "Is there anyone else in there?"

Fear had plastered the man's face. He shook his head and pulled away.

Seeing a door to his right, Otis rushed through it and found himself standing at the edge of a cellar that looked like a long airline hangar. A line of brand-new fermentation tanks still wrapped in plastic ran down one wall. Stacks of new barrels covered the other.

"Is anyone in here?" His voice echoed off the metal walls as he raced inside with his eyes peeled.

A minute later, the door flew open behind him, and a firefighter appeared. "I need you out of here. Let's go!"

Otis followed him back through the tasting room. The wall of fire had grown and was consuming the building. His eyes stung as they pushed through the smoke and ran back out into the night. Coughing, he stumbled away from the building and up the driveway toward the crowd of people standing on Sunset Road next to a line of fire trucks and police cars.

He turned back and watched as Château Smooth became engulfed in flames. Fire trucks were shooting blasts of water into the worst of it, but Otis knew their efforts were futile.

$\sim$

THOUGH BROOKS WAS no stranger to the night, he rarely stayed up past midnight. The life of a wine farmer didn't allow it. Tonight was different, though. Brooks had mentioned Otis's offer to sell him Till Vineyards, and it had launched into a two-hour heated discussion about his and Adriana's future.

At one point, Adriana edged away from him and said, "Maybe you shouldn't come to Florida."

Those six words stuck in the air.

Brooks lay on the bed with his ankles crossed and his eyes focused on the spinning ceiling fan. Over the course of this two-hour conversation, he'd come to the same conclusion.

"Maybe you're right. I'm done trying to convince you that we'll work," he said. "I know you have stuff going on, and I'd love to be there for you. I'd love for us to overcome all of our issues together. But you don't let me in. Half the time, I'm five feet away from the tight circle that you and Zack have created. I can't go to Florida with the hope that it will change. This has felt like a one-sided relationship all year, and I need more than that. I deserve more than that."

He glanced over. Was she listening or stewing?

It was time to say exactly what had been wearing on him. "I'll tell you what all this feels like, A, and you may not like it, but I'm not going to Florida unless we address it. I think that, in your eyes, the best thing about me is my relationship with Zack. I think you're afraid that Zack would lose another father figure."

Brooks wasn't surprised when she didn't argue. He pressed on. "I'm guilty of the same fear. Every time I start doubting us, my thoughts go to Zack, and I can't bear to think of saying goodbye to him." He whispered, "But the thing is, he can't be the reason we stay together."

Showing a side she protected with all her might, Adriana burst into tears.

He could barely handle the sadness in the room and grabbed her rigid arm. "Tell me I'm wrong. Tell me that my relationship with Zack isn't the reason you love me. The only reason."

"I don't know how to love anymore." It was the truest and most authentic thing she'd said in months.

Brooks chose his words carefully. "I love Zack like a son, but I can't follow you to Florida for him." He rolled over to her. "I almost would. You two mean more to me than just about anything in the world, and I'd honestly sacrifice my life for you. I'd move down to

Florida and pretend that you and I are happy just for Zack. But then what?"

He shook his head. "I've spent a long time thinking about the merits of that decision, and I've finally realized it's a terrible idea. Zack deserves better than to grow up in a superficial world where his mother pretends to love a man..."

"I'm not pretending," she spat.

"I believe you want to love me, A. But you don't love me. That's the difference. I can't rip up my life here to gamble on you one day coming around."

"I need time, Brooks. I need time for me."

"Then take your time. I get it. You know I've been there. But I can't wait around and pretend to be a father to Zack in Florida while you try to find yourself. It wouldn't be right for Zack or for me." He fell back onto his pillow. "I want to love someone who loves me back. Not when the moment suits...or for her own agenda. I've spent too many years alone. Only now do I have my parents and brother in my life. It's been a long broken road, and I'm tired of going it alone. I want a family that will be mine forever. I want a woman who—for some crazy reason—is crazy about me."

He looked at Adriana and knew this might be the last time they would ever share a bed, but he'd mustered the courage to be real with her, and he couldn't stop now. Ultimately, it was better to address these issues now rather than later.

"It doesn't seem to me you want the same things, and I just didn't want to see it. I'll never forget your face when I brought up our having a baby. That should have been a warning bell, but I was so desperate to have a woman like you love me that I ignored it. Just like I ignored every other sign. The fact that you're not disagreeing says it all. Our entire relationship is built around your amazing boy, and I finally know how unhealthy that is. As much as I love him, I am not a part of your family. Not totally—"

Brooks's phone rang on the bedside table. Zack had recently changed the ring to the chirp of crickets. He recognized the irony as he reached for the phone before it woke up Zack.

It was Joan. "What are you doing up this late?" he asked her.

"Brooks, there's a fire. Otis needs you."

Brooks jumped out of bed and nearly dropped the phone. "Where?"

She spoke quickly and nervously. "Château Smooth is burning down, and the fire's spreading."

"Has anyone called 911?" Brooks pulled up his jeans.

"The firefighters are already here, but I don't know exactly what's going on. Otis just ran in and woke me, told me to call you. Then he said something about turning on all the irrigation and ran back out the door."

"I'll be there in a few." When he hung up, he reached for a shirt and said to Adriana, "Château Smooth is burning. Sounds like we have a possible wildfire on our hands. I'm going up there. Take Zack and get out of here. I don't know how bad it is, but it's dry out there, and the fire could spread quickly."

"What about everyone else on the mountain?" Adriana asked. "What about Épiphanie?"

Brooks's heart was racing so quickly that he hadn't gotten that far. "Call everybody. Spread the word. Please tell Jake to turn on our irrigation at Lacoda." He suddenly remembered Shay and Abby's new house. "Call Shay and Abby first, please. If the fire jumps Sunset Road, they'll be in trouble."

"I'm on it."

"Make sure you have your phone on you, okay?"

She was telling him to be careful as he rushed out of the room and down the stairs. He laced up his work boots as the garage door opened. The idea of the mountain burning—the wineries and vineyards—was nearly too much to comprehend. They'd worked too hard to lose it now.

He climbed onto his Triumph Scrambler and darted out to Demoss Road. After a short run on the paved road, he cut left and sped up into the vines.

51

SEVERE BURNS AND HOW WE TREAT THEM

Margot opened her eyes to find Philippe barking in her face. She'd been sleeping on her side, and the last thing she remembered, he'd been snuggled up against her leg. Now he was face to face with her, apparently desperate for a midnight bathroom break.

"What's going on, Philippe? Do you need to go potty?"

Margot sat up as he jumped off the bed. He ran around in a circles while he waited for her.

"Okay, okay, I'm coming." She looked at her digital alarm clock. "One-thirty in the morning, and you have to pee? You're lucky I love you so much."

Pulling on her robe, Margot followed Philippe down the steps and to the door. "I might start taking your water away at night. You're as bad as Remi."

Her dog squeezed out the door as she opened it. The cool air pushed in, and it felt rather refreshing. She cinched her robe tighter and stepped out into the night. While Philippe did his business, she put a hand on the rail and looked up. The full moon explained why the coyotes were so loud and almost devilish. She wondered if Otis might be out there singing with them. It was a circulating rumor that he, on occasion, would take to all fours and let loose his inner demons with his own howls.

Breathing in the cool desert air, she smiled at her life. Sleep or not, in a few hours, she'd become Margot Valentine, wife to one of the most caring, chivalrous men she'd ever met. Even after all her silly attempts to run him off, he'd chased her relentlessly, and she was thankful to finally quit playing hard-to-get.

As she stared at the constellations, she wondered how his night had gone with the Guardians of Red Mountain. Hopefully, Remi was sleeping soundly in his RV by now. She'd warned him against showing up hungover to the afternoon wedding. "Don't you let me find you at the end of the aisle all green and sweaty. I know *aaaaalllllll-llll* about the Guardians of Red Mountain."

"Oh, c'mon," he'd said, "we're just sharing a glass of wine and throwing something on the barbeque."

He'd crashed in the Airstream so that he and Margot could avoid any bad luck. Before retiring to her own room at Margot's house, Carly had joined the other ladies of the mountain for Margot's bachelorette party—a youthful and perhaps misleading name, considering they'd gathered at the inn to prepare a vast array of dishes for the wedding the following day. The get-together wasn't without a thousand laughs and tears, and Margot couldn't have imagined a better evening with friends.

They'd behaved, though, and by ten o'clock, Margot had snuggled next to Philippe and was trying to fall asleep despite the electronic music coming from Château Smooth's grand opening nearly a mile away. Eventually, she'd fallen into her bridal dreams, only to be torn away by a dog she'd let drink too much water.

Philippe suddenly raced toward the inn.

"Philippe!" she called out. "Stay where I can see you."

She didn't like him going too far with the coyotes out there.

Calling his name as she rushed toward Épiphanie, she thought she caught a whiff of smoke. Was someone burning a fire at the inn?

Philippe's bark startled her. He was somewhere off to the left of the inn, perhaps in a neighbor's vines. She called out and went in his direction. "Get back here right now! It's dangerous out there."

He barked again, and she followed the sound. As she reached the end of her driveway, he showed himself and raced to her side.

"Don't do that to me, honey," she said. "You'll give me a heart attack."

After scolding him, she glanced at Château Smooth. Though the music had died, it was the loudest vision she'd ever seen. Referring to it as an eyesore would be comparing cancer to the sniffles. Whatever it was, it was lit up like Times Square—if Times Square were entirely pink.

The sound of sirens suddenly filled the near silence, and she swung her head about, searching for their position. A moment later, a fleet of fire trucks and other vehicles came racing up Sunset Road. She looked right, wondering about their destination. It was hard to see any other lights at all with the brightness of Château Smooth stealing the darkness.

Setting her eyes on the pink behemoth again, she noticed flapping sheets of red and orange that looked out of place. Were those flames? When she breathed in another round of smoke, she knew for sure.

She'd watched the horrid fires in California this year destroy thousands of acres and had always worried that the declining precipitation rates could cause problems around Red Mountain. As one talking head had said when referring to the Tri-Cities area, "It's not a matter of *if*, but *when*."

Taking one last look at the fire trucks, she knew that "when" was now.

As the fear of losing her inn and home climbed up her throat, she called for Philippe and raced back to her house and up the stairs. "Jasper! Carly!"

She knocked hard on Jasper's door. He'd only just returned from Boston two days ago for the wedding. "There's a fire, honey. Please get up."

"Huh?"

She pushed open the door and repeated herself. "Get dressed. I'm running to the inn to wake the guests, and then I need to figure out what to do with the animals."

"Okay, I'll be right there," he said, clearly trying to shake himself from a deep sleep.

She rushed to Carly's room next and rapped on the door. Once Carly was awake enough to understand the severity of the situation, Margot said, "Call your dad, let him know what's going on. Tell him I'll talk to him once I get the guests up. This thing could really spread."

Carly wiped her eyes. "All right."

Margot ran into her room to throw some clothes on and then, like the captain of her ship, she raced to Épiphanie to ensure the safety of her guests.

～

BROOKS RODE HARD through the darkness, trusting his instincts as he bounced over the gravel, winding his way through the vineyard blocks. He slid to a stop outside of the Foresters' house. He saw lights on upstairs. Finding their gate closed, he pressed on the bell.

Their Weimaraners started barking somewhere inside.

"C'mon, c'mon," he said, desperate to continue on.

When Jake's voice crackled through the speaker, Brooks said, "It's Brooks. Château Smooth is on fire."

"Yeah, I talked to Adriana."

Jake sounded cool and collected. "I'll turn on the irrigation and start waking neighbors."

"And then get your family out of here," Brooks said. "This could get bad."

He spun out of their driveway heading east. When he reached Sunset Road, he swung a hard right, nearly scraping his knee onto the pavement. Working his way up to fifth gear, he pushed his Scrambler to the limits. Coming up a hill, he saw a long line of flashing lights along Sunset Road. Looking right, he felt sick as he saw the big ball of fire that was Château Smooth burning to the ground.

He ran the bike wide open and only slowed once he could feel the radiant heat of the fire. Smoke hit his lungs as he surveyed the landscape. The wall Otis had built looked like it had kept the fire from spreading in that direction. Brooks was relieved to see fire trucks surrounding Château Smooth, and it looked like the firefighters had somehow taken the upper hand. Two trucks were drafting water from an irrigation pond and shooting giant streams into the flames. Other fire trucks were focusing their efforts on the ground around the winery, most likely dousing it with water and fire retardant.

"I think they have her contained," he heard a voice say. Turning, Brooks saw Otis coming up from the direction of his property.

Brooks turned off his bike. "Jesus, man. I've never seen anything like this."

"I'm just grateful it wasn't worse. This could have devastated us."

"Any idea how it started?" Brooks asked, swinging a leg off the bike.

They both watched the building burn as Otis said, "No idea."

Brooks looked at the crowd of people watching safely from the other side of Sunset Road. "Was anyone hurt?"

"They just wheeled Bellflour out on a stretcher. Looked like he had some pretty bad burns, but he was alive. I don't think anyone else was hurt."

"How about your vines?" Brooks asked. "Looks like the wall was worth all the pain after all."

Otis adjusted his cap. "That wall is the reason I'll have fruit left to harvest. Might taste a little smoky, but what do you do? At least the vines are alive."

"About that," Brooks said. "It probably isn't the best time to bring this up, but would you still be interested in selling your place to me? Adriana and I just had a serious heart-to-heart."

"You're not going to Florida?"

Brooks shook his head. "It doesn't seem so."

"You're damned right I'm interested," Otis said. "The place is yours for whatever you can pay me."

They stopped talking for a moment as the right side of Château Smooth collapsed, sending a shuttering roar and another blast of hot air toward them.

"I'll pay you what it's worth," Brooks said. "As long as you'll give me some time."

"You carry on what Rebecca and I planted up here, and you can have all the time you need."

Brooks offered his hand. "I'll make you proud, Otis. I promise."

Otis pulled Brooks into a hug and kissed his neck. "You already make me proud, son. No matter what you do and where you go."

They turned back to the fire. Château Smooth would be nothing but ashes in a matter of minutes. Otis asked, "You sure you want to put up with another vintage? They're not easy around here."

Brooks looked deep into the orange flames. "What else do I have to do?"

~

A CROWD STOOD out front of Épiphanie a safe distance away from the action to the west. A firefighter in a red pickup truck had just come by to let everyone know that an evacuation wasn't necessary. Château Smooth was no more, but they'd contained the fire.

Remi had reached Épiphanie from the eastern entrance to Red Mountain, and Margot stood with him watching the last of the flames die. He had his arm around Margot's waist. "I know what they say about rain on your wedding day. How about fire?"

In the back of her mind, Margot had been thinking about the wedding, but hadn't yet shared her thoughts. Though no one had wanted Château Smooth on the mountain, it was still a sad time.

"I know we're feeling lucky, but I think we should postpone the wedding." She turned to him and put a hand on his chest. "Even though some of us might be silently cheering, a lot of people worked hard to make what they did happen. It wouldn't feel right."

Remi nodded, as if he'd come to the same conclusion on his own. "As much as I want to lock you down, I agree." Something occurred to him. "Gosh, I hate to waste all that food."

Margot was thinking the same thing. "I think we should still have a party, but not make it about us. Let's make it about the mountain. We'll invite the firefighters, the Drink Flamingo employees, and anyone else who wants to come."

"This is exactly why I love you," he said.

EPILOGUE

The Tweed Cap

Four days after the fire, Brooks was in the cellar of Lacoda, tasting through their new harvest, with Emilia when Jake came walking in. "Harry Bellflour and Drink Flamingo are pulling out of their Red Mountain project."

"What?" Brooks said, spinning around with a glass of grape juice in his hand.

"It just came through on *Wine Business*," Jake said, smiling. "Bellflour gave a phone interview from the hospital. He says they're selling the land and closing down the project."

"Did he give a reason?" Emilia asked.

"He was pretty brief about it, just saying that he accepted responsibility for the fire and that it was time to find a different location."

Brooks smiled back at Jake. "The mountain wins again."

"Yes, it does," Jake agreed. "I'm just surprised Bellflour wasn't canned over the whole thing."

Brooks dumped the contents of his glass back into the fermenter. "From what I've heard, he's taking some time off and going to Europe."

"Interesting," Jake said. "Where'd you hear that?"

"That vineyard consultant they hired from Napa mentioned it to Otis. Said Bellflour was pretty shaken up by the whole thing and was planning on taking some time off."

"Europe will be good for him," Jake said. "Everything I know about wine I learned from the old world." He looked at his daughter. "Anyway, I hope you're soaking up everything you can from this guy. You'll be in charge of this place soon."

"I'm learning as fast as I can, Dad" Emilia said.

Brooks had agreed to stay on at Lacoda until Emilia was ready. Though it would be a busy few years running both Lacoda and Till, he was excited for the challenge.

"She'll be there soon," Brooks said. "I have a feeling she'll earn a place among the greats one day. Who knows? Maybe they'll start calling her the grapemother."

Emilia rolled her eyes and they broke into a good laugh.

A few minutes later, Brooks looked at the time and excused himself. There would be no more laughing today.

~

WHEN ZACK HOPPED off the school bus, Brooks and Adriana were waiting for him. They sat him down at the dining-room table. Recalling the countless times he'd chased Zack around the house, Brooks fought back tears. "I need to tell you something, Zack."

"What?" Even at his age, it seemed he could sense bad news coming.

Brooks's voice cracked. "I'm not going to be coming to Florida."

Zack looked relieved. "I know, I know. Not until after harvest."

"No, kiddo. I've decided to stay here on Red Mountain for good. You and your mom are taking this adventure by yourselves."

Zack seemed to understand the implications. "But you and my mom..."

Brooks had no intentions of sugarcoating the situation. "We're breaking up."

Zack looked at his mom with confusion. "I don't want to go to Florida. Not without Brooks. Why can't we stay here?"

Adriana frowned. "I can't stay here, *mi amor*. I'm not happy."

"I am, and I'm not leaving."

Brooks knew he had to do something. He didn't want Adriana to look like the bad person. "Zack, sometimes we have to do things we don't want to do for the ones we love. Do you love your mommy?"

He nodded.

Brooks reached for his little hand. "Then take her down to Florida and take care of her. She needs you right now."

In a defeat that rang in his words and pushed down his shoulders, Zack asked, "You're breaking up, like, for good?"

"Yeah," Brooks whispered.

Zack bounced his eyes back and forth between them. "Will you come visit?"

Brooks reached past Zack and took his mom's hand. "I'd like to."

The following days were filled with tears and heartache, but when Brooks finally said goodbye to Adriana and Zack on the first Saturday of October, the three of them shared a hug and smile that he'd never forget.

~

IN THE LATE afternoon on November 3, Margot stood in front of her long mirror in the dress Carmen had given her. She had never felt more beautiful in her life. Though she would have rocked the polka dots, the Parisienne wonder that now covered her body was just the right balance between sexy and elegant, and Margot couldn't wait to walk down the aisle. It was no surprise that Carmen had guessed the perfect size, and she'd matched the dress with the most wonderful pumps and a long strand of pearls.

"They're ready for you," Jasper whispered, poking his head into her bedroom.

Margot adjusted her crown of wildflowers, picked up her bouquet, and turned to see Jasper in his tuxedo. "Let's do this."

An exhilarating wave of the jitters rushed over her as they walked down the stairs and out the door. It was a little chillier than Margot would have liked, but there was no way she wasn't having her wedding outside. A light rain the day before had knocked down the dust, and the air was clean and crisp. A strand of cirrus clouds to the west decorated the striking azure sky.

They entered Épiphanie through the big wooden doors and passed through the brightly lit lobby and dining room toward the back patio. Margot—and her heart—stopped when she saw all their loved ones sitting in chairs under the tent.

She reached for Jasper's hand. "Don't let me cry. I'll get mascara everywhere."

"Save the crying until after the pictures," he said.

She breathed deeply and shook off the emotions rushing through her.

When Jasper opened the patio door for her, everyone under the tent stood and turned, as if in slow motion.

There was nothing fake about the smile that rose from within and plastered itself on Margot's face. Not only did she feel beautiful, but she felt proud and confident. She followed the path they'd practiced the day before along the brick and grass and reached the back of the tent. She looked to the end of the aisle, and for the first time that day, saw the man she would spend the rest of her life with.

Remi Valentine took Margot's breath away. He wore a perfectly tailored black tuxedo with a magnificent white-rose boutonnière. He was her future.

Jasper offered her his arm. "You ready, Mom?"

Margot placed a hand on his arm and proudly walked down the aisle. Though she wished her parents had lived to see this day, she was so happy to see all the faces of Red Mountain supporting them.

When they reached the front, Margot saw Henri and Philippe sitting at Carly's feet. She offered Carly a smile and then laughed at the adorable wildflower collars the dogs were wearing.

Leaving Jasper, Margot approached Remi and took his hand.

"Hi," Margot whispered.

"What did I do to deserve you?"

Margot nearly lost it and dug a finger into his palm. "You're going to be in so much trouble if you make me cry."

The preacher standing next to Remi said, "Let's get started."

Thinking of new beginnings, Margot looked at her fiancé. "Yes, let's do."

~

THE MORNING AFTER THE WEDDING, Brooks hosted all their friends at the Till tasting room. He and Otis had worked out a deal on the property and, in the middle of October, signed the papers. Brooks Baker was the proud owner of Till Vineyards, but he'd never change the name.

There were hugs and tears, but what Brooks would most remember about that chilly morning was the powerful and loving way Joan and Otis had been looking at each other.

He'd sadly watched over the past months as Joan had grown terribly irritated with Otis as he'd nearly lost his mind over Château Smooth.

None of that seemed to matter as the two of them giggled with each other that morning. Seeing their love reassured Brooks that he'd made the right decision in letting Adriana and Zack go. It also filled him with hope. Sure, he hoped for fifty more wonderful harvests, but most importantly, he hoped he'd find the kind of love that could survive the hard times and that he'd one day raise a family of his own.

Sticking to their schedule, Otis tapped his watch and asked Joan if she was ready to go. He wanted to reach California by nightfall.

After a round of hugs that lasted ten minutes, Otis and Joan walked with the Great White Beast known as Jonathan toward the Winnebago.

As Joan climbed in, Otis turned back. He wasn't wearing his eye patch this morning. "Hey, Brooks."

Brooks, who was standing next to Emilia, was trying to imagine what the mountain would be like without his mentor. "Yeah?"

Otis removed his tweed cap and slung it to him. Brooks caught the cap with one hand and looked at it for a while. What a grand responsibility he'd taken on. There was no way one person could wear this hat.

Brooks slapped the cap on top of Emilia's head. "I think this might be a better fit on her."

Emilia touched the cap and threw her arm around Brooks. "Don't worry, Otis. I've got his back."

The grapefather brushed away a tear and smiled. "Take care, you two." He looked at the larger group and waved one more time, then said, "Let's go, Jonathan."

Otis followed the huge dog up into the Winnebago.

Brooks watched through the open door as Otis took Joan's face with two hands, kissed her, and then whispered in her ear.

Joan grinned and pushed him away.

The grapefather turned back and winked. Brooks had never seen him so happy in his life.

"So long, sensei," Brooks said. He'd never met a better man and didn't believe he ever would.

With a big bright smile and rosy-red cheeks, Otis whispered, "*Adiós, amigo,*" and snapped shut the door.

The people waved and cheered as the Winnebago's tires kicked up a cloud of dust, and the maestro rode toward his next adventure with the woman he loved. And the crowd doubled over in laughter when Otis stuck his hand out the window and conducted one last symphonic honk of "La Cucaracha" for Red Mountain.

If you enjoyed this story, please take a moment to leave a review on Amazon. It makes a world of difference.

~

For more novels, free stories, updates, and my newsletter sign-up, visit boowalker.com.

ACKNOWLEDGMENTS

I am endlessly grateful to my beta readers, who selflessly slogged over the early drafts of this novel and pushed me to my best. Y'all mean the world to me.

Thanks to the editing team at The Pro Book Editor and also my cover designer, J.D. Smith.

I will forever be in debt to my friend, Christophe Hedges, for his contributions. It was over our many long lunches and dinners around the world that the seeds of these novels took root.

Speaking of guardians of Red Mountain, I tip my hat to all of you who make the real-life Red Mountain such a special place. I can't wait to see what the future holds.

A fleet of hugs and kisses to my wife, who patiently puts up with me under deadline, which is a Herculean task. To say I'm a handful is a tremendous understatement. My love, you are the reason I write. Thank you for giving me the courage to chase my dreams.

And to my readers, thank you for supporting my art. You are the fuel that tears me out of bed every morning. Sharing the stories of Red Mountain has been the highlight of my artistic pursuits, but it's time to say goodbye to these characters and explore new frontiers. I hope you'll follow me, as I'm just getting started.

ABOUT BOO

Boo initially tapped his creative muse as a songwriter and banjoist in Nashville before working his way west to Washington State, where he bought a gentleman's farm on the Yakima River. It was there amongst the grapevines that he fell in love with telling stories.

A wanderer at heart, Boo currently lives in St. Petersburg, Florida with his wife and son. He also writes thrillers under the pen name Benjamin Blackmore. You can find him at boowalker.com and benjaminblackmore.com.

CPSIA information can be obtained
at www.ICGtesting.com
Printed in the USA
LVHW092343310320
651840LV00004B/1210

9 780999 712634